Plank Fence

Plank Fence

a novel

Paul Pioszak

Copyright © 2001 by Paul Pioszak.

Library of Congress Number: 2001118522
ISBN #:   Softcover   1-4010-2849-7

All rights reserved. No part of this book may be reproduced or transmitted in any form or by any means, electronic or mechanical, including photocopying, recording, or by any information storage and retrieval system, without permission in writing from the copyright owner.

This is a work of fiction. Names, characters, places and incidents either are the product of the author's imagination or are used fictitiously, and any resemblance to any actual persons, living or dead, events, or locales is entirely coincidental.

This book was printed in the United States of America.

To order additional copies of this book, contact:
Xlibris Corporation
1-888-7-XLIBRIS
www.Xlibris.com
Orders@Xlibris.com

Thanks to Joel Lake for the cover illustration, to Joel Hathaway and Holley Duffield for editing, and to my Polish friends who helped me get things done there. Thanks to my mother who has always supported me.

To Jane

Locals often forget about seasons. They walk through them without seeing their light or smelling their dust, and they say silly things, "Sure is a hot one t'day" or ask meaningless rhetorical questions, "Is it cold 'nuff for ya," without any consideration of the grandeur of hot or cold. Their bodies remind them that there are seasons—seasons to run fevers, seasons to sleep lazily in hammocks under willow trees, seasons to splash in cool, deep waters, seasons to smell the sky changing hues—but often the mind reduces seasons to temperature, like the seasons were an oven. Eyes do not connect to the mind, though they see. So, the world passes—tilting back and forth on angles and spinning like a ballroom dancer, and the eyes and ears and noses miss the world passing through the cycles. They miss the moon and the sun and the sky and the dirt doing all of those beautiful butterfly things that they do—alone and together. Many people realize only four times a year that there are seasons. It's winter. It's spring. Look over here, it's fall and then it's over—sudden realizations like waking after twenty years—Rip-Van-Winkled. The seasons seem not to arouse the sleepy people. They sneak by. Unseen and unheard, they don't chime like the living room clock. So why bother to look up? Thomas Gern saw the seasons; his mind saw them and his body felt them sting with hard sleet or dry, lip-cracking cold. He saw them come and go and come again. He found them new every year and lost them in the fleeting moments between each—somewhere between end and beginning.

In fact, all he had seen for years were seasons; he hadn't see anything else. For Thomas Gern it was as if there were only seasons and nothing more.

Tom leaned against the fence that outlined what was left of Gern property—flat, captured grassland that spilled from the mountains and washed toward the Raspberry River. Behind him stood the white, misplaced, Indiana house. The yard was truly a field and behind that was the freshly cut hay and in the middle of that sat a six ton rock that had been dropped like a pebble from a shoe out of a passing glacier ten thousand years ago. The mountains, old and worn by time and wind, weren't much more than hills that rose out of his field and into the sky fifteen hundred feet. In Michigan they were mountains, in Indiana they'd be the Himalayas in Appalachia they'd simply be hills. All the same, they stretched quietly, rolling over craggy miles to the western coast where they dipped into the water and ran thirteen hundred feet into the lightlessness of Lake Superior. If the water hadn't been there, the mountains would be the Smokies and Tom Gern would live on a high plain halfway up a northern slope.

He was looking across the street at Toclep, which never seemed to make any noise. The town slept the entire year. Even during the tourist seasons, the town barely huffed with life. It struggled to stay alive.

It was that in-between time now; summer was over and fall hadn't started but something had. For this month was the twentieth anniversary of death and disappointment for Thomas Gern, and for the first time in years Tom would do more than say to himself, how many years has it been? Eleven? Seventeen? His life had changed as quickly and dramatically as a tree struck by lightening and like lightning, the flash had been forgotten by the sleeping town, however, this summer had seen an eye flutter, blink, and open. Summer knew, like all seasons know all things. Soon more eyes would open, not everyone's but certainly those eyes that sat in a corner near the mountain, officially out of Toclep city limits, corralled by thin planks of dry wood.

* * *

Tom stretched his leg up to the top of the first plank and was posed in statuesque immobility. He hadn't moved from the time a Ford Taurus had thumped its flat-tire-self to the side of highway 52, had its tire changed with the efficiency of turning water into gold (squawks of "damn" and "shit" blowing across the fence as the tire iron clumsily bit into five rusted, hexagonal bolts), and then rolled into Toclep, turning right onto Clarion. Tom remembered when the road had been gravel and how the car would have thrown up a cloud of sand, gravel, and dust that would have drifted to the fence and to the house, coating both with another skin of gritty, brown-gray. He pulled a piece of grass from the ground and slipped it under his tongue like a thermometer. He tried to suck the sweet milk from the base of the stalk, but the grass was dry and there wasn't much milk to be had. He tried anyway.

If it had been summer, Thomas Gern might have found himself looking the other direction—across the green field to the fence that separated a man-made meadow from a mountain. He'd see the morning shadow of his house stretch, as it did everyday, across the field like a cat arching and extending every muscle and bone. He'd be able to see his four cows (there had been only four this summer), looming with long, morning shadows. He would know that across the road to the north, hidden by grass, past a thin line of pines and popples, was a freshwater ocean larger than Ireland. His tin cup would brim with thick black coffee and the warmth of the summer sun would be working to pull the dew into the sky. There would still be drops of night clinging to the un-mowed grasses and rivers of smoothish-hawkweed, ox-eyed daisies, and second-crop dandelions. He would take deep breaths of damp, coffee-flavored air. That's how it might have been if it was summer. But it wasn't summer. It wasn't fall either, though some of the maples were already blushing red. Tom used to enjoy the sorrow of fall. In those years before the disappearance of his family, he had sensed aging in the leaves and watched the trees. He had listened to the wind and quoted "Thou, from whose unseen presence the leaves dead are driven, like ghosts from an enchanter fleeing." He had embraced the cold nights and ghastly feelings of time that the earth never seems to feel. Then, after his father and mother and brother were gone, the pleasure of fall had too been stolen from him. All he saw in the air was the pale and the hectic red and there was nothing enchanting about it. Thomas Gern felt the seasons. He didn't necessarily like them, but he felt them. He did not see them as he had seen them in his youth. Now, when saw red, it was simply the red of work—a gasoline can or tractor or barn.

He needed to get ready for winter, today. But for now he would just lean against the worriless fence. Summer was over. He had saved a cow and her calf with the help of his neighbors. He had brought in the hay. He had tended the garden. He had stayed, for the most part, within the fence working. He did not pay attention to what happened beyond the planks; rather, he watched the seasons paint and fade. This summer had been similar to other summers—summers when he was a kid rushing with his brother to ride the horses, summers when he brought in the hay all by himself, summers since his wife had packed and disappeared beyond the bridge that led south—but he would discover that this autumn would not be the same, not for him anyway. It would be as hectic red on the inside as it was on the outside and he would be part of the red.

* * *

He looked over his shoulder at his house whose empty eyes peered out as if gazing into nothing. The house sat silently, unaffected by the wind. To the human eye, it had finished settling long before Tom was born. It had lived the lives of his parents and continued to live. It would outlive Tom as it had out lived his grandfather and his uncle and his father, mother, and brother.

The fence was a shoreline, the field a lake, and the house an island—a refuge of quiet safety, untouchable, unreachable like the Isle of Avalon. Tom had no idea what autumn would bring nor did he expect anything from it. There was a world beyond the fence that was alive and breathing, a world to which Tom only belonged like a television watcher belongs to a docu-drama. It was there; he was here and to him it seemed that all the king's horses and all the king's men could not bring those two worlds together again. Tom had lived his life like there were two worlds, but there was only one world, and he would be swept back into that one world by the autumn winds.

Summer was over.

Lydia looked through the window of the second-story pharmacy and could see sand blowing up Clarion Street. Sand, the tumbleweed of Toclep, blew out of Superior and sneaked under the scattered leaves on the September street. There wasn't anything to stop it from creeping through the spaces between the buildings and swirling aimlessly up the street, out toward Crescent City where it would waterfall into the Raspberry River and wash back to the place from which it had come. If you were outside, it would slap at your ankles and dry spit into your face with defiant whispers, "You can't stop me. Whatever you do will fall short. You might be able to dam rivers and repel mosquitoes, you don't even do that well, but you can't stop me. You can't stop me." The whisper would echo as you walked into Rae Miller's for a beer, as you scratched the part it had put in your hair, and feel the tiny grains of nature under your fingernails. It would mock, "You can't stop me; you can't stop me."

No one had been to see Lydia today, which wasn't unusual for Toclep. Insurance had become a commodity of the past. The more the copper mine tightened and suffocated itself, the less the health of its workers mattered, the less insurance was a priority. Not as if any of that mattered, anymore. For the mine had essentially closed on August first and the unemployment would, like the sand, blow into the sky—unattainably—by April Fool's Day. It was good that the citizens of Greenstone County had Lydia. She had been an asset to everyone's health for years. She had been the specter of health for generations in this part of the country. On the waxy, creosol-covered wall of her office hung the conjured piece of paper from some unknown East Coast college, which indicated her qualifications. In her heart hung the memories of misunderstood medical attention that had forced her into this nearly forgotten county, tucked into the northwest corner of Michigan. The yellow parchment of the endorsed diploma mirrored the yellow coating of nineteenth century plaster in the Jacobson building. The building was the oldest in Toclep; it was one of the remaining buildings from the lumber boom.

Lydia saw Brenda Cafus walking with the wind, arching her back as her hair reached around her like black branches. She didn't have anything in her arms, but Lydia could sense she was carrying something. Brenda, determined in her step, was pushed by the wind to the street-front door of the pharmacy. Lydia liked to look out the window onto Clarion Street and see her next customer coming. That sight allowed her to sense the severity of each oncoming storm. If the people of Greenstone County had ever taken the time to examine her diploma, they might have known she wasn't a doctor or pharmacist, but no one had. Lydia had been assumed into her position. Even the staff at St. Patrick's Medical Center in Ironcloud thought she was a doctor, and why shouldn't they?

The door downstairs flew open with the wind. Its knob hit the worn hole, evidence of years of a pounding doorknob. Flakes of dry, plaster gathered behind the door in a meeting on the landing. Lydia could hear the sand running up the steps toward the Persian rug, racing Brenda to the top. Brenda stepped into view; her wind whipped hair made her look like a coyote with the mange.

"Hey, Brenda. You don't look so good. What's up?" Lydia didn't have the thick yooper accent the rest of the townies had. She spoke softly with something of an unidentifiable European lilt, a mixture of accents. Lydia was aware of Brenda's problems with her husband, Rich, even though they had not talked about it. She was like that. She could sense.

"Really? I don't look good. Shit, I was afraid of that." Brenda's accent, on the other hand, was thick with long internal vowels. When she said *that*, it sounded as if she was taking a breath in the middle of the word.

"What's the problem?" Though she asked the question, Lydia already knew the problem. She had seen it in Brenda's wind-whipped walk.

"I'm pregnant."

"How could you be? You're on the pill."

"You're not s'posed to say that. All these years the damn thing has worked without fail. Without fail. Then, boom, I'm pregnant. I thought I couldn't get pregnant?"

"Got hit by the one-percent, I guess. You want me to do a pregnancy test? Make sure?"

"I already know for sure. I think you know the problem, Lydia. I don't need a pregnancy test. Already done that."

"So, what do you want?"

"I don't know. What are my options?"

"What do you mean?"

"You know Rich." Brenda was trying to hold stiff-lipped composure. Though she was hard and emotionless, her voice, wavering on the edge of vertical hold, told another story. "The problem is, it's not Rich's baby. If it were Rich's baby, I'd want it less than I want this. But it's not, and I'm afraid of that. I'm not afraid he'll kill me. I wish he would, sometimes. I wish he would kill me. I'm afraid of things worse than death. Things that lead to death and then death itself." Brenda eyes weren't looking outside of her body. They were looking inside.

"How often do you see things worse than death?"

"It depends. Been worse lately. Thought it would all stop. Like it was a phase or something. But it's been worse since they announced the closing of the mine." She looked confused. "I used to love him, Lydia. But it's been worse and worse and on top of all that now I've sinned."

"Good God, Brenda, don't hang that on yourself. I don't know my Bible as well as I used to." Lydia remembered a time when all of life had been swallowed by the Bible. The Bible had been the fire that had destroyed her people's way of life. "I think all those commandments are over-shadowed by the do-onto-others. You haven't sinned, Brenda. You've simply done onto Rich as he would've done onto you. And even if you had, you shouldn't be punished by the hand of Rich." There was a pause. "How many times has he hit you? How many times has he . . .?" Lydia couldn't say it. Not to Brenda, so she pulled up short and stopped. They sat. Neither looked at the other. The sound of sand slapped on the window.

After a moment Brenda said, "You know, I'd rather carry Ted's baby than his, but I don't want to carry any. I don't want to end up like Ezra Gern because of what I did or what I didn't do." The comment had slipped unconsciously out of her memory like a slick fish and fell like a two hundred-pound sturgeon into her words.

"I don't think you have much in common with Ezra, Bren."

"But I do. I saw him that day and I carry him around with me. I can't get rid of him."

"What?"

"I saw him that day. Hanging there like . . .like . . .a bird...like a bird or something. I remember." She thought back to the morning scene so many years ago.

The scene plastered in her memory like it had been on newspapers the next day: "Double Suicide: Occult Strikes Toclep." That was the scene that brought her fear today. All she could see was what she had seen twenty years ago on a September morning. "I wandered by the school after hanging out all night with Katrina. She was wild then. You remember? Not like she is now."

"Yeah. Intense. Emotional. Zealous."

"Zealous?"

"You know, like . . . um . . . obsessive."

"Yeah. More than just tourists on her mind back then, eh? I don't know if you remember this or not. Were you here, then? I guess you were. You didn't leave until after. Like the rest 'em, right?"

Lydia felt uneasy to be reminded of her leaving this place like she had been forced to leave others. In the back of her mind she said, yeah, but I'm back, aren't I. I'm back. "Right. Couple weeks after that with the rest of 'em." To clump herself in with the rest of the runners made her shift uncomfortably.

"Anywho." Brenda continued.

* * *

"I wanna learn Spanish," Katrina said. "I'm in love with Jano, and I wanna learn Spanish."

"I've never heard him speak Spanish."

"Me neither." Both girls laughed. "Jano's so, free. He doesn't want anything. He doesn't want to be tied to anything at all. Not even me. He told me so. He said, 'Trina I love you. I really do. I love you like you're chocolate and I'll always love you like that. But there's so much out there. Not just people but so much everything. Too much to be tied down. We're tied to each other forever, anyway. All people are once they've connected.' And you know what, Brenda, he's right. And someday I will show up on his doorstep in Wherever, America, and we'll fall right down on the floor of his living room and make love like rabbits. Because we love each other and love is everlasting."

"Don't you wanna have someone forever? You know, like we talked about when we were kids."

"We will have each other forever. Just not like our parents do. God that's awful. They don't even talk to each other."

"You're so unrealistic, 'Trina. It's just like you to fall in love with someone you can't be with."

"But I will be with him. Whenever I want to. I'll just show up. It'll give me something to look forward to, all the time. Like going to the movies."

"Love is s'posed to be special. What's special about that?"

"It's unpredictable. It's fresh."

"Sounds impossible."

"Things are only impossible if ya make 'em that way."

"Lots of things are impossible and having a relationship like that is one of them. God your dad would kill you."

"Ya, well my dad can take a swim for all I care. That's why I'm not going home anymore. My old man tells me that I'm hurting Mom. He never says one thing about himself just that I'm hurting Mom. And that's bullshit, Bren. Because the only thing my mother has ever wanted for me was for me to be happy. Jano makes me happy."

"I'm sure that's what your dad's all worked up about?"

"Not like that." They laughed.

"You mean you haven't? You know?"

"Brenda. I'm sure. Jano's right over there." They both turned from the fire. Their faces went black. Slowly, the darkness lightened and they could see the outlines of Mose and Jano."

"Where do you think he is?" There was something of the city in Mose's voice.

"I don't know, man. He and Patty probably shot down to the beach. Nice night. Cold. Crisp. Wouldn't mind watching the sunrise myself."

"I'm happy." Katrina continued. "My mom can see it. But, this whole thing has nothing to do with my mother." She imitated her father's voice; "You know everyone in town, in fact, everyone in Greenstone County is talking about what's going on out there." She finished then started again in her own voice. "So I asked, if everybody's talking about it, then what's going on out there? Well, that made him stumble a little bit and he huffed and gruffed then said, well I don't know exactly but it's a bunch of communist hippie crap. He's so full of it that he doesn't have any idea what he's talkin' about.

"So after that he says there are going to be rules around here and if I intend to be part of this family then I'm going to have to follow them. That's when I told him that if that was the way he wanted it I would prefer not be part of the family. He was fuming, Brenda, simply fuming. Then he said, 'if Matthew Gern were alive right now.'" She huffed up and actually did look like her father. "'That crap wouldn't be going on in his backyard. I ought to go out there myself and take care it.' He probably will come out, the sonofabitch."

"Just looking out for his baby, 'Trina."

"I don't need him to look out for me. This is my family. Jano and Mose and Ezra and Daisy and Kristie. We are a family. Ezra says if we just stick together everything will be all right. He's talking about windmills for power and farmin' for food and pitchin' in here and there to pay the taxes. Water's free, wood's free, air and sunshine—all free. That way, we're always together. Enjoyin' ourselves and our lives. Bein' part of it like the seasons. Not part of it like a spark plug or something. Eventually everyone out there will want to be like we are. They'll see that what they think matters, doesn't really matter at all and never has."

"It's a bit idealistic, isn't it? No wonder your dad's all freaked out. You're not gonna work. You're not gonna get married. Sounds crazy to me, too."

"Maybe for some. Ezra says that everything will work out. It's like an apple seed. When you hold it in the palm of your hand it doesn't look like much. But when you plant it and it grows, it will fill lives with apples for generations. Least that's what Ezra says."

"It's all talk, 'Trina."

"No. It's not. That's just what everyone thinks. Ezra even said that people would say that. But we have to believe. If we believe, it will work. If we don't believe, it won't."

"You're talkin' about magic."

"I'm talking about faith in ourselves. It ain't all sunflowers and daisies. You heard what happened in June, didn't you?"

"Yeah, sort of."

"You know Kristie and Daisy."

"Yeah, I do. Not good, though. Can't remember which one has dark hair and which has light?"

"Hey what are you two talking about?" Mose and Jano sat down at the fire.

"That time at Rae's"

"Oh that again."

"Well, Brenda hasn't heard it."

"Remember where you are. I'm sure she has."

"Don't listen to him, 'Trina. Go ahead."

"Anywho, those two, Kristie and Daisy that is."

"Hey, where are those two?"

"I dunno, Mose. You keep askin' me where people are and I keep sayin' the same thing."

"Hey, Jano, where are we?"

"I already told ya I don't know."

"Quiet down you two; let me tell my story."

"We were up to Rae's. It was late because we were there to see if Rae wanted to stop out after work. We had ourselves a little fire, and Lydia thought Rae'd like to come out.

You were gone somewhere—downstate. I'm not quite sure how it happened but Lydia didn't end up going over to ask Rae. So, the three of us went and we were waiting for Rae to close up. We were just talkin' about this and that, you know. Those two bought a couple of beers. Well, right before Rae is ready to push Scott Mohoney out of the bar, in comes John Bower, Brian Wiles, and horse-fuckin' Stststststephenson. Bower can barely stand up he's so drunk and he's leaning against Wiles. Well, it's like they're all stapled together and within a second they're all standing around us breathing their one-too-many breath on us. Bower is leaning over Daisy, but she ignores him and continues to talk to us about nothing. It really wasn't nothing, but I can't remember what she was talking about. So he reaches out, I can't even believe this; he reaches out and grabs her tit! I'm not joshing, either. She pushes his hand away, but he's so drunk insteada goin' backwards he falls forward right on top of her. Now he's down on the floor feelin' her up. Stephenson says something like 'come on baby let us all touch your tits.' Kristie stands up in

Seiler's face—you know Seiler, he's a pretty big guy. She stands up and puts her hands on his chest like she's gonna shove him away. He grabs her wrists in one hand and says ooh you want some action, too? Then he slid his hand up under her shirt. Rae Miller's gone. Disappeared. Then Rae's there with the shotgun. Bower is trying to get away from Daisy so quickly that he falls twice getting off her. Kristie didn't give Seiler a chance to get away. She booted him in the balls. He fell to the ground like a potato bug, all wrapped up around himself. Rae says, 'you boys better get out of here before you get into something you can't handle.' But that's not the end of it. Seiler says in his slow, stupid methodical way. 'We'll get you for this.' Like we did something wrong."

"So Katrina thinks those guys are the ones who started the fire out here." Mose interrupted.

"I know they are. I heard my cousin, Rich, talking about it. He was bragging it all up with my old man. The both of 'em yuckin' it up like it was funny. My dad says, 'there's been too much shit going on in Greenstone County.' And Rich says, 'we'll put a stop to that real soon.' That's what he said like he was gonna do something about it. Then as he was leaving he said, 'as for you cousin, I'd be careful about the company I keep.'" The fire snapped and pinesap fizzled as it boiled out of the logs.

"That's it? That's the story?"

"You had to be there. You don't know my cousin and his friends."

"That guy's got a screw loose."

"You don't know the half of it, Jano. He's been riding Ezra as long as I been coming up here. Ezra looks him full in the eye, not like he hasn't seen scarier shit, ya know, and says let's try to like each other, okay Rich. That steams that Cafus guy, man. He doesn't know what to think. He's afraid of Ezra, but he's not dangerous. He's just pathetic."

"I think he's cute."

"Okay," Mose says, "cute and pathetic."

"You always did like the dorks, Brenda."
"Hey, that's not true."
"All I know is he sides with my old man all the time. They think there's something big goin' on out here. Like we're sacrificing little lambs or something."
"Morons."
"You can say that again."

* * *

After Brenda left Katrina, she wandered home through the trees. The light of the sun was bright in her face. She saw two birds glued and stuck to something, hanging in the distance. The September sun silhouetted the birds in three-dimensional yellow. She thought kids could be pretty cruel as she walked home that morning. But she had always known that. Her taunting of Larry Erst rang though her morning memory. It should be an after-school special, she thought: *The Taunting of Larry Erst*. She shook her head and continued walking down Centerline.

Brenda couldn't tell what it was, maybe blackbirds, stuck somehow in mid-flight, without life. The black silhouettes in the distance looked remarkably like human figures. They were too big to be crows and no one in their right mind would string up a pair of bald eagles, not around here. She had seen the birds all right. But as she got closer she noticed that they weren't birds at all. They were Ezra and Patty. Hung by their feet from the high school backstop.

The newspaper reported alleged sado-masochism and sexual misconduct. It stated that an investigation of Cult-like activity in the deaths of Ezra Gern and Patty Ballantine was already underway. Allegations of drug induced suicide with, by, and involving others of a possible "cult" was the theory cast in the paper the next day. "'At this time information is being withheld pending further investigation,' stated Officer Richard Cafus of Greenstone County."

Poor Patty Ballantine hung arms down, reaching for gravity, tied by the feet. Ezra Gern with arms snagged and caught out at his sides, defying Newton, had been hoisted nearly to the top of the backstop. It was Ezra that Brenda had truly mistaken for a bird. That and the angle of the reflecting sun gave the eerie vision of the two black birds. Two black birds that she couldn't wash from her memory or her fear. "Nevermore."

* * *

"Okay, so what do you think you want to do?"

"About what?" Brenda responded as if she hadn't been part of her own conversation.

She could hear her heart pounding; she could feel it in her arms and fingers. "Oh. Oh Yeah. I don't know. I can't carry it. I can't let Rich know. Hell, I don't know what to do, Lydia. You're the doctor." She breathed in a tight-nosed squeak. "Abortion. Sooner the better, I guess." She would have liked to tell Toclep that she hadn't, of her own consent, slept with Rich in what seemed like years and that she and Lydia had a little secret of contraception. She would have liked to flaunt her affair with Ted in Rich's face so everyone in town would know, for spite's sake. However, underneath, in the webbed layers of her soul, crouched a dark creature she couldn't see but could feel. Fear. She couldn't feel it then but next to the creature of Fear was another, Hope. She couldn't feel Hope or sense Hope's presence. She could only sense Fear. "Can you do an abortion?" Brenda wasn't sure if she should say make or give or do, but she settled on do.

Why everyone in town knew everyone else's business but hadn't known about Ted was a mystery to her. Especially with Mr. Berge always steaming up his living room window to watch her every-morning move. Where had he been?

"Maybe, the baby will get you out of it." Lydia didn't say what was on her mind. She didn't say, don't you think that's a bit hypocritical? You were just talking about sin and adultery. She knew that was not for her to say. It was not for her to judge.

"Out of what?"

"Out of your troubles."

"Maybe it'll get me into 'em, too. I don't want to live in fear. I rather disappear, but I don't want to die." She would have started to cry if she could have, but she couldn't. She chewed her bottom lip and anger seethed within her. Maybe she did want to die. Maybe dying would be the answer to her fear, to her loneliness.

Brenda had told Lydia about how Rich treated her, yet there was much Lydia didn't know, too many trees for her to see through Brenda's forest.

"Does Ted know?"

"Of course he doesn't know." She acted disgusted. "What good would that do? None!" Lydia guided her to the over-stuffed leather chair on the other side of the room. "You remember this summer?"

"I remember." Lydia said. And she did know because she had been there and because Roadside Girl's walk around back had been her idea. What she didn't know but could only figure is it hadn't mattered in the long run anyway.

"We were at the Rae's and the bar was packed with trolls."

* * *

It was mid-summer. One of those late-setting-sun nights when Rae's filled up with tourists and locals alike. The only other time the bar saw as many people was for weddings, which turned into open bashes where all the men kissed the bride four times because they couldn't remember that they had already kissed her. It was one of those northern nights that fool people into thinking that it's only eight o'clock when it's actually ten-thirty. The day had been beautiful because the wind had blown out of the north, taking the stable flies off the beach and whisking them somewhere to the south. It was hard to tell where the flies had been swept. If the wind had been pushing up from the south, the stable flies would've covered the beach like a living blanket. Stabes, as they were known in the area, would tear at flesh, and there wasn't a human alive who could stay under water long enough to fool them. One quick breath above the surface would see five of the monsters light on the unfortunate swimmer. In the morning, the cool air would capture the stabes in sleep as they covered cars. Everyone in Toclep and probably anyone in stabe country knew that you could run your car up to fifty miles-an-hour and the stabes would hang on for the ride. They would stare with their fragmented, million eyes knowing that you had to get out of the car at some point and when you did, they were going to get their fill. They were going to clean your bones. Stable flies were an unknown phenomenon to downstaters because they never congregated by the trillions downstate. When told of the stabes, trolls would shake their heads like it was nothing but a thing, like you were talking about slow moving horse flies or easy-to-kill bee flies. However, that wasn't the stable fly. The stabe was the scourge of hell that blew in with a south wind, like the devil himself. Today there were no stabes because the wind had come cool out of the north. The beach had been a haven all day and the water, well the water had been Lake Superior water, swim if you want. It's cold. It numbs you through the bone and out the other side in the hottest of summers. It shoves your eyes back like powerful blue thumbs and shrinks and shrivels some things while making other things hard; it depended upon your sex. It had been a seasonably nice day, everyone would agree. However, for Brenda the day had been like other days filled with anticipation of nothing and anxiety of everything.

The locals crammed around the bar and everyone was trying to get everyone else to head down to the mosquito-infested beach to gather wood for a fire.

Mark O'Teegan was on his fourth beer and second shot, "I'll go and get us a pile of driftwood stacked up so high that they'll see the pup burnin' over in Canada. Pesky mosquitoes don't bother me none." In his yooper accent the go sounded as if Mark had been talking about ghosts. As he pushed away from the bar, he tipped over Rich's beer. It sloshed over the bar onto the floor at Rae Miller's feet.

"Thanks for the tip, Otter." Rae Miller was smiling. Rich was not.

"Jesus, Otter. Are you always so drunk that ya can't leave the bar 'thout a disaster?"

"Another beer for the man," O'Teegan called.

"I wouldn't need another if ya hadn't of spilled mine all over the place."

"You shouldn't of left it there." O'Teegan emphasized the of. However, Rich didn't catch it. "No use crying over spilt beer, Rich."

"Whatta ya going t'do give him a ticket? Drinking and spilling?" Roadside Girl's extended and stretched her internal vowel sounds. O'Teegan laughed at her comment and slapped her on the shoulder as he passed. He grabbed Frank Lampardson and, buying a bottle of Christian Brother's, the two men ushered themselves toward the waiting beach of driftwood.

"Did ya see there what the *USA Today* said about Michigan this mornin'? Can ya believe that?" Katrina had been the receptionist at the park for five years. She had heard every customer complaint imaginable. "Said, thanks to the new computer-reservation system, state parks in Michigan have had a dramatic rise in revenue. What bullshit. Do ya know how many bumbled reservations I've had to fix since that new computer system complicated something that already worked?"

"No kidding. Not s'posed to fix things that aren't broken. Those yahoos down in Lansing got everything so screwed up that no one knows whether they're pissin' or lookin' out the window," Rich added.

"Ya remember when Morairity took that job down there to get more administrative experience and they had him working on the hunting 'n fishing brochure?" Katrina asked the question and answered it in the same breath. "Hell, he found out that there were three groups of people working on different brochures that all said the same thing. Bureaucracy at its finest."

"Left hand don't know what the right hand's a-doing."

"Do we always have to talk about the bureaucracy?" Lydia asked. "Isn't there something else we can talk about that doesn't circle around government policy and how the trolls down in Lansing have no idea about what's going on over the bridge. Hell, we all know that. Any of you Libertarians don't know that?" She shouted to the bar. It didn't take much influence to get the crowd rocking in another direction.

"Anyone see that flick with Ben Stiller? Something about something. Hilarious." And they were off talking about the eighties. A discussion about movies might take all night because in order to see a movie, you had to get in your car and drive two hours one-way, for some choices, or one hour the other, for no choices. It was drive, movie, dinner, bar, and drive, and it was three a.m. before you got home. It wasn't something you did on a Tuesday evening. Therefore, no one discussed it as if it was.

The more the people drank, the more they slurred into their ideas until finally the conversation would be about something that no one could keep their mind on for more than the initial main point and that main point would circle around the group and keep coming back to same people. They would comment and pass it on. It was like a game of tag where touchbacks were allowed.

"To regret," Rich swayed in half-time not being able to find the rhythm of his words or the rhythm of the music, "is a mistake."

"How can ya say that?" Katrina asked.

"I never regret anything."

Brenda tried not to listen, but she knew what Rich was saying was true.

"To feel sorry for something that you've done. For something that is over and done. For something that ya didn't accomplish.

Hell, we'd all have to feel sorry about our whole lives. Nope, not me." Brenda looked the other direction, down the bar. Her eyes caught those of Roadside Girl. Roadside Girl furrowed her eyebrows and tightened her lips in a grimace and rolled her eyes toward Rich, and absently Brenda, whose eye contact went through Roadside Girl and rested somewhere on a knot hole in the paneling behind her, could only nod her head. She was having a conversation with herself.

"What about remorse?" Someone asked.

"Remorse is a different story," Rich said. But he really didn't know whether remorse was a different story or not because Rich, along with the rest of the bonfire intelligentsia, was neither Samuel Johnson nor Noam Chomsky.

Brenda regretted her marriage. She would've asked herself if Rich had regretted the way he had treated her, but she knew the answer. She was thinking about the affair that had begun in May with Ted Russell. Brenda could not keep her mind on the conversations as she thought about what might happen if Rich actually found out. Though Rich had not followed any of the biblical ideals of marriage, he had clung to the puritanical roots of patriarchy: spider to web. He had used those roots to push Brenda and her feelings down like stuffing garbage into a paper bag. It was not her infidelity that bothered her about the affair; the ideas of sin would come to her later. It was Rich's plumes of rage that crawled up her spine. It was the demands Rich had forced upon her under the guise of playfulness or manliness. It was simple for her. It was rape—rape of her mind and soul and spirit. She couldn't even think about her body, because she had discarded that. She had folded it so far within herself that even she couldn't see it. She didn't feel rage because she couldn't sort anything out of the fear she felt. That was what kept her where she was.

"Hey, Bren', Brenda ya in there?" Roadside Girl waved her hand in front of Brenda's opaque eyes. "Hey, that's some nasty bruise, eh?" She pointed to a blue bruise that was fringed by jaundice yellow.

"You know Brenda." Rich, who had been in his own conversation, snapped around to Roadside Girl like a dragonfly. Brenda opened her mouth but didn't say anything. "Stepped on one of her shoes. Thought she was gonna break her frickin' neck. I'm always telling her to put the damn things away. Aren't I always telling ya that, honey?"

"Yes, ya are." She felt his arm slip around her and then his fingers softly squeeze into the bruise.

"She stepped on one of those shoes and woof her legs went out from under her and down the stairs she went. Ass over applecart. If I hadn't of been so worried about her well-being it would of been a funny sight. Kinda Abbott and Costello like."

On the inside she kicked herself. What did I ever do, she thought? What did I ever do to deserve this? The only thing she hadn't done was to see clearly from the beginning. That was her only sin. Unfortunately, it was a grievous and unforgivable sin that she wouldn't allow herself to forget. It was a sin that was slowly peeling away and eating the lining of her soul.

When Ted Russell stepped into the bar Brenda's eyes stopped looking through people and started focusing on the finish of the bar. Then they dashed around, never stopping to make contact anywhere. Brenda had tried to avoid situations where her husband and her lover would be in the same room. It wasn't as if they were going to strike up much of a conversation. Ted was not a local. He was a troll—a downstater—who had only moved to Toclep last August. Ted was held on the edges by Rich, who believed strongly in the rites and rituals of locals. It wasn't like she was afraid that Ted would saunter up to Rich at the bar and say, "Hey, Rich you know that thing that Brenda does when . . . ." It was that she couldn't trust her eyes. That and she just couldn't take having all the Robinson's over for dinner. But there they all were at Rae Miller's, slopping beers down, easing into the numbness of a bonfire night.

"What's up with Brenda?" Roadside Girl whispered to Lydia.

"Got things on her mind."

Rich also noticed Brenda's eyes. With the addition of one person to the crowd, Brenda felt so cramped she could hardly control her anxiety. Ted had been her sanctuary from Rich. He had been the light in her sordid and dark life but when he entered the bar it was as if all the light had been sucked out of her world. Now, as Ted and Rich faced each other in the smoky, yellow light of Rae Miller's, Brenda suffocated.

"When we going down ta the fire?" Brenda was trying to move the party to the open air. She was trying to take it outside. She was hoping there was a chance that Ted would not be included.

"Beachfire tonight?"

"Sure is, Ted ole boy, why don't ya join us? Ya gotta stop being such a troll if you're gonna stay in Toclep."

Brenda swallowed her beer in one gulp.

In the bathroom she washed her face and talked to her reflection without moving her lips. When she had gone to the bathroom for the third time in thirty minutes Rich asked, "What's up with you? That time of the month again?" Brenda was just about to say, yes when he added, "I thought ya just had that thing." After two more times to the bathroom Rich grabbed her by her bruised arm. "What're ya doing running back there? I just went to the bathroom and ya know what I saw?" Brenda moved her shoulders just enough to indicate she didn't know. "I saw a line of women at that door. You're not going in and out of the john that fast, so what the hell are ya doing?" He was speaking in a lock jawed voice that wasn't audible to anyone else. He looked as if he was chewing on sunflower seeds, trying to separate the seed from the shell.

"When are we heading down ta the fire?" She announced her question to the crowd hoping to have Rich's question swept into movement. But her tone sounded weak and frail and it broke halfway through. No one moved.

"Just one more and that's it," somebody said.

"Or two."

Rich reached around Brenda, "We're gonna step outside for a sec'; Bren' needs some fresh air." Brenda had a sickly look on her face and everyone in the bar could see she really did need some fresh air. What they couldn't see was by stepping outside she wasn't going to get any. Lydia threw a glance into Brenda's eyes but Brenda only dropped her head, which in itself was an admission.

The back of Rae Miller's was an isolated, unlighted grassy area. It was more of a volleyball court than a courtyard and was some of the finest real estate in Greenstone County. It was used for the end-of-season chicken bash, which was an all out eat-a-thon of barbecued chicken, potato salad, and rice crispy treats. Other than that not too many people went around back of Rae's unless it was to use the largest bathroom in the world.

"Okay what the hell's goin' on?" He had her by the arm and was pinching deep into the soft, banana bruise.

"Ouch. Easy. Nothing's goin' on."

"Why's it that as soon as Mr. Teacher-man came into the bar ya got all clammy and started ta run off ta hide in the bathroom?"

"I wasn't hidin'."

"No? Then what were ya doing back there? Cuz ya weren't goin' to the bathroom." She was trying to come up with the best response. She no longer had the same feeling of drowning she had had within the bar. But that didn't help her think any quicker or more clearly. "I asked ya a question." His spit sprayed her face.

"I just don't feel good."

"Come on Brenda. Don't lie ta me. I'm the one who said ya didn't feel good."

"I had a couple too many. My head's swimming. I needed some space." The last part of her statement was true. She needed about a thousand miles of space.

"I'll tell ya what was swimming," he said. "Your eyes were

swimming all over the bar. But ya know where they never stopped? They never stopped on teacher-boy in there. Nope, ya avoided all contact with him. Why do ya think that's so? Is it cuz ya want to screw him?"

"I don't know."

"Oh, so ya do want to screw him."

"I didn't say that."

"What are ya saying? I don't know Brenda. Ya know I'm a detective and it's easy ta tell by someone's eyes and body language that they're lying. And you're lying. Whatta ya thinkin' about? Ya thinkin' about getting that young teacher into bed with ya?" When he said it, she jerked her arm free.

"Don't be ridiculous."

"That's what you're thinkin'. I can't believe it. Jesus you've got fifteen years on that kid. But that's what you're thinkin', isn't it?" She didn't respond. She just stood with the eyes of a dog. "I can't believe it. Right in there in front of all our friends." His voice got louder. "Damn it. I'll kill ya for even thinking, about another," he brought his arm up like he was getting ready to serve at Wimbledon and that's where his arm stopped, caught in mid air behind his head. He was confused and angry and jerked around but that only twisted his arm in a way that he couldn't easily break free. When he spun around he was face-to-face with Roadside Girl who stood an inch taller than he was, and she was looking down into his eyes. She had his wrist and in his anger, position, and state of inebriation he couldn't quite figure out how to break free. "Let go of my fucking arm. This isn't any of your business. Go back inside." He wanted his arm, but she was not going back inside without it.

"I think it is my business, officer." Rich's arm went limp. Roadside Girl tightened her grip then she thrust his arm away. As a police officer, Rich had always hated domestic calls. They were dangerous. They were volatile. They were explosive. He didn't turn to look at Brenda. There would be a time and place to finish this later. Just like there would be another sunset and another moonrise. There would be a time.

* * *

Lydia remembered that night. She had remembered because she had told Roadside Girl to see if Brenda needed anything, and she had. Again, the sound of the sand against the window rose in the room. Lydia moved from where she was leaning against the counter and walked over to Brenda.

She put her hand on Brenda's stomach. "Five and a half weeks." Brenda wasn't too surprised. After all, Lydia was the doctor. She should know. Lydia walked over to the window and looked down onto Clarion, again. "Come here." Brenda would have asked why but she couldn't think of any reason to, so she walked over to the window. "Lean your head against the window. Feels good. Feels cool and young and free of worries, doesn't it? Feels like coldwater breaths." Brenda didn't respond, but it did feel all of those things. "How long have you been thinking about this?" Lydia could barely hear her breathe. "Go home and think a little more. Think clearly. Lean your head against a window and let the coolness fill you and then think. That's the prescription."

"But I can't think clearly. I can't think; I can't even sleep. Haven't slept in nights."

"Lean your head against a window in your house. Do it today. You'll be able to sleep. Guaranteed." She raised two fingers in a Scout's honor sign. "Does Rich have any idea?"

"No, I hope not. No."

"Are you sure?"

"Pretty sure," but she really was only sure of the childlike fear that poked its head from her dark closet.

When Brenda was gone, Lydia stood at the window again. This time she watched Brenda walk into the wind. Her hair didn't fly into her mouth or across her eyes. Instead it followed her like a cape as she leaned into, instead of arching with, the pushing wind. The wind on the windows sounded stronger than it had sounded earlier and the sand hailed against it, even there on the second floor. Lydia felt bad for Brenda; she always had. But everything would be okay, in a sense. Next week would not be just like last week; unfortunately, that didn't make Lydia feel any better about Brenda.

Roadside Girl sat on Sunset Rock waiting for the morning fire to break over the trees. The nights were cold, but the great water would hold the temperate daytime warmth for another month before the tipping earth and shifting sun would give way to the frights of winter. The breeze pulled off the land, which usually meant stable flies, and left smooth water out beyond the tiny inlet of sandstone. The cove was a miniature model of the Canadian Shield basin that swung its pendulum from this edge of Superior to the banks of Isle Royale.

Roadside Girl waited to take a morning swim so the sun's hand could warm her when she came out of the icy waters. In the shadows of the hemlocks she shivered, even with the south wind. But a little sun would warm her skin and sweep the goose flesh out beyond the ripples, which formed just after the sandstone break wall. She squatted on the edge of the sandpaper that angled into the clear, cold water. The front of her skirt dipped into the glass and made ripples run from her until they disappeared. The bottom of her skirt was dirty and a cloud of swamp mud drifted over the silt-covered rocks, changing their shape and appearance as the water breathed beneath the tiny rolls on the surface. Soon, she would dive down to the stark coldness, to the underwater canyons of rock. She would dive through the five inch frosting of semi-warm water that napped on the surface of this little inlet. She would swim out to the deep water to her own private island and lie in the sun, but not yet. Not until the sun changed the light swamp-breeze into warm, low air.

She stood. She looked for the shoots of white. Behind her were the black, eighty-foot sentinels rising out of the gray-skinned sugar maples and the scrubby swamp cedars and jack pines. They didn't let sun through. They kept ground cover from growing; they sheltered the hidden path, never allowing it to dry. They hid the bit of sand that washed over the rock and formed a small beach. She was looking for windows in the arms, for the laser of light that would tell her it was time to join the water. Then she felt it, one warm finger pushing her dishwater hair. The pressure of the warmth tingled down her neck and raised goose flesh for a flash through her arms and ribs and down her legs into the brown, waxy, leather boots that were covered with swamp-black. It's almost time, she thought.

The isolation of this place used to frighten her; it used to Hansel-and-Gretel her imagination. Walking through the cave of trees was dark and cold, even at mid-day. The ransacked, overgrown Ramsey house—the house tipped sideways from winter ice and Superior winds, the house built far too close to the edge of wintry hell, the house with black, barren arms of ash pitching through the windows reaching for the distant and ill frequent sun, the house with the ghosts of fifteen-year-old boys looking at the pictures in 1973 *Playboys* and drinking their parents' liquor out of mayonnaise jars—used to startle and strangle her. What if someone in there was watching? She laughed to herself, now. What if? Give him a thrill wouldn't it?

Since she started coming here, she had rarely seen anyone else. No one walked this isolated stretch of craggy rock. The only prints she had ever seen on the charcoal, cedar-swamp path were those of black bear, marten, and coon. When the teenage partiers stopped coming to this place was not exactly clear to her. The mouth of the path on Bayside Road had grown over. Two green ash trees symmetrically imitated each other and marked the way. To her, they stuck out in the foothills of white pine that eased into the great hemlock mountains that separated the road from the lake. The land was private. The Ramsey family of Somewhere, Georgia still legally held title to this stretch of coastline. No one seemed very interested in the land, because it was too low to build on, with the modern codes, and there probably wasn't any way to get water from the sandstone and bedrock that lay three inches below the swamp mulch. In the summer, black flies and mosquitoes regulated woodland travel, especially in swampy areas like this. Stable flies ruled the beaches and drove the few brave tourists back to their tents or hotel rooms or to Rae Miller's to drink beer. Roadside Girl had found, though, that the winds in this cove were directed differently by the lay of the land and swept most of the stabes down toward the Raspberry River. That's where the sand beach was and that's where the tourists would say, "It's only a few flies. No problem." Two minutes later they would be flailing their arms like fancy kites and running their welted bodies into their stabe-filled cars. Sometimes tourists unknowingly left the windows open, and they'd be striking at their ankles as the innocent looking housefly tore painful pieces of flesh off their lower legs. Though the slight breeze may have brought stabes in the summer, the flies were now out of season.

Mosquitoes had never bothered Roadside Girl, a fact that she attributed to her intake of garlic. Black flies, too, must not have liked her smell for they would rarely light on her. Of course, she knew not stand around the edge of a woods where they were worst.

In the seventies many people, struck by poverty and ghost stories moved from this area. The townies had forgotten about this place, too. The entry grew over, the ash sprouts turned into trees and the vanished path became a secret. She had seen an occasional kayaker paddle around the cove and had come across a fire pit on the beach a couple of times; however, it wasn't like locals to walk all the way down here when there was a rarely used easement just this side of Rae Miller's. Though the easement was close enough to the Raspberry River to attract tourists, it had the distinct look of private property. Locals kept themselves to Rae Miller's or to the easement. It was a shame for them, but a godsend for Roadside Girl because this place was one of the few from which one could witness a sunset over water. The narrow cove jutted out two hundred feet into Superior then fish-hooked around an expanse of water about the size of a football field. The cove locked in the little bit of warm water and was fairly shallow between the arms that corralled it. This allowed the bottom rocks, with the help of the sun, radiate the trapped water. But out where the arms opened into the Great Lake, the water sprinted downward to cold depths. That's where she soon would swim.

 The sun was washing her body halfway down her blue patterned skirt. She squatted and rolled gently back to a smoothed barkless log, untied her dirty boots, and tugged her feet out of the leather boxes. I wish I never had to wear shoes, she thought. But she did have to wear boots. In the summer she could get away with being barefoot if she wasn't working in the woods or chopping wood. Her skirts would hide most of her legs and no one seemed to notice or care that she didn't wear shoes. No Shoes, No Shirt, No Service didn't apply to Roadside Girl. Mrs. Tiffelson was about the only person who would comment, "you're carrying all kinds of germs on your feet. Act like you live in the twentieth century for heaven's sake, put something on those feet." It made Roadside Girl laugh. People often worried about germs, refusing to live life because some microscopic, paisley fish might jump up and bite them. After all it wasn't as if she ate with her feet. And as far as the twentieth century was concerned, Roadside Girl questioned what Mrs. Tiffelson knew about being a modern woman. The woman routinely cleaned the rooms of her four boys because they were too lazy to do it themselves. They knew that their mother would do it if they didn't. They were right. Mrs. Tiffelson was a mother who worked like an indentured servant, preparing meals and washing dishes and doing laundry and ironing shirts and mending tears in John's or Dan's or Mike's or Mark's

Wranglers after they had been out under-age-drinking or raising havoc with Peterson's cows or fences or mailbox. Mrs. Tiffelson was not the example of a modern woman that Roadside Girl wanted to emulate. If Roadside Girl didn't have to live through the aching winters of the north and the ongoing chores around the house and in the woods, she never would've worn shoes.

She threw her wool socks into a small pool of warm water—trapped from the last winds, walked over—her bare feet slapping and flattening on the sandpaper-like rock, happy to be released from their prisons, and bent to slosh and wring her socks a few times in the warm water. She then took them to the big water and rinsed them clean. After wringing them, she brought them up to her face and smelled the wet wool. It was a smell that most people thought dreadful, but it was a natural smell, dirt and sweat trapped in fiber. It was one of water and air and animal and one she loved. She draped the socks over an arm of the dead and barkless tree and the white heat of the sun blazed on the scraggly fibers and glistened like slivers of glass.

It was warm now and she slid out of her faded Carhartt and turned it inside out to the sun. The worn flannel looked like an old Mackinaw blanket. She had turned her jacket lining out toward the sun maybe a hundred times and never thought about it being like an Indian blanket, but now because of Dave, she couldn't help but see it any other way. She listened for the lapping of water against rock, but the water was being quiet. All she could hear was the light breeze at the top of the trees; the breeze was starting to put edges on the water fifty or a hundred yards out. She slid out of the patterned skirt and let it sit in a pile of sunlight on the brown rock. The sun washed her entire body and hugged her with warmth. She turned her back to the heat for a moment then swung around facing the sun head-on. It felt good on her skin, like putting her hands up to the flame of a campfire. She knew that the water would be cold. It would be a good cold, a cold of invigorating senses, a cold of forgotten knowledge, a cold of silent intercourse. Sometimes, it was easy to dive in without thought and other times it took standing and premeditation as if standing would somehow heat the water. Standing was the dare of the action, the push from the back.

She pulled off her undershirt, pushed her underwear to the rock, and stepped into the sun. She was naked. She felt like she had stood on this very rock in this very way a hundred years ago, a thousand years ago, a million years ago as a naked fish climbing to land, seeking the same kind of freedom she was seeking now from the water. There was a sense of strength in standing on this rock naked, with no fear. She felt warm. There were no shivers left from the pre-sun wall of hemlocks. There was only warm freedom.

She broke through the five-inch layer of warmth on the surface—the layer of lies which told a testing hand that the water wasn't that bad, that the water would be fine for playing beach games and swimming for hours. However, underneath that layer slept the truth, as it had always silently slept. Lightening cold water swept from the depths of Gitchee Gumee and formed the place of no decay. Her heart seized from shock and her eyes bulged in clear pain, gripping her brain with cold truth. She glided through the water and came to the surface with an urgent gasping breath, "whhoooa," and shook her now dark hair out of her face as she tread water. It was deep between the two break walls, maybe twenty feet. She turned like a dolphin and dived down, feeling the pressure in her ears and on her skin, yet seeing farther because of the cold. Because of the reflection of light in the clear water, she could see farther than one could see with a mask in Lake Michigan. Sometimes, she would fright when below water. What if she swam into a Sturgeon? What if she swam into something down there that no one knew was still around? These icy waters preserve. Bodies in sunken ships don't rot; it's too cold. They just stare out into icy blue with cloudy bulged eyes. Maybe creatures from the past had the same luck. Today she wouldn't think of such things.

She ran her hands over her naked body and pushed all the

air bubbles away from her. Her skin tingled like being rubbed with alcohol. The bubbles raced to the surface looking to merge back with their mother sky. When she reached the rock on the outer rim of the cove, she was tired and though she wasn't numb-cold, she relished the thought of climbing onto the baking sandstone and having her body sponge the warmth from rock and sky. The sun had just come over the hemlocks on shore, but it had pounded this sliver of rock for an hour. Her body felt as if it was glowing as she pulled onto the rock, scrapping a thin layer of skin from her shin.

She was away from land. She was on her island in the middle of the ocean, an ocean she could drink from if she wanted. She looked inward at her socks that hung and waved from the outstretched arm of the bald tree, to the small pile of blue in front of them, to the wall of hemlocks that somehow had been dwarfed by the sky and were no longer overpowering. She could see the bright green moss on one edge of the Ramsey house and knew that not even ghosts looked out at her nakedness because she wasn't naked; she was simply free.

The water was still. It moved away from her, unnoticeably. In here, in her fresh water lagoon was peace. She closed her eyes and still saw shifting water behind her eyelids. A slight warm breeze blew over her body and galvanized it in the sun. No goose flesh, only the warm soft fingers of September.

Brenda Cafus was in the kitchen of her one and one-half story house. She had done everything she could to make it a home, but the comfort of love, of real care, did not hang in the framed needle-point caption above her telephone: "home is where the heart is." If that were true, she wouldn't be here. She wouldn't be peeling the nutrition off carrots so they would be orange—the way Rich liked them. "Come on Bren', you're jus' being lazy. I like 'em orange. You know that. Not brown like they come out of the ground. What are we, animals?"

She had bigger problems than carrots, now. She was not only cooking on the outside but she was cooking on the inside and that was the cooking that had her thinking. I know he'll find out, she thought. I know he'll find out and he'll beat me again. After the incident at Rae Miller's Brenda started lying about having some sort of infection and had denied Rich sex, for his own good. "You don't want to get this on your mick," she said using his terminology. "Then go to the doc an' get her fixed up," he had said. And she did. She went to Lydia and they talked about Roadside Girl and how Brenda wished she were young again and knew what she knew now—which, she admitted, wasn't very much. Brenda never mentioned the non-existent infection. Lydia figured she simply needed someone to talk to. When Rich talked at Brenda, she in turn talked in her head. She replayed stories in her mind, as if they had actually happened to people she knew. Lydia had told her the story of Francis Macomber, replacing the name Francis with Rich and chuckling with the outcome. "That's a hoot, isn't it?" Lydia had said. "Shot by his own wife, poor guy." A tragedy, Brenda thought. She could see herself saying, "The buck was comin' right out of the woods at me. Biggest one I ever seen, ten, twelve points. It was moving fast so I, quick, pulled up the shotgun and let loose." She envisioned tucking the slug into the single-shot twelve gauge, clicking the barrel up like folding an ironing board, and drawing a bead on Rich who was walking with his Remington on his shoulder whistling his way to the River Kwai. *Bang.* It would echo through the trees and send birds into flight and stop a few autumn birds from chanting for just a wink. Then they'd start again. "I couldn't tell it was him. He was jokin' around; you know Rich—always jokin' around." She would be able to use the same story-telling device that Rich always used on her. "He had taken his orange off and was carrying the buck over his head. I didn't know it was him."

She looked at the mound of naked carrots. The bright orange reflected off the white porcelain of one sink and the discarded coats and trousers of carrots sat in the trap of the other. She had not been paying attention and, subsequently, had peeled enough carrots for ten people. "I'll make cole slaw and carrot cake," she sighed.

The kitchen, with its sinks and stove on one side and the table with three good chairs and one wobbly-legged chair on the other, was too clean not to be on television. Brenda felt like she was Mrs. Cunningham. However, Rich was no Mr. C. "You're here all day, whatdya do? Watch soaps?" The truth was she only liked television when Rich was home. Anything to occupy his mind. Anything to lock her shell. Anything to keep him from the womb she tried to create. He would come home and be soaked into whatever was on the screen, unconsciously hypnotized by colorful moving images like a dog watching squirrels. She got into the habit of turning on the television just before he was due home. She also got into the habit of keeping things clean. Not for him, but because it was easier. It was easier than the humiliation; it was easier than the hand. Two weeks ago he had slapped her hard enough to knock her to the foot of the bed.

* * *

"So you have an infection, that's down there." He pointed, "Get on your knees then." She was bleeding from biting her tongue.
"But I'm bleeding."
"Make it taste better. New and improved."
"Not now, Rich. Please, not now."
"You're my wife and I won't have you telling me when." He slapped the side of her head and the pain rang through her tongue like the noon fire-whistle. "What would my friends say if they thought my own wife wouldn't have sex with me?" He put his hands on her shoulders and pushed her to her weeping knees.

* * *

She was jerked back to the kitchen, which was too bright, by a wrenching feeling in her lower stomach as she threw up onto the discarded carrot clothing. The thick liquid climbed and splattered all over the counter and splash walls of the sink full of carrot skins. It wasn't the pregnancy. It was the thought of Rich shoving her to her knees, always shoving her down. This needs to end, she thought. It wasn't that the actions happened everyday, it was that they replayed every second—over and over in her mind like stop action photography and in the same images she saw Ezra Gern, an upside-down black bird. I'm not sure how to end it, but it needs to end. The words were inside her head, but she was not sure whether she had said them aloud or not so she looked around the room, unsure if the refrigerator or the stove would repeat her thoughts when Rich was there.

Unconsciously, she thought about her brother Tim who worked as one of Greenstone County's deputies. Not that the county, with its seven shrinking villages needed many police officers but nepotism was alive and well in Greenstone County. Rich had gotten Tim the job. It was what people did for each other. What would happen if Tim found out how Rich treated her. What would happen to Tim if Brenda ended the marriage? Brenda only thought about it momentarily because what was more pressing to her was what Rich did to her. And what he would do to her if she had a baby that looked just like Ted Russell, knowing full well they hadn't had sex in months. His ruthlessness shined through like blinding flashes of lightening whenever something did not go his way. The beatings, the threats, the rapes, the emotional fear and scare tactics of sub-human warfare were a matter of course to her. Only recently had she started to climb from her hole. However, he scared her. She wasn't sure she could stop his actions toward her or anyone else. What would happen to Ted? He couldn't just leave his new job. Jobs in this part of the country were breadcrumbs; they disappeared fast and didn't sustain much.

She wiped the mixture of tangerine, coffee, and toast, out of the sink wringing the hand-knit washcloth as scalding water poured from the faucet. "Damn water heater." Taking bleach from under the sink she doused the rag and disinfected the blue counter top and sink.

For the second time in two days she thought back to the morning scene. She wondered why the image seemed to connect for her. She didn't know why she was afraid, exactly. A little slip of the tongue and a nearly forgotten phone call were bothering her even though she couldn't exactly put her finger on why. Brenda startled as a featureless Ford that cried, "salesman," pulled into her driveway, clunked into reverse, backed out, and went the other direction. She was absently chopping cabbage for cole slaw. The reality pulled her instantly back to the present and she said, "I hate cabbage," before dropping back into her thoughts.

Katrina would have disappeared into the nooked woods off highway 52—dancing and singing all night with Jano and Mose and those two girls. All of them lived with Ezra in the cabin that hid from the eyes of Toclep behind trees and fence of Gern property. Brenda remembered what she needed to remember. Katrina would have done that but she never got the chance. Two black birds stopped her.

"I don't want to be a bird," she said. Again she jerked her head around to make sure no one was there, that no one had heard her. But there was no one. There were only the ghosts in Brenda's mind—cricking and cracking, settling and shifting in the sand and wind around the house. She felt warm and realized she was sweating. "I didn't see anything, just some birds."

That was the year that the town had cleared out. The double suicide and ghost stories therewith had steered visiting families from the path of Toclep. It was fear of the occult that kept families from moving anywhere in the general vicinity. It was two black birds that helped ten good Lutheran families pick up a century of life and disappear into the ocean of people in St. Paul and Grand Forks and Eau Claire. And it was the quiet investigation that blew Brian Wiles, John Bower, Eric McCrogey, and Seiler Stephenson quietly and namelessly north, south, east, and west without anyone ever taking notice, without anyone ever asking, "how come those four boys up and lit out of town?" Toclep became a ghost town.

Brenda cut her finger with the serrated knife she was using to cut onions. "Wrong tool for the job," she muttered as she turned on the cold water. It mingled with the cherry-red blood and blushed, then swirled down the stainless drain trap. "Second incident of the day. Can't wait for number three."

All this because she had missed her period and a thirteen-dollar ph strip had said, "Yes, indeed you are pregnant." She couldn't have a baby and she also couldn't have any sign of a baby because then she'd have to have the baby.

She had stopped in Houghton that day. The day before she would be shoved to her knees. She picked up Rich's new gun case, which the people at Hanley's were happy to load into the white pick-up bed, purchased the pregnancy test with her eyes down, and quickly exited the store as if someone in Houghton might recognize her. After she took the test, she wrapped the plastic and paper stick along with the box and instructions loosely in newspaper, squirted a little lighter fluid on it as she passed through the garage, and incinerated it in the burn-barrel. She cleaned the bathroom and retraced her steps from the truck three times to make sure she hadn't dropped a receipt or the instructions or even a sticker from Rite-Aid. "What'd ya buy at Rite-Aid?" The question stiffened her. Lying on the spot showed in the eyes, the lack of assurance and confidence in the wavering vibrations of the voice. She already knew that from the incident at Rae's. She had looked up that day to see Mr. Berge standing in the window and watching her pace the driveway as she frantically searched for pieces of paper that didn't exist.

Abortion. That was the only answer. Could Lydia do it, Brenda wondered. It seemed like she could do just about anything. Best doctor this county had ever seen. Brenda wondered if she would be strong enough to hide it. Her strength had increased lately, her stoicism and detachment worked together to form oblivion that Rich had somehow mistaken for menopause even though his mother had told him Brenda wasn't experiencing menopause.

She feared Rich. There were things about the black birds that swooped around him. There were hushed undertows swimming beneath her, ready to suck her into the depths at any minute. She had evidence of his rashness, his violence. She had those weeks when she couldn't leave the house because she didn't want to raise attention to the fact that she had fallen off the unsteady chair and had banged her mouth or cheek on the faucet or the side of her head on the back of a chair or her lip on the counter. She didn't want to have Rich stand beside her at Murphy's and say, "You know Brenda, clumsiest woman I've ever known. You ought to see her bang around the kitchen," he'd laugh. "It's a wonder she's not sprawled out in the hospital with a concussion half the time. I'd have to cook for myself then. Or have your Mary come over and help me." He'd chuckle as he nudged Harvey with a wink. "Mary and me we could cook something up, eh." He'd laugh as if the sexual innuendo was funny. "That's why we're out tonight. Can't have her cooking in this condition, can we honey?"

She knew him. She should have seen it when she married him. It felt like a thousand years. "Eternal damnation for your sins." Bamboozled, she thought, the lies, the deceit of courtship and early marriage. I'll go see Lydia again today. I'll tell her it's life or death. She was sitting on the unstable kitchen chair, the chair of lies, looking out onto Pine Street wishing that the window shined out onto the lake or onto some brown autumn prairie—space before trees. It did not. She put her head to the cool window.

She looked out at Berge's bright, blue house that sat nosily across the driveway. "You never see anything do you, old man?" Then her eyes focused through the window on the sagging man with his hand down the front of his striped boxer shorts. He smiled as if to say, yes, I actually do see quite a lot.

The small log house sat in the nook of Gern property and had become a museum of the seventies. It was nestled into a two-acre panhandle, which hid behind a stand of old growth and now grown scruff cedar. It abutted and peninsula-ed the strip of national forest between Gern property and the Crescent Mountain land that Matthew Gern had donated to the state in 1958 after his Brother John's heart unexpectedly stopped ticking. The nook was linked to highway 52 by an overgrown two-track and was hugged by the deep crook in Owl Creek. This was one of only three or four places deep enough to swim from where it began to trickle out of the mountains to where it flowed into the Raspberry River. Lydia's house sat on the far edge of an old mining meadow across the creek. Neither her house nor Tom's, which sat in the next field over toward the lake, could be seen from Ezra's cabin.

Ezra built the house when he returned from Vietnam and no one but Tom had entered it since the brief investigation of Ezra's death in '78. Painstakingly, Ezra had chopped and hand hewed logs the way pioneers had. He didn't really know how to build a house, but he set to this project like a missionary to the conversion of people ignorant of the word—selecting trees to fall, stripping bark, weathering wood, and treating with pitch for longevity. He measured with precision. He drilled holes for plumbing and electricity. Ezra was a naturalist but he couldn't live without his stereo nor was it practical to try to get water from the outdoor pump in the sixty-inch snows and twenty-below blows of winter.

He started the cabin in the spring of '72 when he had finally been sent home from the military hospital. In the four months before he started college again, he selected, felled, and de-barked five large hemlocks of which he used every last scrap in building his house. He used the solid bottoms to set his foundation. The thick legs of dinosaurs, which he covered with dirt and let sit while the other wood cured, settled into the rocky soil. They situated themselves like they were snuggling into a blanket. In the summer of his junior year at Kalamazoo College, he put the roof on with the help of Moses Paxton. Mose was a large veteran who had survived two AK 47 slugs in the back and had dragged himself through unremembered miles of leech-infested swamp with holes a man could whistle through in his chest and stomach. How the bullets had actually missed his lungs, heart, liver, and kidneys was nothing short of a miracle. "Praise God, son. It's a miracle you're alive," the doctors had told him. Ezra met him in the infirmary with his own rather interesting whistling hole.

Mose Paxton had not been a student nor for the sake of miracles had he been a carpenter. However, he could lift logs as if he were a forklift and tell stories as he did it.

* * *

"One time we were in the ranks. Damn, we were scruffy. Guys in shorts and cut off shirts. Hotter 'n hell. No one ever wore their flak jacket or helmet anymore. Looked more like a pick-up football game than a military operation. This spiffy looking Australian officer comes out with the C.O. He's all dressed pretty in long, green knee socks and shiny shoes. Uniform's got little brass buttons, shinin' all over. He's got an ascot on. Look's like Dick Van Dyke for God's sake, and he's wearing a neat little beret. It's about 120 degrees and humid as all get out. He's even got one of those silly leather horsewhip things like he thinks he's Patton or something. He comes out there and the C.O. lets him have the run of things. The guy yells, 'Attention!' But no one does anything. We're all standing around tired and sweaty, looking at each other, smoking cigarettes. So, he yells it again, and we kind of straighten up, everyone's looking at everyone else, wondering what's going on and who the hell this spiff is. The officer in all his spiffy looks yells out, 'Well this group wouldn't make it in the Queen's Army.' He says it all proper-like, sounding like James Bond and whatnot. So someone behind me says, 'Ahhhhh, fuck the Queen.' The whole squad breaks down laughing. The Aussie officer is up there yelling, 'Attention! Attention!' And this is the good part. Our C.O. walks over to him and puts his arm around the guy and says, 'I think you lost 'em, sir.' We were all bustin' a gut. 'I think you lost 'em, sir.' Someone else yells out from the ranks, and we all crack up."

* * *

Mose was a man whose spirit of life outweighed any concern for the future or care for others' expectations. "I can't do it." He once said to Ezra's father. "I can't settle into anything that promotes one man killing another. If I have a job, I have to pay taxes. If I pay taxes, it goes into the war machine. I can't do it." Matthew Gern commented that it went to other things, too. Schools. Roads. Libraries. "But there's that one machine. And you've seen it. You know what I'm talking about. I won't do it. And you know damn well why, Mr. Gern. I can't. I just can't." His ideas were not pathos. Mose was alive, unlike many of his non-returning friends from Hammond, Indiana. He questioned the walking disconnected who stumbled through the good life here in the States wondering if it was hot enough for you—unaware that not only on the other side of the globe but also right here in America, brother was killing brother. Aware only that enemy killed enemy, and as long as it was the enemy it was okay. Mose Paxton was looked upon with grumbling discontent in Toclep. He was one of two veterans who grumbled in their own way. He was an outsider. He didn't want to have a job. And, he was black.

* * *

Today Tom, followed by two cats and the near deafening sound of crickets, walked the fence line, which enclosed the Gern property, to the cabin. He didn't go inside this time. Rather, he just walked around the perimeter looking through glass, tipping his head sideways to see through the curtained windows. He would go into the cabin on occasion and sweep some of the dust, though there rarely was much, out the front door and finger some books that he had patiently re-shelved after the investigation. Occasionally, he would take a book from the shelf and carry it over the field to his kitchen table and read it. He would return it to the dark hole in the bookshelf the next time he went by the cabin. He stepped onto the frontier style wrap-around porch and making a glare shield with his hands, leaned against the front window. With his head tipped toward his shoulder, he looked into the house. He could see over the half-wall into the kitchen. The kitchen begged softly, "somebody . . . anybody . . . turn on the stove. Cook something. I can't smell anymore. Somebody . . . anybody . . . I'm dying." The refrigerator door was open but no light shined from it. The faucet was as dry on the inside as it was on the outside, and there wasn't anything left for bugs, trapped mid-way down the kitchen drain, to eat. So they died and turned to dust there. Tom could see the olive-drab military-issue jacket and the Levi-issue denim jacket hanging on the support posts between the living room and the kitchen. He could read the calendar's forgotten letters, September 1978, in bold, lonely print on the back wall next to the smothered light of the curtained back door. "Sure is a beautiful house, Ezrie." Tom's accent had been softened by college and reading. He checked around the sides to see that none of the windows were broken. There had been some trouble like that shortly after Ezra's death, but people forget fast and the house was left to sleep off the seventies, but it never did. It became the focus of all and any ghost stories that surfaced during the twenty-year sleep.

Many people in the area were of Finnish descent and had brought the traditional winter sweat with them. They had sheds connected to their houses or out back to enjoy the cleansing sweat and heat of a sauna, pronounced "sowna." Ezra did not have a sauna in back of his cabin but he did have a large dome-shaped sweat lodge, which he said was for spiritual growth. Ezra adopted his great grandfather's beliefs, though he had never met the man. He tried to identify himself with the Ojibway rather than the Laplanders. His dome sat a good distance from the house in a small clearing that he had surrounded with cedar trees. The trees were towers of shapeless green now. Some were almost twenty feet high, but they formed a scraggly and unfit barrier for the domed willow branches. There was a path leading from the sunrise-side door to a fire ring crested by a moon shaped "It's an altar," Tom heard the voice of his brother say. Tom knew about the sweat lodge. He had been in a couple of times when Ezra had first built it. Though he hadn't embraced it spiritually like Ezra had. It was probably little words like altar that had slipped into the craw of Toclep. "Christian altar?" They would ask. "Not exactly." Ezra would respond. He had been particular about having strips of basswood bark for tying the frame together. The basswood grew on the other side of the mountain on the interior where the soil was clay. It had taken Ezra two years to hunt and tan enough deer hides to cover the structure even with the use of Tom and his father's hides.

Tom looked down at the pathway between the lodge and the fire pit; "I don't know why you refuse to grow any grass." The path had not been used for twenty years, yet still no grass had grown there. The cedar trees had turned into looming giants, the grass around the cabin was like a fire running amuck, some small apple trees had sprung up on the edges of the yard—evidence of deer droppings, and daisies and black-eyed susans had swallowed and replaced the dandelions. Yet this short path, stretching from the lodge to the fire ring, remained a fringed desert. Tom bent over on the path and had to interrupt the crickets to say,

"Can I come in?" He didn't really remember but he thought he was supposed to ask permission or give salutations or something upon entering. He pulled back the ragged leather at the door and peaked in. He was checking to see if raccoon, squirrel, or fox were using the lodge as a home but amazingly it appeared unused: quiet, destitute. The same way it had every time he had stuck his head into it. He walked over to the altar and unraveled one cigarette down to the filter. Dumping the contents onto the rock he said, "I guess," shrugged his shoulders, and wandered over to the outside pump. Pumping the once red-iron like an old, two-man rail car, he shifted the work to his right arm and sucked water out of his left. "Best damn water in the county. No sulfur, no salt, no rust. Customers down to Coppers would kill to have this water. Might even want water with their dinners if it tasted like this."

Tom walked around the house and headed toward the two-track that led through the old growth forest out to the road. He swung around and said to the house, "How come you never need fixin' or cleanin'? How come that grass never grows out there?" He pointed a finger, grunted, and turned. "You always were hard to understand." He directed his comment more to Ezra than to the house. As he turned onto the two track an owl call echoed through the trees, "Who you warning?" He had his head up and was searching the branches. You warning wisdom or death?" But there wasn't another sound; even the crickets had stopped to wonder about their lives.

The two-track was dry this time of year. Dust clouded out of the gray sand as he dragged his feet down the lane toward the light at the end of the tunnel. The trees joined hands and canopied the entire stretch to the road—pines and cedars, hemlocks and maples, ash and birch all holding hands, hooking arms, entwining fingers. He remembered cars had come down the lane and parked in front of Ezra's house. He wondered if a car would be able to make it down that two-track now. Some of the people came and never left, never left 'til the end, that is. The cabin was isolated. His mother never took notice of the nook. There never had been any real commotion—a fire in the woods once but mostly campfires she couldn't see and voices in song that carried across the hay field to the backside of the house or softly ricocheted off the bark and up the silent slopes of the mountain. Tom tried to remember everybody who had moved in back here. Phil Harding, whose speech impediment left him nearly mute, would "uh huh" or "ont ont" with a shake or a nod through most conversations. Jano Garcia whose name sounded distinctly Mexican but whose Irish blood had made him completely American. Daisy Grass, Tom never was sure if her name was really Daisy or not, but suspected not; her friend the guitar player, Kristie, who had gone with them to drop Ezra at Sawyer; and, of course, Mose Paxton. They were all living out here. There were also a couple of locals like Katrina Bauman, Frank Lampardson, Lydia LaChapelle, and Rae Miller, who—though she was twice as old as any of them—had a special relationship with Ezra. On top of the ones who stayed, Ezra had people coming and going all the time. Some were people Ezra knew from college, others were acquaintances from the riots and protests, and some were soldiers who had different ideas of war and "the Man" since they had returned from Vietnam. Tom remembered the time he had run the fence line to the back nook in order to tell Ezra about his father's stroke.

* * *

"Mom just got a call from St. Pat's. Dad's had a stroke. Dad's had a stroke or some . . . " before he could get it out, he was struck, dumbfounded and dizzy, as he watched Daisy and the guitar player, Kristie Lamar, dance around the two foot orange arms of the fire. They were both wearing long dresses that hung in the wind as if animated. Tom was hypnotized by the fact that he could see right through the dresses. Mose was backed against a log, smoking with some unknown girl sitting between his legs and Tom could hear some unidentifiable laughter coming from the bend in the creek. "Where's Ezrie?" Tom's eyes darted around the fire trying to find his brother. The girl's stopped dancing and stood motionlessly staring at Tom. His glasses reflected pure yellow like his head was full of light.

"I'm in here, Tom."

Tom pulled back the flap on the lodge and stuck his head into the darkness to see the whites of eight eyes momentarily before his glasses clouded over with moisture. "Hey." Ezra's voice was soft like horse's breath. "You need to ask permission before you barge in." Tom jerked his head back, trying to keep the hands of fog from stealing his glasses, but he was too late.

"Dad's had a stroke . . . come on . . . we gotta go."

"Hold on little brother," Ezra's voice again breathy and angelic, "Dad'll be okay. I'll pray for him. He'll be okay." Ezra signaled with his hand, "Come in here and we'll send him a messenger, someone to help him. Then we'll go." Ezra had been overseas. His accent had become less pronounced but was still present in certain words like go.

"We gotta go. We gotta be there for him."

"Hold the pony, Thomas." His voice was soothing. "Dad's not dead. He's only sleeping. We can help him from here."

"Stop that shit. I swear, Ezrie you scare me sometimes. Are you comin' or not? Mom's hysterical." Tears stood in Tom's voice.

"Whoa up, you're in a house of spirits. Keep that badness. I'll come. But I need to pray for him first. Don't be afraid. Just believe. We can help Dad."

"I've got no time for this, Ezrie. I don't know where the fuck you've gone, man. I don't know where the fuck you disappeared to after 'Nam." Tom hit himself in the head twice with his palm. "I'm takin' Mom to St. Pat's. You do whatever your freaked-out head tells you to do. I'll tell Mom you weren't here. You go ahead and pray. While you're at it, pray for yourself."

"You don't have faith, Thomas. Don't lie for me, man. I don't want that on my head. I'll pray for him. He'll be okay. I'll pray for you too, Thomas. And if he isn't okay in this place, he'll be okay somewhere else and that's what matters."

"Screw your prayer, Ezrie. Dad may be dead by the time you get your Hail Mary out."

"Ye of little faith. Prayer is my David, sickness my Goliath. Prayer can help us all. You go along, I'll be there."

Tom hadn't heard Ezra's last statement because he had already turned and let the flap of the sweat lodge fall back, producing complete darkness inside.

Ezra was right though. Their father was alive. By the time Tom had gotten his mother to St. Pat's his father, though not fine, was better than he'd been in weeks. In fact, miraculously the stroke had pulled him out of the semi-consciousness, which he had softly slipped into the week before. Short as it was, Matthew's state had stolen ten years of Marguerite's life as she sat nervously wringing her hands and watching his chest rise and fall. Unfortunately, the short breath of renewed life would not last. Matthew's cancer was at an all-you-can-eat bar and it had already paid its seven dollars for dinner.

* * *

Tom's foot caught a blown down branch; he stumbled and was pulled out of thought to the path in front of him as he put out his arms to slow the fall. "Gotta watch where you're going," he said.

He was almost to the road and wasn't sure where he was going from there. He could hear the soft babbling of the drying creek to his right. The water, never standing still, flittered around rocks in constant movement to get to the Raspberry and then to the lake. Tom thought about Ezra and his friends; they were like the creek. They never hurt anyone. They never hurt themselves, and they never meant anybody any harm. They merely flowed. All they wanted was to skirt around the rough edges, the hard rocks, the jagged branches, to go through life unscathed. Ezra and Mose had already been scathed, had already seen death, had already tread through a hundred generations of hell in the black forests of uncontrolled hatred toward an enemy who, just like themselves, only wanted to protect his own life—had only wanted to head, like the river, to the safety of the lake.

Tom splashed from the cool darkness of the trees into the bright white of sunlight. The paved road was radiating heat that miraged up his body and formed water on his brow. It was the kind of heat that made school children wonder why they had to go to school in September. There were no cars on 52 and Tom turned right, away from his house. Away from town. Away from his memories.

Roadside Girl swung the ax in a smooth, nearly never-ending arc, not from straight overhead; rather, she swung off her right side. Her left elbow led the motion and she dipped her knees for the extra power she needed to hack through the large maple log. The double-edged ax head was sharp on both sides. She had kept it that way since she had started chopping wood for Lydia when she was ten. She had been small then, eighty pounds of lanky arms and over-sized feet. With work, she could still pound through the sixteen inch lengths Lydia had sectioned from the blow-downs that she, Sam Adams, and Roadside Girl had dragged out of the creeping hillside behind her house.

At ten, there were times when she had to use the sledge and wedge method. To see her swirl and wind the chunk of hardened steel, like Thor stirring the clouds, then throw her momentum over her body where the uncontrollable head sought the heavy hand of gravity and dove nearly undirected toward the ground was a sight. She used to miss the wedge and, many times, the log altogether leaving indentations all around the chopping area. That was then, though. Now, the ax was her fencer's blade.

Sam Adams was a large roan whose back was more than shoulder high to Roadside Girl. Gray flecks spattered the roan and accented his gray goatee. Sam Adams should have worn a straw hat with a daisy pinned to it like horses in comic strips and black and white movies, but he didn't. He was indispensable when it came to dragging firewood or pulling Lydia's truck out of the bogged two-track that snaked the small piece of property. Lydia's house hunched behind the trees across the stream and out of sight of Ezra's cabin. The clearing had been one of the housing sights for the Ohio Copper Company and was dotted with lilac trees and rose bushes, living remnants of the prior occupants. Behind Lydia's house, between what used to be a sauna and the horse shed, Roadside Girl and Dave chopped wood.

"When do I get to chop? You been chopping all morning."

"When I'm tired, you can take over." Roadside Girl leaned against the ax. "Throw me the water bottle, will ya?" Dave grabbed the green plastic used-to-be Mountain Dew bottle and tossed it to Roadside Girl. It moved like a buoy, weighted on the bottom and swaying back and forth in the air. She pulled the blue handkerchief from her back pocket and wiped the sweat off her face.

"Gonna be hot today, ain't it?"

"Gonna be nothing. Already is." She looked at the sun overhead and finished the half-full bottle and threw it back to Dave. "Run up to the house and fill this up, will ya?" He turned and ran for the house. "Remember to dump the spit out first." She yelled but he hadn't heard.

Dave shrunk as he approached the square house. The clearing bootlegged away from the creek and the small house sat on the corner of the clearing. Dave's black hair stood out against the white of the house as he jumped over a couple of rock piles and disappeared behind the back corner. She heard the slap of the screen door echo from the trees and could almost see the sound coming before it got to her. "Don't slam the door."

Roadside Girl began to swing the ax again. Splintered wood shot from the log and landed on the already split pieces that lie around her. The white wood clapped in repeating intervals after each swing, ricocheting off the trees as the sound disappeared. Sound carried to the house and reflected back into the woods. She chopped, and the echoes were uninterrupted until Dave came back with the green water bottle. "Better start stacking some of this so I don't bury myself. Then I'll let you chop for a while." She continued to swing the ax and Dave scurried around like a squirrel collecting acorns and stacked the split pieces next to the graying wood that readied itself for winter fires. Roadside Girl had lived with Lydia as long as she could remember. Until recently, she and Lydia had shared the house to themselves. That was before Dave had come to live with them in April. Now, Roadside Girl slept in the sauna and Dave slept in her old bed. Lydia wanted her to feel independent, so Roadside Girl moved into the two-room sauna shack, which gave Dave his own room in the house. Lydia had reasoned that Roadside Girl was a woman and she needed space. However, Lydia was thinking more about Dave when she offered the sauna. A twelve-year-old boy with picture ears and wandering eyes couldn't help but be curious. So Lydia moved Roadside Girl to the sauna and hoped to confine Dave's girl watching to school, where it belonged, and not to his newly adopted sister.

When Dave started chopping, Roadside Girl thought it comical to see him unskillfully wield the ax, which was too big for his body and too big for his hands. His effort was grand, though. Each swing, he grunted. Each swing, the ax got stuck in the log and had to be rocked from the grip of the wood. Each swing, Dave said, "One more and that's it."

She remembered when she had first started splitting wood. Lydia had been gone all day and Roadside Girl had gone out to the tool shed and gotten the ax. She ran her finger across the jagged edge, "No wonder it looks so hard. Dull as a butter knife." Roadside Girl remembered watching Lydia sharpen knives on a wet stone and so she went in search of a file. She sat in the open doorway and patiently slid the file over the rough edges, as if petting a dog, until the dings disappeared. The ax gleamed a sharp smile. It thanked her by shining. She laid the ax on her shoulder, felt like Daniel Boone, and unlocked the gate. Sam Adams, a foal then, slowly stepped through the fence and followed her as she walked to the log pile. "I never do anything,

Sam." The lean roan bobbed his head in acknowledgment as he bent for grass. The girl balanced a small log and swung the ax in uncoordinated effort. She held the ax directly over her head and umphed as her two hands strangled the neck of a wood and metal goose. The steel glinted off the edge of the log, peeled bark from the side, and knocked the log off balance. The first few swings saw the log knocked off balance; then she connected and the ax, stuck in the center of the log, had to be rocked out. She had been Dave.

The boy's dark skin glistened in the growing heat between summer and autumn. His arms sweat and the ax handle was slippery with salt water and gritty with dirt. Every so often he switched sides with the ax. First swing right-handed then left then right again. He didn't swing with both his hands together. Rather, one hand started high on the neck and slid in contact with the other. He had been watching Roadside Girl. He had watched her since he had moved into Lydia's. He was a quick learner.

"How long you been here?"

"Toclep?"

"No. How long you lived with Lydia?"

"Forever, I guess." She had to stop and think. How long had she lived with Lydia? She hadn't thought about it in a while. Even though Lydia had said she wasn't her mother, it took a long time for Roadside Girl to understand what that meant. At that time she stumbled around wondering why other kids had mothers and fathers and she didn't. The kids, when feeling especially cruel, would tease her and tell her not only did she not have any parents but she also didn't have a name. "Nameless, nameless, that girl's nameless." And the taunting finger of the demonstrative pronoun pounded the lonely pain into her like a hammer. She was nameless. She was parentless. She was without identity—the girl without a history. "You can choose any name you want," Lydia had suggested. Roadside Girl settled into her Taurean stubbornness; she grew accustomed to her lack of heritage and could not forsake the name her mother had given her. For it was all she had. She could not help it if her mother had been part of a rainbow generation.

* * *

"You have a birth certificate. It says Roadside Girl." Lydia pulled drawers from their sockets in search of the folded yellow square of paper.

"Why would anyone name me Roadside Girl?"

"Why would anyone name me Lydia? It's not the name that makes the person. It's the person who makes the name. Besides, it's not the strangest name in the world. How'd you like to be named Dick? Or Quasimodo? Now those are names with connotation."

"Oh great, so what does Roadside Girl say?"

"What do you want it to say? The beauty of your name is that it says something. It says a heck of a lot more than Tom or Mike or Paul. It's got character like an old house. You ought to try to think of yourself that way."

"That's it? Think of myself as an old house?"

"That's it. I don't have a legacy for you. You have it. You're an old house. You can fall apart or you can refinish your floors. But whatever you do, it's all up to you."

* * *

"How long's forever?" Dave interrupted Roadside Girl's thoughts.

"Well, I can't remember ever living anywhere else. My mother lived in Massachusetts. I guess I lived there for a while, too. But I was too young to remember anything. My mom was sick. Then she died. Lydia said she didn't know what the sickness was, just that she died. Then a couple years later they started talking about HIV and Lydia thinks that's what it was. But I don't know. I don't remember ever seeing her 'cept in photographs. So I guess, I've been here forever."

"What about your dad?"

"Ran away, I guess. Didn't know anything about a baby or didn't want anything to do with one." She shrugged with I-don't-know shoulders. "Lydia said she didn't know who my father was. Said that my mom never told anyone. Always said it was nobody's business 'cept her own." She paused then whispered. "But I guess it's mine, too. She didn't think about that."

"You sure do guess a lot. My Dad. He was the best. Full-blooded, ya know."

"Yeah I know. Ya tell me every time ya open your mouth."

"Well he was. Said I was special. Said I was the only full-blooded Indian my age. Said all the others were wannabees. He was gonna show me the way of our people. Said our people knew how to live with the land and not against it. Always said that the mine was killing the earth. Guess my ma and your dad have something in common, eh? Maybe they're living together somewhere just like we are."

She smiled at him, "maybe." He had stopped swinging and she was picking up the split logs to stack them with the others. "You full-bloods need a break every time you open your yaps."

"Naaa," he said. He hefted the ax and blasted through a solid chunk of maple.

"Dawg. You see that? One swing."

"I saw it Paul Bunyon." She liked Dave. She was glad to have a brother. She liked talking to him. He was a hard worker just like his father had been.

"You think that Lydia really likes having us around?"

She smiled and nearly chuckled, "Yeah she likes having us around. Well, she likes having me around, anyway. She told me that you were a pain in the . . . ."

"Ahhh, quiet down with that. If anyone's a pain in the butt you are Miss Gotta-live-in-the-sauna, house-isn't-good-enough."

"Well, it was fine 'til you moved in and got that full-blood butt all over my bedroom." They laughed at each other. "No, I think she needs us as much as we need her. Makes her life less lonely. Plus, look at all this fuel she gets." She rolled her head and eyes around to the woodpile.

"Think she gets money for us?"

"From where?"

"You know, you think she gets money from the state for us? Eric Linstrom's parents get money for him."

Roadside Girl wished that Lydia did get money from the state. She wished that there was some sort of pay back for Lydia's energy, for her time. "You're not a foster child, Dave. You're adopted. The both of us're adopted. She's just our mother same as your father was your father. He didn't get money from the state, did he?"

"Naaa."

"Unless the police paid him to take you cuz you were a delinquent from downstate or farther yet, Ohio. Not even his son. Not even . . . " She stopped and increased her intensity. "A full-blooded Indian, probably just from Indiana's all. Did the police leave you up here?"

"Naaa, I'm a full-blood. Look how dark my skin is."

"Maybe you're Mexican or," she had to think. "Or Filipino."

"Na uh. I'm Ojibway. Just like my Dad." Dave hadn't been chopping. He was leaning against the ax.

"Okay, full-blood stop yackin' and start hackin'." The boy laughed and he swung, left-handedly, into another log.

"My pop died from coughin'. Always coughin', couldn't stop 'til it killed 'im." This time he was swinging and talking in broken sentences between movements.

"I know. Pneumonia."

"What's ammonia?"

"Not ammonia, Dave, pneumonia. It's a lung disease. Lung tissues fill up or get hard with liquid and you can't breathe."

"What kind of liquid?"

"Don't know, just liquid. Bile or something. Ask Lydia. She

knows all that stuff. She said it was the mining that got your dad." Dave was still swinging and he had worked himself into a smooth rhythm. He didn't seem to be paying attention to the wood or the ax or his sweat. He had become the ax.

"He caught ammonia from the mine, ain't it?"

"Not exactly, just seems that the mine didn't help him get over it, none. Kinda locked it around him or something."

* * *

She remembered seeing Milt Chippeway late in January when he brought Dave out to spend time with Lydia. He seemed to know he was dying and wanted to wrap up the loose ends before he got too sick to do anything but lie in bed, cough, and die. She could see his face in her mind. It had a purple tint to it. Milt would heave into choking, tuberculosis-like coughing fits trying to keep his mouth covered with a white hankie.

"You should be in bed, Bear." Lydia had said. "You shouldn't go into the mine. It's death and you know it."

"I know it. Got a son and don't got anymore sick days."

"You're not gonna need anymore sick days if you keep going down into that dampness. You might as well be digging a grave as digging for pennies. And what's Dave going to do without you? He's already lost Trisha." Lydia was serious. Her warning was honest but that wouldn't matter, because Milt kept going into the darkness and the darkness kept going into to him. He was dead by tax time.

* * *

"Sort of like goin' outside without clothes on when you have a cold in the winter. Sort of like that ain't good for ya?" Dave's voice broke in clearly.

"Yeah, sort of like that."

"Ya think your dad's ever gonna come back for ya?"

"I doubt it. My father probably doesn't even know I exist."

"That's a shame," he said as he swung the ax into a hunk of maple. "He'd like ya if he knew ya. My Ma she'll come back soon as she finds out Dad's gone. She'll be back here to take me out west somewhere. Out to Indian Country. I think she's on a reservation somewhere. That's why she hasn't come back yet. No phones out there. She sure was pretty, you know. My Dad used to say she was the prettiest woman he'd ever seen. She'll be coming back for me."

"Yeah, she'll be back. Sometime. When she finds out. It might take her a while though. I wouldn't hold my breath waiting for her. I'm sure she has lots of things she's got to take care of first." Roadside Girl was lying. She knew that Dave's mother would never be back for him. She knew that she would never find out about Bear's death and that if she did she wouldn't care. "You wouldn't want to go out west anyway," she said. "You're Ojibway. You belong right here where you're people are. Where the fish and the maple syrup run. 'Sides who'd help me chop wood and take care of Sam Adams and drink Mountain Dew?"

"You don't even like Mountain Dew."

"That's what I'm talking about, Dave. Nope you're gonna have to stay right here, where you belong. Where you're needed." She smiled at him and he smiled back.

"I guess so," he said with shucks in his voice.

The heat swelled in transparent waves around them. They had been at it all morning and it was time to stop.

"Let's get some lunch then head out to the Lake and take a swim. Water'll be too cold to swim soon. It's already starting to change."

"Yeah, lunch." Dave was like other boys his age; he was always hungry. He would eat anything and everything that was taken out of the refrigerator and placed in front of him. "Think it'll rain tonight?" He looked into the blue sky.

"Not tonight," she said as she thought about the rains that September and October would bring. He leaned the ax against the woodpile and bent to help stack the last pieces of split wood. They started toward the house with the ax still leaning against the woodpile. "Oh no you don't. Dew breeds rust just as well as rain."

"Ain't no dew now."

"Yeah there is. Just not sopping wet dew that's all. Grab that ax and throw 'er in the shed." He went back and grabbed the ax and laid it over his shoulder.

They walked in toward the house. She walked with her hands stuck in the back pockets of her brown pants. She was at least a head taller than he was but their shadows were the same length.

"We gonna chop wood tomorrow?"

"We'll worry about tomorrow when tomorrow comes, Dave."

Ezra wasn't like the others who surrounded "Fort Daley" in that August of '68. He was astonished. Dazed. He wasn't throwing shit at pigs. He wasn't screaming obscenities. He wasn't being clubbed, this time. He wasn't with anyone. He was gloomy and pensive. He was a bottom heavy hourglass and there were no more showers of sand for him. '63 had been bad, '65 had been bad, but two, two deaths mid-way through '68 had been devastating. The Doves were taking flight. The Hawks were swarming like angry bees. He sensed something. There was a feeling, a welling in his stomach. He felt the opposite of hunger, but not the satisfaction of being full. Something was going to happen, and it was more than the cops attacking the dovish crowd. It was for him and him alone. He knew it.

"Hey, what're ya doing?" A voice broke through the nonsense noise of the crowd. "Hey, you!" His eyes were glassy gray-coated jelly balls. He almost looked like he had cataracts. Then he pulled himself to the surface. His eyes breathed.

"Me?" The question was lost and not really looking for an answer.

"Yeah, you. Look the crowd's goin' forward and you aren't paying attention. You're gonna to get trampled."

"We're all gonna get trampled. We're already trampled; we just don't know it."

"Ok, Zarathustra. Just thought you might want to wake up. Otherwise you're gonna take a pig-stick on the side of your head."

Ezra remembered being caught up in the riots of Detroit the year before. He remembered his father telling him that he had been on the news and that he was lucky his mother had not been watching CBS to see her son walking, stupefied, through the war zone of Detroit.

* * *

"I knew it was you, Ezrie," his father had said when Ezra came home. "I recognized that T-shirt you always wear that simply says, "ONE." It would have killed your mother to see what I saw. I was worried about you when I saw the billyclub coming down. Then when you crumpled to the ground I didn't know what to do. But I did know not to tell your mother. For her sake and mine I'm glad I didn't have to tell her that you were dead. You've got to be careful, son. If you don't watch the tides, you will be swept out to sea. You were lucky in Detroit. You might not be so lucky the next time."

* * *

"You want to take a pig-stick to the head? Are hearing me?"

"Come on Kristie, can't be takin' care of every fool you run into." The girl, whose white tee shirt had been hand painted with yellow daisies, was tugging on her girlfriend's arm trying to drag her back into the waxing tide of people. Ezra turned to her and spoke so quietly that it would have seemed like no one could've heard him, but she did.

"We're all fools." The sound came from deep within his throat. It was as if he was talking through his trachea, as if his throat had somehow opened up. "There'll always be wars. We can't stop it. Why we think we can is beyond me." He stopped and looked up. "The answer's up there. The answer's in the sky."

"What answer?" The dark haired girl asked the question and Daisy Chain interrupted.

"There wasn't any question. What the hell are you talking about? Come on Kristie leave the freak." She was tugging on the belt loop of the dark haired girl.

"Leave the freak," he said. "Go on Kristie." When he spoke her name it was like he had known her all her life. It was like she was talking to her older brother about her parent's lack of understanding. "Freak's got to be goin' soon anyway. Nothing we can do here. Gotta be there." This time he didn't look anywhere. Then his eyes swam up and locked onto her harvest eyes.

"Where?"

"There, you know, the big there." But she didn't know.

"Are you talking about heaven? I don't believe in god, man. They made him up." She was pointing nowhere.

"Heaven's in the mind," he said. "You don't believe in you? There's nothing you can do here. You can hear the wind but you can't see it. You don't know where it comes from or where it goes. But it does both." He started to walk away.

"Hey, where're ya going?" She was following him and she pulled Miss Daisy Chain along with her.

"I'm going home. We should all go home. Everyone in the world should go home."

"Pessimist," Daisy Chain said. "Go home pessimist. Whatcha come here for, anyway?" But his response was not satisfying. She wanted to quench her thirst. She wanted the philosopher to tell her something she didn't know. She wanted a fight. She was following him now, too.

"I thought I would see something. I thought wrong. I didn't see anything, because there isn't anything to see." His voice was patient like he was privy to information she didn't have.

"We're doing something. We've got to do something. The power's in the people and the people are we." Her voice surfed on frantic, but he just kept walking—this time away from the police, this time away from the Hawks.

"The power is somewhere. But it's not in the people. You've

got the wrong idea about power. The boy can do nothing but what he sees his father do."

She grabbed Kristie and stopped. "Fuck you. You don't know anything. You're just a chicken shit. You're afraid of what's up there." She pointed back to the front. "You're afraid of the Man and so the Man will just keep stepping on you. Brother, you're buffing his shoes. You're probably a dirt lickin' narc anyway. Go on pessimist. We don't need your energy here. Come on Kristie, let's go!"

"Go ahead. You don't know me. Go back up there." They were both pointing in the same direction. "The front of one war is just the same as the front of another. It's Wounded Knee up there. Follow your father. Suit yourself." He was done talking. He had talked too much. He waded through the tide of people dodging what they thought was a waxing tide and what he knew was an ebbing tide. His hair stood out among the pale white eyes that faced the other direction.

"Fuck you!" She screamed. But he didn't hear her. He didn't hear anything. He just walked out of the ocean. He was going home. He was going home before the massacre.

Rae Miller was an old woman. She leaned against the bar and her loose fitting skin sagged from the back of her arms. She had been moving slowly and anticipated even slower movement as autumn passed through and winter moved into her bones. The bar was washed with yellow light. O'Teegan sat where he always sat on the curve of the far end of the bar hiding his gout from the breezes that sneaked under the door at the other end. He was the only one in the bar. It was quiet. The television behind him was on but as usual the sound was down. Colors of bass fishing in North Carolina flashed off his flannel covered back and geometrically diffused into the darkness of paneling behind him.

Rae was sorting glasses that had dried and was putting them, by size, under the bar. Probably wouldn't be too many people in tonight—seeing it was a Tuesday before the fall color season, before the snowmobiling snow that would come in November and would bring more people than summer and color season combined. Winter would also bring the cold, snow-machine drunks who bump over winter, warming their blood on loud trails with beer and whiskey and frequent bar stops. Thirty-two snowmobile deaths last year and two-thirds of them alcohol related: a marriage made in heaven.

"Not as young as I used to be, Otter."

"You been saying that for twenty years, Rae. How young'd ya used ta be, anyway?"

"Younger'n you." She chuckled a little without confidence

and drew herself a short draft. She wasn't sure if she had been younger than O'Teegan or not.

Rae Miller had lived in Toclep her whole life. Seventy years, fifty-five of which she had served beer to locals and tourists. Mark O'Teegan was not much different than T.J. Fillipson in the forties or Scott Mohoney in the sixties except that Mark had been to college and was a little better read than the others were. He had been coming into Rae's almost every night for twenty years, give or take. His beer tastes had changed with popular advertisement from Blue Ribbon to Old Style to Bud Light, usually about three a night, and one shot of white Christian Brother's Brandy. That was unless someone came in and tricked him into to staying for a couple more. He usually only had enough money for the three beers and maybe an order of chicken wings. But if someone else was buying, he was staying. He was the regulars' regular.

Rae felt like the leafless reflection of trees just before dark on the mirror of Superior. She recalled looking down from the edge of one of the rocky crags of shore—last year or the year before that or in another decade all together—seeing the motionless water whose ducks had headed south and were flying over Arkansas in a giant determined arrowhead. The black trunks of the naked hardwoods reflected in perfect silence like a Rembrandt painting. Great darkness that went so deep into the gray evening waters that it sifted between the rocks on the bottom and tried to hide, clinging to the underside of them so when the sun came the next day, so when the wind brought ripples to take the painting away, pieces of its shadow would peak out and say, "You didn't get us all." The trees readied themselves for winter. They played dead. Their reflection, like the ducks, prepared not to be seen again until spring. Not to be seen until the fifteen-foot plums of ice and sand melted away like sugar candy, feathering and splintering in the rain and the calm waters of late spring again glassed the coast. Rae felt like the shadows only in part, only in the disappearance, the hiding.

"When I die, Otter, I'm gonna leave this 'ere bar to you. Ya spend as much time 'ere as I do. Anyway, ya know the ropes."

"I know ya been talkin' about dying for twenty years. I know ya haven't aged a day in thirty, and I know this 'ere beer ain't cold. But I don't know nothing about no ropes."

"Well, ya know how ta sort glasses, don't ya? Ya know how ta mix a Bloody Mary, don't ya? That's all ya gotta know. Course you might have ta tuck in your shirt once in a while."

"Do ya put a pickle or an olive in a Bloody Mary?" He asked.

"Pickle or celery, olives are for Martinis."

"There ya go. Besides, I'd have ta get me one of them roly chairs so I wouldn't have ta stand on this gout all night."

"Or stop drinking so much." Rae laughed a quiet mousy laugh that trailed off more than it ended.

"Bite your tongue, woman."

Rae drifted off to the other end of the bar while Mark looked into his beer as if it were a crystal ball. She filled the olive container and began to slice lemons that she wouldn't use tonight or tomorrow night. The paring knife shook in her hands. Her hands weren't steady anymore. They were sore and she was forced to think about them every time she picked up a knife or tried to take the top off an olive jar. Her hands were jerky motion; they couldn't hold anything as tightly as they used to. Damn hands, she thought. Sometimes her mind slipped and searched unaware of destinations. But her body was slipping right from her grip the same as her skin was falling from her bones, and she couldn't do a thing about it.

When I was young, she thought, I had the steadiest hands around. After thinking this, she wasn't sure if it had been her or somebody else who had had the steady hands. She thought about somebody hunting with Harold but wasn't sure who it was. She could see them walking through brown, brown autumn grass— he with his twenty-gauge and the woman with a twenty-two rifle. She didn't need the sprawling throw of birdshot to knock a quail to the ground. One thin slug was all it took. The bird would light to the air in a rush of noise that sounded like a sprung diving board and the woman would raise the rifle. Her eye and the blue barrel would become one and the bird would drop to the ground as if it had been pulled out of the sky on a string. Rae could barely hold a knife to slice yellow and green chunks of citrus. It couldn't have been her. Her hands shook. She couldn't get a good enough grip on the knife to hold it. It hurt. It felt like her hands were broken on the inside of the bones. Rae found that she often sliced the fruit below the bar so no one would see her jumping-bean hands. So no one would really know that she was an old woman. Her mind was a trap but her body was a muskrat and no matter how much she struggled there wasn't a thing she could do.

Seventy wasn't supposed to be old anymore, but she could remember her mother—the shriveled and drying vine at seventy. Her puckered face only released one conversation but changed the names every time, "Sad. So sad. He was only sixty-four. Heart attack right there in the shop. Yep, Andi found him laid out like vegetables for market across the workbench. He was so young." This time it was Sid or Mike or Mr. Rutherford, next time it'd be Harry or Tom or Sylvia, but it was always the same story. "So young." Yet, none of them had been young. At seventy, Rae's mother had seemed like the oldest person in the world. Maybe it had been the cigarettes and maybe it had been the alcohol or maybe it had been the extremes of winter and summer, but Rae's vision of her mother were not unlike what she saw in the mirror. She tried to remember her mother's hands but all she could see were her own: blue veined and cryptic.

She wasn't as young as she used to be, if she used to be young at all. She turned and looked into the mirror behind the bar. I've always looked like this, she thought. Every time I've looked into a mirror, I've looked like this. I haven't changed. I haven't grown old. I've always been old. But that couldn't be true. There were pictures. There were memories. She'd go home tonight and she'd dig them up. She'd look at them. There was proof. She hadn't always been old. However, the mirror staring at her was calling her a liar.

"Think about it, Rae." It was Harold's voice. "Haven't ya always looked like this? The mirror's the truth. I'm the truth. Photographs are fish tales."

They can't be, she thought. She felt like she was hurrying. Rushing in her mind to this memory and that memory in frantic desperation. I was young. I know I was. "I remember," she said aloud.

"What do ya remember?" O'Teegan had swiveled around in his chair and the silent movie about bass reflected off his face.

"Nothin'," she said. "Just talking, ta myself." She hadn't turned from the mirror and it spoke to her again.

"Talkin' ta yourself, that's a telltale sign."

I've always talked to myself, she thought. Nothing has changed.

"That's what I been trying ta tell ya. Nothing's changed. Look." She looked into the mirror. "Not into your eyes. Look at your face." She did. "Didn't ya look this way last year, five years ago, twenty years ago? Haven't ya always looked this way?" She didn't want to agree, but it was true. As far as she could remember, she had always looked the same. Red-rimmed eyes whose white dissolved into colorless centers. Shoulder length white wire that couldn't be pushed with comb or brush in any consistent manner. Narrow cheeks that sucked inward then sagged under a chin.

So, I'm my mother then. I'm seventy years old. I'm a dry, wild grapevine. She thought about the photographs. They were movies. They weren't real. They were what people wanted to think was real. The mirror was real. Her skin did sag around her eyes. She remembered things that had happened but she saw herself in every vision as a seventy-year-old woman: a seventy-year-old woman in the midst of the town council, standing around the new compactor; a seventy-year-old woman sauntering down the beach as the muscle-less skin moved in waves on the back of her legs beneath her bikini; a seventy-year-old woman helping her husband secure the trusses for the roof, a shaking hammer missing the nail on two consecutive swings; a seventy-year-old woman on her wedding night, slipping her wrinkled body into her silk nightgown for the big night; a seventy-year-old woman wobbling without balance on a red bicycle as an eight-year-old boy released his hands with a final shove.

The front door squeaked and Rae turned her entire body to see Lydia pushed in with a gush of cold air. Rae had an exhausted look on her face. She looked like sepia tone memories of the old west that faded in legends and photographs from over use or lack of use.

"Hey, Otter."

"Hey." He didn't turn from the bent fishing rod in front of him.

"I was across the street and didn't have any customers. Saw you didn't have any customers, so I thought I'd slide over and we'd have no customers together. Could use one. Thought you could, too." Lydia pointed to the small glass that had a thin layer of drying foam at the bottom. "Oh, no offense, Otter. Didn't mean to make you a nothing." A dry "none's taken" blew down the shiny bar that reflected the colored hues of the television and sat by the glass like a leaf.

"Could ya see all that from over there?" Rae looked at Lydia; her chestnut hair blended into the dark wall and made her face radiate in the yellow light of the bar.

"Yep, that and a lot more."

"Got good eyes, eh."

"Inside and out," Lydia said. "You know Rae, I was thinking over there," she jerked her head to the side, "people forget how good life is. I've got folks coming in and complaining almost everyday. Folks that aren't even sick coming in to find something that they can complain about because they let their minds tell them things that aren't true." Without tipping it, she sipped a swallow off the top of her glass. Her eyes were on Rae. "Complacency, boredom. Always thinking about right now and tomorrow, but never thinking about yesterday. Mrs. Berge was in this morning told me that her whole body hurt. Couldn't tell me where exactly, just that it ached all over. Said she couldn't keep her mind on anything because of the pain. Said she was worried about having, as she put it, the cancer. Woman is as healthy as a mule and ornery as one, too. I just gave her a physical two weeks ago and everything's as shiny as polished silver. Only malignant cell around her is the rust on her car. I thought to myself, she probably hurts the same way as all of us hurt if we start thinking about our bodies. Same way we hear the high banshee screams when we sit in the silence of the woods. Anyhow, I went into the back room and got her some calcium carbonate pills. You know what calcium carbonate's good for?"

"Nope." Rae had her back to the mirror and was leaning against the bar staring into the light of Lydia's face.

"Good for nothing. Making chalk, maybe. Anyhow, I told her I'd look over her records again. Not that I need to. Make sure I didn't miss anything, which I didn't. Then I told her to go home and take those pills four times a day until they're gone and see if they help and while she was at it to try to think of some things she really used to enjoy doing when she was younger. She looked at me funny, but I told her it would help take her mind off the side effects of the drug."

"Side effects being white lips, eh." Rae wasn't really interested in Lynette Berge's hypochondria, but she was interested in what Lydia was saying. She was interested in looking backwards. She was interested in what was. The truth was that Rae really didn't have that much of a future. At least nothing that was too different than what she had now, except for slower and shakier. However, her past was a rich creamy syrup to be savored if the mirror-voice of her dead husband would allow her to savor it.

"Don't listen to everything your mind tells you. It doesn't always know what's right or wrong, true or false. If it did we wouldn't need psychiatrists. Put a whole group of people at the unemployment office." They both took a drink. Lydia put her hand on top of Rae's. "You remember when you got that letter from Ezrie. The one from the hospital in Camranh Bay. That's the way folks ought to act everyday. Happy for their life. Happy for other people's lives. Remembering what they have and not what they don't have."

Rae smiled. "That was the best damn news I'd gotten in while." She glanced into the mirror and could see herself standing on the bar. Her hawkweed pony-tail bounced off the back of her neck, striking the stretched skin between her shoulder blades as she jumped over the bar with the crumpled letter in her hand. "What a hoot. Listen to this. All of yous listen. Ezra's a-comin' home. Ezra's coming home." She said as she put her hand on the top of Frank Lampardson's head. "'Dear Rae,' it says. 'I'm coming home. Seems the rice pickers and the frog stickers don't want me around anymore. Got me a whole in my belly size of your heart. I just stuff food in without chewing.' How do ya like that? The size of my heart. 'The doc says it's clean as a whistle. Says it's cleaner then any of the wounds he's ever seen. Says it's a miracle. I'm a little sore but if that's what it takes to get outta here, impale me baby. I think they're flying me to Washington next week. Make sure you get some new records for that jukebox.'"

"Hear that, I gotta get some new records, Ezrie's coming back, alive." She remembered her hair—long strands of spun gold, shiny and soft. It hadn't always been white stiff wires. It hadn't always been thin, uncontrollable old woman's hair. It had been spun gold.

"I remember that day," O'Teegan said. "Rae dancin' around like a Texas whore."

"Watch what ya say, Otter. I'll leave this bar ta Lydia if I gotta."

"Well that's what ya looked like. Had that short yellow skirt on. Stomping around the bar and pounding your hands on folks' tables. Everybody looking down your shirt and at your belly button under that knot in your white top. Who wouldn't remember that?"

"You sure got a good selective memory. Can't remember how much money ya got in yer pocket most the time, but remember looking down my shirt. If your old man was still alive I'd have him spank ya. Seeing he's not I just might have ta do it myself." She looked down the bar, and she could see a hundred of her in the mirror. Six-year-old Raes with stark white hair sitting and playing jump rope on the bar. Ten-year-old Raes with the bobbed, short, boy's hair, fishing in bottles of whiskey and gin. Sixteen-year-old Raes standing between the pines and the school—peeking into the boys' shower room—stared out of the mirror. There were Raes with short hair and long hair and permed hair and dyed hair. There were Raes smoking cigarettes and Raes drinking whiskey. Raes dancing and kissing and hugging. The whole mirror was full of Raes. The mirror was telling a story and the story was happy, was full of life; hundreds if not thousands of happy Raes shined out of the mirror. Even the ones that were crying were crying with life.

"Ya'd probably like that."

"She probably would, Otter," Lydia said with a smile. She made eye contact with Rae that said, remember . . . remember all that?

Rae was laughing. "Yeah, it's been a while since I spanked a bad boy." They were all laughing and the voice behind the mirror—the voice of Rae's husband, Harold—drowned beneath the laughter of a thousand Raes and three Toclep locals.

Lydia whispered, "You go away Harold. You leave Rae be now." No one heard her except Harold who was being swallowed by the myriad of Raes.

Rae grabbed Mark's glass off the bar. Her hand wasn't shaking as she popped the top on another Bud Light. Nope, her hand wasn't shaking because Lydia hadn't given her calcium carbonate. She had given her vision. She had opened up the canyons of her life and exposed the shining core of the earth. Lydia had done what she always did best. She saw the light on the inside for what it was worth.

Rae was right. No one came to bar that night. No one needed the yellow or green fruit that had angered her earlier. She closed early after Lydia had added another three beers to O'Teegan's gout and they had relived story after story of Rae's life. She swaggered home drunk with memories of nightshade and lady's slippers and smiled all night long.

Tom Gern liked to read. He had gone to college for one year, and that year was interrupted by the rest of his life. He picked up his books and returned to the house behind the fence and imitated dialects from books that he read like an eleven-year-old playing Tom Swift. He played out the character parts in his head. He became added characters or main characters or sketchy, flat background characters so he could watch the story unfold again and again in his mind. He rewrote plots, enhanced settings, and resolved conflicts. And he did it all in his mind. When he talked—which was usually more to himself than to anyone else because he made it a habit to stay within the fence or to the woods that led up the mountainside because he stayed clear of town like the Prince Prospero of hay and family gardens—he would talk with a thin southern *As I Lay Dying* accent or thick Boone Caudill rhythm as if there was no difference between the Finnish intonations of the North and a southern drawl. He would be true to his accent until the next book came along and pushed his accent from one coast to the other, stealing his natural speech and replacing it with another.

Today he sat with his coffee in his speckled tin cup, dented on all sides from too many drops, and looked over the top of a bent and rolled copy of *The Baron in the Trees* at the weathered fence posts. He was a quiet man whose wife had left him to become a troll: an ogre beneath the Mackinaw Bridge. The North was too one-dimensional for her. She took a job and took a lover and filed for divorce. Tom stayed in Toclep. Alone. It was his home. The loneliness and the solitude were old familiar chairs to Tom.

* * *

He liked seeing the black bear sow and cubs of spring move in their sleek, shiny blackness, like Hawthornian specters, through the woods beyond the fence. Their solitude and loneliness, foreign to the human world, reminded Tom of himself.

He let his mind wander back to late spring. The pips and peeps of crickets and grasshoppers filled the air. It was too early for the cicadas. They would not be screaming for another month, maybe more. He remembered the day because it was the kind of day that people wished they had in July. It'd be a hot day. So hot, that normally the cicadas would scream their violin voices for nearly a minute at a time, telling everyone that it was too hot to be working. It was unseasonable heat that had been swept in from someplace else and would warm the rock and sand on the beach, a day to comb the shoreline looking for agates and not have to worry about being bothered by stable flies because it was too early in the season. He sat against the pump house looking over the field to the mountains and watched a black bear lumber along the fence line away from the campground where it had been feasting in the morning hours, trying to replenish the fat of a long winter. This wasn't a young bear. For the past three summers it had successfully scared people into their trailers and campers, leaving their fatty picnic food for the taking. The park had been trying to trap the bear, but the bear simply sniffed the baited live-traps and said, "you don't really think I'm stupid enough to go in there again. The last time I did that it took me six hours to get back from where you dropped me. No siree, not again." The rangers had constantly warned campers, but campers seldom listened. They would storm into Katrina demanding to see the park manager, saying a bear had ruined their vacation by tearing up their camping equipment and eating their food. The rangers would stand around and shake their heads in we-warned-them fashion and listen to the controlled smoothness Katrina used to calm irate tourists.

Tom loved to watch the bear move confidently along the fence. Its blackness was a dark lake, so deep it swallowed his vision. The bear would walk in straight lines neither sniffing nor turning its head until it was at the end of the fence line. Then it would turn silently into the dark forest and disappear. It was a ghost. It would wait until near darkness to return and nonchalantly stroll back into the campground. Unafraid. Without worry. It made Tom sad to think that this bear, which the locals called Cooler, because it had a reputation for destroying coolers, with all its natural confidence would not make it through another hunting season. It had lost its wild edge to hot dogs and coolers when it should have been eating blueberries. Come Bear Season, it would lumber into a bait pile even though it smelled man thickly in the air and would fall at the report of a thirty-thirty. Tom had watched this bear almost every morning and though the bear didn't know it, Tom knew that it was already dead.

* * *

This morning Tom looked off the front porch; he thought about the bear because bear season was just around the corner. He stood on the porch. His mind jumped back to his childhood and how summers as a child had been far different than summers as an adult. He remembered running through the woods with his brother, kicking down dead trees that stood empty amongst their leaf covered brothers. He and Ezra had run through the same areas over and over, and every time they had, it seemed as if the trees they had kicked over the day before had stood back up to be kicked over again.

* * *

"I'm Superman," Ezra said. He stretched his leg and kicked a rotted tree to the ground.

"How come you always get to be Superman?"

"Cuz I am the protector of mankind, Tom. Come on. You can be Batman or the Flash or Ben Grimm." Ezra stretched his skinny arms over his head. "Up, up, and away."

"Yeah, I guess. I'm the Thing. Superman isn't even as tough as the Thing." Tom grabbed a tree that was not as far gone as the one Ezra had kicked over and shook it until the top broke off and crashed through the live branches around it. Then he and Ezra strangled it together and shook it out of the ground.

"Hey, Tom. You wanna go to the prehistoric forest?"

"That place scares me. Remember that bear track we saw last time we were there. Thing must've been as big as the tractor."

"Yeah, shucks. Maybe we shouldn't go, seeing you're chicken and all."

"Am not."

"Just said you were."

"Did not."

"Did too. Maybe we should wait and go tomorrow morning before the sun comes up and see if we can see that bear. What do you think?"

"Yeah. But maybe we should take the guns."

"Not gonna kill that bear with a pellet gun, Tom. Thing's humong-gus."

"Yeah but if the two us . . . and it . . . attacked . . . then the two of us could get it . . . it wouldn't get us."

"No need for guns. Just got to run down hill, Tom. Bears can't run down hill. They've got to brake. They're afraid of running down hill."

"Heck they are. That's a lie Ezrie and you know it. We saw that sow and her cub bookin' down Haunted Hill last year. Remember? Things were cruisin' fifty miles an hour. Besides, there aren't any hills in the prehistoric forest. Just quicksand to get stuck in."

"There ain't no quicksand out there."

"Is too. Dad says there is."

"He's just trying to scare you like he did with that brown snake. Wasn't no rattlesnake. Aren't no rattlesnakes around here."

"Are too, Michigan Rattlers."

"Na uh, he was just trying to scare you and he did."

"No he didn't."

"Did too scare ya. Ya carried your knife around with you talking about how to suck the poison out of a snakebite for weeks."

* * *

A truck went by and honked, pulling Tom out of his reverie and back to his front porch. He stuck his arm into the air and waved to the passing image of Terry Sikes.

Toclep was waking. If it was summer there might be twenty cars on Clarion in front of Copper's. People would be inside drinking salty coffee and talking about what they would do today or what they might see. Or they would be drinking coffee that tasted like coffee and talking about work. But summer was over. It would be only locals this morning. There would be no tourists thinking about opening a restaurant in the area that had good pizza and quick service and bottled water—things that the people of Toclep didn't care about all that much.

"Hey Tom." Lydia's voice pulled him out of thought and redirected his eyes. She came up behind him from the path behind his house. He stepped off the porch and walked toward her. Tom had known Lydia as long as he could remember. She had always looked the same. He thought that people who saw each other everyday never saw age, that age was something that didn't exist for those people. Lydia was carrying a wicker basket full of roots and dry flowers. She would crush them with no regard for the Food and Drug Administration and would grind them into old fashion natural cure-alls. Lydia was the only pharmacist in the U.P. who could cure a common cold. She had no need for Upjohn or Burroughs Wellcome.

"Kind of early, isn't it?"

"Got work to do." She didn't bother telling him that she was going in to fill capsules so that the drugs she made looked like the drugs people were used to taking. "Roadside Girl's takin' the truck into Houghton today. Need anything?"

"I ought to go with her. I haven't been to Houghton in a while."

"Guess not, seeing you sold that truck of yours."

"Didn't see much use in having a truck I started only to make sure it started, so I knew it would start. That's kinda silly."

"I guess it is. And it's a lot of starts." Lydia knew truth. She knew he had sold the truck because, like everyone else in the county, Tom had had trouble paying his bills. Things were better this year. He had a second crop of hay and the boom of organic goods had helped him. "You want me to call her when I get into work and have her stop by and get you?"

"I don't know? She got plans?"

"Think she just wants to go to a couple of book stores and maybe duck into a record—guess they don't sell records anymore do they—music store or two."

"I wouldn't mind sticking my head into a bookstore. I've read just about everything Ezra left out in the cabin and I'd like to look into a book before buying it for once. Book club, ya know. I order, they send. Half the time I don't know what I'm getting. What time you think she's going? Got some work I was planning to get to today."

"Not sure. But I'll call her and tell her to stop over. You know, Tom, you're gonna fool people into thinking you're an intellectual if you don't watch it. Tom Gern, the farmer who reads. You know Toclep; you'll have the whole damn town saying you're getting to be some uppity academic type."

"Yep, that's me. Uppity and academic. That's why I'm here in Toclep. The academic capital of the world."

"You know people. Give them something to talk about."

"And they'll talk," Tom finished.

People did talk, Lydia thought as she walked away. They had always talked. She remembered when she was young, not young like she was now when looks and age had nothing to do with each other but really young, centuries ago. She remembered how she and her mother, who was like her grandmother, moved from place to place. Moving away from the talk. They moved west each time, following the sun. They had always lived as she lived now, out away from town in the canopy of trees that softened the bright sun, where she could find mushrooms and roots and plants that other people pulled out of their gardens as weeds. She remembered living in a house on stilts in one forest long ago and how the people of the town had talked and talked and talked, telling stories about her mother to each other. "Baba Jaga will get you. Baba Jaga will curse you. She'll eat you." And being young, she hadn't understood why people talked about her mother like that. But now she did. Now she knew that people couldn't help talking and that talking sometimes turned into danger, turned into new lands. She remembered how people had talked about Ezra and how that had also reminded her of her childhood. Yes, she knew that people in Toclep talked. Tom had been mumbled into a Siberia of self by the townsfolk. By winter there would be all kinds of talk floating around Tom like snow, but Tom's Siberia would be melting.

She stopped and turned back toward Tom. "Rae was saying she couldn't get her truck started. Could you wander over and take a look at it?"

"Why didn't she just ask me herself?"

"Not like you stop into the bar very often, Tom. When's she supposed to ask you?"

"Well, I live right here."

"Yeah. Right here behind your fence. Won't hurt you to go over and check on her. It's not like she's thirty years old anymore. She could use the company and so could you." Tom didn't say anything. He knew she was right.

He would fix Rae's truck today and would see her and then in a month or two he would start checking on her again because it wouldn't hurt him. It wouldn't remind him of anything but life. It would take him that long to wake up. He would become aware of more than the seasons. He would remember things he hadn't thought about in years and he would realize that people need each other. He would see that good fences don't necessarily make good neighbors and instead of looking across highway 52 at Toclep like it was a circus tent, he would actually go through the gate and talk to people he hadn't bothered to talk to in years. Tom would do more than just wave to Terry Sikes and fix Rae's truck when Lydia asked him to. Tom would become the seasons and he would remind people, maybe not all the people but some of the people that the seasons were their friends and the seasons were important because they were always there. He, himself, would remember that he lived in the Upper Peninsula, and people in the U.P. need each other. A stalled car in the winter could mean death. Tom would remember that before winter came again.

* * *

An eagle moved in slow circles, floating higher and higher above his head without flapping a wing. Tourists would often point up yelling, "There's an eagle, an eagle." He would walk away from them not telling them that they were looking at a large hawk. Not telling them that the curve of outstretched eagle wings was softer and less obvious than the hawk's. Why should he tell them? Why shouldn't they think they saw an eagle? Eagles made people rich.

Tom Gern was a farmer, mechanic, carpenter, dreamer. The silence, the slowness of Toclep allowed him to do all of that. He had inherited the farm as his father and his father's father had. He had little money and some tax write-offs, but most of all he had time. He had time to do things when he wanted to do them. So he did. He didn't rush and could see no good in rushing. Everything was a slow movement. Outsiders might say that he crawled through life like a turtle-moving potato bug. But he saw everything he wanted to see. At least he thought he did. And when he touched something, he felt it. When he sniffed something, he smelled it. He would say that he could taste work. Thomas Gern moved through his life like some great chefs prepare meals for friends, with aroma. He wasn't conscious of living this way. It was just the way it was.

"I should have fixed that corner in the spring," he said. Yep, it would have been a lot easier to get into the moist non-rooted grasses of spring, pull the three posts, sink the new ones, and attach the planks. But now, in the dried clay-dirt of September it would be work to break through the tall grass into the baked ground.

He had reworked the plank fence again and again. One section at a time, he secured the posts and planks after winter had avalanched on them and broken the flat wood or pushed over the log-like posts. He was glad he didn't have to do it every year. He was glad that they only got two hundred inches of snow and not two thousand. His was one of the last farms in the area with a plank fence. Most people used wire. It was easier. Easier to fix, cheaper to buy, took less time to work. But he had time because, though he had a large plot of land, he didn't have much of a farm—a little hay, a little wheat, and a little garden. The fence had been plank through all the stories his grandfather had told his father. Tom, though he only had four cows, a calf, and two horses, saw no reason to give into the wire of fashion. What would come after that, fiber optics? Nope, he wouldn't be the one to tear down the past.

His coffee was gone. He headed for the barn and thought about buffalo on his way there. I should get some buffalo, he thought. Probably push my fence right over, though. He hitched the planks and posts to the gray horse that stood impatiently waiting by the side of the barn. He released the red horse and started to walk through the brown tufted waves of grass. "Come on old man," he spoke to the horse and it started walking. The other trailed slowly behind. They all headed to the far corner in a parade. He with a hatchet at his side and a post-hole digger, sledge hammer, and shovel over his shoulder: the gray horse dragging a clunky wooden float of cedar, and a baton twirling red horse plodding along in the rear brushing flies away with her tail.

By the time he started working, the sun was sitting on the tops of the shadowed tress like a quarter standing on edge. It angled light toward him and illuminated some of the newer posts of the fence. But looking east, all he could see were the crouched, black shadows of trees that swallowed the town and the road and his land with giant waves of muted sky.

If the sun had been setting, Roadside Girl would never have seen him across the field. But the sun lit whatever was white and Thomas stood out like a beacon in the distance. His brown pants were swallowed by grass, but the white t-shirt seemed to shine from within. She put her arm around Dave, "I'm gonna walk over and see if Tom wants to go into Houghton with me today." The boy hadn't noticed the phantasm in the distance. "Make sure you get that permission slip signed by Lydia before you go to school or you'll have Mrs. McCaffee breathing all over you." He made a sour face.

"Cigarettes," he said.

"And coffee. A deadly combination for secretary breath." She pushed his shoulder so slightly that he couldn't even tell she had touched him, and he drifted toward Clarion like a sailboat in low wind.

She went through the dry ditch and climbed the fence and made her way through the longer grasses that grew along the fence line. She looked down at her skirt and watched unconsciously for ticks.

The horses were finicky as she approached and though Tom

didn't hear her as he heeled the shovel around the base of the corner post, the horses ears jumped abruptly into the air and both lifted their heads to watch Roadside Girl approach.

"Hey Tom."

"Jesus and Mary," he gasped. "Don't do that. Ya scare the bejesus out of me." She laughed as she watched him startle and lose grip of the shovel. The horses moved in disapproval. Then, cautiously, they dipped their heads back to the grass, keeping their eyes rolled up at Roadside Girl. She could hear them rip clumps of earth like hair from the strong dry straws at the base.

"What's up?"

"Nothin'," and nothing was up. "Lydia called. Said you might want to ride into Houghton with me today." Roadside Girl liked Tom. He was quiet. As far as she could tell, he didn't stay in Toclep because he was stuck there; he stayed because he liked it. He stayed because he knew where he belonged. He stayed because the grass was so green here that the other side of the fence looked pale and tomblike. She liked him because he wasn't a liar. He didn't know the great truth and didn't try to fool people into thinking that he did. He was just a man and he was like her.

"Like to. But got some work I gotta do first. What time you going in?"

"Doesn't really matter, long as I get there by four or so."

"So that's one-thirty, two." She nodded her head.

"You need some help? Two's better than, isn't it? Get her finished up and that's it."

He acknowledged the offer with a task. "Here." He motioned to her. "Grab holda this here post." He was standing on one side and she was across from him. "One . . . two . . . three . . ." They heaved once and the pole barely moved in the earth. Then they did it again and again. "Jiggle those planks out and we'll try to pull it."

"This isn't so bad. Why you pulling it?"

"Won't make it through another winter and I'd rather pull her whole than have to dig out the stump after she breaks." They pulled the post with three umphs and he started to clean the hole for the new post. His effort showed in his arms as he banged the handles of the post-hole digger down, smoothed the sides, and pulled out the loose dirt. "Go 'head and clean out 'round those other posts. Have this done lickety-split."

She worked at one of the posts and watched him smooth the edges for the new corner-post meticulously. His dark hair was salted with gray and hung in his face. It wasn't long, long hair, but it was longer than most Toclep men his age, except for maybe Terry Sikes', whose hair sprang from beneath a year-long stocking cap and dropped on his shoulders. She wondered if it was only coincidence that they were both farmers. She had seen pictures of Tom at Lydia's and his hair had darkened dramatically from the hair that ping-ponged between the light and dark of seasonal youth. Now, it was starting to lighten with gray, again. He was thin, and his clothes hung, more from his body than on his body. There were crow-footed lines that flared out from his eyes when he squinted or smiled and though they were visible, she couldn't see them very well. He had gray stubble on his face and every time he thrust the implement into the hole the veins on his neck bulged like fleshy, striking snakes. The skin around his jawbone and chin was tight and he had clear valleys running across his forehead. He looked as if someone had painted him to look both young and old.

"How you like living in the sauna?" He was placing the reddish-yellow post into the hole. "You sweep all the spiders and riffraff outta there."

"I like it. I painted, too."

"Saunas are like weight machines and those Norta-whatevers. Seem like a good idea when you first get one. Then they become hat racks and clothes hangers within a year. Saunas become closets for stuff people should have thrown away years ago." It was like Ezra's house, he thought. "Kinda small, I s'pose. But probably better than sharing a bedroom with that Chippeway kid."

"Dave." She said in a low voice as she rolled her eyes in reprehension. She felt close to Dave. It was as if she had lived with him her whole life. When Tom couldn't remember his name, it reminded her of the tauntings she used to take at school.

"Oh yeah. Sorry. Dave. Always want to call him Bear." He pushed some dirt around the pole so it would be loosely stable until he got the others in and planked. "I know you got that roan over there but if you and Dave ever want to go riding together, I got those two horses, never get rid. No one ever rides 'em and that's a sin cuz they're beautiful horses. Real gentle. I try to put saddles on 'em every so often, but I'm only one person. Can only ride one at a time."

She didn't answer but nodded her head in affirmation. Then she turned the subject like a combination lock and opened her thoughts. "Can I ask you a question?"

"You just did."

"Why is it that everyone works themselves to death?"

"Huh? I'm not sure I understand the question."

"Everyone my age, who could, ran off to college like their house was on fire. All looking for a piece of paper to tell them they can do something even if they can't. Or they dove headfirst into the same pit their parents have been burning in for twenty years—the pit that takes life and returns nothing but telephone wire and pennies. No time to think, no time to breathe, no time to love. Only spiritless, stiff pieces of paper or putrid, yellow mining lights that have all but gone out. I don't know why people want to be adults. I don't know why they want to rush into work the way they do." She shifted her weight from one leg to the other. "Look at 'em walkin' around this town like it's the dawn of the dead or something. Sittin' in their cars with rocket eyes, looking either so far into space that they can't see the stars or so close they can't see the amoebae swimming 'round on the surface of their own eyes. I guess it's not just rushing into work, but it's either, or both. Rushing or dying, all the same in the long run. Why's it got to be like that?"

It took him a second to digest the whole question. "Didn't quite get that last part but I'd have to say that everyone's not like that. Lydia's sure not."

"I know, but she's different. She doesn't count. She always takes her time cuz she's got more time than you and I and all the people in Toclep put together."

"Well," he stopped working and leaned on the fence. "That's a hard question to answer. Most people don't think about it, I guess. Most folks live their lives without thinking, get those . . . whad ya call 'em, rocket eyes. S'pose most folks do what you said your classmates did. Rush out there thinking there's something better, hitch themselves to some train going the wrong direction, spouse, work, kids . . . something they really can't control. I guess I did the same thing. Then they get themselves locked down, locked in, locked out, and spend the rest of their live-long days wishing instead-a doing. They look out their windows and see a beautiful spring rain and think that all that spring rain is doing is keeping them from mowing their lawns. Think they're missing something important, but there isn't much more important than spring rain. Always wishin' for what's not right in front of them. That's what folks do. I guess I do it, too." Today Tom was speaking with a slight southern drawl.

"Or they don't even wish. Doesn't have to be that way, though."

"Nope, s'pose not. But folks gotta eat, gotta live, gotta sleep somewhere. All that costs money. That means having a job. That means playing by someone else's rules, usually. I mean you can live without those things. Doesn't make your life all too comfortable, though. Everybody doesn't have a house and land that their family paid for and passed onto them. It's nice to have a house to live in. It's nice to come home to someone you love."

"But those people, they don't love each other," she interrupted. "Those people never take the time to love. They skip the whole stage of love and jump right into discontent. And they do the same thing everyday." Her yooper accent seemed to diminish with her serious tone.

"Hmmm. All of life is repetition." He rolled his eyes up as if he were looking at the skull in front of his cranium. "Mrs. Jaslo, my old English teacher, would have called that a hasty generalization. You're being a little bit hard on the everybodies out there, don't you think? You're dividing people into thems and yous."

"Baaaa." She laughed. "Us," she said.

"Okay, so you're not lumping me in with the thems. I appreciate it. Still." He hesitated. "People gotta live. They gotta work. They have children and then they have to take care of those children. They don't want the world to crash in on them anymore than you want it to crash in on you. So, they do what they think they've got to do. They work. They pay bills. They take jobs they don't like because there's insurance. They stay married to people they don't love because little Johnny needs both a mother and a father. They sacrifice and work. Time was when they didn't have to work for the Man, but people have always had to work to survive."

"But that was different." She was emphatic. "They also took time to live. They didn't rush into it, throwing the rest of their lives to the wind."

"Maybe, maybe not. Some folks would say if you're not rushin' into life, you're not livin' it. Others would tell you not to live in the shadows of someone else. Marchin' to the beat of another drummer or something to that extent. My Dad worked his whole life on the road. The whole time raping land for the state and farming this." He swung his arms out to the land. "I think he loved my mother but they never saw each other. That was just the way it was. Before that, my grandfather had gotten out of bed everyday at five or so and had gone off to work the land. It was dark when he left and it was dark when he returned. When he stopped in the middle of the day, he ate a cold, Cornish pastry that was dry and flavorless and drank water out of the nearest stream. He came home tired and went to bed and did the same thing the next day. I'm not sure that's what you would call rushing through life, but it also isn't sitting around watching lily pads grow. He, too, loved his wife, my grandmother, but when he got home she was tired, too. Had cooked and cleaned and chopped wood and pumped water and taken care of children. There was little time for what might be the romantic kind of love you're envisioning."

"You say your father loved your mother. But was he in love with her? I mean, if he really loved her wouldn't he have stayed home? Wouldn't he have devoted his time to her rather than to a job? And your grandfather? I don't know, those were different times."

"You saying my father was a louse. A zombie." He held his arms out in Frankenstein fashion. He didn't laugh but he did think it was a little comical. "I just don't think it's that crystal. There's a lot of gray area in there. All the times are different times. And they're all the same, too. I don't think we can say that one way is right and the other wrong. Folks gotta live. Money can't buy you love. You got me and the Beatles believing that one. But love can't buy you food or pay your electric bills or get little Johnny an appendectomy."

"It's the plague of consistency. It's the death of compromise. Everybody's talkin' about gray area. Is gray beautiful? No! Gray's ugly and dead like," she emphasized her clarification, "most gray things. Dead wood, dead fire, dead sky. Not yellow with anger or blue with pride, but gray with death. You know what I mean?" Her voice had intensity and anger.

"Yeah, I know what you mean but it isn't as simple as that. Right now you got a roof over your head. You got food in the 'fridge, and if you needed money Lydia'd give it to you. But that doesn't last forever."

"Lydia said it would if I wanted it to and Lydia knows. Lydia can do anything." She acted like a little, bragging girl tipping her head to one side and smiling.

"Of course, she can. I guess it could last forever except once people get into that tie-down mode like they were paper clips and someone was moving a magnet under them, they forget that they were ever young. Yeah, they remember things they did when they were young, but they forget about being young. They exorcise their past. It's easy to do when you work all day, then come home to a spouse you thought you knew but who you'd left back there with your youth. And then you've got kids and they're pulling for attention in the other direction and you got yourself spread so thin that when your neighbor looks in through the living room window, he can see right through you and out to the Jones'."

"I'll never live like that."

"I hope not. I agree. Too many people allow it to happen. But it isn't just a case of one side or the other. Aristotle said we need virtue in our lives. Middle ground. Not too much excess, not to much deficiency."

"Aristotle can take his middle ground, which I call death, and shove it."

"Maybe you're right and he's right. Maybe the middle ground is the area we never find in life. Always out on the edges moving farther away from the middle because we don't know it's behind us. Probably, most of us can't even recognize what we have or else we see it so clearly, we hate our lives because we can't get way from the obligations that we own. That we bought." He was watching her and she was intent on his words.

"Not me. I'm not buying any of that shit. I'm staying right here with Lydia until I'm ready to move elsewhere. Screw the middle ground."

"Okay, but keep in mind, you don't necessarily have to keep yourself in Toclep. The world is big."

"You did."

"That's different." He said and then whispered, "That's so much different than what you're talking about." However, he was not sure at all that it was different than what she was talking about. He thought about beginning college in Marquette and how his first year he had stepped through the hoops of loneliness and study habits and had made a sanctuary for himself. Then summer came with its avalanche and buried his life. He had found something he didn't even know he had and then one shiny summer took it all away in a drought that lasted forever. That's what kept him in Toclep.

"How's it different?"

"It's different and that's it." As far as he was concerned the conversation was over. He didn't feel like discussing the breakdown of his own life. He saw himself as the trapped animal Roadside Girl discussed. He moved to the work, thinking about hypocrisy. "Gotta get these holes clean," and he handed her the post-hole digger as he took the shovel to the other hole.

They cleared the holes, sunk the posts, and connected the planks that Tom had already honed for the three plank slips. He stepped back and eye balled the planks to see if they were level. Then they packed the dirt tightly around the posts. "Another corner." He picked up the tools and Roadside Girl stepped over and took the sledge and shovel.

"Come on Red, Gray." The horses were already following them.

"How come you never named those horses."

"Got names. Red and Gray." As they angled across the field they looked like two old farmers. They looked comfortable and the tools were fitted into their shoulders like they had always been there. Halfway across the field they became one thick farmer in the light of the distance. She took the yoke off the gray horse then slapped his tail end and he galloped taking the red with him into the shadowed cove of the field that hooked into the nook.

"Those are good horses." She walked toward the house. Tom was cleaning up with the cold water from the hose.

"Damn. Wish this water was a good as that water over there to Ezra's place."

"Cleans all the same."

"Yeah, but doesn't smell very good, does it?" He washed the dust off his face and neck. His hands had dark calluses that didn't wash clean with soap and water, but he didn't notice. "I'll grab a towel." He disappeared into the house while she washed.

He came out and was holding two yellow-green tomatoes and a dingy blue towel.

"Is that clean?"

"Nope, but it's dry." He threw her the towel then tossed her one of the tomatoes.

"Look at that. Damn slimy bastards. Bad enough they leave that phlegmy slime all over the grass. They gotta drill into my tomatoes, too?"

They sat on the front porch and she swung her legs back and forth as she looked out to the road with the tomato in her hand. Terry Sikes drove by again, heading back toward his farm. Roadside Girl waved to him. Tom didn't wave; he was looking at her.

"Think it'll be an early winter. Weather guy says it will be."

"What do mean by early? Geese know better than all the weatherman in the world." He looked into the deep sky. The sun was ebbing from overhead white to the yellow of afternoon. "Be warm, during the days anyhow, 'til October, colors and crisp days'll come before that. Then look out."

She stood up and walked inside.

"Geezus, don't you ever eat? Every time I open the 'fridge, there isn't a thing in there."

"Don't exaggerate. If yer hungry there's cheese, thirsty there's milk or blackberry wine. Bread's over by the stove."

"Well I'm not hungry. Just checking, that's all."

"Don't have to check on me."

She imagined him as a painting she had once seen: a lonely man, sitting at his dark evening table, leaning against his praying hands. His glasses laid on a book, bread and soup in front of him. Tom's kitchen was large and had an old tile floor that had yellowed around the edges of anything that had touched it for very long. The kitchen table was a smooth, old door attached to the wall at one end with two iron legs at the other. It was long and solid and had a dividing brace underneath it that ran the length. Though she wasn't hungry, she sliced two pieces of bread from the loaf and four from the cheese and went back outside. "You know they've got bread makers nowadays." She handed him half of the food and sat down as she swallowed the bread.

"Yep, I know. That's the kind of thing that cuts a little slice off the quality of life. Might as well just buy the bread at the store." He looked into the sky above the trees across the road. "I've got plenty of time to make my own bread. If I didn't make my own bread and can my own vegetables and fix my own tractor, what would I do all day?" He liked making bread for that reason. It took time. And when he was done, there was a steaming loaf. A flavor that no other bread could give and, better than that, an aroma that hung in the air and clung to the curtains. "I sure do sit around doing a lot of nothing."

"Yep, takes away the rocket eyes," she said. He looked at her eyes they were banked in by soft brown feather-like eyebrows. Her irises sparkled and threw dark electric fingers of blue toward the milk white that surrounded them. They sat and watched the wind move tiny clouds of dust out to the road. "You ever get lonely here all by yourself?"

He wanted to lie. He wanted to fake her out like he faked himself out. He wanted to be the heroic protagonist from some cheap novel. He wanted to say, Me? Naaa. But he didn't. "Yeah, I guess I am." He said am instead of do. His voice was soft and drifted into the swirling dust and disappeared. "I guess I am," he repeated.

Neither one of them had anything to say after that. They sat in the clear blue of September, surrounded by life. They sat together. She had never asked him before. And now, now when she did, she didn't know how to react to the response. So, she sat there. She crossed her arms and leaned on her knees and moved the swaying grass with her eyes. Tom just breathed through his nose, eyes made of rocks, and said to himself, yeah.

They would go into Houghton today, but that would be later. That would be after the silence.

About twenty miles north of Milwaukee the ghost of Woody Guthrie, skinny and stretched by the horizon drifted down the road. As the Dodge Dart approached, its lights reflected off the pavement to a white hand and thumb and unconcerned eyes. The hitchhiker didn't truly look as if he cared whether he got a ride or not; he looked as if he could've walked wherever he needed to go.

"Look." Two simultaneous voices pointed and the black roofed Dodge eased off the road a hundred feet beyond the ghost incarnate. The silhouette swayed toward the car, slipped a small duffel from its shoulder, and opened the back door. The dark haired girl spoke first.

"Well, if it isn't Zarathustra come down from the hills. Where you headed, Mr. Optimism?" Her hair clung with friction to the black vinyl and was climbing over the back of the seat looking for magnetic escape.

"It's you. You guys save the world? Fix all the holes?"

"Yep." She reached her arm awkwardly over the seat. "Name's Kristie. Yours?" She was smiling. The karma in the Dart was better than that of the Democratic Convention.

"Already know that. Mine's Ezra. Ezra Gern." He grabbed her hand more than shook it.

"Where to, Ezra?" She paused then added, "Where'd you get a name like that?"

"North. Where'd ya get yours? Hi, Daisy, name's Ezra."

"Sittin' right here. Heard you the first time." She brought her uninterested eyebrows to a furrowed vee that looked like a kindergarten bird. "Name's not Daisy. Where'd you get a crazy idea like that?" She pulled out of the gravel and drove into the oncoming darkness.

"Your shirt."

"What shirt?"

"Shirt you were wearing at Fort Daley." She tried to remember. That had been three days ago and minor details sometimes got lost in the mire of the moment. "White Tee with hand painted daisies."

"Oh, that shirt."

"I kinda like Daisy, Dais." The dark haired girl said.

"Me too." She smiled and he could see her face in the rearview mirror. The dispositions had changed dramatically from Chicago. Mob scenes often made people more violent. They give the feel of indestructibility. Give a purpose that is often forgotten though carried all the time.

"So?" Daisy asked.

"So what?" He was leaning up on the bench seat like a child hovering over his parents.

"So, where'd you get the name?"

"Great Uncle. Died in the Argonne. Canadian Air Force. One hour after the armistice. War was over. Only no one knew it. Pow. Right in the head. One shot. All they sent back was a medal on a colored ribbon and a pair of glasses with no eyes to look through them."

"There ya go. Another war, another death." Daisy was fumbling for something above her head. She pulled the visor down and a pack of Kents tumbled onto her knees and floor. Kristie reached under her legs and groped around on the floor for the pack.

"Smoke?" Kristie held the pack of cigarettes over the seat.

They all took a cigarette. Windows went up as the dark haired girl reached into the glove compartment and pulled out a book of matches. They had lost the train of conversation in the confusion of falling cigarettes and sat silently in the opaque smoke of the car. When another car would pass the inside of their car would light up like a firefly with the white refraction of light through and around the smoke.

"You a student?" Daisy asked.

"Nope. Well, not anymore. I couldn't afford another year. I hope to start up again in January."

Hope, the only thing Pandora had to hold onto, had already unknowingly slipped through Ezra's fingers and was running turn-tail for the woods.

"Hope they don't get you 'fore you can get back in." The "they" swayed in the air like a hanged man, undulating in weighted silence. "We go to UW, Superior. Heading back there, now." The dark haired girl's voice was softer than Daisy's. It seemed to caress the words. He didn't really need to have her tell him the second part seeing they were north of Milwaukee. "You live in Green Bay?"

"Naa. Norther than that. From Toclep." He didn't wait for the question, because he could see it bobbing in the smoke between the two girls. "It's in Michigan. Old mining, logging Podunk along Superior. Nothing there, really. Kinda sleepy. Blue water though. Not like Duluth."

"Superior." Both Daisy and Kristie chimed.

"Yeah." Ezra looked out the window. It was dark, and all he could see was a little bit of the sixty mile-an-hour gravel lighted by headlights. He leaned his arms on the bench seat and looked out the front.

"What ya doing?"

"Looking for eyes. Always looking for eyes." He seemed to speak from a thousand miles away. Daisy and Kristie sensed transformation. Same person they had met in Chicago. They armed themselves and prepared their gauntlet. "Always got to watch. Bambi could jump out any minute." The gauntlet dropped. The car slowed to fifty.

"Guess we're not in any hurry, are we?" It was a question with a built-in answer. "Probably won't go all the way to Superior tonight, anyway. You got to be anywhere?"

"That's the problem," he said. "I don't have to be anywhere. It's good not to be in a hurry. Hurryin' seems like the only thing that people don't forget to do these days. Always in a rush. No time to sit and relax. No time for doing nothin' and nothin's a pretty nice thing to do, sometimes." They rode quietly with Ezra breathing over the seat thinking about doing nothing and Daisy and Kristie both thinking about invisible futures and people they didn't know. No one thought about the war or the convention, which was only an extension of the war to them.

Well out of city lights, sandwiched between Milwaukee and the North Pole, they turned and headed west into the darkness, into the bear-filled pines, into the black darkness of untraveled roads, into the dotted canvas of a moonless sky. Daisy was tired—not the tired that makes sleep but the tired that makes bad drivers.

"We're going west, you know. I don't want to take you out of your way."

"Toclep's outta my way. Can't get much more outta my way than that." The dark haired girl twisted on the seat and cocked her right leg slipping it under her other and leaned against the door. Ezra reached right and pushed the lock down.

"Hey thanks."

"Can't have you spilling out onto the highway like a bag of groceries." Kristie was a Cameo, a statued silhouette of beauty surrounded by black-green light. He noticed her nose, which rounded on the tip like a marble and tucked up before coming back down to join her lip. It wasn't a small nose or a large nose; it was just a nose. Her cheeks weren't high but didn't sag and she had the slightest hint of a dimple on her left cheek, but it wasn't a dimple. More than anything he noticed the curved indentation of her throat. It was shadowed, and he wanted to reach out and touch it. He wanted to feel it slant in and rest his fingers on the soft skin that dipped between the two separated bones of her clavicle. He imagined he could feel her shiver all the way down to her knees when he as he did that. A slight green tinge rimmed her flesh from the faint light of the dashboard. It made her look like an angel.

"Thinking about pulling up. Getting a couple of beers and pitching the tent somewhere." He turned his head toward Daisy. Her face washed pale from the light of an oncoming car. He could see the remnants of childhood freckles. Her copper-blond hair was pushed back on her head with a blue headband. It revealed a smooth flat forehead that eased into the arched top of her head then flowed beneath the headband like water. She had three or four leftover pockmarks, one of which made her nose look like the moon. Her cheeks were full like an old woman's but smooth with youth. He could see the reflection of light in the soft colorless hair under her nose. It was so faint that had it not been for the sparkle of reflection, he would never have seen it. Her square chin was sharply cut and there was no extra skin underneath it. As it turned into neck, it tucked itself away in crisp lines, and disappeared into her shirt. He hadn't noticed before because he hadn't looked. Both front seaters were evening stars.

"Didn't get much sleep the whole time we were in Chicago." Kristie was shifting her legs again. "So intense. Got into a long discussion with this guy about the world being flat. He said it was all a matter of perspective. Lots of conversations like that. All that energy focused in one spot. Too much energy for sleep."

Ezra stared blindly, "didn't get any." His voice pulled a million miles away again. And then more to himself than to them he said, "wasn't any sleep to find." All Kristie could hear was the scratching of a mouse in the walls, somewhere in the back of her mind. Not a voice at all.

Daisy pulled underneath a blood-orange neon sign that was buzzing, "liquor."

"You wanna run in and get something?" She reached into the macramé bag beside her.

"I've got money," he said. "What do you want?"

"Couple of beers or Strawberry Hill." Kristie was getting out of the car. If Daisy had ever had the idea to leave the hitchhiker, Kristie had spoiled it.

"I'm gonna grab something to eat, too."

When they came out, Kristie was holding a bag obviously containing potato chips and a loaf of bread. Ezra had two bottles of Boone's Farm, one pink, one clear green, and a twelve pack of Blatz. "I got some chips." Kristie was pulling items out of the bag with Santa-like gestures. "Some bread. Peanut Butter." She held the bottle, which was glowing with the unidentifiable shade of pink from the neon light. "Cheeze-Wiz." She dropped it back into the bag. "And Quisp for breakfast."

"Cheeze-Wiz? What are you going to do with Cheeze-Wiz?"

"Oh, Ritz, I forgot. They were hiding on the other side of the Quisp." Kristie laughed and Daisy pulled the yellow Dart out of the hued light for which Crayola had no name. "You know where we're gonna stop?"

"Nope. Know that when we get there. Crack that Strawberry Hill, Ezzie." Most people called him Ezrie and when Daisy dropped the formality of the "r," he felt as if he had just been inducted into a new club. He broke the red, plastic seal on the screw-top wine and passed it forward.

"Sign of a good wine. Twist top." He pushed the bottle forward, "Ladies first."

"What're you talking about? I'm not your grandma." She pushed the bottle back into his grip. "Don't spill that shit on me." Ezra took a large swallow and he could feel the bubbles coursing down his throat. "More like it." She watched him in the rearview then inverted her right arm above her shoulder. He placed the bottle in her hand. Kristie was reaching between them, bending over the seat like Mr. Fantastic in a game of Twister, reaching for the beer.

"Not for me. Boone's Farm's the worst sick I ever got." She was pulling herself into the cardboard box that held the beer. The road was black. The light from the store had disappeared and there were only shadows in front of them, like all the trees had gathered together to hide the sky.

As they passed the Strawberry Hill away and chatted words the size of eyelashes, they broke ice and melted until they were all laughing from tired and alcohol and having lived the same lives in different specks of the North. The convention had been serious. The war was an iron-hulled ship of seriousness. But they forgot all about that part of their lives and remembered that they were young. Kristie majored in English but only studied people. She liked literature but couldn't really see the use of a degree that told others you could read. Daisy studied cartography but never thought she would use it, and Ezra, who had finished one semester of engineering and had learned to sleep with his eyes open in Mrs. Jaslo's American Literature class, was thinking about his childhood.

"You know. When I was a little kid, me and my brother had bunk beds." He stopped to see if they were listening. "I was sleeping on the top bunk then. And one night I had to go to the bathroom and I forgot that I was on the top bunk so I just stepped out of bed. And I know this is going to sound funny to you but I didn't fall. I just hung there in the air like I was walking on a cloud."

"Is this a bunch of crap?"

"This is bullshit, Kristie."

"No. For real. I just floated there. Then I realized I had been sleeping on the top bunk. I realized I was standing in air. And I looked down and couldn't believe it. A voice in my head said, 'You don't believe it?' As soon as I said, no, I ceased floating. I crashed to the floor like someone had dropped a rock." Ezra looked out the window and quietly said to himself, "Can anyone understand the spreadings of the clouds." He paused momentarily.

"Tom woke up, Tom's my little brother. Tom woke up in a bolt and my mom came running in and said, 'What happened? What happened?' And Tom said, 'Ezrie just fell out of bed that's all.'

But my Mom, she looked confused and then she said, 'Well how come he's over here by the door if he just fell out of bed?'

"I looked over at the bunk and sure enough I was by the door. I hadn't noticed before she said anything. I sat there on the floor looking up at the bed like the bunk had something to do with anti-gravity and as I was looking up I saw clear as day that I had walked over to the door. Would have walked all the way to the bathroom if I hadn't have said no to the voice in my head."

Ezra opened the apple wine—this time twisting through a green sheath. He passed the bottle forward and watched as the invisible ash at the end of Kristie's cigarette flared into fire then died to invisibility again. A small brown sign, which no one saw but Daisy, said National Forest. She filed it in her mind.

"Ya know, we've been following demonstrations all summer," Kristie said.

"Is that what you've been doing?"

"Not really. I was accidentally or coincidentally down in the riots of Detroit last year. I went down to visit a friend at Wayne State but found I was in the wrong place at the wrong time—more violence than peace there. Whole town was on fire and there wasn't a haven anywhere. Got clubbed there pretty hard. Thought I was dead it hurt so much. Then realized I couldn't be dead cuz it hurt so much."

"Never been to Detroit. Too far away. I heard the Negroes," she was unclear about the correct diction and stumbled a bit when she said Negroes. "I heard the Negroes were fighting everyone. Lightin' everything on fire."

"Yeah I got lost and stumbled into more of a war zone than a civil rights movement. In fact there wasn't anything civil about it. I guess it's all the same. This freedom, that freedom, here a freedom, there a freedom. That mess in Chicago was bad but it wasn't the DMZ. It wasn't Detroit. Blacks are right. They ought to fight. They ought to rise up. That's one thing." He stopped—down shifted in his mind. "But we've got no right to rise up in Vietnam.

But there's always been someone who's said that and that person . . . ."

"Pulling off." Daisy interrupted with a jerking transition from blacktop to sand, which threw Ezra and Kristie to the left. Ezra never finished his sentence.

"Where the Sam hill are you goin'?" The car jumped down a narrow two-track of sand, sliding sideways, displacing moss and rocking as if it were shockless, as if it had no form at all.

"We're setting up for the night."

"Where?"

"Sign said lake." She was pointing over her shoulder, back toward the road.

"What sign?"

"You were jawing. Had your head turned backwards." The car slowed in the sand almost to the point of getting stuck then lurched forward again. It did this three or four times, speeding up, slowing down, lurching until the lights of the car ran like white highways across a small lake. Daisy hit the brakes and sand-dust lifted around the car leaving it in a dry cloud.

"How do ya know this isn't somebody's land?"

"It's not," Ezra said.

"Nope. It's not. It's our land. National Forest." She turned off the headlights. The three got out and were hit by the dryness of the sand dust. Their tongues were sponges rung dry. The sky was glowing and they noticed that the northern lights were growing in the sky—not just streaking from the north but wrapping around them—high overhead, so bright that they blocked the view of the Milky Way. The lake reflected the inverted light, and as their eyes adjusted it was as if a full moon shined in the sky. They dragged shadows around the soft yellow of the car, which glowed in the night.

"Won't need the lantern tonight." Daisy reached into the trunk. "Those lights never last long. Should enjoy 'em while we can." She pulled a heavy canvas tent out of the trunk and threw it on the ground. "Kinda small, but I think we can all squeeze in."

"I," Ezra blundered over his words. "I can sleep here. I mean . . . we don't really . . . I mean you don't . . . It'll be okay. I'll just crash out here or in the car."

"Don't be a martyr. It's gonna be cold tonight and you don't even have a sleeping bag." She was right. He didn't have a sleeping bag. "Where'd Kristie go?"

"Over here. I'm using the john." As she walked back to the car, she fastened her pants. "Want me to get some wood?" They acted as if they knew the routine pretty well.

"Good idea," Daisy was starting to flatten the tent. "Why don't you help her? I got this." They started to walk away then she said, "Watch out for poison ivy."

"I'm immune." They both said it at the same time. Walking into the thick darkness of trees, they disappeared and became the liquid sound of broken ferns and pines needles. By the time they came back, the sky was again dotted and the bright swirling lights of the arctic were gone. It was cold and all three could see their breath in the night air as the tiny sparks turned into flames. The fire popped and spit tiny chunks of lava and ash into the air around them. Two feet away from the fire it was black. But next to the fire a tiny sun breathed into their faces. They were all looking at the fire. All smiling. There was a war in Vietnam, but it was there. They were here in the warmth of a fire that turned their crystal exhales into friendly ghosts.

"Anyone want a beer?" He was moving toward the car in slow motion. No one answered. When he returned he gave Kristie one, then Daisy.

Daisy moved from her crouched position. "Shall we skinny dip?" She asked as she answered the question by shedding her clothes. Ezra watched as her clothes dropped to the ground and her white body vanished through the wall of darkness and splashed into water. "Water'll be getting too cold to do this soon." That was all it took. Kristie and Ezra shed their clothes. It was an exhilarating feeling in the cool night air. The three of them splashed in the warm water, keeping below surface because the water was warmer than the air. It soothed their skin, sunk into their pores, and reminded them, unconsciously, where they were and where they had been.

    The air felt cold when they got out, so they rotated their bodies around the fire as they warmed and dried. Ezra felt good because for some reason he wasn't embarrassed or shy and Kristie and Daisy seemed to be perfectly comfortable as they rotated nakedly around the fire like parts of a human mobile. They were all tired. It had been a long drive. They didn't think of the war because the war was over there. Not in the sky over them, not in Chicago, not in the woods. Ezra slept between them that night. He dreamed of walking in the air, walking just above the tent and warming his feet just above the fire. He didn't have a sleeping bag, but he didn't need one. They were warm. They were all quite warm.

Tom got out bed, as usual, and wandered over to the window in his pajama bottoms. His room was morning dark. On the other side of his house, rays of sunshine streaked into the sky from behind Toclep. His side of the house faced lurid gray, like someone has mixed tarnish with midnight. With his hands on his hips he surveyed the Gern property and when he saw his cows, he replayed a summer day.

* * *

The shadow of the house was long and stretched over to the tree line beyond the fence. It gave the white-green hay a blue tint and merged with the fading obscurity of night. He looked at the hay, which had not started to yellow, and out to the pasture where the two Holsteins and the two red Angus were grazing. They were all standing except one, which didn't seem very odd to Tom; cows often lie down when they are tired. The only difference was that this cow wasn't lying with its legs under it. They were sprawled beside the cow and it was on its side like a plastic, toy cow that had been tipped over. Down cow, he thought. His morning mind slowly moved into gear. Then it registered. "Down cow, damn."

He dry shifted his mind into rabbit. He pulled his pants on over his pajamas, threw on the same, brown shirt he had been wearing the day before, and stumbled down the stairs as he tried to fly. He tied his boots over his sockless feet and powered through the door, slamming it wide open against the back wall. Its spring-chain yanked it closed behind him as he clumped off the porch and into the dew.

Tom Gern had only four cows and he couldn't afford to lose one. He ran as fast as he could past the hay to the pasture that stood in the windless, summer morning. Red and Gray, his two horses, jumped with spastic eyes as he flew by them. The stable flies were just starting to wake and the horses' stopped swatting them when Tom passed. When he got to the Holstein, she was bloated and breathing heavily. "Mary and Joseph." The cow was like a beached whale whose lungs, under the pressure of unsubmerged gravity, were crushed by its own weight. Tom knew that he needed to get it on its feet, but its body was so bloated that the cow couldn't move. "Geez, Margie what'd you get yourself into? Come on," he urged. Tom always talked to animals as if he expected them to answer him with logical responses. As if Margie was going to say, "oh nothing, Tom. Just had a little too much grass I guess. Must've gotten grass poisonin'." Margie moved like she had a broken neck. She rolled her large, brown, egg-like eyes and let out a weak and tortured moo that sounded more like a skinny cat than a cow. Margie was close to the edge of the pasture. The black flies swarmed out of the woods, landed, and bit little pieces out of Tom's forehead. He kept reaching up to brush them away but he couldn't brush them away because black flies could stick to children. Tom looked at the sky. The sun was now up over Toclep and the sky was perfectly cloudless. "Damn it Margie, move." It had been a hot for three days. The wind blew noiselessly out of the south. A sick cow lying bloated in the sun would never make it through a day like yesterday and he was quite sure that today would be just as hot, if not hotter.

Even though he knew he wasn't strong enough to move the cow, Tom tried unsuccessfully. He didn't want to leave her and have her drift into some sort of cow coma. He searched the horizon saw nothing and turned his attention back to Margie, cradling her in his arms.

* * *

Lydia enjoyed the walk to work. She was on her way downtown when she noticed what she thought was a log with its roots reaching around a rock. She turned her head away not thinking twice about the fact that the roots, white with sunlight, looked like the arms of a crouching man. She continued her step. She must have walked twenty-five paces when it suddenly occurred to her that there were no logs in the Gern pasture. It had all been hay field in one generation or another. She stopped and looked again. This time she recognized Tom arching over one of the cows, trying to lift it. Without haste, Lydia jumped the fence and started running toward Tom.

Tom was trying to figure out what he could do for the down cow that didn't even have enough strength to lift its head off the ground. He bent again, trying to lift it and though his mind was saying yes he could do it, his back was saying, definitely no, he could not. Lydia's hair spread out behind her like a cape in the draft. The closer she got to Tom, the more she could see his worried eyes. By the time she got to him, Tom was holding the neck of the cow trying to make it easier for her to breathe. "What is it Tom?" Lydia wasn't winded. She asked her question without hesitation.

"Not sure. Looks like the bloat. Gotta get her standing. Gotta get her breathing full breaths." Lydia got alongside Tom and they both heaved, but a dead-weight bovine was not an easy thing for two people to move. They tried again; the cow was no help and only looked around with its big, brown eyes wondering why it was going to die as the black flies swarmed around like vultures and the stabes multiplied for a free dinner.

"You stay here, Tom. I'll run back to the house and get those kids out here. We'll get that girl up." Lydia didn't head back to the road; instead, she ran to the hay field and jumped the fence. Tom thought she would disappear into the green but she didn't. She seemed to rise above it like she was running on top of the sprigs, bouncing off the spring-loaded straws. He bent back to the helpless cow that was moaning with struggling breaths, trying to clear her nostrils so she could inhale. Then knowing he couldn't do anything but wait, he sat with the cow's neck heavy across his legs trying to comfort her, to say with a gentle, rocking motion that everything was okay. He looked back toward Lydia's, but she had disappeared. How could she have run that fast? How could she be out of the field so quickly? Maybe he had had his head down longer than he thought. However, he hadn't. He looked again at the hay and there was no path going through it. No broken sprigs, that he could see from where he was. Tom wasn't worried about the hay. He was worried about the cow: bloating, choking, dying. "And then there were three," he said as he rocked his half-ton baby on his lap.

Lydia didn't come back through the hay field. She pulled into Tom's driveway throwing gravel into what was supposed to be a yard. Her truck bounced through the furrows behind his house and out to the pasture. There was no two-track to where Tom was but Lydia wasted no time making one. Three heads bounced and jerked in the cab as Lydia brought the truck to a quiet stop that threw no dust in the air because there was only grass under her tires. Come on," she said. Then she, Roadside Girl, and Dave were standing next to Tom, who was buried, under Margie's drooling head.

* * *

They seemed to be pushing the Holstein around in circles, and Margie kept looking at them with her dying eyes wondering why they were even trying. But Tom knew.

"She's pregnant," he said. "I lose one, I lose two." They finally rolled the cow off her side just a bit and Dave got into the crack and thrust his shoulder into her as they pushed.

Margie kept saying, "Let me go, let me go. Just let me lie down and sleep."

The sun grew hotter, which forced the black flies to find cover. Tom was sweating through his shirt. Roadside Girl had a dirt-marked, sweat stain running down the middle of her shirt, Dave had little kid's sweat on his forehead and lip, and Lydia, whose dress was quite dusty, had not released one drop of precious water.

"We need to get her up so she can breathe before it gets too hot." The stable flies were off the lake today. The heat brought them in numbers to the open field that moaned with death.

"It's already too hot," Roadside Girl said and she was right.

After pushing and shoving they got Margie up to where she could get her legs under her. She tried in vain with little uncoordinated movements to rise but her legs were like those of a wet fawn. They sprawled and spread and did everything but support her. Tom was feeling her stomach. Baby and bloat. "She's got the bloat," he said. "Gotta get the air out of her."

"What's the bloat?" Dave asked.

"It's just bad gas. It's gas she can't get rid of, building up inside her, trying to explode."

"Doesn't sound too bad."

"How's it look?" Tom said, not meaning to show his frustration. Dave looked at the lack-luster eyes that were beginning to film over and to the slow movement around Margie's lungs. He listened to the exasperated huffs and wheezing gasps that sounded like emphysema.

"Looks like death," he said and there was no flare in his voice, only sadness. They were all quiet after that, except Margie, who was trying to get some oxygen into her system by taking short, struggling breaths.

"She can't die. We can't let her die. Not like this." He looked over to the house. "Bear run up to my house and look under the kitchen sink."

"It's Dave, Tom." Lydia said in a soft voice. Dave seemed to be looking around for his father with confused eyes.

"Sorry, Dave."

"Nothing to be sorry about," he said but it didn't sound like he meant it.

"I'll go," Lydia said.

"God no. I need you here. I can't have her slide back down on her side. We'll never get her up again. Dave, you run up to the house and check under my kitchen sink. I need a mayonnaise jar and some powdered detergent. Like Tide or All Tempa-Cheer. It seems like I might have been out, so if I don't have any, you need to run home and get some." Tom turned to Lydia, "You got powder or liquid?"

"Tide," she said, which meant powdered.

"Okay. Need that soap and a mayonnaise jar and some gasoline. Check in the barn, Dave. I don't want you to bring me leaded gasoline. You hear me? No leaded gas. Look at the cans. Bring unleaded. Don't want to save her life then have her die of lead poisoning." Dave was standing there as if Tom had more items for him to get. Well, what you standing around for boy, get going." Dave took off sprinting toward the house. He looked comical, jerking up and down as he hit furrows on the upside and the downside. He looked like a truck with no springs. "Be lucky if the damn kid doesn't break an ankle the way he's going through those ruts."

"He's strong," Roadside Girl said. "He's not gonna hurt himself. Look at him go. We're lucky to be able to see him, he's so fast." Her voice was confident and reassuring. Tom thought that the way she sounded, she reminded him of somebody he knew but he didn't have the concentration to think of whom. She was tall but she had a thickness to her body. Maybe it wasn't thickness but toughness, which he sometimes confused as the same thing. She was sinewy. She looked strong enough to lift the cow by herself, but she didn't look muscular. She didn't look like a weight lifter.

Lydia could see that Tom was looking at Roadside Girl. She could see his eyes focusing on her nose and the tiny droplets of sweat on her upper lip. Her nose angled into her face like a thirty-sixty-ninety triangle and forged into her forehead like it was forcing the merge, pushing the other skin out of the way. Her eyebrows were light and wide. They were much darker than her hair, which was almost blond from the summer sun. Her eyes sunk deeply with a kind of seriousness and had their own built in baseball caps. She'd be able to look out toward the sun without shading her eyes. A sweat stain had formed down the center of her shirt, turning the faded blue into navy. And though he probably shouldn't have thought it, he thought that it was sexy. Her shirt was tucked into her brown pants. She rarely wore jeans in the summer, flies like the reflective dyes in denim. Blue jeans are a summer magnet for stings and bites, a flashing neon sign for bugs, and she knew that.

She was about the same size as he was, maybe a tad shorter. But something about her made her look taller than Tom. She wasn't fat and she certainly wasn't skinny, not like many of her under-nourished peers who were competing with magazine waists. A few black flies floated around her head but didn't seem to be landing.

The cow let out a miserable sigh. The sound made Tom shudder, "Oh Jesus." He looked over and met Lydia's eyes. They were darker than her hair. She appeared to have no worry. She didn't have any flies around her, at all. Nor did she have any little pink rashes on her exposed face and neck. He thought about all the years that he had known Lydia as he waited for Dave to return.

"You know," he said. "You never age. How do you do that?"

She smiled at him, "Mighty kind of you to say cowboy. That would be magic." She paused. "Or maybe it's just my Oil of Olay."

"Whatever it is, it sure works good. Wouldn't mind having some of that myself."

"I'll send a little of both down, later. But it might be kind of late, Tom. My secrets don't get rid of wrinkles and gray hair. They stop them before they happen. It's a little late for you. But you can give it a try."

"Thanks for the boost in confidence. Maybe if you . . . " the conversation ended. Dave stood over him with a box of Tide, a mayonnaise jar, and a red, tin, state-regulation gas can that said UNLEADED in large, black, El-Marko letters.

"God, what're gonna do make a bomb?" Tom grabbed the stuff out of his hands as Lydia and Roadside Girl steadied Margie's neck. The stable flies were all over her. They spotted her white coat with thick, moving specks and hid in the black ink spots of her hide. Even if she were up they'd be getting the best of her, like they were getting the rest of them, sucking blood for their short life on earth.

"Nope," Tom mixed the gasoline and the detergent together into the jar. "Need baking soda and vinegar to make a bomb. Used to make 'em for illegal fishing when we were kids. A jar, old light bulb, vinegar, soda, and BOOM. Look mom, no hands. Twenty perch would float to the top of the water. Not very environmentally sound, though." He shook the concoction into a frothy white foam. "Now, if we can just get her to drink it."

"Looks awful," Roadside Girl said.

"It is awful. It's a helluva morning cocktail, but it isn't s'posed to taste good. It's s'posed to make her burp. Next best thing to Gas-X."

"Don't anyone light a match," Lydia said as she pried Margie's mouth open and Tom poured in the thick, stinking liquid. Roadside Girl steadied Margie's head and Dave rubbed her throat to make her choke it down. It was quite a team effort. Tom could never have done alone.

When the bottle was gone Tom said, "All there is now is the waiting. Seems like that's all there ever is, waiting."

* * *

Margie began to lurch and burp. One burp followed the other and Tom noticed her abdomen shrinking. "Put your hand there on her stomach, Dave. Feel it real good."

"Geez, what's going on down there?"

"A little internal combustion, Dave. Do it again in about five minutes and you'll notice the difference." Margie looked like she wanted to vomit, and she probably did, but instead she continued to burp and the swelling went down.

After a little more than an hour of burping, Margie began to look thinner. Her filmy eyes were leaking a gooey, yellow-green fluid but her eyes appeared to have life and, without encouragement, she forced herself to a standing position. "Cow'll stand on its own if you let it."

"Looks like she's gonna make it, Tom." Lydia was relieved because she knew that a man with four cows couldn't afford to have one up and die on him. "I gotta get into work. Probably five or six tourists in there wondering what to do about the stable flies and the black flies." She smirked. "I'll tell 'em to go on home," then she laughed. "Those flies are our secret weapon to keep out the surplus population and they work pretty well. Gotta go. I need to change out of this dirt, first. Anyone want a ride back to the house?" Tom looked over and saw that Lydia's dress was filthy. However, she hadn't sweated a drop nor did she have any stable flies around her.

"Sorry 'bout the dress, Lydia."

"All in a day's work, Tom. Better to be here with you in the dirt and grime than to be in the office listening to tourists complain about nature. Or worse than that listening Lynette Berge complain about dying, again. Sometimes, I wish she'd get the bloat. Then she'd really have something to complain about."

Nobody wanted to go back just yet, so Lydia turned and headed to the truck herself.

"Thanks, Lydia. She would've died without you." Then he

looked around to Dave and Roadside Girl. "They both would've died, heifer and calf, without all of you. Thanks." He looked almost sad when he said it. He wasn't, though. He was overjoyed that Margie was going to live and he counted himself lucky to have Lydia and Roadside Girl and Dave. Who else would have run across the field to check on him? Nobody, because nobody would have known that there weren't any logs in the Gern pasture, because, except for the occasional wave from a car, Tom really didn't even exist in Toclep.

"No problem. I'll send you the bill. Doctoring's expensive business." She was grinning as she backed the truck around in the field and shifted into first.

"What caused her to do that?" Dave asked. He was looking at the cow that was still burping but very much alive.

"I don't know, Dave. Sometimes things just don't work right, isn't really a cause. Lots of things in life are that way. Sometimes there's a blockage, too much grass or something. I don't really know. I'll have to try eating grass sometime and see." Margie wasn't running around but she was standing up and the heat of mid-day was now upon them. The cicadas where screeching long, high-pitched screams. The black flies were hanging at the coolness by the edge of the woods. The sun was hot white.

Roadside Girl looked at Tom. He had dried cow saliva mixed with dirt stuck to his shirt and pants. He had sweat through his shirt probably more from worry than from heat. His hair was stuck to the sides of his head, and he was unshaven. His hands were dirty and he looked like he had lived ten lives that morning. However, thankfulness showed in his eyes, the happiness of doing what you do because you want to do it and not because you have to do it. Tom was a farmer. He was a simple man. Roadside Girl liked that because simplicity made it easier to see the truth.

"Looks like she's going to be okay. Let's go in and wash up." The three of them walked out of the same field that Thomas had charged into in a panic that morning. The sun was hot and they felt good. They all felt like they had accomplished something today. In retrospect, it felt like they had a whole lifetime of accomplishment in one morning that hung on the edge of time. They were all glad to have been there, to have seen it, to have helped. Tom didn't have anything to offer them but both Dave and Roadside Girl had something that was like gold. They took that feeling and they put it in their hearts and they kept it there for the rest of their lives. Every time they felt poor, they remembered that they had gold growing like apples in their hearts. Tom was thankful for their help, but they wouldn't remember his thankfulness. They would remember accomplishing something—saving a life that would produce another life, which would produce numerous lives, which would string out for an eternity. They would remember the gold for it was the cycle of life and they had been part of it. They had helped without thinking about it or about what they might get out of it and that made them feel good.

* * *

With his hands on his hips, he surveyed the Gern property and when he saw his cows, he grinned. They were all standing. His side of the house was light now. The first frost was upon him. He would have to pull the tomatoes before that. However, today he would not. Today he would think about life. He would think about himself. And he would think about Roadside Girl.

Wrathful, dark, November clouds had blown into September from the arctic. Coming all the way from above the sixtieth parallel through Canada, they amassed on the shore of Superior bringing with them large, cold waves that increased in size all the way across the great lake until they pounded onto the north shore of Michigan. They pushed sand into the mouth of the Raspberry, churning and frothing the small sand beach; punching the loose sandstone until pieces dropped into the water that was as dark as the sky. Lydia's hair didn't have the same milk chocolate smoothness in this wind that it had on a calm sunny day. It ran from her head and face like a mischievous child. She could hear the waves thunder onto the beach behind Rae Miller's and the Post Office and Thomson's liquor store. The buildings couldn't stop the reverberation from thousands of millions of gallons of water.

When she opened the street door, again like every windy day, tiny grains of sand tried to barrel in and settle into the calmness of the red Persian rug at the top of the stairs. Most would fall short and bang headlong into the graying, wooden steps. The corridor was dark. It was a cavern that spilled out into lightness at the top where the windows allowed the outside, in.

Lydia checked the messages as she fixed a pot of morning coffee: blood pressure for Karl Natcher, the patch for Bud Wilkinson—again, Orvil for Sheelah DeFore—now, can-I-see-you-today from Mrs. Berge, and an empty, silent click from Brenda

Cafus. She's got to do something, Lydia thought. She's been trapped and flailing and either needs to die or chew her leg off. How long has this been going on? Lydia pressed her finger tight against her head and saw eight, nine, ten years of Brenda's life, in one bolt of energy. One flash in the sky of her mind and ten years of Brenda's life ripped across Lydia's horizon then disappeared, another flash and ten more. Rip Van Winkled. One more and they'd be sliding Brenda into an expensive, polished dresser where Brenda would get to be the old socks that no one wears anymore, pushed to the back. Gone. Brenda was already old ignored clothing. Lydia watched her hang in the closets of their conversations. How long could she hide herself? How long could the affair with Ted go unnoticed? How many more lies could she tell? How long would it be before Rich beat her again? How long was life anyway? And eternity? What was Brenda waiting for? What was holding her in?

A baby that Brenda knows she can't have and even if she could have it, she wasn't sure if she wanted to have it. It might save her, but it might not. How many times would Lydia have to see this story unfold? How many outcomes are there? How many losers? And why was it always women, always women in the physical. Men are different. They take the hit somewhere else. Men bitter-down like they're readying themselves for a long winter. Or they simply disappear with a shotgun in the mouth. Women struggle through it, martyr it out like life was a hurricane.

Lydia pulled the hot coffee away from her mouth. "Damn it." Her tongue tightened in pain. Then she envisioned Roadside Girl married to Rich Cafus. One week into the marriage and Rich pushing her around, two years in and Rich beating her up, ten years down the line and Rich forcing her to have sex. Nooo. Her mind screamed, seeing a young Roadside Girl aged and dry like wood. Not knowing what to do. Not knowing how she had gotten in or how she could get out—A dead, disintegrating, January oak leaf that crumbled, brittle when it let go of the tree that had already let it go. That is what had happened to Brenda. Tricked at a young age. Tricked by youth and lust and dreams of a future that rarely happened in towns like Toclep. Impressionably molded by promises and sweet kisses that hid the truth. Rich was a person who would only let you know what he wanted you to know and who hid reality in a deep, dark well. By the time Brenda figured this out, she was in the well, too; she was so used to it that she couldn't tell that the status quo wasn't supposed to be so status or so quo.

Lydia had been in Toclep as long as anyone could remember. Before this was happening to Brenda, it had happened to Mrs. Handley. It had happened here and, as Lydia could remember, it had happened rampantly like the flu in other towns in which she had lived. But that was so long ago. Maybe she could do something about it this time. Maybe she could stop it. But it was domestic. Brenda had to stop it. Brenda had to hold the knife in her own hand and cut the vampire umbilical cord. Yeah, she would bleed but so would Rich. The town wouldn't turn her out. Not now, not in the 90's. It wasn't the 1690's. Brenda had an opportunity. The knife was growing in her belly.

Lydia filled the pharmacy-brown bottles with blue and yellow pills. She stuck named stickers on a pink plastic slider with white pills. Things had been quiet in Toclep as it slept off the hangover of a dying small town for nearly twenty years. People were afraid to make waves. Let the lake do that. People had gone to sleep and let life drip by like a slightly leaky faucet. "It's not bothering me. I can't hear it," they'd say. But they did hear it. They heard it in their breathing hearts at night when they tossed in their sleep. "It'll go away. Eventually, it'll go away and everything will be okay," wheezed the night breath of the townspeople. Lydia stepped to the window and exhaled a coffee fog. She leaned her head against the glass. Had Brenda leaned her head against a window? Was she seeing cold clear? The solution was in the clean brisk air. It was not in the stagnant air of inside; rather, it was in the ever moving, outside air—the fresh air that breathed life into all of nature. The inside air soothed and rocked insecurity. "There, there." It said, patient like a mother. It hid what the blue air knew was right. "There, there. Everything's all right. This is the way it's supposed to be, for everyone." And so the fresh air never diluted the stagnant air. It never cleared the must from the hidden basements.

The waves were pushing against her window. Lydia could feel them trying to crest and break on her forehead. She remembered the winds of her past—the winds that pushed from the north Atlantic against the darkness of her log house. Wind that said, "get out of here." Winds that told her, "It's not a tiny leak in the roof. It's a waterfall, a tidal wave. It's going to drown everyone in its path. Move." Lydia felt her head against something other than glass. "Protect yourself," the wind said. And she had. That wind had echoed for centuries without anyone ever hearing it. Lydia had learned to listen to it.

Lydia whispered and she saw her breath reach up the window in fingers to her eyes. "Protect yourself." It echoed inside her and jumped two blocks to Brenda, who was washing the morning dishes in her Pine Street house. "Protect yourself." Brenda shivered a Tourette-like shiver that made her drop the plate she was washing back into the dishwater. It made an underwater clunk as it crashed into the other dishes but it didn't break.

"Jesus," she said to the kitchen.

"Jesus has nothing to do with this." Lydia spoke to the window and there was no echo.

When the telephone rang, Lydia knew by the nervous quickness of the rings that it was Brenda. She imagined Brenda fumbling with a pencil, wishing she had a cigarette. She could see her tapping and rolling the dull Ticonderoga in her fingers as the reflective green letters shined onto her hand. Then the image of Brenda bouncing the eraser off the light brown of the 1960's formica table in unconscious nervousness entered Lydia's mind.

"I been thinkin'," Brenda said. "I need to talk this out. I need to," she paused in an I'm-not-exactly-sure-what-I-need silence. And Lydia could hear the tap, tap, tapping of the pencil on the table.

"An abortion?"

"I . . . I don't think that's what I need. I need something else." It was as if her voice was coming from her chest and she wasn't moving her lips. Lydia imagined her draped in a terry-cloth robe and slippers. Still in the satin nightgown Rich had given her as a birthday present for himself, staring without blinking, eyes of obsidian, into a white plaster universe in the corner of her kitchen. "I forgot something."

"What? What did you forget? Is there something else?"

"No." She said in her Major Tom voice. "I didn't forget to tell you something. I just forgot something, but I don't know what it is."

Lydia knew what it was. It was life. It was air, space, birth. It was death.

"Can I come in?"

"How 'bout not in, but out?"

"Huh?"

"Why don't you meet me out at the house? Quieter there, more comfortable. No one'll see you come. People'll start talking 'bout you being sick if you visit me at the shop all the time. Like they do about Mrs. Berge. You can walk over. It's cold but that cold air is good for clarity. Get you outside where you need to be."

Brenda drifted. She had already been into Lydia's once this week. She didn't want people to think she was sick and have Mr. Berge asking Rich what was wrong, and Mrs. Berge telling everybody at the Lutheran church that Brenda had been into the doctor's twice in one week. She heard vacant voices in foggy conversation in her mind. I saw Brenda go into the Doc's again today. Maybe, cancer. Or a baby. Why else would she be in there twice in one week. Maybe she's pregnant again. Brenda shivered as she heard the voices in her head say, "Yeah, that makes sense.

That would be wonderful, eh. Maybe she'll carry this one. Isn't that an awful thing to say."

"Right. nine-ish now." She looked at the large wall clock whose arms were directing the traffic of time. "Eleven okay? I walked today."

"Eleven." An unsure acknowledgment came groggy and ghost-like across the line.

Dave ran frantically with twelve-year-old's legs, that were too long for him, to the sauna but Roadside Girl was not there. He scanned the yard as he made for the path that lead from Lydia's to Gern's. His gangly legs twisted and turned as they broke sticks and slid off rocks on the thin packed dirt that snaked through the woods. He jumped Owl Creek to meet the Gern property behind Ezra's log cabin. He stopped when he got to the clearing. He was gasping for air, as if this had been an emergency, and walked slowly and quietly between the house and the sweat lodge. When he got to the trees again he took off running. "I'm not scared of you," he yelled to the house, but he was scared.

Roadside Girl and Tom heard the clump of uncoordinated feet on the porch and looked up simultaneously to see a dark image flash by the window. Dave pounded on the screen door, which double-slapped the frame every time his fist hit the wood. Roadside Girl got up slowly from the table where two coffee cups and two open books rested. Dave was puffing like a steam engine.

"Come on in, Dave." Tom said from the table.

"Can't," he puffed. "Mom . . . I mean Lydia . . . Lydia needs you down at the store," he breathed. "Says she needs to leave for a while."

"Okay." Roadside Girl said calmly. "It isn't a fire, is it, Dave?"

"No."

"So, you could've just called?"

"Wasn't sure you were here."

"So you decided to run over. That makes sense."

"You want something to drink?" Tom was standing now.

"No, sir."

"Continue this some other time." He closed the two books. Dave noticed that they were exactly the same thick blue paperbacks with white sideway letters on the spine.

"You want to go down with me?" Roadside Girl asked Dave as she grabbed her book.

"If ya don't think I'll be in the way."

She grabbed him by the neck. "You're always in the way. Gotta go, Tom. Later, eh." His eyes responded, "Later." She pushed Dave through the door and off the porch. Dave headed down the driveway but she redirected him. "We'll go kitty-corner. Jump the fence." She pointed. Dave looked at Tom who was standing with quiet eyes in the door and watching them fight their way into the stormy, leaning grasses. Roadside Girl heard the slap of the screen door as Tom turned back to the kitchen and to the cold coffee and silent words of the kitchen table.

* * *

At ten o'clock Lydia was turning off Clarion onto highway 52. She looked at the deserted island of Tom's house in the waves of wicker brown grass. He was sitting inside. Alone. Reading a book. Not hungry. Not thirsty. Not busy. Not lazy. Just longing. Toclep was a macrocosm of loneliness, such a small town and so much separation, so much by-yourself, within and without. Maybe today would be different; maybe there was the hope of a save. She cut along the fencerow and walked. Dust and a spit of rain slapped her face and pushed her hair sideways. She tried to use her back like a sail with the wind. The clouds billowed black above the lake and ushered her to the wind-safe path that cut through the woods. As she turned, she looked one more time at Tom's house. He was outside now. She could see his black figure, leaning in the garden behind the house. He seemed not to move and she turned away.

Brenda didn't have a terry cloth robe or slippers but she did have the red satin nightgown that she used to wear when she silently protested Rich's touch, but she hadn't worn it in months, which was the beginning of outward protest. She was dressed. She jerked when she saw the shadow-less lead beaked crows outside the kitchen window. "Hhh." She couldn't speak. The sound and the two knee-high birds were looking in the window, watching her bend to put her shoes on with their shining coal eyes. She was tying without looking. Now, she was making eye contact with one and then the other. She knew the birds; the devil-like birds were always hovering around her. Inside and out, they were there. Inside and out, they were glaring and had been glaring for years. "Go away." The window stopped her words. "Go away I said." She waved her hand at the window. But they didn't go away. When she stepped outside, she raced at them. They lit into the air, floating in the gray darkness, pushed and shoved by the wind that swirled between the houses. "Damn birds. Eat all my chickadee food." She said looking around as if someone was there to hear her. As if she needed to explain her action to the roving neighborhood eyes or the omniscient windows that saw but never spoke, never acted.

But that's not what the birds were eating. She left them in the air floating around the house: mobiles of fate.

* * *

When Lydia saw Brenda come up the driveway under the waving, angry hands of the windswept trees, she walked out onto the small porch. They walked into the white house without saying a word. Brenda had a monologue a mile long written in the tears that ran down the smooth curves of her meek, chinless face.

After dropping Ezra on a cumulus, cloudy car-less U.S. 2, Kristie and Daisy turned into Superior. Ezra threw his thumb to the east. It was mid-morning when he started walking, and he walked less than an hour before he got his first ride. The air was cool and the sun had the flavor of still-green leaves. The sky had a distinct autumn hue. It was that hard-to-define, in-between blue—not the sharp, lake blue of summer or the ice cold, white blue of winter. It was the fade in the middle. He didn't mind walking. He never had. Walking on U.S. 2 wasn't the same as walking up 43, that busy stretch of highway between Milwaukee and Green Bay with zooming cars rushing into overcrowded cities. There weren't any cars on 2 because there weren't any cities to speak of. Trucks would come in streams heading west, taking supplies into Duluth or northern North Dakota or splitting and running south into the empty-spaced farmlands. His tan Sir Jacket sucked in the light, and he knew he would have to take it off because he could already feel the heat welling underneath it. From the west he was a long man, maybe fourteen feet tall, a colorless dark slice through the sun with no distinct features. From the east he was squat, maybe four feet high and the light colors of his face and jacket took the color of white fire. He was God and the Devil on U.S. 2.

The breeze was coming out of the northeast. He could smell the lake. If he had been a horse and that smell had been the barn, he'd have been running with anticipation for the door—

barn sour. But the smell of the lake told him that he was already in the barn. Ezra Gern wasn't religious in the traditional sense but as he walked down the quiet highway, the bloodline of the North, he looked around at the bowing trees and into the sky, which was larger than all things and said, "Thanks, God." He huffed through his nose and repeated the statement. "All this," and his eyes swung like arms out in front of him, "and heaven, too. You've done quite a job." He didn't have to smile because his whole body, together with the land, smiled.

Almost exactly halfway around the globe were walking men just like Ezra. Walking through forests and openings, different than what Ezra walked through now, but just as majestic. They swung their eyes around like weasels, and they didn't see anything God had created. They looked down a tube to the forests of hell, forests on fire with hatred. And more distressing than that, they were in that same tube. When they screamed, "GOD. HELP ME," sometimes it was in English and sometimes it was not. Their voices echoed through the tube and banged around in their heads but never made it to God. And so, they began to curse God, as if God wasn't there and in the same breath they prayed. "Save me, God save me, save me . . . Please I don't wanna die . . . I'm only eighteen," or fifteen or thirteen. They cried and they couldn't even tell they were crying because that's how hell was. They were confused in the floating fires of desperation, the yearning, the desires, the eternity, the lack of escape, the edge—always on the precipice, always just about to . . . . Always. Unlike Ezra, those fire-toting youngsters noticed the black in the sky. They saw the ugliness of the beast. Even when it was sunny, the slime-green trees of hell enveloped them like bacteria, kept them on the edge, kept them in the fire. The locusts that ate everything in their path were multiplying. Hope was a tiny word, so small that even in their minds they couldn't imagine it. Their sun was black. Ezra wasn't thinking about halfway around the world, today. But he would be thinking about it. He knew he would be. Just not today.

Cars passed and he smiled at the woman or the woman with two children who sped by him. He waved to truckers going the other direction and gave them the international sign for toot your horn. And they would, as they dragged the groaning sound with sand and dust into Ezra's face and swept it along pulling it into the empty lands west and north, the in-between lands of America.

He made his way down the road, and the road seemed like life to him. It stretched out ahead through pine forests that cradled it in their arms. It eased over rolling lands that had lost the trees and had become farms of nothing. An occasional cow and long, uncultivated grasses spattered like oiled canvasses with flowerless lilac bushes and drooping apple trees. And the land said, "I've been here a long time. No matter what happens, I've been here a long time." It told a story about being one land mass connected to all the land like brothers holding hands. The oceans had rolled peacefully over it, making rivers at first, then stretching the brothers apart, and separating them. Glaciers came and pushed it around. Pushed it down, dug trenches, left scattered rocks and then receded back to the North where they thought they belonged, for now. That was okay because they only changed the shape of the land. Then there was the big lake, Lake Duluth that swallowed and spit back land. Superior was left, edged with tiny pines trees that would become giants in centuries, towering over all the land in all directions, spread out to where the soil said, "You can't grow here." So they stopped and looked over the grasses, making sure that the grasses were okay. Before the glaciers, the trees had watched the dinosaur go from fish to lizard to armored monstrosity to gone in a spark. After the glaciers, the trees watched the buffalo come and go in a blinking flash. Then man came and cut some of the giants away and put a black, paved sticker down on the land, but the land was same. It breathed, "I've been here a long time. I'll stretch out, because I'm gonna be here for a long time yet, and I need to get comfortable." The land stretched in fantastic colorful smiles. It relaxed. "And when you leave I'll say good-bye. I'll say my own prayer for you—the prayer of the land. Because you will be staying here only a millisecond." The land knew it would change again. But change lasted through entire species and the land, like someone who looks at herself everyday in the mirror, never really sensed the change. There was no time. There was no space. There just was and there always would be. Ezra could feel it and the land, stretched out around him, was telling him so.

Stiv Magliner, a trucker going east, saw Ezra in the distance and exclaimed, "Jesus!" He had meant it. In the distant sunlight through the waves of heat that rose off the road, he saw a man standing sideways with his thumb up, arm out. That wasn't what had surprised him. What had made Stiv exclaim was that the black figure drenched in light seemed to be holding a crucifix. The long pieces of wood were part of the man, an extension of his shoulders that tailed out behind him twenty feet. Stiv shook his head but that was what he saw. As his truck got closer the crucifix turned into a duffel bag and Stiv grunted to the inside of the cab, "I need to get some sleep." Subconsciously, he thought that if he didn't lend the man dragging the cross a hand he might end up somewhere he probably was headed anyway. If he stopped maybe he wouldn't. So he stopped. He thought about how he had seen the twelve-foot ostrich like dinosaur lurch up to the road and shoot across. That was back in the day breaking light of North Dakota and it made him laugh. When Ezra stepped into the truck Stiv realized that he was just a boy. I've been driving a long time, he thought. I'll pull up in St. Ignace and get some sleep. St. Ignace was over six hours away.

"Where ya headed, son?"

"Ironcloud'll get me where I need to go. Ironcloud then north."

"How far north?"

"All the way." Ezra smiled.

"Beautiful damn country up there."

"Here, too." They both looked out over the sprawling land and nodded their heads. Stiv wasn't much of a talker but he was trying to stay awake, so he didn't stop talking all the way to Ironcloud. Ezra nodded, "uh huhed," and "yepped."

Stiv snorted and laughed, "Thought I saw a dinosaur shoot out in front of the truck back there. Dakota or so, I guess."

"Dinosaur?"

"Yeah. You know one of them bird-like things. Big ostrich with scales about ten or twelve feet tall."

"You stop?"

"Naa."

"Why not?"

"I figured I could make it a little farther."

"No. I mean did you stop to see the dinosaur?"

"Oh." Stiv paused. "I thought you meant did I stop to take a nap."

"It's big country. Odder things have happened than a big bird-like thing.

"Naa." Stiv almost told Erza about the crucifix, but he didn't.

"Ya never know. Maybe we see the truth when we're tired."

The comment didn't make Stiv feel any better. Maybe we do, he thought. He turned his head from the road and stared at Ezra.

"What you looking at?"

Stiv shook his head back to the road. "Nothing."

"See another dinosaur."

"No. No I didn't see anything."

Ezra thanked Stiv for the ride and headed north. Stiv felt rejuvenated as he pulled back onto the highway and drove east. He wasn't tired anymore and he felt, somehow, different after he dropped Ezra off.

This'll be the long hike, Ezra thought. Luckily for him, he was able to snag a ride from Ironcloud all the way to his front door. That was the good thing about living on 52. He scooted by Sike's farm then almost to Toclep without delay. When he came up the driveway his father was sitting on the porch in the shadows of angled hemlocks that crouched on the east side of the mountains. Behind them the sun was bowing to the horizon. It was a ways from setting but it was behind the mountains and, therefore, cast a shadow that stretched across the road and covered Toclep. His father was smoking a cigarette. He was always smoking a cigarette. He sat motionless on the porch watching the sky in the east.

"Hey, if it isn't the world saver. How goes the protest?" Matthew Gern didn't necessarily agree with what his son did, running around the country fighting the establishment, but he had served in the big war and also didn't think running into combat was the grandest idea that ever came down the pike. Ezra, unlike some others, didn't have disrespect for the home, just for the government. Matthew thought it was healthy enough seeing that was how this great country, and that's how he saw it in his mind—great, got started. "Glad you're back in one piece. No unseen wounds, I hope." And there had been none.

"Naaa. I kinda left the fight early. Did some thinking."

"It's a good thing to do. A little thinking here and there would save us all a whole lot of trouble. I was hoping I wouldn't see you on TV, again." Matthew hadn't gotten up; they weren't the hugging type of father and son. He drew off the cigarette and let the smoke seep out of his mouth as he talked. "I won't forget that for awhile. Your mother'd have your head if she knew what happened last year." It was quiet.

"I ever tell you about that time I got clunked in the head with a beer bottle? Your Uncle John was trying to show me the ropes. He was a bit older than I was. I guess five or six years, and he was taking me 'round to all these bars, ya see. It was before I was married to your mother. He used to tell 'em I was twenty-one. Anyhow, we were in Marquette and we went to this bar . . . just before the Fourth of July, I think it was the day before, in fact." Matthew pushed his yellowing silver hair back off his forehead. He held his cigarette as if he had forgotten that he had been smoking. His voice crackled with his story.

"Anyway, everybody had firecrackers because it was the fourth of July, and well, we were in this bar and there were some people sittin' across from us . . . Oh from here to the end of the porch over there, I guess. They were about twenty-five or somewhere's in there and they were throwing firecrackers onto the dance floor. Well, no one knew who was doing it, except your Uncle John and I. The bar keeper come over and accused me and Jack of doin' it. He was yelling at us and I could see this table of people laughing at us as the bartender yelled at us. Well anyway, the band had stopped playing but there were these old folks, I'm not quite sure what they were doing there."

"Old folks?" Ezra interrupted.

"Old folks. You know, gray hair. They were quite old. This place was full of young people. Anyway they were out on the dance floor. Guess it was kind of a hokey dump and those people sittin' at the table threw a firecracker out there. It hit the floor and danced up explodin' on this woman's calf. I think she thought she'd been shot. Well, this ole man, he saw who was throwin' the 'crackers. So, he walks over to the table and gets on these jokers. He was a big guy, too, size of Terry's old man. The guys stood up and was gonna get on this old man—Four on one. So us young guys, there was a gang of us, Jack and me and some others. We went over and surrounded these guys and their gals. Well this one gal, she had this 'ere beer bottle in her hand and was kinda smackin' it against her palm like a billy club. And Jack says, she's got a bottle. Watch out she's gonna let someone have it. And about that time she let me have it all right. Came down with that bottle and let me have it right across here." He took his finger and ran it across the worm like skin just above his eyebrow. "I was bleedin' like a stuck hog." He laughed a little. "Bleedin' like a stuck hog, I tell ya. When your mom saw me the next day she had a fit. She didn't speak to her Jack for over month."

"Uncle Jack was pretty wild, eh?"

"He was pretty wild." Matthew looked straight ahead at the road. His cigarette was nearly all ash. "Glad you're home in one piece. I know you feel like you gotta do what you gotta do with this whole Vietnam thing. I guess I would, too. But I'll tell ya, Ezrie, when you're gone I sure do worry about you."

"I wonder whether there's anything people can really do to end this war. You think there's anything?"

"I'd guess not, Ez. This war, it isn't like the Big One. Different motives. I'd guess this is a people-in-power war not a power-in-the-people war. My guess is that they'll just let it play out and hope it plays out soon, but I wouldn't count on it. Think it all comes down to power, and that is always tied to money. But I'm no rocket scientist. I don't claim to understand the politics or economics of war, only the morals. I'm not like most folks who think this is going to come to a head with a big nuclear bang, but the whole thing scares hell out of me. It could drag on, a standstill of powers and economic systems like the dawning of a new Crusades for the twenty-first century. It scares me for you and for your brother and in a more Christian sense it scares me for everyone your age. If I were your age it wouldn't make a whole lotta sense to me, either. It doesn't make any sense and I'm not your age." Matthew Gern wasn't like many of Ezra's friends' fathers. Matthew believed that life took precedence over country. He thought that whoever the crackpot was who turned the idea the other way around was a fool. He was a patriot, and he believed a man should serve his country, but death and serving your country were two different things to Matthew. This conversation was a never-ending circle of questions, so Matthew ended it with a question that was more pressing to him. "You gonna be around a while?"

It seemed like an odd question, Ezra thought. He did live there. "Yeah."

"Good. I gotta be away. Over 'round Seney for a while and we gotta get that hay in 'fore it starts to rain. Been nice and dry. Perfect weather for haying."

"No such thing as perfect weather for haying."

"Guess not. I was gonna get started on it with Tom, but I

figured, hell, I got two sons who can do that and I don't have to have a sore back or scratched arms."

"Nope, you don't." Ezra sat next to his dad in the shadows that reached across the field. They looked alike except for his father's extra fifty pounds and silver hair. He liked his father. That wasn't an easy thing for a young man to admit at the time, but Ezra did. When his friends complained about their parents Ezra would say, not my dad. My dad's not like that. He's like this, and he would pop his thumb into his chest. The others, the complainers, thought he was insane, but he wasn't. Matthew spent weeks at a time on the road, gone for long stretches. He was a state man and the entire U.P. was his territory. It didn't seem quite fair but the regions came from Lansing and that was in another country. "I met a couple of cool girls," Ezra said then rephrased, "a couple of nice girls. Gave me a ride all the way north to 2."

"Yeah?" His father lit another cigarette before the other one had stopped smoldering in the Maxwell House can by his side.

"Yeah." Ezra told his father about the convention. Matthew told him he had been watching it on the evening news and things looked out of hand what with the tear gas flying and the billyclubs banging their way home. Ezra left the convention in the dialogue like he had in Chicago and gave his father a description of the ride home in the yellow Dodge Dart. He told his dad about Kristie and the driver, whose real name he didn't even know, but whom he had called Daisy for two days and how they had camped in the light of the borealis on a small, Wisconsin lake in the middle of nowhere. He didn't bother to tell him that they had bought wine and were underage drinking-while-driving because some things were best left unsaid. The convention seemed on the edge of a dream. However, everything outside the fence seemed on the edge of a dream.

"Sound like real nice girls," his dad said. "College girls at that." Then he turned eyes down into the shadowed darkness of his feet and said, "You know, you should be in college right now.

You're playing a helluva game of craps, here." Ezra believed him but didn't respond. His father didn't carry it any further. "You ought to invite them girls over 'fore the weather changes. Still swimmable water out there." He looked toward the lake. It was reflecting light back and forth between water and sky, trying to multiply its strength. "Lots of room here. Horses to ride, mountains to walk. And your mother'd love to have the company. Especially a couple of girls."

They both looked out toward the road. It seemed like another world out there, like beyond the gray planks of the fence the reality was sur-reality. Things that mattered didn't happen out there. But that was wrong, wasn't it? The fence was only dead pieces of trees that kept cows in and reminded people that some piece of paper from downstate said the property ended. The truth was that the property never ended. That it flowed like a circular river into itself. It extended through Wisconsin and north pushing the breadbasket up and under the glaciers, through Ironcloud and south slipping under the water of Lake Michigan. It was a bowl that held Superior for the sky to drink and dusted itself east into the sunrise. There were no boundaries to the land. There were only boundaries to the mind and that was what the fence was. It didn't really protect anybody from anything. But illusions are sometimes strong enough to convince people that they are true. The fence had locked the farmhouse into the field so it couldn't up and run away like the cows. For three generations, it told the house "I'm looking out for you." It would do the same for another generation. But someday the fence would just be a fence. And beyond that, in the future, the fence, breaking with dry age, would fall down, crumble into dust and the land would say, "I've been here a long time and I'm taking you home."

"Right you are. I should invite those girls over. Toclep's got quite a bit on Superior."

"The town, not the ocean." His father said.

He would invite them over. He would introduce them to the sylvan solitude of the Crescent Mountains and the ocean that was cold blue, unlike the brackish waters in Duluth. "Superior," he could hear the girls say. He would call them and have them speed over after he and Tom got the hay in, before the weather changed. Unfortunately, he didn't know that the weather had already changed. There was a letter in a bluish envelope *en route* from D.C. He would see the girls again, but it would be under a different climate and that climate would bring anger and sadness and closeness that all disastrous storms brought. It would be closed-time, squeezed between now and then and the then that had seemed so far away was now right around the corner.

The hay would be finished in three days. Well, all but one load that would sit and wonder why it wasn't in the musty shade of the barn. His father would be out on the road inspecting the tragic stripping of land. His mother would be clinging to childhood-Ezra-memories with worried smeared cheeks that screamed for Ezra to stay within the fence. His brother would wander around not knowing what to do because he knew war was death and that death had come for supper.

"Yeah, that'd be nice. I'll invite 'em over."

"What the hell is this?" Rich Cafus stood at the back door with the garbage pale in his hand and a blank question hanging from his mouth. He eyed the top of the full wastebasket where a crushed pack of Marlboro Lights sat. "Throwing away good cigarettes, now?" He was a skinny man. His dark cow-licked hair, parted on one side, was cut short around his ears. He had piercing eastern European eyes, the color of ice and steel. His mustache was trimmed short like his hair and bent just a touch around the sides of his mouth.

"I'm quitting." She moused.

"Well I'm not." He was holding the semi-crushed pack.

"You don't smoke Marlboros." She didn't want him to quit smoking. "You smoke menthol." Keep smoking, she thought. Keep it up, another drag another breath gone. She imagined the Surgeon General, still looking like J. Edgar Coop, shedding off the side of the pack and shoving cigarettes by the handful into Rich's mouth. Rich couldn't even breathe; the Amish looking Surgeon General suffocated him. She imagined him with cylinder hands, full like machine gun canisters with white cancer.

"Well, we got friends that smoke 'em, don't we?"

"We don't have any friends. You have buddies." She said so quietly that he could only distinguish the rumble of words.

"Huh?"

"Guess so."

"Two bucks here, three bucks there and we're in the poor

house. We'll be just like the Morhouches. That what you want?"

She had to think about it. Let's see, does Nan Morhouche struggle through the days worrying about whether Will is coming home and going to slap her around because the carrots aren't clean? She would have smiled if she had been alone, because, of course, Rich had been cleaning his own carrot lately. She could see he was watching her. Nope, Nan and Will had a pretty good life, she thought. Dirty maybe, but happy. Every time she saw them they appeared happy, and she wondered if she and Rich, too, appeared happy. Nan and Will had to do it on food stamps. However, food stamps didn't give bruises. Especially inside bruises that time couldn't heal if God himself were the salve. The ones that hurt like having your twelve-year-old dog die everyday of your life. "Nothing wrong with the Morhouches. Different strokes for different folks." She liked saying that because when she said it, it scraped down Rich's back like a cheese grater.

"Don't think you're gonna make me quit. And don't get uppity." That's what people who didn't smoke or drink got: uppity. So full of themselves, struttin' around tellin' everybody else what was good for them. Or that was what Rich thought.

"I didn't ask you to quit. I want to quit." She didn't want him to quit. Keep going. Keep huffing, she thought. She had to have a plan. She had to make a move. She had to shake the cobwebs clean so she could see if there was anything living in them or if they needed to be swept away. She felt spoiled like a rotting corpse. She needed to cleanse herself. "Doctor says I need to get healthy. She says my blood pressure is erratic, my throat and lungs belong to a coal miner. She says I need to clean out my system and exercise or I'm gonna have heart trouble early. She said it would help me to keep from getting infections, if I was healthier." Brenda didn't say anything about the fact that the fish that was becoming a child inside her would be better off without the tar and nicotine, also.

"Sweet Jesus. She saw all that. She must be some kinda mind reader. Must have crystal balls for eyes."

"She's the doctor."

"She's the doctor okay, but a doctor of what is the question? One minute she's hangin' out with all them hippies, next thing you know 'Ole Jed's a millionaire.'" He sang. "Got herself a degree in doctoring. She's a freak."

"Anyway. She said I need to get healthy, clean it up a bit."

"Great." He had the crushed cigarettes in his hand and threw them to her. "Fine, straighten them cigarettes out and I'll give 'em to someone else, then. Wasting cigarettes."

She missed the pack and bent to pick them up. "Here," she said reaching into her pocket. "Here's two dollars you can buy another pack." She set the money and the cigarettes on the table. She knew she had said the wrong thing at the wrong time. She turned trying to sneak away.

"Don't move." He yelled. He returned the basket to its place by the backdoor. She froze. It was freeze tag. Her eyes sighed and went to the floor. He grabbed her shoulder and spun her back to him. "First of all, that's my money you're puttin' on the table."

"You're the one that insists I shouldn't work." Strike two, she thought. Don't open your mouth, she repeated the words in her closed mouth, don't open your mouth. Don't open your mouth....

"And that's the second thing." He had his lip pulled down over his teeth, furrowed like his eyebrows. "I don't want to hear it. You don't run this house." He was shaking her by the shoulder, and she let all the stiffness fall away from her body like she had no bones. She jellyfished. Her extremities became dangling gelatinous tendrils floating in a sea of misunderstanding. "Do you hear me?"

Her body said, yes mas-ter. I hear and I obey, oh great one. If she could belittle him in the mocking manner that played inside of her like a black and white horror film and not have to have her mouth wired shut, she'd be content. "I . . . I just meant . . . well, the cigarettes . . . are broken . . . I meant . . . ." However, she couldn't get it out.

"I know what you meant. And I'm telling you that's my money you're using like toilet paper. Then after you wipe your ass, you have the nerve to smart mouth me about it." He acted hurt. "Don't you have everything you want? Don't I treat you good? Better than the rest of the folks 'round here. Better'n anyone else would treat you, that's fer sure. Damn it Brenda, sometimes you act like I'm not your husband." He put extra emphasis on hus-band like it was an absolute, carved on the bottom of the tablets from Mount Sinai. "You know I love you, baby. We're just not rich, that's all."

The words "baby" and "love" in the same sentence directed toward her by Rich made her nauseous. She felt her breakfast well up inside her and flood into her mouth in thick ropes. But she didn't vomit. Her cheeks bulged, and her nose flared. Her eyes immediately filled with rain, and she swallowed a bitter, dry braid of semi-digested food and stomach acid. She didn't want him to see her crying, but she couldn't help it. He had already seen. "Gggp." She sniffed the clear mucous back into her nose.

"Don't cry, baby. Everything's okay." He tried to hug her, but she was dead and unmoving. She didn't blink. She didn't lift her arms. She didn't sniff again. "You go up and lay down. It'll be okay." However, she knew that it wouldn't be okay. She didn't want to lie down in that tomb. She wanted to go lay on the railroad tracks by the river and be sliced open like a fish by a three-ton steam engine. Unfortunately, trains never used those tracks anymore. As she voodoo-walked up the stairs, she wondered if she had ever loved him. How could she have? She tried to remember the past, but all she saw were visions of pain. She unconsciously collapsed on the rose colored bedspread.

She was crying as she fell asleep. Tears dried sideways on her face. The webbed phlegm in her mouth turned back into saliva as she passed from crying to sleeping, and onward her choked breathing huffed.

* * *

Her mind sorted through the red-brown fog and stepped into a classroom—a bright outdoor classroom with rows of seats sitting on the sand bottom of a lake and all the desks facing the shore. The lake wasn't one she had seen before. It wasn't dark like the tannin colored lakes around Toclep. The water, like light, surrounded all the students. The teacher stood on shore and held a pointed stick. He pointed at some geometrical figures that moved on a four-dimensional chalkboard and were too complicated even for him to explain. He was a skinny teacher with a brown uniform and a cowlick right where his hair parted. She could hear him repeating, "That's the way it is. That's the way it's always been," as he tapped the pointer on the board. "This equation is the equation of marriage and happiness. That's the way it is." Tap, tap, tap. "That's the way it's always been." There was a colored chalk picture in the corner of the equation of a man with a collar of some sort around the neck of a woman who was prostrate. The man in the animated drawing kept pulling on the collar and the woman choked and spit multi-colored chalk onto the board. He kicked the bottoms of her feet and she whimpered in pain. In the other corner were two plus signs that were longer on the top than on the bottom. They breathed. Inhaling large, exhaling small. Brenda had her hand raised and kept asking the same question. Which didn't seem to be in English and the teacher kept saying, "Cuz. That's the way it is." The dream-Brenda screamed as two black knights swooped out of the sky and plucked two figures, like cherries, out of their seats. She stood, "That's not the way it's always been. Not always." The teacher held his hand in the air and one of the knights swooped and knocked her to the water where she struggled to separate the "O" from the H2O. She couldn't breathe. She sucked, but it was as if the siphon was dry. "That's the way it's always been." The voice snapped like uncooked spaghetti. It was brittle and broke as it came to her. She stood and walked without oxygen to the board and spun it around like a roulette wheel. As it spun all the colors merged into an egg white like consistency. When it stopped there was simply a line drawing of one, lone figure: a woman. "There. You see. There is another equation." The teacher's face changed. It was now black like oil. The knights landed on his shoulders. They were a hundred times bigger than he was. They screamed. It was as if a window had been opened at thirty-thousand-feet. All the desks were sucked out of the water, and the board disappeared into a vortex of invisible brightness. Brenda was standing like there was no wind. "Notheitway isthat's. Onlybeenit's wayit'sthe always," she said. A group of people she recognized gathered, but she couldn't see their faces and the knights on the teacher's shoulders were now five-inch mimabirds. They imitated the teacher, "That's the way it is. That's the . . . .

She felt a hand on her skin, a soft hand with long fingers slipped beneath her denim shirt and slipped under her bra smoothing circles around her breast. She grimaced because it didn't feel good. It was out of place. She was out of the dream but not awake. Then in fragmented frames, she recognized the hand as the teacher's hand, dilapidated and emaciated, and she mumbled aloud. "That's not the way it is. Not the way it's always been."

* * *

"Right. Things are good, aren't they? Not bad. The way we've been acting, let's forget that. Let's make up, eh. Best part of a fight." Rich was talking in a dragged-out child's voice like he was trying to soothe a burn on his tongue.

Brenda's eyes popped open, and she could see his shadow against the wall. Don't touch me, she thought. "Not now, Rich. I don't feel good." She turned fully onto her stomach to stop the caress of his hand.

"It'll make us both feel better—about everything."

"I don't feel good." She was talking into the pillow and he was rubbing her back under her shirt.

"I'll make you feel good." He said softly.

"No. Not now."

His voice lowered. It hunkered down like a cornered animal. "Then when?" His voice sounded more like thunder than man. "There's some making up that needs doing." He was pulling the rest of her shirt out of her pants with angry frantic hands. "Do I ever ask for anything from you?" He turned her by her shoulder and was now looking her in the face. "Do I?" She couldn't answer. He grabbed the collar of her shirt and white buttons flicked against the wall as he tore the shirt open.

"Do you care so little?" The words tried to fight through her anger and her soul, which had shrunk and was standing in a small closet behind her heart. She couldn't cry. There were no tears to be had. The hiding soul had taken them. The soul said in tiny whispers, "You can take from me things you can touch, but things you can't touch—you can never steal. Never." She stopped struggling. She didn't move. "He can't hurt you," the little voice said. "He can only do that." The voice spit the last word. Go ahead she said in her mind. Go ahead if that's how you prove to yourself that you're a man. Then she turned into a jellyfish—dead on the beach.

Rich saw she wasn't struggling. "Good." He said. "You'll enjoy this, I'm sure. Been a long time." He reached between the bed and her back and unhooked her bra and flung it to the floor.

She lay there. She was dead; her eyes rolled back in her head. Go ahead ... fuck a dead person, she thought. When he grabbed her arms they flapped like wet clothes on a line. When he touched her breasts, she didn't move. They didn't move. They were cold.

"Okay." He threw her broken arms to the mattress. "Okay if that's the way you want to play. Do you hear me in there?"

"Just barely," her tiny soul said.

He knuckled her forehead hard enough to leave the red mark of three fingers. "You see?" He pulled his pants down. "You see how frustrated you got me, this time." She couldn't see, however, the tiny person in the closet knew there was nothing to see. Rich was losing his edge. "You know, I don't need this. I can get laid all over this county."

"You probably already do," the little voice said. "He probably does."

"I don't need this." He pulled up his pants and walked out of the room.

The closet-person cracked the door, looked out, and grew. The closet-voice was playing a game and Brenda was Lazarus. She was transforming Brenda back from a fish to a human. Rich hadn't gotten into her soul. He had ripped some clothes, he had touched her skin, but he hadn't broken through her. He hadn't done what he had done before. He hadn't gotten to the little person hiding behind her heart. She heard the truck start and clank into gear. The tires pulled and pushed the gravel onto the street and made a blessed scraping sound as they pulled away. Rich was gone. She was there. A little beat up emotionally, but she was there. She wasn't pulp. Now she could cry. She cried until she slept.

* * *

She heard the truck jerk into the driveway as if the truck itself had been drunk. The boom of the door vibrated through the walls, and she was instantly awake. Her eyes focused on a little light in the eastern sky and she turned to the clock: five-thirty. The refrigerator door opened and she imagined the light running across the floor like mice. The sound of bottles pushing crowded bottles and the clank of the glass Miller bottle kissing the table made her shrink. She listened for what seemed like an eternity. The refrigerator opened again and she heard another Miller bottle hit the table. "Dear God, please help me." She could tell by his slow clumping steps that he was swaying on the staircase, having kinetic problems navigating the treads and risers. She heard the bottle bang against the railing and the wall. He was mumbling. She wondered if she should get up and hide in the bathroom, but the vision of him kicking through the door then pounding her head on the white porcelain stool and seeing the flecked pieces of teeth swimming in her blood made her shudder. She could see her thick, chocolate blood dripping down the front of the bowl and a piece of her tongue floating in the red water. No, she would stay where she was. She could sense him swaying in the doorway as he stood burning holes through her back with his eyes.

He flicked on the lights and she sat up. "Scared ya, eh?" He moved over and breathed rubbing alcohol onto her cheek. "I should scare ya." He could barely get the words out. She wanted to move but couldn't. She sat in suspended animation. "Know what I did tonight?" His tongue was heavy and the words were mashed potatoes as they came from his mouth. She couldn't answer. "Said . . . know what I did, 'night?" He slapped the side of her head. "Got laid, bitch. You hear me, said I got laid." He slurred.

She closed her eyes. My God, she thought. Did he go out and seduce some young girl or did he stick his police issue pistol in someone's mouth the way he did with me. She could hear it, "Bang. Bang. I'm shootin'."

"We still got some makin' up t'do. Don't we?" He had her by the hair and she was shrinking, running, hiding. "Said . . . don't," he only got through half of what he wanted to say before he passed out with her hair in his hand. As he fell over, he pulled her by the roots to the other side of the bed, peeling back the covers where she waited, fully dressed.

"We got some making up to do," she said to the air. She stood at the window. The violet-gray sky lightened to a shade of gray—a civil war in the sky. It turned bleeding red like hell had climbed out of the mines and settled behind the black hemlocks. That red wasn't hell, though, it was a warning bell ringing so loudly that all the windows of her mind shattered and giant waves washed the glass away. "Red in the morning, sailors take warning," she said. "I hear you loud and clear." Rich was out. Even when he did wake up, he wouldn't be able to move. Be no sheriff in the county today. Brenda didn't take the truck. She didn't take the money. She didn't take her clothes. She stuffed a couple of things into a shoulder bag, and she took the passenger who had been hiding in the dark closet behind her heart, and she left.

Morning was end-of-the-world red as one bloody egg yoke spread across the sky. It would never reach blue today. The sun soon would be running behind the distant clouds that were so far away you couldn't tell that they were clouds at all. However, now it was a Martian sky that would blink over the circular star and close down on the gray that had swallowed the water.

Brenda stepped onto Clarion Street. From a distance she looked like she was on fire: a cartoon-hot-face so far above boiling point that steam would come out her ears. There were two unknown cars and one familiar red pick-up truck with a horse trailer attached to it parked in front of Coopers. Brenda looked up the empty morning street, looking at the Post Office and Rae Miller's and the Jacobson Building. "My town," she whispered to the windless street and it didn't argue.

She pushed the first glass door open and could see Terry Sikes sitting at the bar with his cafe-white coffee cup perched in his mustache and beard. His hair, which always looked dirty, flowed out of his maroon stocking cap. Brenda hadn't seen him without the cap since he had returned from college. Behind him at one of the tables were five people she had never seen before. They weren't the salvation for which she looked. Her tan work boots didn't squeak like her sneakers usually did on the tile floor and she noticed the sound or lack thereof of her heel-toe movement, immediately. "Howdy, Brenda." The voice came from a headless half door.

"Hey, Gene." Brenda waved to nobody.

Terry Sikes turned his whole body as not to spill his coffee and said, "Hey there Mrs. Cafus." His missus sounded more like miss than missus. Terry called everyone he knew by his or her surname. It felt funny to him to call people by their first name so he never did. When his old schoolteachers would say, "You can call me Ed" as they turned at his elbow, he would say okay Mr. Smaltz. Even his wife chuckled when he called the high school kids who worked the milkers Mr. This and Mr. That. And though Brenda was younger than Terry, she was no exception to his rule.

"I wish you'd call me Brenda."

"Sure thing, Mrs. Cafus." Terry knew the people in Toclep. His farm sat surrounded by nothing about fifteen miles down 52. He did most of his business over in Falls Creek because it was easier to get there via the back roads. He was usually busy at the farm but that did not stop him from catching the morning chat a Coppers. He wasn't a drinker or a smoker and the occasional times when he came into Rae's he would have a watery-eyed coke with his wife and both of them would try to carve air holes through the blue smoke that lingered head high. He didn't see Brenda much outside of town meetings and church, which he only went to about once a month, but he saw her enough to notice that something was different about her today. "You get you hair cut, Mrs. Cafus?" She answered no. "Dyed?" Again she shook her head. "Hmmm, well somethin' sure looks different." The thing that he saw but couldn't pin the tail on was that she looked taller, bigger, but not in size.

She moved to the rotating green stool and sat next to him. "What's with the trailer?" She asked. She thought about the relationship Terry had with his wife. Everyone always said that Kat and Terry acted the same way they had acted when they first met. When they were around each other they behaved with teenage lust and love. Poking each other, laughing under their breath with secret jokes, holding hands, hugging—everyone who knew them was jealous.

"There's a little girl over to Falls Creek wants a pony. I got that small painted pony out there," he motioned toward the trailer in the parking lot. "I'm slowly killing that poor horse cuz no one rides her. You know, no work for a horse is just as bad as all work. Anywho, I figured that little Barber girl ought to have a horse if she wants one. Every little girl ought to have a horse."

In one blink Brenda saw herself on a horse, riding freely over some rolling treeless plain, parting the brown grass with a spotted horse and flowing hair. "S'pose you're right Terry." Through the half door, she ordered black coffee. "I saw your truck down here and thought you might be going into Falls Creek." She could hear the people behind her complaining about the salty coffee and she yelled back to the half door, "From the blue-topped pot." There was bottled water in the back but if the customer didn't ask, Gene just used tap water, much cheaper and much saltier.

"Of course," the voice responded.

"I was wondering if you could give me a ride into Falls Creek. Rich is going to be coming back through there this afternoon, and he thought we could have an early dinner at the Riverside. And I thought it would be nice if we could ride back together. So, when I saw your . . . ."

She didn't get a chance to finish before Terry said, "most definitely. Be glad too. Always glad to see someone go out of their way for the one they love."

"It's nice isn't it?" Brenda smiled and Gene set the coffee in front of her and she pulled it to her lips and sipped even though it was hot enough to blister the roof of her mouth.

"It's mighty early, though. What're you gonna do all morning?"

"Oh I told the folks at the Spotlight, you know the Wentworths?" He nodded. "I told 'em I'd come in and work on curtains for that front window of there's." She knew that Rich would not be up for hours and when he did get up every step he took would rattle through his body like a ball-peen hammer pounding on an anvil. He'd look around. Yell her name a few times. Say god damn it. And every time he would, the ball-peen would strike against the iron in his head. "Beautiful thing, love." They sipped their coffee. Brenda talked nonchalantly. Gene joined them for a discussion the bear problem Les Smalley was having over at the Picnic Basket, because he left his dumpster open like a giant, black bear lunch box.

"It's a crying shame," Terry said. "Bear aren't s'posed to eat garbage. They're s'posed to eat berries and nuts and insects. Mr. Smalley be killing that bear just as shootin' him would. First thing you know some tourist'll go over there and that bear will get daring and charge someone. Then the rangers and the rednecks, like me I guess, will have to go out and kill every bear within thirty miles of here to take care of something that should've never been a problem in the first place."

"The sheriff," Brenda said as if she didn't know the sheriff. "The sheriff ought to slap a hefty fine on Smalley for not keeping his dumpster chained."

"Good idea, Mrs. Cafus. Mr. Smalley and your husband are friends; you ought to suggest that to the sheriff."

As she climbed into the cab of the old F250, Terry asked again what she would do all day. Brenda gave him a listy lie about finding material for new curtains and getting groceries and going to the library and, she put special emphasis on, get my hair done, for tonight.

"That's nice." Terry always sounded like he had a fourth grade education. The truth of the matter was that he had an agricultural degree from Michigan State and had graduated with honors. He ran his farm with state of the art milking machinery and did his book keeping on his desk-top computer that forecasted the bovine milk output and held data files on yearly and monthly milk production. He had always been a farmer and he liked being a farmer. He could play the part quite well. No one really knew the sorts of things that he and Kat did because they were quiet country folks who were in love and who kept, for the most part, to themselves.

It was twenty-six miles into Falls Creek. Brenda noticed Terry's strong weathered hands. His knuckles bulged like metal gears as they gripped the large steering wheel. He had two white scars on his right hand that stood out on the tanned skin like high beams. His beard was untrimmed and started just below his glasses and tucked into the stained, blue work shirt with a combination of red, brown, and gray. He was a strong man and he was quiet. He had gone to college on a wrestling scholarship. Brenda wondered whether he had ever hit his wife or forced her to make love to him. It's hardly love at that point, her mind added. She envisioned herself matter-of-factly asking Terry, you ever beat Kat? You know, just for the hell of it. Smack her around a little bit. Or just kick the living shit out of her just for the fun of it. But his face held the answer to the question.

"You know," Brenda smiled when he made the comment because she could tell he didn't have much interest in talk. "Mr. Cafus is one heckuva a good sheriff. Don't hear about any rowdy kids stirring up problems around here, like over in Ironcloud. Yep, he does a good job, all right. Works hard for this county. Of course, that's not to say your brother doesn't do a good job. He does."

Brenda let a "thanks" slide out between her lips and found herself wondering if Terry Sikes ever said anything bad about anyone. She couldn't remember one town meeting or one church function when Terry had ever put anyone below himself. He was always saying to the men who complained about so-and-so or what's-his-name that as far as he knew so-and-so, who didn't have a job, was a great father and spent countless hours with his son or what's-his-name might drink a lot but he sure took good care of his mother. And the men would look at him as if he couldn't see. However, Terry Sikes saw just fine. He just saw more good than bad and wasn't afraid to say what he saw because everyone in the area knew Terry and everyone liked him. He was likeable because he didn't see any reason to offend others. He wasn't swayed by opinions and he wasn't intimidated by anyone. When he brought the red haired woman named Kathy back from MSU, everyone acted like they had gone to elementary school with her and, as far as Terry was concerned, they had.

When Terry dropped Brenda off in front of the Spotlight Grill he told her that if anything came up and she needed a ride that she could find him at Matt Barber's, "the insurance guy," he added. Terry saw Brenda walk into the Spotlight through his side view mirror but he was looking up the road when she walked back out and headed to the Shell station where the Greyhound stopped.

"Hey, Mariam." It took the woman a moment, then she recognized Brenda's face and her eyes lit up. "I need to catch a bus to Marquette," she paused then added, "Rich is over in Munising and we're going to meet in Marquette for dinner. How long 'fore that bus goes through." Mariam didn't have to look at anything because there were only two buses that stopped at the gas station: the Marquette at eight-thirty a.m. Mondays, Wednesdays, and Fridays; and the St. Ignace at eleven p.m. Saturdays and Sundays. She would have to buy the ticket from the driver. Brenda turned to get one more cup of coffee before she disappeared.

At the Spotlight she pulled an older zipper pouch out of the oversized shoulder bag she was carrying. She hadn't used either in years. She checked her money. She hadn't taken anything from the house but the clothes she was wearing, a green and yellow cloth pouch, a couple pairs of underwear, and a blue fitted baseball cap. She unzipped the purse and counted through the bills they had squirreled away to buy a new water heater: three hundred and thirty-seven dollars and twenty-one cents. That would be enough. She wasn't going far. She had a plan. It was half-baked but at least she had one.

When the bus stopped in Neguanee, she slipped off while the driver was in the gas station and never made it to Marquette.

Rich was probably stirring. Tim had probably called to see

why he wasn't at work and he was now realizing that Brenda was not in the house. Or, his head hurt so much that he couldn't bother thinking about it and he slipped his clanging head back under the covers to hide from the gray-skyed brightness. Brenda wasted no time. There was an old U-Haul step-van that had the word U-Haul painted over in white house paint sitting at the pump. It faced toward Marquette. She waited by the pump until a young man, maybe twenty-two or so came out of the station. He was trying to eat a steaming, microwave burrito, but it appeared to be too hot to put in his mouth.

"You headed south?" The man looked around and when he figured out that Brenda was talking to him, he nodded. "I know this seems a little odd, but my car's broken down," she pointed over at a beat-up Delta 88 that was sitting on the side of the parking lot. "I've got to get down to Escanaba today for a job interview and I can't worry about that silly car. I sure could use a ride."

"Not going all the way to Escanaba. What time's your interview?"

Brenda had to think. She paused because she didn't know what time her interview was. "Three-thirty."

"I'd like to drive you in but I got to head down state, Petoskey, for a gig. Rest of the band's coming later. But I can take you to Rapid River. How's that?"

"Perfect. That's right on U.S. 2. It'll be easy enough to get a ride into Escanaba from there. Thanks." She tried to open the passenger seat door but it was locked. He jumped in and unlocked the door, "You ever heard of the Meat Monks?" They cut through the middle of the U.P. toward Lake Michigan.

* * *

U.S. 2 sprawls across the top of the United States from Michigan to Washington. It's a one-way, non-stop highway to freedom. A truck driver, whose name was Bob Hedgway, pulled into the station in Rapid River and found Brenda with a thumb going west. He was on his way to Williston, North Dakota and had been driving since Ann Arbor this morning. He appreciated the company as much as she appreciated the ride.

"I'm headed to Ironcloud. Bought myself a car there and going to pick it up."

"Whatcha buy." He had a distinct southern accent.

"1968 Camaro. A classic. Mint condition. I didn't feel like hauling it back to St. Ignace on a trailer. Too nice a car for that."

"You a collector?"

"How'd ya guess?"

"Not everybody buys a '68 Camaro."

"Well you know there's that big auto show every year in St. Ignace. You ever been to it?"

"No Ma'am. I'm not from around these parts. Tennessee. I love checking out old Mopars, though."

She wasn't quite sure what a Mopar was so she said, "If you ever make it to the show, you make sure to look around for all the Camaros. Last year I had six of them there. Next year I'll have seven." She looked over at Bob from underneath an old, fitted Tigers cap with a dingy, white "D" on it.

Bob dropped her off in Ironcloud. Bob Hedgway continued west to his destination in North Dakota. From there he would go to Texas before returning to Tennessee. It would be another two years before he drove his truck through the Upper Peninsula. Brenda crossed the street and walked into a youthfully staffed Dairy Queen and had one Coney Dog and a coke. She had ridden with Sikes to Falls Creek; he knew that. Mariam had seen her get on a bus and presumed she was going to Marquette. Then, unbeknownst to anyone, she had headed south and backtracked the southern route to Ironcloud. Now, she just had to get home. She had figured it out. Where would Rich look for her? Everywhere. Everywhere except in his own backyard and that's where she was going.

She crossed the street with a pocket full of quarters and pushed eleven numbers.

"Hello." The voice was quiet and seemed to be already hanging on a question.

"Tom?"

He waited for the voice of a telemarketer to say Tom Jern, instead of Gern but the voice did not. "Hello, who is this?" There was a pause and then he said, "Hello?" He thought for a moment that he recognized the voice then said to himself, no. Thomas Gern didn't get many phone calls and he didn't have many conversations outside of those with Lydia and Roadside Girl. He had kept himself and his memories locked behind the plank face and away from Toclep for nearly twenty bitter years. In those twenty years he believed that no one in the town had done anything to help Ezra when he was alive or find the truth when he was dead. The town had been a lie and he closed himself away from the lie behind a fence that no one crossed—no one except Roadside Girl and Lydia, anyway. And that's why Brenda called him now.

"Tom it's Brenda Muran. I need your help."

He tried to remember. Muran. M-U-R-A-N. I don't know any Muran's he thought. Only Muran I know is Lawrence and Bev Muran, drunk-driver dead for ten years and Tim Muran Deputy Sheriff of Greenstone County. "Brenda who?" He asked. She repeated the name and he said to himself, nope don't know any Brenda Muran. Then he saw her sitting next to him in math class and he remembered a Brenda Muran two years his senior. "Oh . . . Brenda . . . sorry I lost myself for a minute."

"Tom, I need your help."

Thomas Gern had no reason to help Brenda. No one in Toclep had ever offered a finger to help him during or after that tragic summer late in the seventies. Now a long-distance voice was whispering a request for aid. "What's wrong?"

"I can't really tell you that right now. I need help and . . . ." Her voice broke to a tear for the first time since her sleeping tears of the night before. "And well, Tom, we went to high school together. We're friends."

He tried to remember. Friends, he thought. I don't have . . . and then it swooped on him like a bat in early evening. They had been friends; they had sat in the back of two years of high school talking about boys and girls and parents and teachers and . . . . He hadn't talked to her for more than three minutes at a time in over ten years. In Toclep, a town where no one lived out of earshot of anyone else, he hadn't heard a whisper from her.

"My time's almost up," she said. "Can you help me?" The operator interrupted in a mechanical voice, *"please deposit seventy-five cents."*

Tom didn't think. He simply said, "What do you need?"

* * *

He had to call Lydia and ask her for her truck, which he did every time he needed a vehicle. He justified having no truck because he said he didn't need to own one when all he had to do was walk a quarter of a mile from his driveway to Clarion Street and down the street to Ed's Groceries. He already had two horses he never rode.

"Sure. What do you have to do?" Lydia asked.

"Just need to get another LP tank. Don't want to wait for the company to get around to changing it. You know how that goes."

She gave him a yes-I-know-how-that-goes then said "I walked into town today. Take a hike over to the house. Keys are in the truck if not Roadside Girl has 'em."

* * *

"You want me to go with you?" Roadside Girl tilted her head sideways and her face looked like it was made out of cream.

"Thanks, but I gotta screw around in there and pick up a bunch of stuff for the tractor."

"I don't mind."

"Not this time, okay?" It was a rather disappointing response and she dropped the keys in his hand and drifted into the high gray sky. He watched her as he left the driveway, watching in the rearview mirror until he turned out onto 52. He felt bad.

Thomas Gern hadn't lied. He didn't know what Brenda needed or why, but he was going to get a new tank of LP just in case. He turned left out of the driveway and left again two hundred yards down the road and drove the truck down the overgrown two-track that hadn't felt the tires of a car or truck in a decade. Thomas mumbled "damn it" all the way down the two-track as the branches that had advanced into the clearing scraped the side of Lydia's truck. It's been a while, he said to himself.

At the same time, Rich Cafus, his head being one large bell, was yelling to the empty staircase. "Br-en-da." The stairs sighed and mumbled carpeted responses but the only thing Rich could hear was the swinging arm of the wall clock as it pendulummed back and forth. His unsuccessful search of the house forced him to realize that no one else was there except the beast of a blood pounding pain in his head. "You're not gonna like this." He yelled to the refrigerator, who sat humming a low vibration but didn't understand how it was affected by the situation.

Thomas Gern didn't know exactly why he was doing it, but he had a monkey wrench in his hand and was loosening the fitting on the gas line that ran into Ezra's cabin. He lifted the old tank and dropped it, metal against metal, into the back of the truck. "Damn," he said, "I ought not do that." He imagined the tank of LP exploding and taking the truck and its twenty gallons of gasoline with it as he drifted to the ground like a cigarette ash. As Tom pulled into get the LP refilled, Rich Cafus was at Coppers dropping uninterested questions like loose raisins from carrot cake to Gene who had been there all day as usual.

"Back early, eh? Saw her this morning. She caught a ride into Falls Creek with Terry." Gene didn't seem too concerned about Brenda because he had no reason to be and added, "You know he's gettin' rid of that spotted he has. Damn good lookin' horse." But Rich Cafus didn't hear him because he was walking out the door. He had to call several times before Terry returned from Falls Creek.

"Said you were out of town, Mr. Cafus. Said she was meeting you at the Riverside, but you got back early, eh?"

Rich covered, "God I thought we were s'posed to meet at the Forrester for dinner and dancing. Good thing you told me. I'll catch up to her either way. Thanks Terry."

"You bet, Mr. Cafus. Bye now." Terry got no response, just the empty click of the receiver at the other end.

Rich and his jack hammer brain that seemed loose in his head, raced east into Falls Creek. Rich had a tear-like flavor of anger in his mouth as he mumbled in phlegmy words, "you're not gonna like this. You're not gonna like this one bit, you bitch. You'll see not to fuck with me." At the same time Brenda sat, her hair still stuffed up under her hat, silently staring out the window of Lydia's truck as Tom, who was not bothered by the lack of words, drove back toward Toclep.

I hope you're doing the right thing, she said to herself. She told Tom what she thought he needed to know. While she talked she thought, I hope this doesn't back fire on you. How can it, another voice said. No one will know where you are except Thomas Gern and how often have you seen him running a drunk mouth at Rae's. Not in years. She wondered if she was schizophrenic. At the same time Tom was thinking. I hope you're not afraid of ghosts, not that I'm saying that cabin has any ghosts in it but . . . .

He hooked the gas back up and unlocked the door for an occupant, which made the stove and sink cheer with joy. "Turn me on first," "No me. Turn me on first." And she walked into the wax museum that wasn't musty or damp but should have been.

"I don't know you, Brenda. I don't really know what's going on and I'm not sure I want to. I'd guess you think backyard hidin' is the safest place for you." She didn't say a word or shake her head. She was tired. "I wouldn't turn any lights on in here during the night. Cover the windows with something and use candles."

He looked around. "This scare you?" He wasn't pointing at anything but was motioning to the room with his words.

"Nothing scares me. Not anymore." She lied.

"I'll walk out here once it gets dark. Bring you some food."

As he pulled off the two track, Tom was glad that it had been dry and that there wouldn't be any sign of a car having been down the canopied cavern. He dropped the truck at Lydia's. Roadside Girl was not there, so he walked the path back to his house. He didn't see Brenda's shadow inside as he passed the cabin. When he came back later he would have to tell her that Roadside Girl and Dave and even Lydia, sometimes, walked the path. He would tell her she'd have to be careful. But she already knew that.

Brenda didn't bother covering the windows. She sat on the couch looking at the faded light through the windows and fell asleep imagining Rich racing now toward Marquette, swearing under his breath with ballpeen brain and her dream smile twitched like her closed eyes.

PART TWO

By mid-afternoon Ezra and Tom had finished the hay and were coming through the cropped field taking off their shirts and letting the sweat dry the dirt and hay dust to their arms and chests. They would let the cloud settle and bring the tractor and wagon, with the last load, back after lunch. They had seen Mr. Lukis drive by in the fog of dust that rose out of the shaken, shifted, and stirred hay that was bundled and spit into the air. His nearly invisible, right-sided, white, mail Jeep had gone by on the other side of the cloud of hay fog. They would've waved to him, but they were too far away for Mr. Lukis to see their images through his perpetually dirty, Mason-jar glasses and the cloud of dust. So, Ezra and Tom waved in their minds. As they walked in, their arms splattered with pockmarks from the straws, covered from head to toe in the pollen and hay dust, they were happy. The hay was up. Only one more load needed to be moved and thrown into the barn. The bulk of it was in. Only one wagon but that would wait until after sandwiches and cold milk.

When they walked into the house, Marguerite was standing in the pale yellow of the tile-floored kitchen with sunken cheeks and skeleton eyes. She had been crying and was on the verge of whimpers when they came wrestling each other into the kitchen. The sandwiches were quietly whispering stories to each other on the table. The milk was still in the 'fridge wondering what was happening. The table looked plastic and hollow like if one of the pieces of food were lifted, you would realize how light it was.

Nothing to it, just empty plastic. The boys stopped dead as the screen door slapped behind them. They looked at their mother, who stood in the buzzing silence that screamed like a thousand cicadas on a hundred-degree day. She opened her mouth. Nothing came out but tears. Ezra tried to soothe her with rocking hugs as Thomas stood intimidated, trying not to make eye contact, and wondering what to do with his lanky arms.

"What? What is it? Is it Dad? Is Dad okay?" He rocked her back and forth and the questions made her wail. She let loose one of those sobs that sounds like suffocation and lost motor control, and Ezra could feel the nickel sized tears making paths through the dirt on his neck, sending a muddy stream over his shoulder and down his back. She let him rock her back and forth until she stopped. He didn't ask again. She would get control. She would speak, when the speaking time came. He thought she had fallen asleep but then felt her tight fingers kneading his gritty, salt covered skin. He finally pulled away and she pointed with her eyes to the table. What Ezra had not noticed before, he now noticed in slow motion. Leaning against his glass like a birthday card was a bluish envelope with a printed return address in the upper left-hand corner. All he could make out was *Department . . .* but he didn't have to read any more because he knew the rest of the words were . . . *of Defense.* Northern had contacted the D.O.D. and the D.O.D. had finally sent the letter. It had only been a matter of time.

"Oh," was all he could say. The 'oh' bounced in low tone off the roof of his mouth and he could see Tom lip it at almost the same time. They all stood in the malaria light of the kitchen. No one moved. The cicadas in their heads screamed louder. And the din of the sandwiches' stories stopped. The milk in the 'fridge was still wondering what was going on. The room felt just like death.

It might have been ten seconds or ten minutes, it seemed like forever. "Guess I knew it was coming." He picked up the envelope in toneless words and examined it as if he wasn't supposed to open it.

"Maybe it's a release." Tom said trying to sound encouraging but his words hung in the air like a swatted fly and fell to the tile with futility.

"Don't open it. Don't open that envelope, Ezrie. Pandora's everything is in there. Everything but hope. Don't open it." She pleaded.

"Won't matter if I open it or not. Still says the same thing." He reached for a butter knife off the table to shimmy into the envelope.

"Don't open it. Throw it away. You'll hide. I haven't seen you. I haven't seen you since Graduation Day." She believed what she said. "I never saw a letter from the government. No. Don't open it, Ezrie. Just hide. Hide in the attic."

"How long could I hide?" He wasn't trying to respond to her. "Hide until Tom gets his letter."

She was crying again, "Tom's not gonna get a letter. Don't you say that. This war'll end soon. Isn't any reason for you to," she gulped, "go."

"Never been any reason for any of this." They were still standing. The hay that waited to be moved until after lunch would wait the rest of the week, baking like bread, in the sun. Tom stood with his arms waiting to develop and fill out. Ezra floated in a paddle-less canoe to the oceans of his mind.

I knew in Chicago. I knew then, in the swarming Hawks, that something was coming down the pike for me and here it is. A nice cheery letter from Uncle Sam. An invitation to the big party saying, don't miss the event of the century. And the Let's make a deal, "tell him what he's won, Johnny . . . ."

"Well today, behind door number three, we have an all expense, paid trip, which includes airfare, tasteless starchy meals, a six-week workout program, and two sunny years in Southeast Asia."

Every time I stood up against the war, I knew it was coming.

Why am I doing this? I knew, I knew. I could've stayed college. I could've worked that out, but I didn't. I was waiting and, now, what I've been waiting for is here. Should I be glad? He wasn't glad. Should I be angry? No, I knew, I knew it was coming. Nothing we can do here. Gotta be there. I said it. As soon as he thought the words a *deja vu* dropped into his mind with the slow swooping low noise of a helicopter. He already heard the swarming. He saw the dark haired girl being pulled back to the crowd by Miss Flowered Shirt. He hadn't been talking about heaven. He just hadn't known for sure what he had been talking about, and now he had some idea. He had a press conference in his mind.

* * *

"What are you going to be doing over there in Vietnam?" A black microphone was shoved into his face by an olive-drab war correspondent with a light, red-gray mustache.

"I'm gonna save the world."

"You hear that folks. He's gonna save the world. That's excellent son." The reporter gripped his shoulder in you-go-get-em fashion. "And how exactly are you gonna save the world?" The microphone was again thrust into his face.

"Well, I'm gonna end the war."

"Commendable, commendable. Will there be a winner?" The ping-pong microphone jumped back and forth.

"Well, yeah. Everybody will be the winner." The reporter looked dumbfounded and confused like someone had just told him that two plus two was seventeen and he wasn't sure if that was correct or not. His next question was no longer full of excitement, but breached on tentative.

"Everybody? And how, exactly, will you end the war, son?"

"I'll stop the fighting." Now, the Ezra in his mind had the same dumfounded, Catch 22 confusion rolling around the whites of his eyes. He felt like a dog that stumbles away in scrambled disorder after being hit by a car, wondering why he was going to die and why he wasn't already dead.

The reporter, in a patronizing voice, asked, "and how do you plan to do that?"

"I . . . I guess I'll just ask everyone to put down their guns."

"Then you speak Vietnamese?"

"No, sir."

"Sounds like a foolproof plan, son." Again the reporter put his hand on Ezra's shoulder in good-ole-boy fashion. "That was Ezra Gern, draftee from Toclep, Michigan. Sounds like he's got a plan to get things under control and this war'll be wrapped up real soon, over to you, Walter."

As the reporter walked away Ezra stood with his arms at his side whispering, "you don't believe me. I will. I will end the war. That's what I said I'd do." But even the Ezra in his mind didn't believe his own words. Even his own voice betrayed his faith. His mind went black then yellow and he woke to everyone still standing in the kitchen with the unopened envelope and the butter knife in his hand. "Guess we should all sit down and I'll see if I won the lottery." Marguerite didn't think the comment was funny, and Tom didn't even hear him.

* * *

They ate quietly like moths, putting the food in their mouths and chewing unaware of flavor. The envelope was sliced open like a dissected pig and its guts were spilling all over the table. Marguerite was staring into the past, seeing images of a five-year-old Ezra saying in tiny five-year-old words that he was too old enough to have his own bike, even though there was really no place to ride one. She saw the same five-year-old boy in an over-sized army uniform, the sleeves a foot too long and the helmet rocking on his head like a lampshade, carrying an M-16 like she had seen the others, the TV soldiers, carrying. She saw him walking through mud and water with a bunch of men four times his age and twice his size and him saying all the time he was too old enough to carry an M-16. She felt like she was pregnant, again. She felt heavy in the womb—her body pulling and pulling. Unfortunately, this was a different kind of pulling. It wasn't the pulling of her life to give another life. It was the pulling of her life to give up a life. It was growing. It was eating. It was an anti-pregnancy that was stealing her life from her. She felt herself age as she sat on the worn, wooden chair and watched one son look at his milk as if it were another universe as the other slowly pushed soft bread and ham into his unsuspecting mouth which took the food but didn't know what to do with it. She could feel the gray hairs growing out of her scalp and the arthritis growing into her joints. The lines on her face deepened and furrowed in seriousness. They sat like that, soaking in the yellow light of the kitchen for an hour.

Ezra stood up with the envelope and put it with the bills in the wooden bowl on top of the refrigerator. He looked down on Tom and his mother, and they looked like they were miniature models of themselves. They were both looking into the table, somewhere, and when he spoke their heads mechanically moved so their eyes could gaze up toward him. Their lips were identical. Mirrored symmetry of pursed lips. Inside their mouths was a web of sour gum-like saliva, thick and rubbery. Their eyes focused just beyond the tips of their noses so neither one of them could really see Ezra as he spoke.

"I think I'll go for a walk." He said as he already moved toward the door. He noticed for the first time that he had eaten lunch without a shirt on which, even in the heat of late summer, was not an acceptable Gern behavior and he said, "Tom. Tom." Tom's eyes pulled away from his nose and made contact, "put your shirt on. You're at the table," and without thinking Tom stood up and grabbed his shirt and put it on. But it didn't matter to him.

"Doesn't matter," his mom said in a dry, toneless voice.

Ezra disagreed. "Yes it does. Everything matters."

As he pushed the screen door open and stood in the shaded, open light of the porch, Tom said, "You want me to tag along?" His mother reached over and placed her hand on his.

"Not this time, Tom."

"No I guess not," he said absently.

Ezra was holding the door open standing between outside and inside and Marguerite didn't think to tell him that he was letting flies in. She didn't say anything. She simply looked at his shape and held Tom's hand. With the outside sun shining in, Ezra, surrounded by light, looked like Gabriel. He looked like he had been sent with something to say and was holding his horn at his side. Then, like an angel, he disappeared into the light and was gone.

Marguerite got up and moved plates from the table to the sink and even the plates didn't make any noise. Everyone was being extremely quiet, the plates, the glasses, the refrigerator, who usually hummed softly in the background, had all ceased their usual chatter. Tom went to the barn after lunch but he didn't restack any of the disorganized hay. He just sat in the sweet smelling shade, in the perfect peacefulness and wondered why his brother was going to die. Marguerite sat in the kitchen glass-eyed, wondering the same thing. And no matter what either one of them did there was only silence around them, deafening, ear-breaking silence.

When Lydia came in the back door, Dave was sitting with a book in front of him on the kitchen table. Dave had never liked to read before he moved in with Lydia, but Lydia received only one channel on the color television and that channel came in fuzzy and black and white. Unless he wanted to be bored, he had to learn to like reading. Through the kitchen in the den were three walls of books that stretched to the ceiling. There were classics and contemporary, religious and theological, critical and science fiction, medical and occult. The room was dark with books. They sponged up the light and shadowboxed the windows. The den didn't have an overhead light; rather, it had three floor lamps that surrounded the couch and easy chairs with different colored antique shades. Dave wasn't sitting in there. He was sitting at the kitchen table, leaning on the edges of a large book to keep it open.

"What ya reading?"

"Some book about how to fix motorcycles. But it's boring. Doesn't even talk about motorcycles, really."

She peeled back the cover and said, "You might want to find another book. You're right this one isn't really about motorcycles as much as it is about quality and life."

"Quality?"

"In a few years," she said. "There are a few good Hinton novels about gangs and growing up in the city, in there," she encouraged. "Think you might like one of those?"

"Well, it's got to be better than this." He let the cover flop itself shut and she walked into the den and pulled *The Outsiders* from the shelf. Lydia didn't have much adolescent literature. She had skipped that section of literature with Roadside Girl and had jumped her directly from children's books about foxes in boxes into adult books about that and everything else. Roadside Girl had on occasion gotten in trouble at school when she had asked her teacher, Miss Sytel, and the whole fourth grade about her independent reading, wondering what a boner was. When Miss Sytel told her it was a blunder, Roadside Girl responded by saying that she thought it had something to do with the human body. Dave started reading and Lydia shelved the Pirsig novel.

"Have you seen Roadside Girl?"

Dave hitched his thumb at the wall, "out back, I think." He was lipping his way down the first page and Lydia was backing out the door.

The inside of the sauna looked pretty good. Roadside Girl had a small fire going in the wood stove; the nights were now chilly. The stove sat in the actual sauna room and Roadside Girl had the door open, letting the dry heat take some of the dampness out of the air. The sauna, sitting in the back corner of the yard, didn't get much light and had a certain mustiness because of that. So she kept the air dry. She was reading in a hammock that was strung above her desk and bed next to the back window.

"What ya doing?" It was kind of a stupid question and Roadside Girl acknowledged that by rolling her eyes. "I was wondering if you'd do me a favor?"

"Sure." Roadside Girl didn't care what the favor was she was always willing to do whatever Lydia asked her to do. She checked her page number, closed the book, and swung out of the hammock.

"Tom's down there. Got all his storms out. Always makes me nervous to see someone on a ladder that isn't being steadied." She didn't have to finish.

"Say no more, I'd be glad to." Lydia could have asked Dave

to run down and help Tom but Roadside Girl seemed to be about the only one in town, besides Lydia, that Tom would go out of his way to talk to.

Roadside Girl hadn't really thought about it before but the Gern house was quite old. Tom's great grandfather had built the house and the repairs that Tom made usually took the form of old-fashioned construction. It dawned on her that Tom's screen door slammed the same way Lydia's did. They weren't like the newer aluminum storm doors that most people had with the black, enclosed, piston hinge. They were wooden frames with screen. Her's had a rusty spring about half way down that slapped it closed as soon as anyone let go of it. She guessed Tom's did, too. Roadside Girl liked throwing open a window at Tom's house. Until now, she had never noticed that they weren't the standard double or triple-pane Anderson type window in which the other houses of town were dressed. They were old single-paned, caulk on wood, double-hung windows. When she wandered up to his house, he had just begun to work on the front. This time, he did see her before she could surprise him.

"What're you doing here?"

"I thought if you wouldn't let me help you get the LP tank filled, maybe you would let me help you put the storms on."

"You just can't stay away from me."

"That's it all right." Her response had more truth to it than either of them knew. She added, "I was reading and had a sixth sense that you needed some help, and poof—here I am."

"Sounds like living with Lydia is rubbing off."

She asked what she could do and he directed her to the storms. There were only seven upstairs windows and eight various sized downstairs windows. The storms fit very tightly into the frames around the windows and had to be lightly pounded into place with a rubber mallet and piece of wood, as not to damage them. He locked the storms in place with four butterfly screws.

"Isn't it kind of early to be putting these on?"

"Nope." He said it as if nope was a descriptive and defining answer to his action. He carried the windows to the top of the ladder with his arms outstretched, holding tightly onto the frames. He climbed with no hands; she balanced the ladder and watched him fumble with not enough arms for the job. "The rains will be coming soon. The nights have already changed. I pulled the tomatoes yesterday. Lot of half-green ones, but the frost has come." He did all the upstairs windows first, and then they manipulated the large downstairs windows into place as they looked at each other across the old, waved glass.

"What about this one?"

"I need to be able to open the kitchen window. Still gotta can."

When the job was done they carried the ladder back to the barn together.

"Ya wanna stay for dinner? Pay ya for your work." She called Lydia and told her she was going to hang out for a while. "What d'ya want?"

"Nachos." She knew Tom pretty well. She knew that he was a loner. She also knew that he was lonely. "Rae's? You can be my date as long as you pay." She was smiling and though he hadn't been to Rae's in over a year, he agreed. As they walked up 52, Roadside Girl thought about Sunset Rock and the sun dipping into the icy waters of Superior. I need to go swimming before the cold nights steal the little warmth there is, she thought as she imagined the green spot after sunset hanging in the air just above the waves.

"Hey Rae." Tom said it like he was in everyday drinking beer and swapping stories with the other regulars.

"Well Thomas Gern. Ta What do I owe the pleasure?" Rae slapped her hand against the bar.

"Simply missed ya."

"Not true, Thomas. If ya did, ya'd walk across the street more often. All the same it's mighty good to see ya. I guess I owe ya some thanks for getting my truck going, eh."

"Wasn't anything. Faulty regulator. Got five more of 'em in the barn. Leftovers, ya know."

"All the same."

"Your welcome, Rae." He head-nodded to four people bellied up to the bar and he and Roadside Girl took two stools. "Couple of Old Muds and two orders of Nachos." Tom's yooper accent stuck out. He didn't use the mixed dialects from fiction when he was around other yoopers. Rae Miller didn't see Tom as much as she wished she had. She no longer came across the road to watch him weeding his garden. For a while after Ezra died, Rae used to wander across the road to see what Tom was doing. He didn't have much time that year. He farmed his land all by himself, and it was the start of his retreat inward that was only briefly interrupted by his marriage to Sarah. Rae wished that he had been more like Ezra, somebody to help her and to share her time. She had lost that when Ezra had gone to Vietnam and she never found it again. Whenever she saw Tom, she beamed. Not because it was Tom, rather, because it was a little part of a good life from another time, a time she would have almost forgotten if it hadn't have been for Lydia.

"One, one order of nachos. Beans, no meat." Roadside Girl corrected. Rae looked at Roadside Girl, remembering her own youthful days of drinking and dancing. She set two glasses and two cans of Old Milwaukee on the bar. In the semi-darkness Tom looked like he was twenty years old. The lines of weather and age blended into the dimness and the subtle shadows from the bar hid any sign of the age difference between him and Roadside Girl. She was glad for the lack of light, but it didn't matter to her.

"Dave and I were talking a few days ago; did ya know my mother?" The question seemed to come out of nowhere. Tom, suddenly, had a sneaky suspicion that Roadside Girl had stayed on for dinner in order to raise this question. However, that was not why she had stayed.

"Yeah, guess I did. Not as good as my brother did, but I knew her." He reached back and tried to pull the scarf of images out of a closet full of old memories. "Yeah, god that seems so long ago. Daisy. That wasn't her real name, ya know, but nobody ever called her anything else. She wasn't from 'round here. Wisconsin. I never really had a conversation with her about her family. I have no doubt that Ezrie knew all that. Nice enough girl. Her friend played the guitar. Remember she could play some pretty intricate stuff. Lot better player than I was."

"I didn't know you played the guitar."

"Played is the operative word here. I don't play anymore. Haven't picked the thing up in years."

"You still have a guitar?"

"Yeah. It's upstairs sleeping in Uncle John's bedroom. Anyhow, she disappeared with the rest of 'em when the shit hit the fan and the locals and police broke up their little commune. I really wasn't part of all that. I only knew her through Ezrie. I was actually at college when all of that happened."

"Disappeared. What do you mean? Lydia said she died. Said she was sick with something, then died."

"That was later. That was after they all disappeared. Lydia would know more about it than I would. She hung out with the rest of 'em out there. Like I said I was at college. Had to come home early. Then I had my hands full with a million tiny details."

"Seems like you were rushing around just like we were talking about when we were sinking those new corner posts."

"Not quite. They weren't those kinds of details. Death brings work. Especially so much death at once. I told ya it wasn't so simple. We all got things we need ta do. It's just a matter of when and how we do 'em. It used to seem odd to me; how Lydia disappeared and reappeared without anybody really ever noticing she was gone. But she managed it somehow. It's like she cast a spell on the whole town so no one would remember her being a part of . . . ." He didn't know how to say it. A part of what? "Ya know they were all out there. The whole bunch of 'em. Lydia and even Rae, too. She was out there, just nobody seem to care about her. She been a fixture for a while, I guess. They didn't do anything. Campfires and sang. They had a small garden that everyone worked in. S'pose some of 'em were smokin' dope, but not all of 'em. When everyone skinned out of here Daisy didn't look anymore pregnant than you do. In fact, I never even heard about it until Lydia came back with you. That's when she told me that Daisy had passed away.

"It's okay. Ya can say died."

He didn't. "Well, Lydia came back with ya. God ya were small. I sold her that house, I s'pose I thought that's what Ezrie would have done. Plus, what was she gonna to do with a baby and no place to live? She needed something. I couldn't use all the land. It was odd though. She wasn't gone that long. It seemed like a year maybe a tad more. But she came back with you and a degree. Seemed hardly long enough for Daisy to have had a baby and pass on or long enough to go to college. Oddly enough, the town had lost its old pharmacist about the same time the rest of 'em left. An old woman. Had the same eyes as Lydia. Same straight hair, too, now that I think of it. Anyhow, Lydia slid right in without anyone really knowing that she'd been gone. It was as if she wasn't gone at all." He had never really bothered to ask Lydia about Daisy. There were other things more important like getting Lydia's house ready. She was lucky Tom's father hadn't parceled that piece of land in with the rest it that was donated to the park in '58. Out of all those people who had stayed out in the nook, the only one ever to come back was Lydia. Some of the locals never left, but they were swept back into their families and cushioned. Lydia was the only one to run and come back. "They were all trying to salvage their lives at that point. Get out and not get hung by the law or by the locals. Locals were worse than the law." He was talking louder than a regular speaking voice and was directing his words toward ears down the bar.

"Let's leave the past in the past." Rae nodded to the door. "Ya know what happened the last time ya started that." Rae was whispering. She thumbed in his direction and continued to Roadside Girl. "Tom hasn't been in here in a while. Damn good to see him. I wish he'd come in everyday. One time he came in stirring up the past like a hive of bees they," it was an indefinite they, "dragged him out kicking and beat the shit out of 'im. I thought I was gonna have to shove his parents and brother over and find a place for 'im in the dirt. Damn good thing Lydia came by," she laughed, "never seen anything like it. Well, maybe once. She grabbed Sam Booksen by the shoulder and spun 'im 'round dizzy and clocked 'im right in the nose. Busted the damn thing right open and knocked 'im through the rest of 'em." The rest of the boys were laughing at Sam." Rae bent over and whispered, "He called her the nasty C-word and a whore but the boys were mocking 'im. She said ya all wish I was a whore but I'd rather fuck a stump than the likes of you. Somebody else said, 'ya probably do' and when she stepped toward them, they all backed away like she was a rabid dog. She came out quite a bit better than Tom with his bruised ribs and loose teeth." Rae reached out to grab his front teeth, "Them real?"

"Yeah, they're real. Jesus, Rae, that was fifteen years ago." He jerked his head away. "They were all lucky it was five of 'em."

"Ya never were a fighter, Tom."

"Why don't you go get us our food?" He was smiling at her because he liked her and always had. Plus, she was right.

"I can't imagine you in a bar fight, Tom."

"It was long time ago. I was young. Anyway, Daisy was someone Ezrie met in," he had to think, "Chicago, I think. She always seemed to have guarded disdain for Ezrie. It was like she was mad that he knew something that she didn't. But they were pretty close. They, she and that guitar player, came up here to see him off to Vietnam even though they were calling him a traitor the whole time. A sell-out. Soon as he got back they were hanging around summers and when he finished the cabin, they moved in with the rest of 'em. They always said they were like brothers and sisters, a family." He remembered Daisy dancing around the fire pit the night his father had had the stroke. He hadn't really ever looked at her body, but now he saw it clearly in his mind—the young curves of her body through the loose dress. He imagined her as art, Rubenesque, with full arching lines that danced with the shadows of the fire. She was beautiful. He looked at Roadside Girl and he saw her dancing now. But she didn't really look like Daisy and the imagery disappeared in his mind. She did look like somebody. Somebody he knew, but not like Daisy. Not much, anyway.

"What about my father? Any idea who that could've been? Was it one of Daisy's brothers?" The last of the questions was asked in a grin.

"Like I said, I don't know that much. When they were all playing commune, I was trying to take care of my mother and father and a struggling farm while I was in college, and I was yer age. A little younger, a little older. It depends upon when we're talking about, exactly. Least in the first summers. By the time the whole thing exploded my Dad was dead and Mom . . . " he almost didn't finish. "Well, that was Ezrie's fault, I guess. Unintentional, but the result is the same."

"Do ya think your brother could've been my father?"

"I hope not." It sounded like he had said I hope not for her sake but what he really said was I hope not for his own sake.

"What's that s'posed to mean?"

"Nothing. Never mind. No, I doubt it. Daisy and Ezrie, they liked each other but I can't see those two ever . . . course they were all sleeping with each other. S'pose anything is possible." The nachos interrupted the dialogue momentarily. But Roadside Girl kept pushing, looking for something she could get a hold of, something that Lydia might not have known.

"What about some of the other guys? Did ya know them?"

"Well, it probably wasn't Mose Paxton." He laughed and she looked at him with frustration.

"Why not?"

"Well," he gave a little nose snicker, "He was black. Don't know how those genes work exactly but ya don't look like you're a mulatto. And Jano, he was Mexican guess ya can put an X through that one. Phil, maybe. Frank." He was shrugging his shoulders because he couldn't remember all the names. "Murph? God there were a lot a people that were in and out that I never knew. Hard to tell. Not much help, I guess."

"Ton of help. Least you're giving me something to chew on. Something's better than nothing."

"Sometimes. People get used to nothing." He seemed to be talking more to himself, but he said it out loud and she heard it. He munched on the chips, soggy with beans, and thought about how his ex-wife, Sarah, gave him a whole plate of nothing-to-chew-on. He never saw the telltale signs and then, boom like thunder, there was a rift of space between them. It was only a small rift but it grew the same as an unattended hole in a radiator grows. He never even realized that they were no longer alike. It was just like the conversation he and Roadside Girl had had. He hadn't changed, just gotten a little older, and that was probably what upset the delicate plate tectonics of their relationship, his lack of change. She drifted quietly out of reach like an unanchored boat on calm water. It was slow and smooth and, as he saw it from the biased inter-sanctum of his mind, only painful for him. She pulled the plug on the relationship he thought would last forever, and he never even realized what was happening. And now separated from love and severed from Toclep, he had gotten used to nothing. "Nothing ain't so bad." He said quietly.

"Huh?"

"I said ya got something to chew on then." They finished the nachos that were almost too much for two people and had another beer then walked out into the gravel parking lot to a new night sky. There was a slivered Turkish moon that had scooped Venus into its sideways smile coming up over the trees. The sky was already blanketed with stars. It was somewhere between dark and light but the light was fading fast on the western shores of the lake.

"Do you like stars?"

"One of the things I loved as a kid. All the stars. No city

lights. Sometimes, I just stand behind my house at night and count the stars. I just count until I can't count anymore. You know, what comes after seven? I always get stuck there." They were both looking up into the sky.

"You wanna see something?" After she said it, she thought she had sounded stupid. You wanna see something? As if they were six-year-old kids and she was going to pull down her pants for him if he did it for her. However, she did feel somewhat like a six-year-old right now.

"Sure. What you gonna show me?" He, too, felt like he was a child.

"Something special. Come on." She grabbed his fingers until he started walking and then she let go.

He was sorry that she had let go. He liked the feel of her hand in his. But then his big logical mind jumped in and said like a radio announcer, 'you're twice her age.' Then the big radio voice said, 'what would the town think? What would they say?' "Screw them," he whispered. They walked down Bayside Road as the sky darkened with every step and past 52, past Rae Miller's house, around the bend. Then he broke the silence of their footsteps. "The Ramsey place?"

She stopped. "How'd you know?"

"I grew up here, remember. I go there all the time."

"Me too."

"I know."

Though he couldn't see her complexion in the night, she blushed and wondered if he had watched her take her morning swims. The pile of clothes sitting patiently on the rock or draped over the barkless log and she . . . It didn't embarrass her though. Instead, it sent a series of small shivers through her body, and her extremities felt like they were full of sand. "How do you know?"

"I've seen your footprints, both bare and booted." And he thought about the imprint of the bare footprint and again he had a Rubenesque vision of the artful human body in his mind. The circular roundness of all the indentations the foot marks. It's a nice foot, he thought.

"I've never seen yours." It was almost defensive like it was impossible that he had seen her prints and she had never seen his.

"I walk on the side of the path. I walk in the grass."

They turned in at the ash trees and entered an unfiltered blackness. They were both sticking their hands out in front of them as if their fingers had infrared eyeballs at their tips and would help them not to stumble over a new fallen branch in the path. It was the kind of blackness that didn't even leave a shadow to be seen. It was darker than having their eyes closed.

"You've been here so many times, you lead the way." She pushed Tom in front of her and held lightly to the back of his jacket. Even though she had been here a thousand times, the quiet darkness spooked her. Quiet darkness has that effect on most people whether they admit it or not.

"Sure that way you can shove me into the mouth of the bear and run and I'll end up being the evening snack."

"Yep." But it wasn't bear that gave her the eerie feeling. It was the cold dampness of the cedar swamp. It was Young Goodman Brown stumbling unawares into Goody Cloyse. It was what was out there that she couldn't see but that could see her. She was glad that Tom was with her. Likewise, he was glad that she was with him. When they stumbled out of the cave of trees onto the rock, the night sky's reflection off the water made it seem almost like daytime, and they both sighed.

"Damn Ramsey house always gives me the willies." He shuddered.

"Me too." They walked out onto the sandstone in the calmness of the night air and sat on the rock and looked east into the moon. It was a chilly night. Autumn was upon them and the nights of being in shirtsleeves had ended. "You believe there's life on other planets?" Her voice was a dream, and it made him feel clear like the sky.

"Yeah, don't see why not."

"You think we, maybe not you or me, but somebody, will ever see an alien?"

"Maybe. Not sure about all that big head, flying saucer, space modulator shit we see on the tabloid covers. But maybe." He thought about *The Martian Chronicles*. He hadn't read it in years, but he could remember the kid telling his father that he had always wanted to see a Martian and his father, having the boy on his shoulder, pointed straight down into the water. Into their reflections. "Yeah, I guess someone'll see an alien."

"You believe in ghosts?" She wondered if she was steering the conversation in a juvenile direction.

"Why d'ya ask? Ramsey house?" People in Toclep had told ghost stories forever, like in any small town, but since the late seventies there had only been one ghost story—the story of how one bad ghost had killed everyone at his cabin and strewn the bodies throughout the forests.

"No. I thought I saw something moving around in Ezra's cabin. I thought I saw a light then the light was gone. It wasn't a big light and it disappeared in an instant but not like it was being turned off. I was a little freaked out but I went up and looked in the side window. I picked the side window closest to your field so I could make a quick run for your house if I needed too. Kind of silly, eh."

"Not really. Lot of stories about that cabin. No ghosts there, though. Just emptiness. You think you could outrun a ghost?" He wanted to lighten the conversation.

"Never thought about that. Anyway, I thought I saw something shimmy into the loft. Probably just the light and my imagination or maybe a bird or something."

"Yeah."

"Yeah what? You think it was a bird?"

"Yeah, I believe in ghosts." When he said yes they both sat speechless and watched a shooting star streak across the high sky. How many things could be mistaken for a ghost, he wondered. There were a billion tiny dots above their heads and Venus was starting to run out of the grasp of the moon. Then Tom added, "I don't doubt that you saw what you saw. I don't think it's anything to be afraid of though."

"Casper?" Her voice wanted an affirmative answer. It was looking for some sort of assurance.

"Could be Casper. Could be Lizzie Borden."

That didn't make Roadside Girl feel any better. "I'm cold." With two words she had drastically redirected to conversation. "Probably should head back."

"Conversation making you cold?"

"No, the air." The soft lapping of the waves ran down the beach and gave her a chill and she jerked.

He stood up and she did too. "I don't want to leave, yet. It's too nice out here, and I never come here at night . . . I'm not trying to . . . ." He couldn't bring himself to say the words pick you up, so he didn't finish the sentence. "Or we can just walk back."

"I think we can stay." She took his hand and guided them both down to the sandstone. He leaned against the same log from which she usually hung her clothes, and she leaned into his chest. He put his arms around her waist to keep her warm. They watched the slice of light from the moon reflect over and over across miles of water in multiplying smiles. They sat. They didn't talk. They watched the sky like some people look at paintings, all wrapped up in the lines and textures, envisioning themselves on the canvas. They were afghans for each other. Sometimes, people get used to nothing, Thomas thought. And sometimes they don't. Pain is never that easy to get used to. But for right now his pain was gone. For right now he felt like a light in the sky. Roadside Girl sat embraced and felt warm and comforted. She closed her eyes every once in while and could still see the stars through her eyelids because they were the stars.

Rae Miller had beautiful, long, yellow hair that faded to white in the summer sun. She came into the mid-day heat that swelled and hovered like summer gnats around the boys, who worked behind the fence across the road. Rae grabbed her mail and walked across the road in her shorts and bare feet, climbed up on the fence above the growing stalks of soft grass, and sat with her hands tucked up under her legs, balancing. She wasn't sitting entirely on the fence or entirely on her hands. She swayed somewhere in-between with a clump of mail shoved under one leg, throwing the scales off balance—cock-eyed. Ezra was on his knees buried in corn, pulling the blood-sucker weeds that he couldn't get with his hoe. The garden was never overgrown with weeds because Marguerite wouldn't allow that to happen. She had the boys out there constantly, making sure the rows were clean. Tom, at the other end, worked his hoe around the tomatoes. The garden had a temporary fence that moved from year to year around it and the horses walked up and down the sides snorting finely as Ezra and Tom worked.

  They could have sprayed the weeds away, same as some, but Matthew was always saying that the spray would get into the ground and seep out to the woods, "You don't want a woods without weeds, do you? Whole damn thing is weeds. We'll have hemlocks tumbling over and then you boys will have to be out there fixing the fence. Lesser of two evils, I guess. The earth's done just fine by no sprays up until now." And so they hoed.

Tom didn't mind the garden, but Ezra would have rather been brushing the horses or working on the fence or barn or tractor, anything less back intensive. Bending and bending and bending, the garden was a gym class of toe-touchers that lasted all day.

    Rae and Ezra had become close since Harold's heart had stopped cold one night, two winters ago. Rae woke up next to an open-eyed husband, who was neither snoring nor breathing. Rae had been thirty-eight when that happened, a young widow in Toclep. She had to take over the bar, running that and the rental cabins, by herself like she had when her father died. She had worked in that bar since she was fifteen and when she married Harold, she thought she would be able to step right out of it and be a housewife, take care of the cabins, that's it. Unfortunately, she ended up working at the bar as much as he did because he didn't know how to run a bar, and the first year they had the place was the only year that it lost money. Before Harold died, Ezra had done the yard work at Miller's Cabins. He was in high school and he'd go over anytime the lawn needed mowing or the flowers needed tending. He was better at it than Harold. It seems that Harold wasn't much of a gardener or a bartender, "I'm not much of a farmer," he'd say and laugh and Ezra would quietly agree.

    Since Harold had died, Rae had gone through fits of unidentified loneliness and Ezra had started taking care of the cabins and filling in the space that Harold left. Even though neither one of them realized it; Ezra had become a better husband than Harold had been. It wasn't that he even knew he had. It was a case of simple circumstance and, of course, necessity. Had they slept together the circle would have been complete, but they didn't—not that she hadn't thought about it. But her nights were filled with people who, after three drinks, would progressively get more daring with their propositions and her days were full of sleep. On top of that, the mumbling Toclep women's voices jogged through her head every time she even considered the prospect. The whispers, "Geez Helen. Do you see what's going on with Rae Miller? Playing mommy-love with that little Gern Boy. She's more than twice his age." Even if she had considered it, in a town like Toclep, it would have been slow emotional death. She always wondered what age had to do with love and, more accurately, sex, in the first place. It had absolutely nothing to do with either, she thought.

"Ezrie, I need to get one and two cleaned tomorrow. Got some more people coming in on Thursday."

"All right." He looked up from the garden. He knew that when she said she needed to get some work done, it meant that he needed to get some work done. It didn't bother him though. He liked Rae.

She was forty-one years old and she acted like she was eleven. It seemed like everything was funny to her, like everything was a joke. She had a way of taking a serious issue and ushering it into a vaudeville stage show, laughing and smiling with her sparkling eyes. Along with her disposition, she was striking. People turned their heads when they saw her, saying to under their breath that she should be in Hollywood. She was a blond Audrey Hepburn. Her hair reached to the middle of her back in the straightest yellow lines anyone had ever seen. The women in Toclep talked jealously about her under their breath because she wore short-shorts. If she had been in New York, she would have worn mini-skirts and hot pants. Their words were sometimes harsh, but it was jealously in their eyes, in their yearning. "She's trying to act like a kid," or "I just think it's disgraceful. It's sad." They'd say. What they really knew was that Rae Miller had not lost her early-twenties body or her eleven-year-old spirit. She hadn't sagged down with gravity. She hadn't metamorphosed from a butterfly to a dung beetle.

She was never much of a housewife no matter how much she wanted to be one. She enjoyed staying at the bar until morning, drinking and smoking with the town. She enjoyed sleeping past noon. She enjoyed putting on her wool pants and tucking them into her boots to go hunting, something she had done every season, faithfully. She wasn't like other women her age for those reasons. But there was one more thing about Rae Miller that made her different from other women in Toclep. Rae couldn't have children, and that's what separated her, more than anything else, from other women. She couldn't have babies and, therefore, she had no reason to settle out of childhood. Life was her university. She was a professional student—in for the learning and the beer drinking. When she had married Harold Miller, she did settle down somewhat, acted more like an adult but she didn't like it very much. She only liked it when she could choose when she had to do it. But when Harold died, the straps, if there had ever been any that bound her, were broken. The styles had changed throughout the years but Rae hadn't, that's why she kept wearing them. Death in this case brought sorrow and second childhood.

"You know I got to get in and get some wood to fix that table and bunk in cabin five. Those guys who were in there last week completely destroyed the place. I think they were confused as to whether they were sleeping in your cabin or your bar."

"Well boys'll be boys." And that was exactly the kind of outlook Rae had on everything.

"Do you have people coming into five this week?"

"Not booked. But you never know. Maybe you could take my truck into Falls Creek and get what you need. Do one, two and five tomorrow."

"S'posing I could. All day affair, though."

"Well, Barb's on tomorrow night. Long as I can go in and get some paper work done in the afternoon, I can help you in the evening." That was how it was. That was how they spent so much time together. That's how Ezra had eased Rae's loneliness.

A carload of kids zoomed around the corner; Ezra could see the rising dust behind the car. It ground to a sliding stop in front of them, "Hey, Ezrie." There were at least four voices bellowing from the car, cat-calling at Rae because she couldn't see their faces. "Hey, we're going up to Rodos Falls. You wanna come with us?"

"Got work to do, Terry. You know people don't pick figs from thorn bushes. Look at me, I'm neck high in corn."

"Neck high by the fourth of . . . shit that July thing doesn't work, does it? My old man gave me the afternoon to play cuz the milker went down and he had to run into Ironcloud to get the parts. So I picked up these bums. Maybe later, eh. Get you're work done and try to zip up." Terry Sikes had a flattop. His ears stuck out of the side of his head like ping-pong paddles just like his father's did.

"Maybe."

"Maybe I should go with you boys. Sounds like there's a lot of excitement in there." Rae chuckled.

"Whoa, Mrs. Miller. Yeah."

"I'm a little old for that," the convenient use of age when you want it, she thought.

"Okay. Don't know what you're missing though."

"I think it's the other way around, isn't it boys?"

The Maverick tore off and in the flag of wind Rae could hear them yell "Whoa, Mrs. Miller. Eewww, Ezrie and Mrs. Miller. Get it, Ezrie." The car disappeared into the praying trees on Bayside Road.

"That Terry Sikes is one of the nicest boys around. Just like his old man. But the rest of those hooligans, I don't know. Looks like you're about done here, how come you didn't skin off with 'em?"

"Always got work to do."

"Yep. Which reminds me I've got work to do, too." She pushed up with her arms and lifted her lithe body, like a gymnast, into the air. She held there for a second and Ezra watched the muscles in her arms control and balance her weight. Then she swung her legs back around. She was on the outside of the fence sunk up to her knees in the green water of grass. She leaned against the fence pensively for a moment. "You know, everybody in a small town is beautiful." Ezra wasn't quite sure why she was saying this but he grunted as if he guessed he knew that. "I mean it. You're all done with school now but think back to your spring classes. Look around the room at the girls in you class." He didn't close his eyes but he was sketching and shading and putting the lines together in his mind. "Look around the room. Do you see 'em? Not just the girls but the boys, too. Do you see 'em?"

Tom could hear Rae and he, too, was painting the faces behind his eyes. He could see them. He looked around the room. Vera Berge with her chubby arms and pointed nose, Tim Wiles with his thick square head, Kathy Lampardson, he thought—well what can one say about Kathy—whew. Then, chinless Brenda Muran, pimpled Scott Whalmers, freckled Jeff Asher; he looked at them all and in every aspect that was bad there was three that were good. Thirteen that shined outward, three hundred that said, "Can you see me? Can you really see me?" Rae was right. Everyone is beautiful. Tom had never realized it before because he had never bothered to look, but now that he was looking.

Ezra stood up. The knees of his jeans were dirty from today's work and yesterday's work, and the work from all the days that led up to yesterday. He wasn't wearing a shirt and his upper body was the color of baked bread. "I never really thought about that before. You're right."

"Well you ought to think about it. If you could see inside those people you'd see the same thing. That's what small towns are. They're what's left of Paradise."

Ezra imagined all the small towns in the world. That's all there is in some places, small towns. In fact, that's all there is in the Upper Peninsula—small towns. "The whole damn world is small towns," he said.

"That's right." Rae responded in a matter-of-fact-it-is tone that said that's what I'm trying to tell you. "Isn't that picture. Everybody in the whole wide world is beautiful. If we could just convince Ho Chi Minh and Richard Nixon," she sighed. This was a rather serious twist for Rae. "If we could just convince them that the whole world, the whole darn thing was just a bunch of small towns, just a bunch of beautiful people all clumped together. Look around you guys. Yep, easy as pie, isn't it." She pushed off the fence like it was the wall of a swimming pool and turned to cross the road. She didn't complete her thought. But the seed was growing in the minds of Ezra and Tom. "Stop by the bar later, if you want."

"I'll try ta run into Falls Creek, get that lumber if I have time later."

"If ya want. Swing over and get the truck. You know where the keys are."

He watched her cross the road and walk into the shadows of her driveway. She didn't gingerly limp when she hit the gravel in her bare feet. It was as if she was walking on sand. He hadn't noticed that she was wearing a halter-top, but he did, now. He focused his eyes on the skin that tucked itself into her shorts. She's right, there are a lot of beautiful people in the world and she's one of them. When her door slammed he went back to his knees, back to the dirt, back to the weeds. He heard the slap of her door again and looked up over the grass through the gray fence planks. He could see her sitting on the one square of concrete at her side door. She was sitting and smoking a cigarette. He could see the white stick in the distance. She didn't have her mail anymore, just the cigarette and she sat there and blew smoke into the sky and looked down the road to where Bayside turned into Clarion, which turned into town. Ezra wondered if that was the work she needed to do.

Across the street, Rae sat chilled by the cold cement against her legs. The hushing, trees blocked the sound of waves and sent a shiver through her bones. "Well Harold, here I am. Quite a sight. Forty-one years old and no one to kiss." She knew that as long as she stayed in Toclep she would never marry again. Maybe there would be an affair or two. Maybe not. However, affairs didn't take loneliness away. They only entrenched it deeper into the soul—made it harder to shuck. She knew that she wouldn't leave Toclep. It was her father's legacy. She had inherited Toclep from him and then, again, from Harold.

Besides, where could she go? Where could she go where she could hear the fresh water lips kiss the stone shores, where winter brought deep snows even in April, where fall gave fire that didn't burn, and where spring brought tumbling water and bayberry and lady's slipper. There were trades to be made and things to be sacrificed. It was true that paths diverged in yellow wood, but there were more than two and all of them were untrodden. She would stay in Toclep. She would wait but not wait for anything in particular. She'd just wait and there was nothing wrong with that.

It was nothing, Roadside Girl thought. It was fresh air and big sky and that was all. That didn't make any sense, though. It was always big sky and fresh air on Superior, but if that was all it was, how come she felt like spring? She felt like lilacs were growing in her soul and, at the same time, she felt like she was waiting for an algebra exam for which she hadn't studied. This is crazy; he's almost twice my age. However, it was not an old man who had held her in his arms in the dark North, fighting off the clear cold that fell out of the sky. She saw his face in the muted light of Rae Miller's. It was that of a twenty-year-old. She was twenty, and last night he looked twenty; what's the difference? Time. It's a blink, a quick nap, nothing. They were the same age. She knew they were.

Questions. All these questions. Did he hold her in his arms or did she simply dream that? Was it anything more than simply wanting to stay on the lighted water of a calm night? Did he hug her or was it simply an old man keeping a child warm? He's not old. I'm not a child. That's how the coursing argument continued in the lilacs of Roadside Girl.

* * *

Over a clump of trees and a quiet brown field, past a square, white farmhouse in an old, red, hand-hewn barn Tom was brushing a gray horse and there was more spring. He wasn't quite sure why, in fact. He didn't even realize that today, he was happy. Not happy like he was everyday, not content this-is-the-way-of-my-life happy, he was child-at-Christmas happy. Little waves of stored energy jolted through his body and though he really didn't know how, he was whistling. The horses even sensed his overflowing and were adjusting to the brush, which seemed like part of Tom's happy hand.

There was something missing in Tom's day this morning, and he couldn't quite put his finger on his lack of loneliness. His body and subconscious knew more than his conscious. Often times, his psyches would keep such secrets from Tom's conscious because his conscious was kind of daft and didn't adapt well to everything on the inside. It was a little game of which Tom was privy only to the side effects. As Tom walked out of the barn singing, "I am a child, hmm mm mm mm, you can't conceive of all the pleasure in my smile." The horses laughed. He couldn't remember when he had heard that song last, probably in the nook. That's where he had heard all the music he knew. "I haven't listened to music in a long time," he said to himself. The fact of the matter was that Ezra had taken all the music away with him like he was the pied piper. Even that didn't change Tom's mood. "I wonder if I could still play that one?" The horses behind him seemed to nod.

* * *

Roadside Girl couldn't keep her mind in one place. She put her book down on her bed. She had just read the same four lines over and over fifteen times. "Outside," she said. "I love September. It's a great month, cool nights, clear days." She stood on the small decking in front of the sauna, stretching. She wanted to walk down to Tom's and talk to him and watch him work and lend a hand. She wanted to lean against his sweat-damp t-shirt while helping him pull a fence post or move something in the barn. She wanted to go by the road rather than by the path, as to see him from a quarter mile away, where the trees broke onto his field, sitting by himself on the front porch having coffee. She wanted him to look up and smile all the way through his body because he could see her coming down the road and he knew she was coming to see him. She wanted to pour herself a cup of coffee when she got there and sit right next to him feeling like the caramel-colored coffee—warm and strong. She wanted him to put his large callused hand on hers and be soothed by its roughness.

But what if it had been nothing, she thought? It could have been nothing. Deep inside the truth was hiding, teasing her with punishing insecurity. She had dated in high school but after a couple of watch-how-many-beers-I-can-drink-before-I-throw-up dates and more than a couple of let-me-feel-your-breasts dates, she decided that she could wait. Maybe she had stronger feelings and intuition than her dates and, therefore, always felt awkward. Who didn't feel awkward? Almost every high schooler in America lived with the insecurity of thinking that she was different than everyone else. There were a few lucky ones who didn't live with that insecurity, but Roadside Girl hadn't been one of them. In fact, she still told herself that she wasn't like other people. Albeit, that's not right, is it? Because people are similar. People do have the same experiences and feelings. They just don't want to admit that someone else could feel what they feel. That would be too dangerous. That would allow everyone to know that everyone else was vulnerable.

Roadside Girl did carry the name of something odd. It put people in awkward stand-offs as they tried to get out of saying it or tried to shorten it. "Hey Road" or "Girl" but neither was her name. Nevertheless, in terms of emotion, her name was the only thing that was different. She had graduated with a small class. There were only forty students and out of that forty there were about three who enjoyed reading and three more who forced themselves to read. Lydia never turned on the TV and Roadside Girl grew up reading. She had digested approximately one book a week since she was ten. Fifty books a year times ten or so years. This statistic didn't leave her much to discuss with her classmates, most of whom had read two books, one being *To Kill a Mockingbird*, required in ninth grade—the other, *A Separate Peace*, required in tenth grade. She was lucky that she had a horse and a little farm knowledge, otherwise, because she didn't like sports and she didn't go hunting—she would have had absolutely nothing to say to her classmates. No common ground. Most of the people in her class would've bet money that Roadside Girl was bound for college. She had stayed, though. It did not surprise her that her classmates had miscalculated.

So why should it seem odd that she had these feelings for Tom, she wondered. Tom was like her in some ways. Tom read. They sometimes sat in his kitchen flowing over identical books, both trying to learn something. He would talk about the rush of life with her. He didn't try to act her age, and he didn't scurrying around like a rodent trying to prove he was or wasn't this or that. He understood how she felt about her classmates who had run off to college so they could drink beer and lie to each other about how great they were. They would fool themselves into thinking they were better than the other rodents who stayed and scurried themselves into that hole over in Crescent City into which some Oz-like figure behind a corporate curtain was pouring acid. Roadside Girl didn't feel better than the other rodents, she simply felt different. It was country mouse and city mouse to her; except, the feeling had little to do with location. It had to do with how mechanical life, as she saw it, became to the people around her. She wasn't positive that Tom wasn't like the others but to her he didn't seem to be. That's the way infatuation was though. The truth isn't always clear. Rather, it is like a morning mist on an autumn lake. Feelings sometimes mask the truth. Maybe she didn't love Tom and maybe she did, but one thing was sure, she had strong feelings for him.

She wasn't ignorant enough to walk down the road hoping for Sir Galahad to be drinking coffee on the front porch. Therefore, she skipped, actually skipped, down the path between Lydia's and Tom's. She increased her gate when she got to Owl Creek and jumped from one bank to the other, getting one boot wet. She was surprised at how easy the leap had been. As she approached Ezra's she slowed down. She hadn't thought about what she told Tom until she saw the ginger-bread house with the deer skin dome standing like a two stone, family burial plot. She walked so slowly that she was nearly walking backwards. The daytime windows were reflective and black. The cabin crouched silently, lonely on the edge of the trees. It sat patiently like a spider waiting, ready to pounce on something. There had been many ghost stories about this little cabin, and when she looked at the windows she couldn't help but see the eyes of a spider. She couldn't see in the windows from where she was and maybe that's what sent the almost unnoticeable fringe of electricity through her bones. She moved up to the cabin like a deer and placed her periscope hands on the black window. Nothing. No more haunted than it had been last year or the year before that. No signs of chain-dragging specters that go bump in the night. "Just a house," she said to herself, "no different than any other house." No one died here. All the same, it sure is perfectly lonely. It sure is a step out of time. As she slowly moved away from the house she thought she saw something. She wasn't quite sure but something about the upstairs window made her uneasy. Nothing had moved. She had stopped skipping. She had forgotten why she was going over to Tom's until she stopped looking behind her at the dark old cabin and focused her eyes on the house—the square, white farmhouse that belonged somewhere in the middle of Indiana more than it belonged here.

    No one answered when she knocked on the door. She pushed it open and called, "Tom? Thomas?" The house remembered the calls and was sure that Roadside Girl was Marguerite. "It's Marguerite," the walls whispered. The kitchen anticipated her entry and the aroma of fresh baked cookies. Tom didn't answer and Roadside Girl, who wasn't Marguerite, closed the door and left the poor interior walls weeping as the screen door smacked shut. She stepped around the back of the house and scanned the entire field to see gray plank and dry grass. When she got to the barn, she noticed that the door was unbolted. "Tom?"

"Huh? Down here."

She saw a light shining out from under the tractor and heard Tom humming. It was the first time she had ever heard him hum. "Whatcha doin'?"

"I'm putting a new field catcher on. You want to hand me the skyhook out of the toolbox?"

She walked over not wanting to tell him that she didn't know what a skyhook looked like and dug around banging the open-end wrenches against each other. "Where is it?" She was searching for a hint that would point her to it.

He sniggered. "No such thing as a skyhook or a field catcher," he said. "I'm working on the PTO. It doesn't seem to be working right, but I don't quite know what's wrong with it."

"Yeah, right the PTO." She laughed back at him. "That sounds more like a 70's band than a tractor part. You can't get me twice with that."

"Serious this time." He scooted himself about halfway out from underneath the tractor. "See this here." He patted the chipped and dirty arm that jutted from the tractor. "This is the PTO. That's Power Take Off. It spins like this;" he made a spinning gesture with his fingers. "It's what powers things like the mower. See over there," he pointed to the mower. "That arm's female this one's male. They attach and poof—instant power."

"Guess I don't know that much about tractors."

"Me neither. And I've been working on them my whole life. I can't figure this damn thing out." He pulled himself from under the old Case with grease black hands that had rocks and tiny pieces of straw stuck to them. He wiped them on the ground and brushed his pants off with the back of his hands. "What's up?"

She wasn't sure why she started where she did, but she did. "Ya know what we were talking 'bout last night," she asked. "About ghosts and such." She was tentative. She seemed unsure of herself. Was this the right way to start this conversation? Wasn't there another reason she had come over? Like to say, I like you do you like me—check the box next to your response? "I walked past Ezra's again today."

"Seems like after you saw a ghost there you'd want to take the road?" He cleaned his hands with turpentine.

"It sounds kinda stupid, but something looked funny. I didn't see anything, just . . . something looked odd about the upstairs window."

"You saw right. I was over there this morning and cracked that upstairs window to let some air in. Gets kind of musty in there," he said. Even though that was one of the things that spooked him about the house. For being closed up all the time, it never smelled musty.

"Sure. Like the sauna. I knew it was nothing. Don't know why I even brought it up."

"Well somebody's got to keep an eye on that place." He knew that somebody was. "Hey, you know what time we got back last night? I didn't see my clock before I passed out on my bed. Man, all that sky."

He had brought it up. Unfortunately, she was a bit disappointed because he didn't say that he had a good time or enjoyed their time together or indicated that he was glad she had stayed there with him. Like she had thought earlier, he only mentioned the sky and how the air had put a spell on him, which made him fall asleep before he could see his clock.

"Not sure. I didn't check before I went to bed, either." He had walked her to the sauna by the way of the road because it was easier to see. They had stood between the sauna and Lydia's in an awkward adolescent-like stupor and then he said I better let you get to sleep. She was fooled and agreed. However, she didn't really want to go to sleep at all, she wanted to talk but that hadn't happened.

"Last night was nice, eh." She urged ever onward.

"Yeah. It was beautiful." That was it. She thought, yes it was beautiful and that was it, eh. "That sky as open and unending as it was . . . sure was . . . ." he searched his mind for the words. "Well it was . . . but it wasn't . . . it wasn't as beautiful as you were . . . or are, I mean." There he said it. He felt as strange as a four-eyed egghead at a logging festival when he did.

But it was out of his mind and into the air. He didn't say it as if saying you sure look nice today. He said it with feeling, and she was glad he had said it. It made everything easier for her. It made everything clearer. It relieved her.

They looked at each other. Energy buzzed between them like a cloud of mosquitoes, vibrating the air around their skin, making them feel like they were both full of gritty sugar. Sugar crystals shifted under their skin and raised soft bumps and gentle hairs all over their bodies. Both felt like they were on a swing-set, passing each other on every swing, climbing higher into the air. They would spin around the top soon. They would defy gravity. They had already defied gravity. And they floated there in the barn.

He broke the magnetic friction, "So do you want to go steady?" He said it as a joke but meant it in a not-so-silly way.

"I'm not sure I'm ready for that commitment," she said and they both laughed.

Now he knew why he had been whistling this morning. Now he knew why he was singing some song that he would never have remembered on any other day.

"I'm glad you had the nerve to ask me to stay last night. I was cold. I was thinking the whole time . . . if he just held me close to him I'd be warm. I'd be warm outside and inside." She seemed surer of herself than he did and she had every right to be. She was young. She had never had someone get in the untied boat and float, slowly, out to sea as she stood on the shore wondering why she wasn't in the boat, too. She had never had to say, what have I done to make it float away. "I don't think this has to change the way we act toward each other." It was kind of a stupid thing to say and she regretted it as soon as it came out of her mouth, because it made the situation seem serious. However, why shouldn't they act differently toward each other? Why shouldn't they be more open with their emotions?

"No." He was Thomas Gern again—man of short answers. Reserved. Inside he felt like he was shaking, like he was looking up to her because she was older and she knew what to do. "But it does." She was glad he said it. They hadn't kissed. They hadn't really held hands. He had just cradled her close to his body and their heat had flown like one river and they were together, floating on the moonbeams that glimmered across miles and miles of open water.

It was still morning and everything about the day made it seem like it was late afternoon. The sun was overhead and the air was crisp. The blue sky took a golden tint. It wasn't warm, yet somehow it seemed warm.

"Do you need to do anything today?" Her words asked one question and pointed in another direction.

"You should know. I never have anything to do. Unlike most folks, time is what I have." They weren't looking at each other. They were looking into the future but there was nothing there for them to see because unlike the past there were no distinct images in the future. There were only heat-like mirages that wavered off the ground in transparent snakes. Even if they could see into the future, how far would they want to look? Do people really want to know what's down the road?

Tom could remember feeling the way he felt at that moment before, but he couldn't remember exactly when. He thought about that time he and Sarah had gone into the park in Falls Creek and had played on the merry-go-round for an hour, believing they were both kids. Roadside Girl had never felt like this and didn't know that this was a way to feel. The frenzied buzz of unknown happiness, the anticipation of a carnival, frayed their edges. They had racing hearts and edgy confidence.

"Wanna go for a walk?"

"Just point the direction." It didn't matter to him. He thought she might want to wander down the beach in a romantic hand holding scenario. He had, until now, forgotten what it meant to walk down the beach with a woman.

They walked through the drying grass to the protective planks that were the force field of Tom's life and climbed over them. They weren't holding hands. They weren't talking. They were both thinking of the same thing with completely different, elaborate scenes and outcomes from different aged minds. They vanished into the trees and became a part of the woods. She was a fern and he was an autumn flower. They both shined their nature into the woods, which magnified and reflected their feelings. On that September day there was a light ushering from the woods like someone had accidentally knocked the sun out of the sky and into the hemlocks. They didn't come out of the woods until the sun had ducked behind the mountains. And when they did they brought sunshine with them.

Tom knocked on the cabin door for the first time in his life. Even when Ezra and his friends were around no one ever knocked. Tom tapped softly. He didn't want the pounding to drift through the trees and whisper to someone in town, "Brenda Cafus is in Toclep. She's out in dead ole hippieville." He waited. When he tried to use the key, the door swung invitingly open. Unlocked. There was the smell of cooked food, and since he had primed the pump, there had been a drop of water hanging from the faucet. The spigot was like a magnet, "don't let me dry up again. I don't like to be dry." He looked around and saw that everything else was the same as it had been before. There were books missing from the shelves. He noticed this easily. He had looked at those bookshelves, which never changed, for twenty years. There were times when he had come in and sat on the arm of the couch and stared at the bookshelves for an hour or more, just sitting there like he was waiting for the books to say something.

The plates, cups, and silverware were sitting on counters screaming, "There's someone living here!" One small, white candle had been burned down to the holder. That was the only wax item which had changed in this museum.

"Brenda? Brenda?" Tom over-cautiously whispered through his cupped hands to the ceiling, but there was no response. He climbed the steep, loft stairs that angled in the corner of the living room at about seventy-degrees. She wasn't there. The open loft had a large window at one end by the bed. It was cracked, not wide open, but cracked and he could feel the cool, morning air sweeping through the loft and running down the stairs. That's what's different he thought. There was air in the cabin. It was breathing. It hadn't breathed in years but now it was breathing. It was no wonder Roadside Girl thought she had seen a ghost. She had—the ghost of the old cabin.

The bed was not made and that sent a glow through Tom's bones. There were three books on the floor next to the bed and one resting on the pillow. On the pillow was a broken-spined copy of *The Little Prince* that looked like a sunning butterfly. He wondered where she would go in the daylight, which seemed to hold danger for her. There were two candles half-melted, one on the floor and the other on the dresser next to an open notebook with a knife-sharpened pencil on it. He flipped the cover back to see that it was a new notebook with a big, shiny badge of a price tag. He read:

I haven't kept a diary since I was a girl. I hate Rich ... For years I've been strapped and bound now I'm unstrapped but still bound. I should kill him for doing this to me. I should sneak in and get his pistol and shove it in his mouth and make him get down on his knees. It makes me sick just to think about it. The slimy fucker made me this way. He stole from me. He always said paybacks were hell. Hell would look good compared to him. Hell would be frosting for him. Who's right—what right does he have to steal from me? Is this my fault? Did I do this to me? No! No! I wouldn't have done such things to myself. No one would. But I wasn't me. I was someone else. I was a puppet, a toy. God forgive me. I let these things happen. It can't be. I can't be to blame. It's not right! I'm going to kill him. But a bullet's too good for him! Death is too good for him. Misery. Misery is what he needs. I've been haunted but the haunting has just begun. He'll wake up swinging at spiders when I get done. He'll talk to dead people because he's dead and those are the only people he can talk to ...

Tom stopped reading and flipped through a couple of pages:

What am I doing here? What do I think I'll accomplish? I hate this. I hate the loneliness. Do you think this will make things better . . .

Tom put the notebook down. He was unsure about whether he put it back the same way he found it.

Two large towels lay on the floor by the window. Good, he thought. She's covering the windows. Downstairs he noticed that Ezra's green, military-issue jacket was not on the hook. I need to find out what's going on he thought. He had not asked any questions and he hadn't said a peep to anyone, to whom would he say a peep? He had dropped off food, mostly things he himself, had canned or made. He found it odd that the desperate voice that had called him was now out of the house. He closed the door. The only sign of life was a smell trapped inside the house. It's in there, he thought as he walked away.

* * *

Brenda was wearing an oversized pair of brown overalls and a rather thin flannel shirt. She had made a new hole in one of Ezra's old belts, which was holding up the overalls. Over everything was the faded-green jacket that said GERN on the breast. This morning she had walked into the woods thinking that if she didn't get out of that cabin her head was going to split open and a hundred little hers were going to jump out and scurry around the wooden floor. It would be okay, she thought. Not many people around this time of year, especially mid-week; I'll stay off the trails.

She eased through the dewless, morning grass into the trees that were desperately trying to hold their color, and slipped into the world of nature. She had marked her path with pyramids of gray sticks against periodic tree trunks. It's easy to get turned around when you can't see the sun through the trees. It took time, but she had time. I feel better today than I have felt in years, she said to herself. I think I am alive.

She stopped in a grove of hemlocks and sugar maples and sat at the base of a hemlock that swallowed her body. *My Side of the Mountain*, she thought. The image of that boy living in the tree with his friends who chattered and snorted other languages made her smile. The furrowed bark of the tree caressed her back through Ezra's jacket. I'm free. I'm free, her mind whispered. I'm pregnant. I don't think I want the baby but I'm not going to give the baby up because the baby is giving me life. She kept repeating baby and every time she heard the word it was as if some woman from New Jersey had invited herself into Brenda's mind to say baby. She spoke aloud. "I don't love Ted; I just needed something to hold onto that wasn't Rich. And now I'm done. I'm sure Ted's figured out that I'm gone. I wonder if he's called and talked to Rich." She laughed because she could see it.

"Hello. Rich?"

"Uh Huh."

"Yeah, Rich this is Ted Russell over at the high school."

"Uh Huh."

"Hey, I was wondering if you'd seen your wife?"

"What? What do you mean? Of course, I've seen her. See her everyday."

"Oh, is she there? Can I talk to her?"

"What do you need to talk to her for?"

"Well we've met a couple of times over in your bedroom. And... well Rich, I'm kind of lonely, you know, and if Brenda's around... well, I'd kinda like to stop on by."

"You son of a bitch. I'm gonna kill you. You hear me. I'm gonna kill you. And when I find her I'm gonna kill her." The kill her echoed in Brenda's mind.

"Oh, so she's not there. Well, excuse the ring." *Click.* And then just the buzz on Rich's end and him pounding the phone against the wall, marring up the drywall he was so darn proud of having done himself.

She laughed because for the first time in years she knew that Rich wasn't going to kill her, because he wasn't going to find her. She drifted away from her story as she watched the sun try to cut through the quaking leaves. Every so often a flash of a star would jump through the movement and light on her. This used to be an ocean, she thought. All of this was covered by water, every bit of it. These trees used to be towering seaweed, under water. She felt the water all around her. She wasn't cold because the water was her life and she was the life of the water. She breathed in water and it felt like everything because everything was water. She breathed out bubbles that disappeared as they clung to the bright green sprigs of the giant seaweed. I can see the surface up there, but I can't tell how far away it is. Arms reach? And she held her arm out over her head. Miles? Light years? How deep is the water? How deep is the life?

She didn't imagine; she saw. There were whales. Whales the size of apartment buildings, whales the size of canoes, whales the size of hotdogs all swimming in multi-colored majesty through the seaweed that reached toward the great light beyond the water. She could swim with them, weaving grand baskets through the evergreen that was so bright that it radiated. However, she didn't swim with them; she just sat and watched them and they looked down on her with approval. They were her siblings.

She wasn't sure how long she sat there watching the whales but finally they disappeared and she held them in her memory like an epic film. Sometimes, you need to go into nature and take nothing, she thought. Sometimes, you just need to sit. She had, and she saw her past, but her past was not what she had lived in Toclep. It was what she had been a million years ago. It was beauty.

She looked back to make sure that she knew where her last pyramid was. She could just barely see its gray arms waving to her through spaced legs of giant elephants. The woods were different from within than they were from the path. There was somehow more to see even though you couldn't see as far. The canopy blocked the sun and the ground was covered with blow-downs and small ferns in places. This is an old forest, she thought. She stood and then continued, deeper into the trees, leaving little gray tents of wood to guide her home. When she came upon what she figured was the Greenstone River, she watched the sand colored water move over the carved rock like it wasn't moving at all. "Where do you come from?" She asked. "Where does all the water come from? Always flowing, never stopping. Different water and, in never stopping, it stops." The water looked fake. It looked like one of those cheap paintings that restaurants sometimes have—the kind with a light behind it that rotates and is supposed to look like flowing water. Is there only one water, she wondered? Only one water that is connected to itself everywhere.

* * *

By the time she got back to the cabin it was evening. She was hungry. She would wait for all the light to disappear before she started moving around, before she covered the windows. She would wait until the shadows surrounded the cabin. She would wait because she could wait. Waiting was good. It bred patience.

* * *

Thomas Gern faintly knocked on the cabin door for the second time that day. The interior was dark and Brenda woke from a dreamless sleep in the loft. Tom stuck in his head, "Bren? Brenda?" He whispered. "Brenda, are you here?"

She didn't bother whispering, "I don't think anyone will hear you, Tom. We're about three lumberyards away from the road. Sun's down in Toclep, I'd guess most folks are watching TV."

He grew up instantly from the crouched whispering eleven-year-old to his present slightly crow-footed age. "Oh, I guess you're right." She was looking down on him in the darkness.

Both of their eyes had adjusted and she could see the ghostlike outlines of him.

"I brought you some food."

"Great, I'm starving. Must've fallen asleep." She felt her way along the handrail to the stairs and descended.

"How you doing?" He had a gunnysack with him and began to empty its contents onto the counter that was a half wall between the kitchen and the living room.

"Okay, I think. Not eating very good. I should be more aware of that."

"Probably good for you. No offense, but we could all use to shed a couple of pounds."

"You shed any pounds Tom, and you'll be able to play the scarecrow in the stage version of *The Wizard of Oz*."

"Don't think I'm that thin. It's kind of cold in here, eh.

"Yeah. I've been keeping bundled in clothes and blankets." She watched as he unloaded pint jars and bread and some other unidentified dark shapes. "I'll draw the curtains." After she did, she lit a candle and set it on the floor. It was astonishing how much light the quarter-roll of wax gave. She could see rice, pasta, canned tomatoes, bread, cheese, butter.

He set it down and said, "butter's better for you than margarine. The closer to earth, the better it is." Then he continued unloading rice crispy treats, and, ironically, two jars of homemade pickles. Next to all of that was a duct-taped casserole dish with warm lasagna. "Geez Tom, did you bring me the whole back storeroom?" She immediately dug into the lasagna.

"It's none of my business." He stopped to think. "Except you're holing up on my property in my brother's house."

"I don't think he minds," she said in garbled mouthfuls.

"You want to tell me what's goin' on so I know exactly how I should treat this situation? By the way, if you're trying to stay out of sight, you've already been discovered." The last sentence seemed like it fell out of the sky into his words.

She dropped the fork, "What?"

"Yeah, Roadside Girl saw you. Lucky for you, she thinks you're the ghost of my brother."

"I'll be more careful."

"It's none of my business. We don't really know each other, haven't for years but . . . ."

"You're right, it's none of your business." A blanket of silence fell between them and Thomas felt bad and awkward. "But . . . I need to talk to somebody and, right now Tom, you're the only somebody I have." This didn't comfort him much but at least he would have something more than a handful of angry lines in her journal to help him understand.

"You were right when you called me a runner. Kinda reminds me of *Logan's Run*. Remember that movie?"

He shook his head. "No."

"Rich has no idea where I've gone, just that I have. Tom, I can't tell you the whole story right now. I'm not ready for that. But I will tell you that I made a mistake when I married Rich. I read him wrong. I believed in marriage and I wanted it to work but then I just forgot, ya know . . . I forgot and forgot and forgot and before I knew it I was forty-years old . . . I forgot how things were really s'posed to be."

Tom thought about Sarah. How things are supposed to be. What did that mean?

Is this how Sarah felt while we were married? Like running away? He knew that the answer was yes. Maybe not so emphatically yes, but it was yes all the same. "So . . . "

"Let's see, how do I say this?" She suddenly became stoic. Her posture stiffened and her voice harshened and she spoke with dead words. "Rich rapes me." Her eyes were tiny charcoal dots. "It's been happening off and on for years. It's gone too far. I've had my limit. It's over now. He's never going to touch me again. I needed to get away. But this is my town, Tom. It's my town." Strained emotion stood behind her rigidity.

Tom dropped his head. He wanted to believe that things like that didn't happen in Toclep but he knew so much better than that. It was his town, too. Though he wasn't very connected to it, he loved it, too. He looked at it everyday and knew that he couldn't run away from it. "Sorry."

"No sorries needed, Tom. I can't run away from this. I've got to solve it. I've got to sort it out, come to terms." She hated the sound of that, like it was some sort of twelve-step plan from Alcoholics Anonymous. "I can't let that fucker win. I can't let him steal my life. But I don't know what to do right now. I need time. Time to think. Time to sit. I might want to talk, but right now I don't. I gotta think it out. I gotta fix it. It's mine."

He noticed a distant familiarity in her, the cut of her face. The dark shadows gave certain definition that he might not see in the light. Tom had not seen much of Brenda over the years. He hadn't seen much of anyone except from the other end of a wave from a car. But Brenda's face had an oddly familiar shape. It was a photograph from his past. "I can't say much."

"I know. There's a lot to say but the words, they disappear like clouds."

"What do you need? What can I do?"

"I don't think Rich will ever look for me in town, especially if there are no whispers. I gave him a trail and that trail headed east. Besides, Rich doesn't like this place. Thinks all the Gern property is haunted and always has been. Gives him the jitters."

"He's living on Gern property."

"Yeah," she wasn't quite sure what he meant but agreed with him so she could continue. "I don't mean to offend you. But he thinks you're a crazy, living over here all by yourself in your low profile, field wanderings. Really thinks you're a homo. Thinks Sarah left you cuz you were and that you never took a second wife cuz, as he put it, you were over here Homo-ing down."

He didn't care about what Rich Cafus thought of him; what bothered him was the thought of Sarah leaving him. "Who was I supposed to marry?" He asked but not to her.

"Doesn't matter. Doesn't matter much to me whether you're gay or not. He doesn't talk about you much, but when he does it's the same old thing, no wonder his wife left, mother fucker's a fag." She could see Rich squinching his face and rolling his eyes in loony imitation of insanity. "I think he's afraid of you. I think he thinks you're your brother. I think he thinks you're a ghost."

"Sometimes I am a ghost." He mumbled unemotionally and thought about the truth behind what Brenda was saying. Probably most of the people in town felt that way. "So that's why you called me. I'm the ghost your husband's afraid of?"

"He's not my husband. I'm not sure he ever was," she wanted to make that crystal. "I called you because I thought you'd help. And I know you don't talk." She was right. Her senses had clung to a weak vine since her high school days but she had remembered him as the boy who everyone trusted—the boy who went out of his way, not the man who locked himself behind a fence of history. They were quiet for a moment as the candle illuminated the legs of their pants in spits of flame.

"Okay. So, what can the ghost do?"

"You're not a ghost, Tom." Her voice had changed again and had a friendly warmth like they had been friends, forever. "I . . . I didn't tell you one thing. I'm pregnant. Not very far, but pregnant's pregnant. It's not Rich's child, thank God. It's mine. I need food. I need vitamins. I don't need people asking you questions about why you're buying so much or buying things you don't usually buy."

"I've got a pantry full of food, Brenda. No problem, two can eat just like one. I'll bring you food everyday. I don't know what I've been doing."

"I don't know what I've been doing, Tom."

"The garden's dead from frost but the cellar is full, and you can get what you want from there. I don't have a mercury light if you were looking to do a little cellar shopping at night. What about this place? Does it give you the willies?" She hadn't thought about it. She had been in the darkness of the house going about her sorting for days and hadn't noticed any willies running around.

The cabin had hugged her and soothed her. "People might have forgotten this place. I doubt it. Probably stuck in the sticky webs back behind their fleshy cranial matter. It's haunted, you know."

"It's haunted all right. Roadside Girl was right. It's haunted with me." She was warm even though the air was cool. The house had welcomed her and she felt clearer, more able to breathe and think. She had been here before and it was comfortable in those days and now she was here again. It was the same. She knew haunted because she had lived in a haunted house for years on Pine Street and now she felt like she was in the sanctuary of a church. She felt protected. She had fooled the ghosts, too. They hadn't followed her with any more success than Rich had. "I'm fine here. I like it. It's quiet."

"I don't know how long you think this will take. I don't really see how this will work out but it's gonna be getting cold soon. The nights have already changed; you can see it in the leaves. You start using the heater and you'll run through gas like crazy, you start having smoke drift out that chimney and you will have a proverbial fire. Electricity's feeding from my line, a fridge don't eat much but . . . Hell, I don't know what I'm trying to say. Anyhow, you can't hide here forever. It won't work."

Brenda was almost perturbed but realized that he was only seeing the situation in realistic terms. "I'm not planning on hiding. I just have to know how I'm going to handle this or what I'm going to do. I've got one thing figured out but have to work out the details."

"You're not thinking about doing something . . . " he didn't say stupid. But the word hung like a lynched man in his mind. "You're not thinking about . . . " he swallowed because now he felt stupid. "Murder."

"Good idea. I hadn't thought of that." She smiled at him and her stoicism had run to the turned corners on her mouth. He recognized her from high school. He saw blinding familiarity. "Divorce. I'd like to surprise him with a nice letter from the county.

But seeing he's the county government, I'm not exactly sure how to do it."

"Letters can be a helluva surprise," he said as he pictured the bluish envelope leaning against the empty, milk glass yelling, "Surprise! Surprise!" And saw the surprise in the blank eyes of his mother.

When he left, the night was black. The sky had clouded and had trapped the light on the other side of darkness, and the coolness in the air calmed the bugs to silence. He walked along the fence, listening to his silk steps, knowing it was there, and knowing that it was the fence that protected him and now her.

Brenda stored the food away and put the butter, cheese, and lasagna in the refrigerator of which she had unscrewed the light bulb. She couldn't see very well and she didn't know it but the fridge looked almost the same as Tom's did. Empty. She opened the curtains and climbed the stairs in the smoking blackness of the candle on the floor of the kitchen. She had time. She would read. She would write. She would fall asleep and the ghosts over on Pine Street would drift through the one and a half story house trying to find her, but they wouldn't. Not tonight.

On a Friday as September merged into October, Rich Cafus dragged into Rae Miller's late in the afternoon. Everybody at the bar looked gray faced and dead like they had never seen the sun: Morlocks of Miller's. They looked at Rich as he entered, as if he was dinner, then they turned their gray faces back to short glasses of beer and long conversations which they had had with each other numerous times before. Rich sat away from everyone and didn't bother to say hello to the people connected to the bar, all of which he knew. When Rae walked down to him, she saw a red-eyed strain that made Rich look like he had a cold. It was the head holding, I've-got-a-fever-and-don't-feel-so-well look of desperation that says somebody bring me some soup, I can't move. It was that look which made Rae ask, "Rich, are feeling okay?"

The truth was that he wasn't feeling okay. He had a sick worry that felt like tapeworm gnawing away at his insides. Chewing its way out of his intestines and starting to munch away on his heart and lungs. He wasn't sure what worried him and at the same time he did. She's out there somewhere, he thought. Maybe she's just gone to Canada to wait for a pardon and won't return when she gets it. Something was eating him. A big-old scandalous, ruin-your-career type lawsuit that would drag him through the news and have uppity feminists and sexual abuse mongers dropping their larva like flies on road kill—and the tapeworm kept chewing. But that wasn't all that ate at Rich. Around the last slice of cheese, which he had eaten for breakfast, scrawled in blue ink on the wax paper were the words: I know something that you don't want anyone to know. He had read it, threw it to the floor, kicked the wobbly chair, and swore.

"Yeah, I'm okay," his voice didn't sound okay. It didn't sound like cocky Rich Cafus, either. It sounded like it was hiding behind a schoolteacher so it wouldn't get beat up when he went out for recess. "I'll take some coffee and a cheeseburger basket."

"Eatin' out again, I see." It struck him that she had seen. They all had seen and in their little bedroom voices, behind the heavy veil of night, they were whispering questions and making accusations and pointing fingers and saying desertion and cringing murder and seeing Poe-like scenes of a blanketed corpse carried and cinder-blocked into a corner of Rich's cistern. She set a whiskey down in front of him, "You're eyes are tellin' me that ya don't need anymore coffee." He didn't argue. He looked down the bar, and the small group of locals seemed to be whispering. They seemed to be pointing with their eyes. They seemed to be saying, that's him, that's the guy. So, Rich looked down into his shot of whiskey like it was going to tell him a story, like it was going to tell him the story of his life and he was going to listen and he was going to say, yep, god damn, you're right I am the sheriff of this county and a damn good one at that. I got nothing to hide. Although, he knew that wasn't true. He did have something to hide. He just didn't know how much he had to hide. "Brenda still not feeling good? Maybe ya got the same thing she has. The two of ya should go over and see Lydia. She's mighty good at fixin' things." Rae remembered how Lydia had come from nowhere to fix her broken ego that was having an argument with the mirror.

"Maybe you're right." Lydia knew. He could see Brenda sitting in the cordovan leather chair in the office across the street telling the witch lady all about the little misgivings of her relationship. Then a large, black-beaked crow flew into his mind and he visibly jerked on the barstool. His neighbors down the bar turned their heads and looked at him for a full two seconds, then slowly went back to their whispers.

"Ya all right?" Rae put her hand on his and realized that her hand was warm. It was wrinkled but it was warm. There was still blood moving into the cracks of her veins and that little warmth made her bright inside. She glanced over her shoulder at the mirror. All she saw was her own reflection.

"Yeah, fine. Just a chill." Lydia knew something, he thought. Probably knew where Brenda was. They were probably plotting and planning a feminist lynching. He remembered what Mrs. Berge had told him about having seen Brenda go into the doctor's office. How long ago had that been? Mrs. Berge had been at Coppers and watched Brenda look around before entering Lydia's. "It was as if she was looking for something." She had said. At the time he shrugged his shoulders and said, "Probably some woman thing," and Mrs. Berge shyly agreed, "we got places you can't see," and she giggled. That was a pretty accurate picture to him now. Places you can't see. Deep dark pockets all right, but not down there. The egg white of his eyes bulged a bit as he swallowed the burger with a throat-wrenching hiccup. "Think you're right, Rae. Think I'll stop by Lydia's and see if she can make me feel better." Tomorrow, he thought. Tomorrow I'll find out what the hell's going on. Tomorrow I'll put an end to this bullshit. He looked down the bar at the patrons who weren't looking his direction, whose voices sounded like barnyard animals.

When he walked out the door he could feel rain in the air. It wasn't raining yet, but he could smell the yellow, dusty smell that comes before rain. He didn't walk home. He strolled down Clarion toward the Raspberry River, smelling the rain. He stood on the bridge for a moment then walked across and down to the mouth. He could see the sheets of rain in the distance, water falling to water, and he looked up the coast to see the rain was falling on land, too: the dust of ten thousand years that had been stirred again and again from postglacial rains. There was a sliver of sun that reflected off the drops and made them easy to see even though they were ten miles away. The rains a-comin'. The rains a-comin', he thought.

"I sure wish I was a fisherman," he said as he threw a rock out into the water—just a fisherman with a fisherman's wife who missed him and loved him and wanted to see him when he came home. He threw another stone. What the hell happened? What hell is going on? I feel like killing her, but at the same time I feel like holding her, but that hasn't happened in a while. Something is mighty wrong. I'm not sure I can fix it but it will get fixed. And though he thought it and believed it, he didn't know what was wrong. He only knew that his wife had mistreated him and was forcing him to take action. He could hear the rain approaching. It thundered onto the glass-like water, breaking and splintering as it ran across the undisturbed surface to the shore. He stood there until the rain, the cold, almost October rain, pounded the darkness through his jacket and into his skin. "Tomorrow," he said as the rain knocked his words toward the ground. "Tomorrow I'll find out, and tomorrow I'll start fixing."

* * *

When he walked into his house he was greeted with the smell of unwashed dishes and spoiling refrigerator scraps. They weren't table scraps because he had been eating as he stood in front of the 'fridge and had never really sat down. "This isn't the way it's supposed to be," he said. From outside the kitchen window, a movie showed a man, wet like a dog left out in the rain, strip down to his white briefs, which clung indiscriminately to his body. All the neighbors could have gotten a good picture of Rich Cafus that evening, but only one did.

"That man ought to put some clothes on." Mr. Berge said even though he, himself, often stood in his underwear and, sometimes naked, in front of his picture-glass front and side windows. He remarked to himself that he liked it better when Mrs. Cafus would come into the morning kitchen in only her underwear and bra. He would look at her legs and say to himself, mmmm, as she reached above her head into the cupboards, stretching her body, making the muscles in her legs and under her panties tighten into smooth tight balls.

"Come away from that window, Harold. Whole world'll know you're staring at 'em." He backed into the darkness continuing to watch Rich talk to himself in the light of the kitchen. He wondered, where's Brenda's been? Haven't seen her in a while. I miss my peeks.

Rich Cafus left his wet clothes on the kitchen floor and went upstairs. "This isn't going to eat at me. I'm not gonna hang out here with your eyes glaring at me all night." He was talking to the wedding photograph that hung on the wall. Brenda's hair was long and hung straight down her neck, mid-way between elbow and shoulder. She looked like a teenager and her marriage eyes now, somehow, looked sad and disapproving. Still talking to the photo he said, "I don't need you. You need me. You'll see. You need me." He wasn't going to sulk or be angry. He was going to forget about Brenda and drop himself into another world, a world he could get to from there—a world that reminded him of him and not of her.

He closed the door of the truck and snuck, incognito, out of the county with his low beams flashing off the black mirror of pavement. When he got to Buck Up, a bar he sometimes visited after shifts, changing out of his uniform and into his smooth talk, he pulled the truck into the gravel alongside four or five others and went inside.

* * *

Rich was a liar and Buck Up was just another fish on the line. When he walked into the bar the regulars accepted him as somebody who stops by every so often and tries to pull one of the lonely wives of an out-of-town husband out the door under the pretext of a safe and sober lift home. Though the truth of the matter was that he was rarely sober and safe was relative to his cause. The regulars, who thought it was none of their business whether John's wife slept with another man, and who saw the entire game as a possible opportunity that they, too, would get to sleep with John's wife, didn't seem to be bothered that Rich extracted women from the bar. However, in the back of their minds they wondered whether their own wives snuck down for a beer or three when they were out of town and got a safe and sober ride home from a stranger. They pushed the thought to the back of their heads by repeating to themselves that they never went out of town. Then they would hmmph and think, except for that week at deer camp. So, Rich entered with semi-recognition and squeezed between the regulars into the night.

There were only three women in Buck Up and it appeared that they were all with men but that didn't matter to Rich. If nothing else, he would sit here and get drunk and go home with no memory and no sight and fall into a hazy bed that would take him into drunken dreamlessness until morning. He had been drinking much more than usual to help fight off the horrors of the night. Morning would be Saturday and being on-call in Greenstone County meant sleeping 'til noon. He wondered if Lydia would be in on Saturday and thought briefly about an afternoon meeting until a small argument in the back of the bar by the pool table stole him away into the night.

He had been wrong. There were five women in the bar, and two of them had been hiding behind the pool table wall and now were arguing with a large bearded man in very dirty jeans. Maybe it would be more than a drunken night after all, Rich thought. He turned back to the bar and gulped his beer in large open throated swallows. He would wait out the argument. He wasn't a hero. He wasn't an argument stopper. He was a waiter. He could wait out almost anything, waylaying and stalling and letting time slide and memories ease into unassured questions of what was real and what was not. After two more games Mr. Dirty Jeans walked out of the bar like he had just been spanked. The two girls continued to play pool as the regulars shot wanton glances past their wives and their wives whispered soft words, "whores" and "sluts" beneath the rims of their beer glasses, even though the girls were neither. They were just drunk and too loud and probably out past their bed times.

"Those Wash Bremmer's girls?" Rich heard a sandpaper smoker's voice through the indistinguishable din of the bar as the man looked over his shoulder watching the short, blue haired girl bend and reach over the pool table.

"Naaa, what are you blind?" Said the other. "Christ, they don't look anything like the Bremmer girls. "Bob says they're staying down at the Twin Lakes. Been there a couple of days I guess."

"Wish I was staying there with 'em." The smoker's voice said. He was still watching the pair maneuver around the green felt-covered table.

"Don't think Aggie would like that any."

'S'posin' not. But what Aggie don't know won't hurt her." They both laughed and went back to talking about bow season. But the smoker had been wrong. What Aggie didn't know would hurt her. It would tear her heart into strips and feed it to swooping, criminal seagulls.

At a stumbling quarter after two, bar time, only the smoker—Aggie was probably wondering when he'd be home or if he had hit a deer in his swerving, blurry drive home; the bartender, washing glasses; a face-down head that was suffocating in it's own hair; the bartender's daughter, picking up glasses; and the two girls were left in the door-closing bar. Rich was there, too, but he hadn't counted himself.

The girls walked out of the bar and did something a local would never think to do. They walked out to the road and headed back to their motel. They hadn't driven. They were smart enough to know that it wasn't worth the hefty fine or the pine box to drive the drunken half-mile back to Twin Lakes. You were at the bar, you drank too much, you had to get home, so you drove was the standard operating procedure of drinking and driving in the area. Besides, there wasn't anybody on these roads at night.

When Rich stopped next to the girls and offered them a ride, they said no. After looking at each other in come-on-we're-together eyes, they drunkenly decided that nothing could happen in one-half mile. At the same time, they drunkenly forgot why they hadn't driven to the bar in the first place. So they slid across the bench seat into the truck and Rich watched the taller one's skirt shimmy up her legs as she slid onto the cloth seat. She had to adjust herself and arch her back to grip the skirt under her legs. As she did that, Rich watched, imagining her writhing in sexual pleasure and stretching over him, arching her head to the ceiling. "Kinda cold for a dress." He said, looking at her legs.

"Skirt," she said. "Not in there it's not."

"Or in here," he said and chuckled a little. The two girls looked at each other.

When he pulled into the Twin Lakes Hotel, he left the truck running.

"Thanks, Mister."

"It's Mark." He said.

"Then thanks, Mark," the tall one said.

"Hey, you wanna come in for a beer?" The other asked.

"Come on Suse. We've had enough. I'm tired."

"One for the road," Rich said.

"Don't be a prude, Lynde. You only live once." The taller girl headed for the room and unlocked the door.

"Okay. One beer." Before she could get out the entire affirmation, Rich had already turned off the truck.

The taller one kept adjusting her skirt. She felt uncomfortable and it showed in her constant adjustments. The shorter one with the Mary Tyler Moore haircut was flirting with Rich as he thought about sex with two young girls. Rich stood up. "What do you two gals think of a little game of two on one? Odds are in your favor."

"Is that your pick-up line, old man?" The taller one said. "That's pathetic."

"I think it's cute."

"I think you better leave."

"She's game for a little adventure." Rich said.

"Well you're a bit old for my liking." It was the second time she had said the "O" word, and Rich didn't like it when he heard it the first time. "Look, you gave us a ride. That was cool. We gave you a beer. Even Stephen." She was trying to be diplomatic. "You made your pass and we're not catching."

"Well, Suse is catching. Maybe you should go take a bath for a while." Rich said. With that he backed Suse onto the bed. "You're up to play, huh?" He reached out and put his hand on her breast and pushed her over backwards.

"What are you doing? Get off me!"

"Come on baby. You're the one who said it was cute." He pushed against her harder and tried to kiss her and though she didn't know why she did it, she screamed. "What're you doing? Don't do that."

"Quiet. You sound like my wife." He tried to put his hand over her mouth, which only made her scream louder. The taller girl opened the door and screamed down the empty porch. "Jesus Christ!" Rich stood up and made a move for the door but his beer-filled legs didn't allow him to move as quickly as he would've liked to. As he got into his truck he saw Ernie Marquort coming out of the office door with a shotgun in his hands. "Ah Fuck," Rich moaned but Ernie didn't lift the gun. The truck pulled away, throwing giant handfuls of gravel out behind it that screamed, look at me go. I'm a big man.

"You ladies okay?" He called to the open door.

The taller one stuck her head out the door, "I think so. Thanks. Just a drunk and a bad move on our part."

"You want me to call the police?"

"Probably won't do any good."

"Well, it ain't the first time something like this has happened," he mumbled as he turned back into his apartment. Both doors closed at the same time and locked the night out behind them.

On highway 52, Rich had to pull off the road and pee. "Teases." He emptied his bladder. It was late when he pulled into his driveway. He had forgotten to turn the kitchen light off and the front window was a beacon of emptiness. "Tomorrow," he said in anger. He remembered what time it was. "No, today." Things weren't going his way. However, later today he would get this straight. He would fix this like it was a flat tire. In the fog of alcohol he wiped his hands and said, "That's that. All cleaned up."

Two black crows hung upside down in the air. They were two upside-down plus signs longer on top than on the bottom. They floated. They weren't dead. Their large, black beaks moved—cawing loudly, but the caws were really voices and the voices told Brenda they were coming and she was confused because they were already there. Then the two black crows turned into people. She recognized them but didn't know who they were. Only one cawed and his caw was soothing and gentle. He said, "Everything is okay." His voice sounded like he knew something she didn't know. Brenda reached out to touch the bird but the bird shattered like a piñata and little moths of light flew out at her as someone grabbed her wrist. She saw a uniformed arm and looked into the face that went with the arm, but there was no face. The uniform's arms appeared to be large sticks. They weren't arms at all; rather, they were ax handles. The handles came down with unearthly strength and splintered the bones in her forearm. Brenda could feel the pieces breaking-up and swimming in all directions as if she had dropped a paper bag full of silver fish on the floor.

Brenda breathed heavily and was sweating. Her arm was broken and she screamed and her scream turned into laughter but the laughter wasn't hers. There were blank, pale faces behind the uniformed man and they were all laughing. She didn't know how many faces there were or who they were but she felt like she knew them. She recognized a distinct cartoon chuckled. She struggled to her feet and began to run. Her crushed arm, its bones a bunch of chipped pieces, swayed uncontrollably. She had a hard time keeping her balance as she tried to run. She stopped because she knew there was someone else there who needed her help and she turned noticing that no one was chasing her. The faceless figures gathered around a light that blazed like a campfire. They seemed to be throwing logs onto the fire with savage gesticulations. As she got closer, she noticed that they weren't throwing logs onto the fire, instead they were pounding long sticks into the fire. They were trying to put it out by beating it, but it wouldn't go out. Even when they had crushed it down to dusty ash, it wouldn't go out. Then she watched in stupefaction as the campfire came off the ground and floated over their heads. They swung their heavy sticks through it. Now they were scared. She was standing there because she couldn't move. It was reverse serendipity. She saw that they were scared and they saw that she saw. She couldn't move as they descended on her. She felt like a deer trapped in headlights, knowing damn well that its life was over but not being able to do a thing about it, not being able to move a muscle. As the group came to her she recognized the uniformed man. The uniformed man was Rich. He was younger, he didn't have a mustache, and his eyes were different, but it was Rich. He came at her with the stick held high and hit her on the shoulder. She dropped her to her knees. She was still conscious as he put his hand on her head, like he had done so many times before, and swung again. That's when she awoke in a puddle of sheets.

Brenda didn't know where she was. She had to get out of bed because she was trapped between a soaking wet quilt and a drenched sheet. Before she could put both feet on the floor her sweat had gone cold and she shivered in the dark. She looked around for the shadows of her wedding photo or the floor lamp or the dresser by the window but they weren't there. Her t-shirt was gripping her skin as tiny trickles of cold ran down her legs. Then she remembered where she was. "They found me," she whispered in hard breaths. She had to feel her way down the stairs to the bathroom where she lit a candle. She was glad to be awake. She removed the oversized t-shirt, which she had taken from one of the drawers upstairs and dried her upper body with the hand towel. She pulled out of her wet underwear and dried below her waist. She was cold in the dampness of her skin. She was scared. She had to feel her way back up the stairs in the nude and had an eerie feeling that someone was watching her from behind. She stared at the bed. "I don't want to go back there." She went to Ezra's dresser and pulled out another large t-shirt. She pulled the towel curtains from the window to have some outside light but the overcast sky was inky black. She pulled the quilt off the bed and slipped the dry side around her body. She sat on the top step looking out from the loft in an envelope of fabric.

She didn't want to go back to sleep. She didn't want to go back there. She was covered with goose bumps. "Just a dream. Only a dream." She said reassuring herself. She was right it was only a dream. The only problem was that *they* had come often to her dreams, which meant that the ghosts had found her. Only a matter of time, she thought. With her eyes fully open, she tried to remember the dream. It wouldn't be able to hurt her now though, because she was awake.

She shook the dream loose from her mind and tried to watch it from the outside rather than the inside. She tightened her grip around her bent knees and tried to stuff the quilt into all her cold crevices. Unlike most dreams this one didn't leave her five minutes after she awoke. She kept seeing the images over and over in her mind. The more she ran the images, the clearer they got, until she wasn't even in the dream. Instead, she was watching it like a football fan watches the game from the bleachers. She was standing off to the side, watching. She wondered if she was just adding details so she could see Rich as the Devil, but she realized that wasn't it. The details were coming out of the light that had floated above the heads of the dream men. She had somehow held onto that light.

Brenda replayed the images until she fell into a quiet sleep. She was curled on the floor at the top of the stairs when she awoke. She wasn't sure whether she had had the dream or whether she had only dreamed she had had the dream. However, none of that mattered because the images were now clear in her mind and, for the first time, she understood the ghosts. She understood the crows, and the crows weren't waiting for her. They had come to tell her so. They had come to tell her they were waiting for Rich.

She stumbled, nearly falling down the stairs and had to jump with a woofing clump to clear the last four wooden steps so she wouldn't break her legs in the fall. Her loose footedness had shaken and boomed inside the empty cabin. Dave, who was down by the creek, heard the noise and jumped. He thought he saw the cabin move and before the thud could echo into the trees he was running for his life. He was glad he had been on his side of the creek and didn't have to try to jump it. When he threw himself into the sauna shack, Roadside Girl was standing in her underwear brushing her hair. He didn't notice.

"Something's in that house." She could see he was winded and he wasn't looking at her. He was looking behind him like the bogeyman was chasing him. "Something's banging around in that house."

"Whoa, slow down. Our house?"

"No, that house." He pointed but didn't realize that he was pointing straight out the door to his own house. "The one all the kids talk about." He was too frantic to think about how they all knew so much about this haunted house when none of them had ever seen it.

"Calm down. It's probably just Tom. He told me he was in there the other day."

"Well he isn't in there now, cuz he's out plowing the field behind his house." It was almost comical because Dave was acting horror-movie scared in broad daylight.

"I don't know what you're all worked up about. It isn't like there's a mass murderer in there."

"Worse. The ghost of a mass murderer."

"Ghosts don't kill people, Dave." She was trying to remember a story where a ghost had actually done anyone any harm. Maybe ghosts scared people enough for those people to do harm to themselves, but ghosts themselves did not kill people. "It's only ghosts from urban legends that ever do anything and those aren't ghosts at all; they're people."

"How do you know? You ever seen a ghost before?"

She thought quietly that she had seen a ghost. Unfortunately, it was probably the same ghost that he had seen. Dave had a good question, and Roadside Girl tried to remember ghosts from books she had read. Marley seemed pretty harmless and even the ghost of Christmas yet-to-come didn't kill anybody. "Lydia says ghosts are good. Says they come back to remind people of their past. She says there are ghosts in the woods that help people when they get lost—help them find their way." Lydia was right to some extent. There were ghosts flying around Brenda's dreams, stirring up hornets in Rich's dreams and those ghosts were trying to help both of them remember the past, find their way.

"She never told me that."

If Roadside Girl was trying to calm Dave, it wasn't working. He still had the jitters. She noticed she was still standing in her underwear, turned around, and said, "let me get dressed and we'll go over and see what all the commotion is." She pulled on the brown pants she had worn the day before and grabbed her blue flannel shirt that was hanging on the door.

"See what? I'm not going over there."

"God, Dave you act like you've never heard a book fall off a shelf before."

"This wasn't no book."

"Well, it wasn't a ghost, either." She said and she believed herself.

They wandered down the path together and stepped through the creek on a natural rock bridge. The creek was low this time of year. Even the swimming hole was only about thigh deep. Dave didn't want to go back to the cabin. He had heard the story from kids at school.

* * *

"My Dad said back in the seventies he snuck out there one night. Said they were all tripping on something. All whacked out of their minds on drugs. That crazy guy who lives behind the fence and never comes out he and his brother got 'em all stirred up on spirits and drugs. Tricked and hypnotized them. I guess they gave him all their money and he took it and hide it out in the woods. My Dad says it's still there, but it's guarded by ghosts. He said he snuck out there one night and they were all dancing around the fire. The girls were all naked and had painted their bodies white with something. The guys were naked too but their bodies were painted with swamp sludge. He said they were all dancing around the fire and that Gern dude was sitting at the head of the fire on a stone altar-like thing and all these whacked out people would come up and kiss him all over, even the guys. He'd touch their hair and say stuff, but he wasn't speaking English. Then he would stand and move like a snake. And they would all imitate him."

"My Dad says Gern led them all into the house one night and he was doing that thing like a snake. His naked body all covered in green-black sludge and he was smoothing his hands all over their bodies as they licked him. They would move with his hands then violently freak out kicking and screaming. My Dad says that's because their souls were revolting. Then he would touch them and, one by one, they climbed up on a chair and slipped a noose around their necks. He kicked the chair out and the others all watched the body swing until it stopped swinging. He did that seven times. My Dad says if you go into that cabin you'll be hypnotized by the spirits, and there's nothing you can do to stop it. You'll hang yourself, too. That's why that Tom Gern is so crazy. I've heard he's had to pull two or three bodies out of there. Tourists, I guess."

"After seven people hung themselves, the Gern brother took the body of one of his girlfriend's down and had sex with it. Then he dragged it through town cursing everybody. They say that he cursed the Lutheran church and that no one could get the doors open on it until all the bodies were buried. That took awhile because someone came to get one of the bodies to bury downstate. Anyway, they say he dragged that girl all over town and finally ended up at the high school. He hoisted her body to the top of the backstop and hung her from her feet, but not before he slit her throat and drank her blood. They said he was covered with blood. Then he climbed the backstop and stood on top. He had tied a short rope around the top post and jumped. I guess his arms got caught on something as the rope tightened because they were straight out at his sides, like he was trying to do jumping jacks. He was dead in the morning."

"That old cabin had seven bodies strung up on the rafters swinging back and forth for days. My Dad says they beckon you with their arms, hypnotize you with their dead eyes and you can't help it. You just climb up there, too."

"He says that's why this town is so quiet. Everybody shuts themselves in because the ghost of Gern is dragging around the night, looking to string up another. My Dad won't even let me walk on that side of 52. Says the whole area is haunted."

* * *

"Kids say that there were seven people hung in that cabin."
"Same old story. Who told you that?"
"Kids."
"What kids? Who? Nobody ever died in that cabin, Dave. That story's been hanging around the school for twenty years." She hadn't meant the play on words but she had said it, and she was pretty sure he hadn't heard her. She thought the stories were

like *Little Red Riding Hood,* stories parents told their children to keep them in line, to keep them from joining any "crazy cult," to keep them from veering off the path.

When they got to the cabin, Dave stepped behind Roadside Girl. She didn't bother with the windows and was a little surprised when the doorknob turned freely in her hand and the door glided open. Brenda turned around in the kitchen and they both saw each other at the same time. Brenda gasped just short of a scream. Dave jumped backward off the porch and fell into the sandy soil. Brenda dropped the cup she was holding, and Roadside Girl, shocked, did nothing.

"Jesus Christ. What are you doing here?" Roadside Girl had dropped her head a little and had her hand on her chest.

"You scared the shit out of me," Brenda said. And without thinking they both laughed at their reaction toward each other.

"What is it?" Dave asked.

"Nothing. Come on in."

"It ain't nothing. You're talking to something."

"It's not a what. It's a who, Dave. Stop being a chicken and get in here. I told you it was nothing. And it's nothing."

"Heck if I'm going in there."

"Dave, stop being a baby and get up here." Dave trailed up to the front door like a beaten dog.

"Oh!" He expelled. "Hi, Mrs. Cafus." He seemed confused. "What are you doing here?"

She had been found. Now, not only did the silent Thomas Gern know she was there, but so did Roadside Girl and Dave.

"Come on in and close the door." Her voice was solemn and serious because even though she didn't consider Roadside Girl a child, she did consider Dave one and kids don't keep their mouths shut very well. She looked at the broken cup on the floor. "You want coffee?" She asked as she bent to pick up the thick chunks of glass. Roadside Girl didn't know they were staying but figured there was a reason that she was making breakfast in a cabin that had been closed for twenty years. It was quiet for a moment and the air in the cabin seemed not to move at all. "It's all I've got."

Dave noticed sadness in her voice. "That's okay, Mrs. Cafus. I'll have coffee." He didn't know why he said it because he didn't even like coffee. However, he would have a cup and he would act like he liked it.

She poured three cups of coffee out of the speckled enamel-coated coffeepot and set them on the counter. In a sad voice she said, "I don't have any milk. Sugar, but no milk." Brenda tried to tell a story that would explain why she was living in the cabin. She left out major details like the dream and the crows and the rape—details that followed her around. She thought that was best for now. After all, Dave was a child and children didn't need to know all the sordid details of life—they'd get them soon enough. He tried to understand why she had to leave her husband and lay low for a while, as she had put it. The story somehow reminded Dave of his mother, though he didn't know why. He sat through the whole thing and finished his coffee and didn't squirm on his stool once. When she finished the story no one moved and no one spoke. They all stared at something that was in-between them, with blurry eyes. She hadn't told them that she was trying to work out a plan—a fix of sorts. She only told them that this was her hometown and she intended to stay here until she wanted to move. Roadside Girl felt some sort of instant connection to Brenda because of that, and she thought that maybe everybody in this town wasn't as different from her as she had thought, after all.

"Mr. Cafus can't find out." Brenda said. "He's not a good a person and if he finds out . . . ." she stopped because the fear was dripping back into her. Then she realized she didn't have to say it. "Let's just say it'll be very grave." She thought that was an appropriate way to phrase it. "No one can know I'm here. Once one person knows everyone will know and that won't be good."

"No one will hear anything from us, right?" She turned to Dave who had already locked the knowledge of Mrs. Cafus deep in his heart.

"Buried." He said in stern-faced seriousness.

"No one. No one can know. Whispers get around this little town faster than sand." No one would know because neither Dave nor Roadside Girl would say anything to anyone. At least, not until it was all over.

"We thought you were a ghost."

"Dave thought you were a ghost," Roadside Girl corrected. Even though on two separate occasions she had mentioned to Tom that there was something, as she put it, in the cabin. He had known all the time that there was something in the cabin but the something didn't go bump in the night. She thought he lied to me by not telling me. But that thought lasted only long enough to disappear. Tom had protected Brenda that was the kind of person he was.

"There aren't any ghosts around here. Leastwise no ghosts that you need to be afraid of."

However, there were ghosts somewhere, maybe not the ghosts of the campfire stories from childhood, maybe not the chain-dragging ghosts that sucked the breath out of people while they slept. But there were real ghosts that lived in people's minds and told them what to do and how to act and that things were right or things were wrong. Brenda had had a visit from those ghosts in the night and those ghosts had told her something that she should've already known. Those ghosts weren't there to get her; they were there to save her. For the first time in her life, she understood that the ghosts had never been there to get her.

The three of them sat in the semi-darkness of the unlit cabin and let some small talk break the tension of the morning. They could see Tom, a dark speck on a toy white and red tractor, in the distance dragging a plow and dust behind him. They all thought about losses. They all thought about secrets that they had or that others had from them. They all thought about dreams and how it would be nice if good dreams came true and bad dreams came never. And for the brief morning that they were together, they felt like a family, all of them together—a family of misfits.

Roadside Girl thought about all the people closest to her and they were all misfits—Dave, Lydia, Tom, and now, Brenda. They were all alike in one way or another and none of them even realized it. All of them thought they had to face the world, the cruel world where they didn't belong, alone. But they didn't, because they were part of the world and the world was part of them and they had a finger on life that, like others, they had forgotten. Yes, they too had forgotten that finger or hidden it, and they had forgotten that they held the pulse and could share that finger. And they would share it. Eventually.

The windows in Tom's kitchen were steamed closed. All he could see from inside was the moisture fog that lined the kitchen side of the windows. Even in the living room the windows were building a white, moisture frame around the edges and closing like an eye into the center. Tom had sweat—not outside work sweat that was mixed with dirt, grime, and work—he had clean, clear sauna sweat dripping down his arms and soaking his white t-shirt and making his pants grab at his legs. He was wearing an old Carhartt cap to keep his hair out of the pale, blood vegetables that ultimately became his winter spaghetti sauce. On the yellowing linoleum sat a bushel basket of ripening tomatoes that he had pulled from the garden when they were still green before the frost had come. Today would be another hot-sweat, lid-sucking day of canning. Tom always grew more tomatoes than he needed. He couldn't help it. He loved watching the tomato vine stretch out to the sun. He loved being on his knees between those plants and pulling the tiny, green weeds that tried to steal nourishment. He loved the sweet, nearly mint aroma that wafted from the plants. For years, he thought the smell was that of the marigolds that walled the bugs away from the garden, but it had been the tomato plants.

  Canning was a yearly ritual that came in waves as different vegetables became ripe. It marked the seasons for Tom. There was no tradition or ritual Tom held with greater esteem than canning. He did can too much, but Lydia had always received those spoils. Tom was seldom left with any extra vegetables. He enjoyed doing it because it was a hot and laborious all-day task of bubbling and boiling pots and pans. It was slimy, naked tomatoes that slipped and slid from his hands uncontrollably. In the past he had enjoyed the sloppy, gushing heat of canning.

He remembered Sarah and himself canning in their underwear because it was so hot. Moving the hot pots and steaming tomatoes and clean quart jars from place to place trying to find space for the bottled gold. Both of them sweating, ungoverned by the normal laws of human perspiration. Sarah's hair would be netted back in a babushka. The two together looked like a power duo from some Marvel comic book: CanMan and The Pickler. Sarah had liked canning, too. That was when Sarah still enjoyed being a farmer, before the lack of dimension, as she put it, had stole her away, beneath the bridge, to the land of Billy Goat's Gruff. She was never really a farmer's wife; she had always been a farmer, herself—in the dirt, in the work. Tom remembered them skimming over the floor after the sweat had rolled down their legs and they had spilled water here and tomato sauce there and the yellowing floor had become an autumn ice rink. Their feet skated, gliding on the film of moisture that had covered the floor. Sarah would push off from the stove with hot bottles burning her hands and slide to the screen door. She would bang it open, and set the shiny, brass-capped bottles of life in rows as they winked light back at the sun. Then she'd skid back through the door like a five-year-old on clear, January ice, sliding up to the stove to grab two more hand-burning bottles. She would laugh the whole time. "Look at me, Toclep. Look at me out on the porch in my underwear." She would laugh and dance with the bottles burning her palms. "Don't you all wish you were me?" Tom, draped in the cloud of steam that billowed off the stove, knew that that was what everyone wanted.

Even though Tom still enjoyed canning, it had ceased being a game and had turned into simple necessity when Sarah left. There was nothing really fun about it when you did it all by yourself. It was like a balloon without the air. At the same time, he knew if he didn't do it the tomatoes would wrinkle and die from frostbite on the vine and he would feel guilty for the waste. "There are people starving in China." He could hear his mother say. People starved everywhere, he thought. He heard his own version of Eleanor Rigby, "All the hungry people, where do they all come from? All the hungry people, where do they all belong?" He knew if he didn't do it, in January when he wanted chili, he would have to trot down to Don's and buy canned tomatoes that tasted like tin or the not-so-fresh tomatoes he could pull out of the bin and use for baseballs. They were bland rubber in the mouth. So he had done what he needed to do. What he had to do. He canned. In those Sarah-less years the bottled gold had tarnished and turned to bitter fruit. It had rusted. He plodded through the task of canning, which sometimes lasted three or four days depending on the season and the fruit or vegetable. It was harder to do with only one person—washing bottles, slipping the hot tomatoes out of their skin, chopping, keeping four pots boiling, capping, finding someplace to stack the hand-burning bottles. It was a two-person job. It was necessary. He hadn't done it alone since Sara had gone. He had done it with his old buddy, loneliness. And in those years his sweat had felt just like tears.

After Sarah left, he canned only pint bottles: pint bottles of salsa, pint bottles of fresh basil and tomatoes, pint bottles of onions, beans, and squash. Pickles were the only thing he still canned in quart jars. Pickles didn't last. He could finish a bottle of pickles in a week or less. The other hundred unused quart bottles lined the top shelves of the pantry. The shelves he couldn't reach without a chair. The shelves that would cry to him, "remember when?" He would turn from them trying not to remember and close the door of the pantry on their voices. But it was impossible not to remember. In those early days he had to go out and buy pint bottles and lids and rings, his canning sweat mixed with tears and he didn't even notice, but he could taste the salt in his mouth and never knew it was the salt of loneliness. In January he could taste the tears in his soup and in his spaghetti sauce.

This year was different, though, because in the early-morning kitchen, wondering what to do as she began to sweat, stood Roadside Girl. She had her hair neatly tied in a backwards babushka like southern black women in some old Shirley Temple movie. She was watching Tom, his clothes clinging to him like wet crêpe paper, and was learning the fundamentals of food preservation *a la* Gern. This year along with the tomatoes, he would drop in some sunshine. In the harsh winter winds of below-zero January he would be able to crack the top of one of the pint bottles and the sun would rise right out of the mouth and hang in his kitchen saying, "spring isn't so far away. Start plotting the garden. Where did you plant the corn last year? The peppers? The sunflowers? Stir it up. Plot the garden. Remember not to replant the same crop in the same spot." He would remember that January was only thirty-one days. January didn't last forever.

Roadside Girl was like the skinless tomatoes. She was slippery and sly and dipped in and out of the canning like it was a basketball game. Tom watched her and he couldn't help but smile. He laughed. It was like when Sarah was there, but it was fresher. It had even more energy. Though he didn't hold that against Sarah. Her leaving him couldn't force a wedge between him and his feelings. This year canning wouldn't be lonely. This year canning wouldn't be a chore. This year canning would be life.

The bottles were hot in Roadside Girl's hands and she did something that was more like circus canning than the traditional, good-old Marguerite Gern canning. Roadside Girl took three glowing bottles and she juggled them over to the screen door, which she kicked open with her bare foot. She stopped juggling and one, two, three; she caught the bottles a hair off the surface of the porch as she set them in rows. Tom had stopped skinning tomatoes, and he stared at her with his bottom jaw, broken and hanging open like someone had cut the tendons that allowed it to close.

"Good thing these aren't quart jars. Never be able to get a grip on 'em." She said. Tom hadn't thought of it before because there had never been any reason for him to think of it. For the first time in his life, he was glad that the quart bottles were hiding in the darkness of the pantry. "Never seen so much life in this kitchen," she said. "Usually you're just sitting there drinking time and coffee like they went together." He didn't respond. He just smiled into the boiling blood of the tomatoes. Canning is life, he thought.

"Okay master of Ringling Brother's Canning. Remind me to check the seal on those bottles so I don't get sick and die midway through winter." He smiled and smiled again when she smiled.

She pushed the metallic tin buttons on the lid of all three bottles. "Broken," she said. "I'll juggle softer next time."

"They haven't had time to seal. We'll check 'em later or tomorrow."

As far as Tom could remember, he had never missed a season of canning. He drove his mind back over the years and there hadn't been one year. Even the year he spent at Northern Michigan, he had come home to help his mother put up tomatoes. It was a two-person job. He knew that, and somewhere in the past five years he had forgotten it. He had forgotten that it was going against the Ten Commandments of canning. A reading from the Gospel of Marguerite Gern in her letters to Aunt Lorraine: one must not can as one but always as two for in two the light of the summer can be preserved but in one only the darkness. This is the Gospel of Marguerite in her letters to the relatives. Amen.

Canning was noisy and sloppy and busy and hot. Canning wasn't really the time to start long, drawn out dialogues about Dante's visions of hell. Though the heat of the kitchen was probably a bit like the mist above the lake Dante had to cross. Between the banging of bottles and Roadside Girl's juggling, between the spitting and sizzling potted water, between the "Oww" and the "Damn," between the busy movement of bottle and hand coordination, between the visible happiness of the players in the game of canball, there were single words or shouted comments that were answered with head shakes, arm gestures, and "uh huhs."

Roadside Girl disappeared and Tom frantically searched for her as he pulled the bottles from the water while he tried to de-skin steaming tomatoes. He was an Octopus in over his head. She had only stepped out of the room for a second, probably to use the bathroom and already his work had ganged up around him. How had he ever done this alone? It was impossible. But he had, because in all impossibility there was possibility.

"Too damn hot for that ensemble." Tom's grin stretched across his face and looked like that of a cat, stealing the dinner trout off the counter. "Don't get any ideas." She giggled through her nose. He wasn't getting the ideas that she thought he was. He was grinning out of pure joy. He was grinning out of her shear sense of comfort. A flash of Sarah jumped through his head, but it wasn't that the action was like Sarah, it was that the action had been natural and uninhibited. Roadside Girl wasn't in her underwear. She was wearing cut offs and had pulled off her shirt and had on a sports bra. She was barefoot, which was normal for her, though not this time of year. She looked a little bit like something out of *Lil' Abner* except, of course, she wasn't over-proportioned. The thing that struck him most was that he could not remember ever seeing her not in pants or a dress of some kind. She often wore long summer dresses to work in. He had seen her riding the roan in a dress, chopping wood in a dress, cleaning the shed in a dress. After she had told him about her morning swims, he had even pictured her naked. But he hadn't pictured her in shorts.

He wasn't back at work because his mind was running from year to year trying to remember her wearing shorts. Then he saw her in junior high with her long skinny legs peering down in whiteness under the shorts that were too short. He saw the teenage girl trying to be like other girls her age that she was somehow not like at all, because her body was longer.

"All right. Stop gawking. I know they're white." He wasn't gawking at the whites of her legs; he was gawking at his memories. "Don't know how you can work over that boiling water with those clothes sticking to you like wet papier-mâché." He looked like a drown muskrat. "Only gonna get hotter in here today. Why don't you go put some shorts on?" She stepped in front of him facing the bobbing, tight-skinned tomatoes that were breaking out of their skin. "Get goin'. I can do this." She dipped her hands into the scalding water and eased a tomato out of the hard orange-red skin until it was a heart in her hand.

"Okay, but you better prepare yourself for some reflective skin. I'd better run out to the barn and get you a pair of welding goggles."

"Just get goin'. You're slowing down the production, Henry. Gotta keep the factory rolling." He disappeared behind the wall and she could hear his Frankenstein boots pounding up the uncarpeted stairs.

When he got to his room he wondered if he still had any shorts. He was trying to pull out of the wet shirt and the sticky pants but they felt like they had shrunk and he had to sit down to get out of their wetness. He found some old shorts. When was the last time I had these on . . . '80 . . . '82? He couldn't remember. He tried to pull into them but they were too small. "Must've put on some weight."

"Hurry up." Roadside Girl's voice filtered up the stairs into his room like the steam from the kitchen.

He grabbed an old pair of jeans and took the scissors to them. He cut uneven lines. The sheerness of the lines would make the chicken white of his legs even starker. He changed into another t-shirt and flopped, barefooted, down the stairs.

"That's more like it." She laughed and turned her head so he wouldn't have to see her trying to hold back her laughter. He had a hard time remembering daytime bare footedness. His feet looked like they had been soaking in water all morning. But they swelled into their skin and the heat wrapped around him and sucked his dry t-shirt into the dampness of his body. "I've never canned before. First time."

"Well if Lydia didn't get all my leftovers and if I didn't over plant every year you'd know this game inside and out, as if there's anything to know. Skin 'em, chop 'em, throw in a little salt, top 'em, and submerge 'em. Can't get much simpler than that."

"Yeah, but there's more than that. I always wondered why people still did this when they could just walk into Don's and load up a grocery cart full of stewed tomatoes for a buck a can. Seems kinda stupid. Seems like a waste of time."

"But . . . ." He had to shift his ideas around to get them to come out. Then he said in a prideful and selfish voice. "But these are my tomatoes. I grew 'em. With my sun and the ground's water and a little talking to . . . ."

"You only talk to 'em cuz you don't have anyone else to talk to."

"Yeah."

"Got ya."

"They're mine. I did the work. They grew right out there. They would've grown without me, but I helped 'em along," and he gestured with his nose. "It's like; well you can make chili with those store-bought tomatoes that taste like aluminum, sure. But it's not the same chili. It doesn't taste the same. It doesn't go down the same. It ain't the same. You really didn't make anything at all. It's not your Michigan sunshine in those tin cans; it's California sun. That ain't the same." His words sounded like the closing statements of a criminal lawyer, like someone had told him that canning your own tomatoes was against the law and he had become Daniel Webster and was trying to forge a case out of Michigan sunshine trapped in mushy, tomato redness. "These tomatoes have my life in them. I played in that dirt out there. I've moved that garden all over the back acres. Those tomatoes have my mother's eyes and my grandmother's hands and my great grandmother's singing voice. They have the muscle of my father, the consistency of his father, and the stick-to-itiveness of his father's father. They have the history of this family and the history of this dirt. Those tomatoes that I'll start eating and you'll start eating in a month will have the taste of the land and the sun and the lake—that big lake, right out there." His voice, which was usually low and scratchy, took on a stern yet bouncy tone. It was so unlike his usual voice that Roadside Girl found herself staring at him with lack of recognition. "That lake that used to be a chunk of ice a mile high and it'll all be in the tomatoes. These tomatoes can't get rid of that. They can't spit the history away from themselves. They can't say their not the life of this land because that would be a lie. They are the life of this land. They're your life and my life, now. And in fifty years they'll be somebody else's life, just like fifty years ago they were somebody else's life."

He stopped and she thought his defense was over. Then he breathed and said, "Right now your sweat is dripping down you arms and mingling with those tomatoes. You can try to stop it, but it won't work because that's where your sweat belongs. Kissing those tomatoes. And when we close the tops on those tomatoes there'll be a little you and a little me and a whole lot of sunshine and history in those bottles. When you crack one of those bottles in the warming snows of March next year the sun will step right out of the bottles and kiss you full on the lips and you will say, that's me in there. That's my kiss. Your chili won't taste like a tin can; it will taste like you. And there ain't a sweeter taste in the whole wide world."

Her mouth was open and her eyes were smiling and she didn't have a word to say. She knew why people still did this. She knew why Lydia's winter stew tasted better than anything she could get at Coppers or Rae's. She knew why those cans at Don's were sub-par to these clear pint bottles that had been used over and over. Those tin cans had lost their soul. They were purgatory tomatoes wandering aimlessly across the salt plains and prairies to grocery stores and then into the soulless kitchens of America. She wondered how many times mothers across the country had dumped in half a pound of powdered garlic and dried basil and granular iodized salt, and other nameless spices, taken the wooden spoon up to their lips, gave a quick blow, and said, "this doesn't taste like anything." They were right; it tasted like nothing. It didn't even taste like air because air has a piercing, acute flavor like sharp cheese. Air makes your nose twitch. But nothing...nothing is nothing and it doesn't do anything. It doesn't taste.

Tom, surrounded in the cloud of his kitchen, stopped cold in the mist. He looked at Roadside Girl who was skinning and chopping, her hands plastered with translucent red epidermis. "I wonder," he said then paused like he had made a mistake.

"What do you wonder?" He looked as if he wasn't going to say any more, then he looked her in the eyes, not like he was going to say something serious, but like he was swimming in her soul, like he was looking from her heart out, like something had been lost.

"I wonder . . . if . . . I wonder if we shouldn't can some quarts?"

"I can't juggle them. But other than that, I don't see why not."

And neither did he.

It was dry enough for a grass fire when Daisy and Kristie got in the September Dart. The car's dull, creme-yellow finish seemed to absorb the gray, which the lake shined into the sky, and the sky shined back into the lake. It had only rained twice in a month and the pine needles felt slick like ice on the hard ground. The grass slowly danced a parched waltz. The Smokey the Bear sign in front the Amnicon Falls State Park read, Fire Danger and then, in bright red: HIGH. The fire danger was high. However, it wasn't high for the earth that lived through natural disasters like tornadoes and earthquakes the way babies fall down. It wasn't high for the earth that was born again and again. Fire was like spring for the earth. However, fire for mankind was not like spring. A fire already burned for Ezra.

When Ezra called Kristie, he had sounded farther away than the long-distance party line that stretched down U.S. 2 to Ironcloud and then up to Toclep. He sounded like he was calling from another century. His voice crackled like someone was standing behind him crinkling a paper bag. He'd be done with the hay, he said. And they could come, and he would show them the mountains and they would eat Marguerite's apple-raisin cookies and ride horses and walk the rocky shores. They could stay the weekend in Uncle John's room. He did not add that it was a quiet, unused room with a bed that was always made and a dresser with an odd corner that somehow looked like someone had hit his falling head on it and had died on the floor. The dresser didn't have a mark. It just had the glowing corner that seemed to pull the young boys' eyes saying, "Right here, right here. This is the corner that kills. Look right here." And they would. Every time they walked into the room their eyes were magnetized to the spot, to the unmarked corner. Ezra wondered whether the girls' eyes, too, would be lured by the whispering corner. When they came into the room, would they stare in awe as they set their bags on the floor, the whole time watching the corner like it was a horror film too frightening from which to take their eyes?

He had called only Kristie but he had invited them both as if they were sisters or roommates. They were neither. The drive wasn't that long from Superior to Toclep. The girls left in the yellow car on the gray morning that blanketed the dryness and threatened rain. They rode with the windows up even through it was warm. A certain feeling that said, "you'll need the windows up." By the time they got to Brule it had started to rain, first in puny spit-like drops that washed the windshield with dusty, brown tears, then in a steady drizzle that misted like fog and, finally, the rain that tells everyone, "I'm an all day rain. Stay in bed. Pull the covers up over your head. Sleep." Daisy drove and Kristie watched the windshield wipers push the drops in arcs and sweep away blurriness, blurriness would come again and the arms of the wipers would sweep it away. She was hypnotized. It was still raining when they pulled onto highway 52 and drove passed the Gern house and into Toclep.

"Must've missed it." Daisy stopped in the dustless, wet gravel near the corner of Clarion and 52. "Didn't he tell you that you couldn't miss it? Well, we missed it." In truth, they hadn't missed it. Not really. Ezra had seen the Dart from the barn where he had been sitting on the tractor in silence. "What did he say about some fence?" That was when Kristie looked across the road to the sprawling mule-gray boards that stretched around a pasture with mute arms.

"He said plank fence." She was pointing.

"Guess that would be it." As they turned their heads back

down 52 they could see the fence disappear into the trees, wrapped around the field like a blanket. Toward the back of the land was an empty wagon waiting for two boys to finish the job they had started. By the time they pulled around, Ezra was moving through the rain to the fence. In the grayness of the day, he seemed to be glowing—not glowing with happiness, just glowing. His white t-shirt took in water and released light. When they pulled into the driveway he ushered them by like a landing strip director. They were both smiling and he was smiling, too. His smile held the look of I-know-something-you-don't-know and both Kristie and Daisy recognized that look and shrugged at each other.

"Hey, Ezra." Kristie jumped out of the car and skipped over to give him a hug, which Daisy thought was kind of weird. Didn't they just meet? Or did they? Though she couldn't identify why, she felt like they had all known each other forever. She found herself giving Ezra a hug even as she questioned the action in her head.

"Hey, Ezzie. Thanks for the invite to beautiful Toclep."

"Sorry 'bout the rain. Could've been a better weekend I guess."

"Why are you sorry? You don't make the rain." The word sorry, that overused and under-honest word, was one that scraped across the chalkboard of Daisy's soul. She saw no reason for people to use the word so much. "What you mean is that it's a shame that's it's raining."

"Yeah. Isn't that what I said?"

"We didn't come to see the weather. We came to see you." Kristie was holding a small canvas rucksack that was so faded you couldn't tell what color it had been and a flaking, leather guitar case. "Little rain never hurt anybody. Besides we need it." She was right. The driveway had soaked every drop of water into the cracks and crevices of rock-hard earth. It appeared to be softening, breathing. There weren't puddles on the driveway, though it had been raining for hours. Yes, the earth did need the rain.

"I forgot you said you played." Ezra's arching arm pointed toward the guitar case. "Tom plays, too." Again the girls looked at each other and shrugged. They couldn't recall that Ezra had told them about his little brother before, but he had.

When Kristie and Daisy came inside, Ezra introduced them to his mother, who was watching the bread dough rise. The whole house smelled like yeast and flour and the kitchen seemed like a human heart. Pounding with life, that was the kitchen. It wasn't Ezra's mother—whose childless eyes pondered the rising, crusted dough like it was God—who was pounding with life. Marguerite smiled at the girls with skeleton eyes. She was looking somewhere; she was looking into the future and the future scared her. She was detached and the girls noticed it in her eyes and in her voice and in her handshake. They had never met her before. They had no basis for their reaction but when they were turning around in Uncle John's room they looked into each other's eyes and said, "She's spooky." They both agreed, spooky—the quivering, ghostly handshake—the broken, drowned, emotionless welcome, the thousand-mile stare. They didn't say anything to Ezra, but he heard it in their speechless chatter. They would learn why she was spooky. They would see that she herself wasn't scary. She was simply scared.

Marguerite stood motionless in the thumping, headache kitchen as Ezra pulled the girls back into the heart of the house after the two-dollar tour. There was no time for coffee or small talk. Ezra had Kristie by the hand and she in turn had Daisy by the hand as he dragged them passed his mother.

"Gonna show 'em around the property. Show 'em where I'm gonna build my house."

"That's nice," she said in a foggy voice to her apron. Then she turned like an automaton to the window and said, "it's raining." However, she really wasn't talking to them, and they never heard her say it. All the same, she heard it over and over and over in her head. It's raining. Stay out of the rain. It's raining. The child's nursery rhyme chimed, it's raining, it's pouring, the old man is snoring. He bumped his head." God not his head, she thought. He bumped his head, he bumped his head, he bumped his . . . .

Ezra took them to the barn and showed them the tractor like they had never seen a tractor before. He showed them the horses that nodded a salutation and the cows that seemed helplessly forgetful. The cows just kept staring at the three of them, in disbelief, as if they weren't really there or as if they were there but the cows had forgotten that they were. Ezra was excited to show them his land. He had friends in Toclep but they knew the Gern property well enough. Their town was built on Lionel Gern's foresight and the townspeople had peered across the road into that fenced land for what seemed like centuries. The three of them walked across the hay field, through the short, sharp straws that poked into the soles of their shoes enough for them to feel. The rain had eased back into drizzle that would slowly fog the day into night. It was a North American rainforest mist that enveloped the coast of Superior.

When they got to the enclosed nook, the sunless corner of hidden property that was tucked, like the panhandle of Oklahoma, into the trees, Ezra stopped.

"Right here." He spread his arms out wide. "Right here's where I'm gonna build my house and live my life, when I get back. I'm gonna live my life and pretend there isn't anything else, that's what I'm gonna do." Kristie and Daisy looked at each other. Pretend, he thought. Pretend that nothing exists beyond the fence. Of course, that was pretending and Ezra knew it. The world was beyond the fence. Life was beyond the fence.

"That's good," Daisy said. "You're gonna hide in the shaded quiet of your dad's land and pretend the world doesn't have any troubles, eh? That'll help solve all the problems. That's the answer. Just hide yourself away and close your eyes. Let someone else worry about the holes. Good God, Ezra, I don't know about you. You're . . . ."

"What d'you say, Ezra?" Kristie interrupted with a confused look on her face.

"Hopeless." Daisy finished.

"Huh. Oh." He sounded sad. He was listening to Daisy and had his head down like he had struck out with bases loaded at the little league championships. "Oh, just that I . . . ahh . . . I was . . . am gonna build my house here." He nudged the ground with his foot. If it would've been dry, he would've kicked up a cloud of dust but in the mist his foot simply slid through the wet grass. "Live in peace."

"No. Something else. Something 'bout when you . . . ."

"Come back." He said. "Yeah, that's when I'll build it, when I get back." He was looking into the grass that was soaking their shoes.

"What're you talking, Ezra?" They said it at the same time with the same look of I've-heard-this-story-before.

Daisy grabbed him by the shoulder and shook him out of the mist, back into the conversation. "What the hell are talkin' about?"

"Yeah. Got the letter on Wednesday." His voice was still distant. Then in a joking manner he added, "In the words of Tom Paxton, I guess this is my lucky day." He hummed.

"Not funny."

"Right, not funny. This isn't funny at all, Ezra. Is this your idea of a joke?"

Kristie drifted down a worn path to the memory of linked arms in the driveway, thinking about a nice weekend away from the world, and into the encounter with the spooky, mother's eyes that cried, "I've lost my son."

"Why didn't you tell me when you called?"

"I thought you might not want to come. You don't know m . . . I mean, well. I thought you wouldn't want to come. The whole thing's kind of a bummer."

Daisy pushed his shoulder, "You're goddamn right we wouldn't have wanted to come. What the hell are you talking about? What the fuck is going on here? Are you yanking our fucking chains? Jesus Christ, Ezra." She was yelling now and stomping into the soft, damp grass. "Call us up, get us to come up to Nowhere, Michigan, and then drop a fucking atom bomb on us. You're god damn right." She marched back and forth, throwing her arms around like a fire and brimstone preacher. Tears of anger held to her eyes and mixed with the mist. "And you're gonna go? Jesus, Ezra. What about Chicago? You're gonna be Hawk, now? You're gonna play their silly fucking games and be one of their pawns?" She had walked up to him and without realizing it, slapped him in the side of the head. "What are you, stupid? Are you?" She still hadn't realized that she had slapped him and silence fell between them. Kristie, who wasn't watching either of them, was looking into the darkness that danced between the tress beyond the fence.

Ezra just stood. His arms draped at his sides, and his body looked boneless. He was still staring into the universe at his feet, into the droplets of water, through the atoms of hydrogen and oxygen into the positives and negatives of protons and electrons and that is where he saw his life: a tiny, gray-white moth fluttering in the plusses and minuses. "No." He finally said sullenly.

Daisy's "what" squeezed between her furrowed eyebrows and her tight-lipped anger and came out in a squirt of guttural Cro-Magnon.

"No. I'm not stupid."

"We know you're not stupid." Kristie turned from the trees and came back into the conversation and hugged Ezra. Her hug was different than it had been in the driveway. It was desperate and calling. It pulled on her and him and on Daisy who was still standing a yard away with the word *stupid* scrawled across her flushed face and forehead.

"God Ezra. I'm sorry. We've got no right. We've got no right to blame you. You didn't do anything." Kristie was still hugging him like he was her child. He was blank and she was dazed, and he was sure that he had been in this place before. "I don't know. I'm not a man. They're not telling me I gotta go." She pointed like Vietnam was behind the large rock that was watching them from its immovable place in the middle of the shaved hay. "Can't you run?"

"I'm not a runner."

"I'm not calling you a chicken, Ezra."

"I didn't think you were. It's just that I have to go. I don't have a choice."

"Everyone has a choice."

"Yeah, everyone." Kristie pushed away from Ezra. "We're right here. Canada, it's right there. Right there. I can throw a stone to it. You could swim to it."

"I can't. I'm supposed to go."

"What are ya talkin' about? I don't understand what you're saying."

"I've known. I've known; it's like floating next to my bunk, I can't explain it. I'm fated."

"You're crazy. That's what you are. Nuts. Wacko." Daisy spun her forefinger around her ear. "You don't gotta go. Nobody's gotta."

"I do. There's something I'm supposed to do there."

"Like what? Fix it? End the war?"

"Yeah."

"Are you nuts?" She shook her head at him. Kristie was watching his eyes. They weren't distant, lost glazes of film anymore. They were poignantly clear. "You can't stop war."

"Now look who's a pessimist," he said.

"Maybe he can . . . do . . . something." Kristie said in broken words.

"No, he can't. You're not God, ya know." She was yelling into his face, again, and the words echoed and quivered through the trees in tiny jumps.

"I didn't say I was."

"Well you sure do act like you think you're God. Gonna walk right over there and a spread peace like it's fucking peanut butter. You're outta you're goddamn mind. Anything swimmin' around in there? Hey," she yelled, again. "I said, hey, anything in there?"

She tried to rap him on the forehead with her fisted knuckles, but he moved away.

"Lay off, Dais. Jesus, he didn't start the war."

"My name isn't Daisy." If there would have been anything to throw at him, she would've picked it up and chucked it at him as hard as she could. "Nope, he didn't start the war. Just gonna add to it. That's all. Just gonna be another piece of kindling—another scrawny piece of dry, brittle kinder. Perfect. Fuck Ezra, why don't you just go get yourself a hunting rifle and come back out here and splatter your brains all over your fucking homestead? Home, sweet, home. Dead Ezra, inside his stupid fence." She was marching lines to and fro across his eyes, making flesh pistols with her hands, and gesticulating her words.

"Enough." Kristie grabbed Daisy's arms that were lost among some stage action of death. "Enough is enough. You think he needs this? You think he hasn't thought about it? You think it isn't tearing his insides to shreds?" She was talking about him in the third person as if he had been somewhere else entirely. "Stop it. Stop it." That's when Kristie slapped her and brought the whole misty ranting to an end. "Grow up. We're fighting. We're letting the war destroy us. Jesus, Daisy. Don't you think Ezra could use a little compassion instead of a fistful of hate?" She still had Daisy's right wrist gripped tightly in her left hand.

They all stood there not noticing that the rain had turned to a soft, petting mist. It brushed their skin and painted their faces. No one said I'm sorry. Kristie stepped over and took Ezra's hand and then forming a circle Daisy took his other. They had their heads down and their long wet hair hung over the edges of eyes in sheep-dog fashion. Ezra had his head up and his eyes were still clear. The white frames looked whiter than usual and lit the small circle with hope.

"Everything'll work out all right. I know it will. At least, there it will." They weren't listening to him. He walked them to the darkest corner of the nook which was by the large bend in Owl Creek, which though they didn't know it, they would swim in when he came home. After that they walked along the back fence line toward the sleeping noise of the lake.

"My dad says that his grandfather built this fence. Surrounded the whole place by himself. Post after post, plank after plank, all by himself. He had four kids, but before the first one was walking he had the fence finished. I'll be back here. I'll do what's right. I'll do what I gotta do and I'll be back here, inside the fence, where I belong. I promise." They passed the Easter Island erratic that some glacier had placed in the middle of the field ten thousand years earlier and which had been watching their angered dialogue in the nook. They passed the empty wagon that waited for the last, wet bails of hay. The hay cried to them, "take us in. It's raining. We don't want to be all wet." They skirted the perimeter of the property out to the corner on Bayside Road and stopped to look across the wet road at the lights that looked out of Rae Miller's small, white house, which seemed to wink its fake, red shutters. "People rent those." He pointed to the empty, little cottages, closed and dark, behind Rae's house that were nestled like little bird's eggs in the nest of trees that separated the lake from her. "I take care of 'em for her. I guess Tom will have to do it now." Unfortunately, Tom never would. Rae would keep them going while Ezra was gone and then after he was gone again she would let them fade away like spring snow. They'd die from lack of use, as they grew old and decrepit.

When they got to the corner of 52 and Clarion, they could see into town.

"That a bar?" Kristie motioned toward Rae's as Ezra nodded his head. "They very serious about checking IDs? You gotta be twenty-one in Michigan, right? Maybe we could sneak in there for a drink or two tonight? Take the edge off a little."

"Naaa. Rae's not too strict about that sort of thing. Besides, I work for her. She says they're gonna change that law, anyway. Keeps saying that they can't send boys off to fight their Fat-Cat war and not let those same boys have a drink first. Doesn't seem rightly fair."

"Nothing seems fair to me," Daisy whispered loud enough for all of 'em to hear.

But something inside of her was now saying in little heart beat words that everything would be all right.

"We can go over there a little later. Mom's fixing dinner for you guys. Might take a little while for it all to dissolve into our systems." They would not make it to Rae's. Not tonight, anyway. They would be locked into the warmth of the living room and the leftover smells of stringy roast beef.

"That's okay." Kristie was holding Ezra's left hand and bouncing her left off the fence. "I'm sure your mom could use a little company right now to help ease her mind a little." She looked across Ezra to Daisy, who had both her hands shoved in her pockets like she was one solid piece of plastic, and exchanged a I-know-the-ghost-in-the-spooky-mom's-eyes-now look. When they entered the house Marguerite was sitting at the table. She looked up with slow reaction, then came alive.

"My Lord. Look at you all. Wet as muskrats. Ezrie, you run up and get some towels for these girls 'fore they catch their death of pneumonia." As Ezra left the room all of the women looked into each other's eyes and told life stories about each other and about their families and stretched their memories into the past through the droughts and the floods and the wars and each saw what the other knew and each lived what the other lived. Daisy put her arms around the kitchen woman who was suddenly her grandmother. She forgot that before this afternoon she had never seen the woman. She forgot that the woman had looked like the ghost off Christmas Past, and she hugged Marguerite as hard as she could. She hugged her so firmly that it felt like their bones had all formed together as one mass of calcium, and she whispered in her ear.

"He's gonna be just fine. You wait and see. Just fine." She couldn't believe that she was saying it to this mother of a man who was going to be trailing off to the other side of the world carrying a black gun in his arms like a baby. She didn't believe she had any right to say anything at all, but she felt compelled to tell the woman what she knew. There was no secret. Daisy had walked into the kitchen and seen into the future. What she saw was Ezra sitting on the counter top by the sink, kicking his heels off the white cupboard doors. She had no right as an outsider, but she wasn't an outsider. She was the angel Gabriel coming down to Marguerite's kitchen with the news of life. It was the second time Gabriel had been in the kitchen in less than a week.

Marguerite didn't cry. She just hugged Daisy harder and Kristie looked into Marguerite's eyes that had mysteriously become the crystal clearness of knowledge not knowing that Daisy had ever said a word. When Ezra came into the kitchen he saw Daisy pulling back from his mother and he saw that the bread zombie was gone and that his mother had returned. The house smelled warm. The kitchen thumped on and on, a healthy heart.

Once, Brenda had been in love. Brenda had been lost. Brenda had been in hell. Brenda had taken to the roads. Brenda had taken to the trees. And, now, Brenda was taking to comfort in the quiet, hushed cabin behind the walls of hemlock, locked in by cedars and ghost stories, and surrounded by gray planks of safety. Dave and Roadside Girl knew of her hideout, and it was simply a matter of time before the entire town of Toclep knew. It was not as if the people of town knew that she was even missing. All they really knew was that they hadn't seen her in awhile and that Rich was holding strong to an under-the-weather story. Lydia knew that Brenda was missing because it had been discussed at the meeting at her house. Lydia had suggested that Brenda camp on the other side of Owl Creek in the dim, little log cabin full of ghost stories. Though Tom didn't know it, Lydia had been talking with Brenda, sorting through her life.

Brenda had used the time to transcend. She wrote her dreams down on thin blue-lined paper then analyzed it as if she was trying to figure out why her chocolate chip cookies were flat. She had started to be more conspicuous. She had gone as far as using electric lights at night. Not that anyone could see that through the yearlong haze of black-green that formed the barrier between her and the road. She had sorted through Ezra's records, stacked collections of plastic that stretched higher than her head in three, square columns. She dusted the shiny, black vinyl with a piece of flannel and spun the grooved Frisbees on an old, wood-grained

Garrod turntable. She sat on the sofa looking nowhere and seeing her life unfold in tragic pages as the turntable played years through her bones. She relived '64 and '65 and '66 dancing around her mind in pre-teenage ecstasy. She spun through her troubled and turmoiled high school days. Who hadn't had those days? Days of wanting something but not knowing exactly what. Days of watching kill counts on CBS. Days of not knowing how to achieve success. Days of wanting to be popular. Days of trying alcohol, marijuana, sex—all of which were Timothy Leary-like experiments into the teenage unknown. Then as she moved into the seventies of music and memory, she started seeing the tell-tale signs of becoming Fortunato. She started to see coughing walks through the catacombs, prodding and taunting, the lock down, the slow mortar of bricks. And, finally, the enclosure—the total darkness.

Soon the time would come, when the winds would blow out of the north and sweep the stable flies of her life away. Her strength had grown. She felt like a woman. She had been beaten, but that was then. Now, she had healed at least enough to feel like it couldn't and wouldn't happen again. She looked into the mirror of the future and could see clearly where she stood. It was almost as if she were in high school again, looking at the bumbled and confused intersections of her life's freeway. She stood on an edge, but was not lost in confusion.

She hadn't had a cigarette; she hadn't had a mid-morning vodka. She had cut down on her coffee. She wasn't thinking about Rich. She wasn't thinking about Ted. She was thinking about herself. For once, it felt good to think about her happiness and not someone else's happiness. She hadn't worked in years but she longed to work and play like other people.

Brenda's thoughts broke. She could hear the fresh impacts of iron and wood shake through the trees and quiver into the logs of her outer walls. She imagined Roadside Girl beyond the trees swinging an ax through the quiet air, sending rushes of rippled sound into the forest in all directions.

It was a white-gray day and the sun tried to punch its fist through the high, elephant sky but could not quite do it. The light left shadows and made Roadside Girl squint as she cleared remnant straw out of the shed to stack the winter's straw for the roan. The dust and flakes of straw floated through the air, drifting in slow circles to the hard ground where Sam Adams packed the grass to dirt and turned the dirt to cement. Dave was splitting wood in his own dirt-packed circle. Roadside Girl was soothed by the crisp sound of the ax cutting through the hardwood. It wasn't like a basketball bouncing in the distance or a roofing hammer laying the squat, flat-headed nails. No, it was the cool separation of wood from itself in the dry, autumn air like the breaking of mammoth bones. She thought she could even hear the air, dividing and pushing away from the filed head of the ax as it split the sky and bit the wood. Her mind wandered back to the day before and her coincidental encounter with Rich.

* * *

Lydia left early that morning. She needed to go into Ironcloud. Roadside Girl was working though it was rather slow. Though she might dole out the already-filled prescriptions to anyone who bothered to come and get them, and she could fill brown bottles if someone needed something else, except narcotics, only Lydia could do that and on occasion she took phone-in orders—today there had been no customers. Lydia had commented, "the place could sure use a little dusting if you have time." Time was exactly what Roadside Girl had that morning. So she cleared shelves and cleaned walls. She dusted everything dustable including the glass fixtures around the lights. She was listening to the Rolling Stones just loud enough as to hear the phone ring and not much else. She pirouetted around and started with the sight of Rich Cafus. He gawked at her from the top of the stairs. His uniform in the shadows of the hall looked coal-black. She could feel his eyes like electric spiders crawling up and down her body.

"Jesus, you scared me." She walked over and clicked the cassette deck off.

"Where's Lydia?"

"And good morning to you." She sung it and waited, hoping to get a response or a smile or something but none of that came. "She had to go into Ironcloud. Be back this afternoon.

"Are you here alone?"

She looked around the room. The answer to his question seemed obvious to her, so she responded by nodding her head. "Just doing a little cleaning 'round here. Sure was dusty." She didn't want to tell him something she shouldn't with her eyes, so she darted them around the room like mice.

"You know, I'm not stupid."

"Huh?" She thought it was an odd way to begin a conversation but under the circumstances, which she knew and he thought she knew, his comment seemed almost logical.

"I mean...I'm not stupid. Lydia knows and if she knows so do you. I wanted to talk to her but you'll do just as well, probably better."

"Knows what?" She knew she would have to look him in the eyes if he was going to believe her.

"Don't act dumb. You know what I'm talking about." He stepped out of the shadow toward her in the main room of the pharmacy.

"I guess I don't."

"Don't I-guess me. Where the hell is Brenda?" There it was. He had spilled the beans all over the rugged floor now she would have to avoid stepping in them.

"What do you mean where's Brenda? I don't get it." She was pouting in Academy Award winning confusion and had both palms facing the ceiling in shrug. "What, you lose her?" Her comment was a bird that didn't fly.

"Goddamn, smart-ass women. Don't get cutesy with me. Just answer the question." For the first time she noticed the smooth, intense lines of cruelty on his face.

"I'm not getting cutesy. I just don't understand what you mean, where's Brenda?"

He was fully into the main room and he swung the frosted, glass door closed behind him. "Look Road-Side-Girrrl, I'm not playing games here." He stepped closer to her, and she backed away trying to keep her eyes full of shine.

"I'm not sure this is a good idea. Maybe, you should come back when Lydia returns. Maybe she'll know what you're talking about. I don't."

"No. I think this is a fine idea. Hmmm, let's see." He rubbed his chin like he had a beard. "First of all it's not really legal for you to be here with all these drugs and no supervisor. Might be some illicit dealings and such without a certified pharmacist. Yep, that's a problem, isn't it?"

"Hold on. You know as well as I do that we've worked like this. It hasn't been a problem before. There isn't anything illicit going on, either."

"Yep, sometimes the illegality of everyday things just slips your mind. Secondly, you're here alone. I didn't see anybody downstairs. That seems to be a different problem." He had pinned her against the counter that normally separated the medicine from the customer. "Don't you think?"

"What do you mean, officer?" She threw her trump card again as she had last summer. She tried to turn the law in her favor, but this time Rich didn't budge.

"That's a pretty fun game you like to play, isn't it? You want to know a fun game that I like to play." He waited. "I like to play truth or dare." She could taste his breath. He had only left a space of shallow air between them. "Truth, Where's Brenda?"

She tried to smile. Her lips were pursed and starting to tremble though he didn't notice. Never let a dog sense your fear, she thought. "What's the dare?" She wanted him to think that it was funny and step back in a chuckle at her defiance. Unfortunately, he didn't. He leaned into her so that they were chest to chest, instead.

"The dare. Oh the dare is this." He put his hand on her shoulder. He could feel her body try to slip away from his touch. "You're a nice little girl, aren't you?" He ran his hand down her arm and as he did mushy slime ran through her whole body. "Pretty, too. Let's see if you can't guess the dare?" Then he released his pistol from its holster. He didn't point it; he just held it in a menacing, barrel-down fashion.

She didn't like the game. "You're not threatening me, are you, officer? Is this harassment? Does my congressperson need to know about this?" She was afraid, but she was also afraid to show she was afraid.

He knew there wasn't really anything he could do. He could slap a fine on Lydia and close the pharmacy, but that wouldn't gain him any points in Greenstone County. He couldn't really do anything to her except try to scare her into talking, which apparently hadn't worked. She had his arm again but not like she had had it in the summer. He backed away from her. "I want to know is where my wife is, that's all. I love her and I'm worried about her. She could be in trouble. She could be laying in a ditch somewhere, raped. I just want to know where she is. How she is."

Roadside Girl knew Brenda wasn't lying in a ditch anywhere, unless she had fallen asleep in the woods somewhere while she was walking. She also knew, because she had been back to the cabin without Dave that Brenda had already been raped and that was why she wasn't around in the first place.

"Sorry. I don't know anything. I didn't know Brenda was missing. I'd like to help. When was the last time you saw here?"

He backed away. He was like a hard-to-read dog—mad, rabid, beaten. About the only thing she knew for sure was that she didn't want to stick her hand out to pet him.

"You tell Lydia I want to see her. You tell her to call me, today."

"Oh, I'll tell her all right. I'll tell her all about your questions and inquiries. You can count on that." And he had counted on that. He knew that the edginess frayed around him. He knew that Lydia would be pounding on his Pine Street door that evening. He turned at the door and she thought that he looked like a piece of cloth that was starting to come unraveled. She watched him go down the stairs and out onto Clarion. Then she went to the window and watched him get into the white sheriff's car and drive out of Toclep toward Falls Creek.

* * *

The sound of the ax and wood penetrated her thoughts. She was nearly finished cleaning the shed when the other memory jumped into her. It was so coincidental that she had a hard time believing that it had really happened. Ten minutes after Rich Cafus had driven down the street, the phone rang in the office.

* * *

"Greenstone Pharmacy."
"Yeah, Lydia. This is Ted Russell, from the high school." She didn't even get the chance to tell him that she wasn't Lydia. "Look . . . I'm a little worried about Brenda Cafus. She's . . . ahh . . . in my book club and well . . . I haven't seen her in awhile. I've tried to call her and haven't had any luck. Doesn't seem like she's been around town. I was just wondering if something had happened or something?"
Roadside Girl responded to the question as if she was Lydia, "I haven't seen her Ted, but I'm sure she's fine. She'd call me if she were having any problems."
"Yeah, I guess she would." Anxiety padded his voice. "Well, thanks, anyway."
"Nice to know the people of Toclep care about each other. Thanks for the concern," and she clicked the phone back into its cradle.
When Lydia came back to the office, Roadside Girl told her about both conversations. The first was volatile and the second,

just the opposite. She also told Lydia that Brenda was living in Ezra's cabin. Lydia told her that she already knew.

* * *

When she finished raking the scraps to the edge of the packed dirt, she leaned against the corral fence and looked to the clear Gern fields through the trees and listened to Dave hack away at the defenseless wood. She took the roan out of the corral and walked it through the woods and through the creek and through the plank gate on Ezra's nook and to the other gate on the property. She had decided that the horse should have some open space, some room to run. Everybody and everything should, really. She slapped Sam Adams' rump and he ran between the fences that separated the hay field from the pasture to Grey and Red and the five cows out near Bayside Road. Roadside Girl was happy to see the calf mingling with the others. Something in her chest felt like it grew. The horses looked mythological. They were dreams in the distance with tails of fire and wings of flight and the gods and goddesses of the heavens floated in the thin clouds that covered the sun.

As she passed the cabin, she heard faint music and looked up to see Brenda standing in the back door watching the day. She lifted her hand and waved, Roadside Girl returned the wave with a smile and a hand. She stopped.

"I'm glad you're alone." Brenda said. "It'd be nice to talk. I need to talk to a woman about the things we think about and not the things we're supposed to think about. I need to continue what we were discussing a few days ago."

"I relationship to that I'll say there are good men out there, too."

"I want to talk about life and death and future and past and me and you. Can we talk about all that?" Roadside Girl nodded. "I feel good here. I feel better than I've ever felt before. I'm not very smart, but I'm trying to read and I'm trying to write. I realize that I'm not lonely because I've been alone for years. I didn't know I was alone, but I was. I see that now. I thought that I had to get married. I thought that's what people did. They got married. They got a house. They had children. I never knew that I was supposed to be happy. I guess I used to think about that, but I completely forgot. Then, well then, I stumbled around as if I had missed an important step in the developmental stages of a relationship. Like I forgot to do step three where you connect love and life and get happiness. Then I got beat up. First, emotionally and that moved smoothly into physically. Then, I got sad and I sat in my sadness because I didn't know what else to do. But I know what to do now. I think."

"What's that?"

"Live. That's what. Just live. One life at a time. Not my life through someone else's, that's not living—that's dying." Then, as if someone had whispered in her ear she said, "I'm not young anymore."

"You're not old."

"No, I'm not old. But I'm not young, either. I'm not twenty. I don't have my youth or my beauty or my strength. Not like I used to have. I've been listening to this music." She gestured with her arms. "I've been listening to this music and thinking that all these musicians, the ones who said they—you know those old people, people over thirty, I guess—can't tolerate our minds and we, the young can't tolerate their obstruction. Well, all those people are old. I wonder what they tolerate, now. I'm like those people. I'm old now. I wonder what I should tolerate? Bad thing is, I've never been young. I've never had a chance to experience anything just for me—all by myself. I've always had to live through somebody else. Well, I don't want to live like that. I never could figure out how to do that very well, anyway. I want to live. I'm alive. I should get that chance."

"Does being in love . . . does having another person in your life mean that you can't experience life? I mean, do you think that if you really loved someone that person would allow your life to be stripped away like old paint?"

"I'm not sure. I've looked at it from only one side. I don't really know. I haven't done anything. Not in terms of living. Only in terms of dying." She said this with up-turned cheeks. She didn't sound like she thought she was Kafka, but she didn't sound like the winner of the fourth-grade spelling bee, either.

"I think you can be in love and have someone you love and still experience life to the ends of the universe. There's no reason you can't. Swans mate for life—always together. But they take turns on the nest. They fly away together to quiet, green, southern lakes and take life in like a fishing line. Then they come back up here, always living life together. And when one swan has to return alone because the other has died, that swam turns gray and withers—swimming around in the same spot, making circles, protecting something that isn't there. Then that swan dies, too, because there is no life without the other, because life is connection. We're not islands." She looked across the field knowing Tom's house was adrift in the ocean of brown grass. "We need each other to experience life fully."

"Yeah. Maybe we do need each other but we also need our own time."

"I don't doubt that." Roadside Girl tipped her head gently to the left.

"That's why I need to talk. That's why I need to write and to read and to think, because I found out, recently, that I don't know very much about life, at all."

"So what do you want? Do want to stay in Toclep?"

"Toclep's my home. My parent's are buried here and their parent's are buried here. I want to fly out of this place because of what's happened but that would be wrong, wouldn't it? I don't think I have to go away. I need to take care of some things, clear some air. Not runaway, you know? I just need to do some of the things I've never gotten a chance to do. There's nothing wrong with that, is there?"

"I don't think so. Sounds right."

"Then there's money. I've never worked. I don't have a dime. I'm not sure I can even get a job."

"You've worked. You've worked until your heart has dissolved into blackness. You just haven't had a job. When you get a lawyer and the divorce, you'll get some of what you've lost your life to. At least in monetary terms, which doesn't have much to do with happiness or life. You might even get alimony. Hell, you never know."

"I don't think there will be any alimony to get when this is all through." Brenda said because she knew something that Roadside Girl did not know. "I wouldn't want it if there was. It'd be like blood money. Rich did absorb all of the money from my parents. I don't think any of that is left. But if there is, it's mine. My father never liked Rich Cafus. He said he was shifty. I didn't listen because I thought I knew more than my parents did, like most kids think. I should've listened to him. I'm listening to him now but he can't talk anymore. It's a little late to hear what he's trying to tell me. I guess if he could speak, he'd tell me that the money from his life should be lining my pockets. You know, I love this place. I forgot I did because I forgot there were mountains and eagles and bear."

"And lions and tigers, too."

"And lions and tigers, too. I forgot there was Superior. I forgot everything. Or I didn't forget it; I just couldn't see it."

"So now that you can see it, is money that important?"

"It's money and principle. I can't live without the first and without the second life isn't worth living. At least, not this new life I'm trying to forge." Brenda wasn't acting or talking like she had weeks before with her buried feelings of insecurity. She wasn't hiding against the inner walls of her soul, the sanctuary of sanity. She was confronting the reality of the situation, and she was doing that by transcending the past. She wasn't sure whether or not a person could live in harmony with another. Roadside Girl seemed to believe people could and possibly needed to. Maybe, she could learn love but if she could, it would have to start where the little person used to hide in her soul. It would have to start deep and swim outward, growing with strength and intensity the entire way. She could learn from Roadside Girl and Roadside Girl from her, because they were the same age of sorts. Brenda had just lived more pain. They could talk. They could learn. They could laugh and they would.

With each day Brenda's interior and exterior melted. She was like April snow that padded the green grass of spring early in the morning. It melted and evaporated at the same time in the afternoon sun. That's what Brenda was. She was the spring thaw and soon her crocuses would be blooming.

A double knocking on the front door, which seemed rather odd, revived Rich. No one ever used the front door. He heard it again as the fist pounded the storm door and the storm door banged into the aluminum frame of the inner door. Though he had expected it, Rich felt annoyed by the banging. He glanced out from behind the one-way darkness of the kitchen window but couldn't see anything. He had been sitting in the subdued streetlight that shone into the kitchen through the large, front window, drinking his third beer and staring across the shadows into the empty kitchen. He wondered if he had imagined the knocking like he had imagined the man in his dreams and then it came again and shook the house. Christ, he thought. There aren't any lights on, don't you know I no longer feel like this encounter. Not now anyway.

"Rich. I know you're home. Open this damn door before I step back and kick the mother fucker in." Lydia's voice was a garden rake that scraped across the pavement of Pine Street and ricocheted off the neighboring houses. It was enough to make Mr. Berge rise off his couch and turn off the living room light so he could see what ensued. Rich stepped to the door and pulled it open. It moved freely on its hinges without squeaking. Lydia thought that probably Brenda had kept the door oiled. She didn't bother waiting for an invitation. Instead, she drew the storm door open and stepped into the darkness of the living room. She could see his outline in the unlit room. "I don't know who the hell you think you are, Rich Cafus!"

"I'm the sheriff, that's who."

"Don't be a smart aleck, Rich. Jesus Christ you haven't changed one bit from the mealy little tick you were back in the sixth grade."

"What do you know? You weren't here when I was in sixth grade." He grunted as if that mattered at all.

"I was here, Rich. Just not like this." The statement rather bothered him, in some intangible way. "Coming into my office and threatening Roadside Girl. For Christ sake Rich, she's just a kid." Everyone was just a kid to Lydia, and, of course, Roadside Girl for all intents and purposes was her child.

"Is that what she said, that I threatened her. Why that little lying bit . . . ."

"Don't even say it." Her eyes had adjusted and she could now see the faint lines of his face. "When are you gonna grow up? When are you gonna stop sauntering around here like you're Wyatt Earp? You piss me off, Rich." She was clenching her teeth so far back in her mouth that they could have been connected to her throat. "You've been a little menacing prick for thirty-some years now. Always thorning somebody's side. Always thinking that you've got something on everybody else. What you've got is shit, Rich. Don't you think you could start to mellow out a bit? I don't know what you call it, if you don't call it a threat or harassment. Telling her you have a game you'd like to play. Making sexual advances on her with a pistol in your hand."

"Is that what she said? Little slut."

"You're the little slut. You fucking putz. You don't even have the balls to come and ask me your questions? She's young and impressionable and you're god damned lucky that she's strong cuz if she was at home crying right now I'd kick your ass."

"Sounds like that's a threat to me."

"Big tough guy like you can't handle some words, Rich. And

the words of a woman on top of that." She could see him shifting in his fury.

"Don't push me, Lydia. Or you'll find yourself in trouble. I'm not up to being pushed right now."

"Yeah? What're gonna do, Rich, hit me like you hit Brenda? I'm not your fucking wife. I won't cower down in some corner and let you kick the shit out me. I don't think you have the balls, mentally or physically, to do it anyway. To top the whole thing off you thought you had to brandish your pistol in front of Roadside Girl. Prove you're tough enough to scare something out of a kid. Is that what you did with Brenda, pulled your little metal phallus out of its holster and waved it around?"

"What do you know about Brenda?"

"Is it?" He could feel the force of her breath from three feet away. "You used to pull your little pistol off your belt and make her have sex with you."

"Shut up. That's bullshit."

"Is it? That's what you used to do. Scare the shit out of her and threaten her. And what's the word I'm looking for, Rich—rape her? Is that the word? I think it is."

"Knock that off, Lydia. You're pissing me off."

"So what're gonna do pull your gun out and point it at me? I'm pissing you off? You come into my office and scare Roadside Girl with power plays and a police-issue revolver and you say I'm pissing you off? You've got some nerve, Rich Cafus."

The words came from deep within his charred lungs. "I've got some nerve? Roadside Girl's a liar. She's full of shit." Lydia could see the thin little lines of white around his eyes and smell the beer on his breath. "All I want to know is where my wife is. That's what I asked her. That's it, then I told her to have you get a hold of me. That's it."

"That's it, eh? I don't think so. I'm gonna say a couple of things, Rich. Then I'm gonna walk out that door and you and your buddy Miller High Life can sit down and mull things over."

"What's that s'posed to mean? You calling me drunk?"

"You said it Rich, not me."

"You . . . you bitch. Tell me where my wife is." He took a step toward her and she didn't move. Dave stepped onto the porch and pushed his face against the screen, making the crushed but visible image of a gargoyle.

"How long you gonna be, Lydia?" Rich was startled backwards. His momentum was sucked out like someone had switched on the Electrolux and cleaned the dust out of a corner.

"You go on back to the truck, Dave. I'll be there in a minute. The sheriff and I are just about finished here, aren't we, Rich?"

"Yeah you go on kid." His voice wavered.

"I can wait right here. I don't understand all that adult mumbo-jumbo, anyway. Won't bother me."

"It's okay, Dave. You go on back to the truck." Dave backed off the porch but he never went to the truck. He stood in the middle of the front yard like a piece of lawn art. Lydia couldn't see him because he was behind her but she could sense that he was there. Rich, however, could see him—standing in the middle of the yard with his hands stuffed in his pockets. It was dark inside but streetlight allowed Rich to see Dave's eyes glaring in on him. He felt like Dave was doing laser surgery on him and it made him uncomfortable. He tried to step out of the line of the boy's eyes but it was as if he couldn't move.

"Let's see, where were we? Oh yes, you were attacking me. That's over now, though, isn't it?" Rich couldn't respond even though anger seethed from his pores. "Okay. First, I know everything about your relationship that Brenda was open enough to tell me. Though I'm sure there are plenty more horror stories that she can't choke through right now. Those will come out down the road, after a little therapy and soul-searching. I must say it's not good. Second, I know where she is, but Roadside Girl doesn't. Nobody does, just me. And Rich . . . " There was a space—a second held in the air for thirty years. "Rich, can you hear me?"

He snarled. "I can hear ya. You're right next to me for Christ sake."

"Rich, I wouldn't tell you where Brenda is if God sent Gabriel down here to tell me I had to. My guess is that God would never do a shitty thing like that. Maybe someone else or something else would, but God wouldn't. The last thing, Rich, hear me well on this one. I let you and your friendly buddies persecute my friends. I watched, Rich. Think I have a pretty good idea of what went down."

"What friends? What're you talking about?"

"I wasn't young then, Rich. I'd seen that sort of thing happen time and time again. And I knew better than to get involved. I'm sure you don't sleep that well, Rich. I think you know what friends I'm talking about. Think about it." She frowned in disgust. "Think back to the seventies, Rich. You remember the seventies? Sure you do. In fact, sleep on it, Rich, if you can. I'm sure it'll come to you. You may wake up screaming but it'll come to you. That'll all come out in the wash in its own sweet time. I can see out there, somewhere. It's foggy though. That'll need some therapy time, too."

"What're you digging up? You got nothing on me." He sounded like a shoplifter that he might have to arrest.

"You're right, Rich. I don't have anything on you. You do. It's all over you and there isn't a thing you can do about it. Let me finish here, Rich then you can get back to whatever you were doing. I let you brow beat your wife. Rape her. Kick her around. Of course, I didn't know it was going that far, but I still could've done something. I didn't. That's my fault. But, and this is the big point, Rich. So get this one." He was still playing an involuntary game of lock eye with Dave, who had not moved or swayed from the center of the lawn. "If you ever threaten Roadside Girl again or Dave or anybody in this town—ever—you can kiss your shit good-bye. Consider that a threat. Bully to bully." She moved toward the door and he didn't move or say anything. "I can do things to you, Rich, that you couldn't imagine in your wildest dreams. And I'm quite sure your dreams are wild." He just stood there. Lydia had the door open and turned back. "In case there's some dried insect of human compassion lurking somewhere in your deep, dark soul, Rich, Brenda is fine. You'll never find her, but she's doing just fine." She let the door be sucked by the black piston behind her. As she stepped off the porch she noticed Mr. Berge standing in the shadowed darkness of his living room. His big ogling eyes said, all the better to see you with, my dear.

She turned from the yard and whispered, "Dream." He didn't hear her say it or see her lip it. Dave didn't move. He just stood there throwing his hawk vision through the screen. He was looking directly into Rich's eyes. It seemed impossible, but Rich knew it wasn't. He felt them. Dave heard Lydia's door close. He turned and was gone without Rich even realizing it.

"She's bewitched him, too." He closed himself within the darkness of his house. He had a lot to consider. Before, it had just been Brenda and he thought no one knew about her. Accursedly, someone did. He was sure the others knew. However, now there was something else. Something that he hadn't contemplated in a while but that had been gnawing on him. The thought was buried so far back in his mind that he wasn't sure if it existed or not. He stood in the living room an eternity before he went back out to the kitchen and opened the refrigerator. It spilled a funnel of light across the floor, up the wall, and onto the ceiling. It was as if he had opened the gates of hell itself. He took the rest of the six pack and shut the light off by closing the door. He sat down on the couch with the beer and turned on the television. It didn't do any good, though. He couldn't watch it. It was simply casting pinwheel colors across his body, so he turned it off and sat in the dark and finished the beer.

* * *

The darkness cleared into light and Rich could see someone hitch hiking down the road. He didn't recognize the person but he felt like he knew him. Then it wasn't a hitchhiker at all; it was

Jesus toting a cross. There were no cars and the road had turned to mud or rock or both, if there could be such a thing. Rich watched him walking now and he noticed that the hitchhiker, who was no longer a hitchhiker, wasn't alone but there were people with him. The Christ was pointing to things, and the people stopped in awe-struck amazement like they were seeing the future or a three-headed giraffe. Rich looked around but he couldn't see anything at all. Then he wasn't walking toward the crowd, but he was standing on a high bank, wearing a brown uniform. It was hot. The sun pounded him with intense desert heat. The white sun shone so brightly that he had to shield his eyes the entire time, even when he was looking down at the man and the crowd of people.

Rich wasn't one but, now, he was many and the many were telling him that something had to be done. "About what?" The mumbles came back all saying the same thing. "That, that, that." With each "that" there was pointing and confusion and Rich couldn't see the problem. What did he/they mean, "that?" There was no "that." There was only a man walking with some people, who seemed to Rich like a group friends. Suddenly, that was what Rich saw—simply a group of high chums gathered around one kid. Rich tried to see. But he couldn't see. He couldn't get close enough to tell.

Then the man was no longer a high schooler and they were all in the desert again and he wished they weren't. He didn't belong there. It wasn't his home. All the same, there was the man again. At least, he thought it was a man. This time he had more friends, and this time they didn't seem bothered by the heat. Rich recognized some of the people. He saw Mose Paxton and was sure it was Mose because he had only met three black people in his life and the other two weren't as big as Mose. He saw Brenda and couldn't figure out what she was doing with the crowd. He saw someone he recognized but didn't know who she was but was sure he had seen her before, maybe upside-down. And there was the man that he could place but couldn't recognize.

Everyone around Rich started to yell, "Arrest the man. He's making a commotion. He's disturbing the peace. Arrest him. Arrest him." Rich had to ask, "Can I do that?" Their voices all said the same thing. "You're in charge, aren't you? You're the sheriff." He thought he was, but he couldn't be sure. Maybe he should just go talk to the guy. When Rich got close to the man the other people backed away, he scared them. He raised his hand toward the man and noticed that his hand was shrunken and crippled. He continued, then he that thought he recognized the man. It was the man from the dentist office, from the large, blue picture book he had seen as a child at the dentist office. The man was friendly and didn't shrink away from him. The man was amazing. He had a presence like he knew something that no one else knew, and Rich liked him. Rich could see no reason to arrest him. "No reason," he said to the man then turned and walked away. When he got back to the raised bank, he could see the man in military trousers. No longer in the desert, Rich recognized it was Toclep. The man was standing on a sandstone stage on the edge of Superior and people were standing around him, tossing little sticks into the water. Rich was trying to figure out why. So he walked out to see what was happening.

When he finally got up to the man he noticed that it wasn't the man from the blue picture book at all. Rather, it was a young soldier wearing fatigue pants and no shirt. There was a hole that went all the way through his stomach, just under his ribs. He wasn't bleeding. Rich bent down and he could see all the way through the hole to the water beyond. It was clean. He noticed that the man didn't seem to be talking to the people around him. He seemed to speak with eyes that knew everything. Then Rich and the man stood by themselves. Alone, except for one crow that landed on the sandstone, stark black against the soft brown. It opened its mouth but didn't caw.

"I guess this is it."

"Yeah, it."

"Aren't you worried? You really should be worried." Rich said.

"No. Not really. I've gone through this quite a lot."
"You never try to get out of it?"
"Nope."
"Why not? You didn't break the law, did ya?"
"Nope."
"Are you an agitator? You stir up a bunch of problems?"
"Nope. Well, maybe I do. I seem to bother people for some reason."
"Why does it have to come down like this?"
"I didn't do anything. And that's what makes people nervous. You don't do anything and they think you're up to something."
"Are ya? Are you up to something?"
"Well no. But you can't tell people that. They won't believe you."
"I'm the law. I can tell 'em. They'll listen. They have to, cuz I'm the law."
"Law's a lot bigger than you."
"It can't be. I'm the law. I've always been the law. I make the rules."
"No. You're a man. You play by the rules that someone else makes."
"Are you sayin' you're not a man?"
"I didn't say that."
"You sayin' you make the rules?"
"I didn't say that, either. You and I don't make the rules. It's not up to us. This isn't an H.G. Wells story. It's bigger than that. Can't you see?"
"So that's it? There's nothing we can do?"
"Whoa, don't use that we thing." He was scratching around the hole that ran through his body.
"What do you mean?"
"Hold it, man. You got a connection?"
"I don't think so. How would I know?"
He shrugged, "You might feel it. I got a connection. But it's

not gonna help me much. Didn't really help me last time, either, or the time before that."

"Why not?"

"Cause that's the way it's got to be. I think it's a game."

"So what happens next? I mean we take care of this business, then what?"

"Well, I guess I go to heaven. Gotta make a quick trip to hell and let some of the others out of there. They're connection wasn't so good. Like yours, I guess. But different. But how would they have known? They wouldn't. Then I head on up the road. Another time. Another place."

"And me, do I go with you? Do I go to heaven?"

"Well, you go with me sort of... But... well, that's the problem, isn't it? No." The man shook his head. "No, you don't go heaven. You get blamed and they keep blaming you and you go to hell. I'd be glad to have you come along with me—I mean besides to somewhere else in the future, but my hands are tied. Figuratively and literally."

"I won't do it then."

"You can't, not do it. It's not in your nature. You go through with it cuz that's the kind of person you are."

"No I'm not."

"Yeah, you are. You can't lie to me. I can do something you can't do. I can see through you."

"I can see through you, too."

"Not like that. Even if you could control yourself, which you can't, you can't control destiny. None of your kind can."

"I'm not gonna do it. I'm not lying. I'm not lying." Rich had been talking quietly; now, he was screaming like a spoiled child.

"You are lying, because you're a liar. That's the way you are."

"I'm not." He was stomping. "I'm not a liar. Fuck you!" He pointed both fingers at the man and then said, "I'm not lying."

The man was non-nonchalant, worry-free. He just shrugged his shoulders. "See, you can't even see it. But I can because that's what I do. I see."

"Liar."

"You can't turn the tables like that." The man shook his head and smiled like something was oddly funny.

"Stop doing that. I'm getting tired of that." The man shrugged again. "Stop it, I said. Take him away," and when Rich said it people appeared and they did take the man away.

* * *

When Rich woke up, he wasn't out of breath or sweating. He had seen this dream before, but it was always a little different. He was never sure if he had it in the first place or not. He woke into the darkness. He wasn't afraid or angry. He was just sad.

"We all kill our own god," he said and got off the couch and dragged himself up the stairs. When he turned on the light, his pistol, that was still in its holster and draped over the straight back chair at the desk, stared at him. It seemed to be calling his name. He looked at the pistol and he thought about hell. He knew he would hear the revolver all night long, so he walked over and took it out of the holster. He felt the weight of it in his hand and it felt good to him like an old baseball bat. He tossed it in his hand a couple of times, then he sat on the edge of his bed. Thinking.

Large, autumn cumulus clouds, puffy and three-dimensional, climbed high into the sky. It was October but somehow these summer clouds had sneaked by the weathermen and had painted themselves in cotton-white stacks across the sky. It was windy on the lake but here, protected by a mile of giant hemlocks and turn-color maples, the wind pushed high above them into the sky. Tom sat on the cliff face and looked over Moose Lake. He sat down off the trail over one of the edges so that passing hikers, not that there would be any, wouldn't be able to see him. This time a year quite a few tourists came into the area for the color season. However, it was mid-week and the cliff trail would see little or no traffic today. The climb from lake level to the rocky cliffs of Moose Lake, which hadn't seen a moose in fifty years, was strenuous but not difficult. The wind coming off the big lake was being pushed over the trees in arching currents and sailed over Tom and Roadside Girl's head by a hundred feet or more. He could hear the wind as it forced the tops of the trees together, but he couldn't feel it.

"Eagles. Look." Roadside Girl sat in the grass behind him. She pointed to the north end of the lake, past the beaver dam that had formed this stretch of river into a lake; the three birds painted great circles in the currents and drafts. They watched the birds climb higher and higher into the sky without ever flapping their wings. "I wish I was an eagle."

"Yeah. That'd be something." Tom held out his arms and

slowly tipped his head from side to side, as he became one of the eagles. His eyes drifted down into the trees from half a mile in the air, scouring the ground for a field mouse and searching the river for a trout that could be snatched near the surface.

"You're a trustworthy man, Thomas Gern." He didn't seem to be listening. He was still holding his wings out at his sides. No need to flap, he had the currents. He was floating in the loud, blue winds that filled infinity. "Are you listening to me?"

"Huh? Yeah." It took him a second to put his arms down. "I mean no. What d'you say?"

"I said you're trustworthy. Helping Brenda and never saying a word about it."

"What're you talking about?" He lifted his arms and was an eagle again. He was now looking into the tannin-brown water that was three hundred feet below him. The sun's reflections looked minuscule as they flashed off the water in little jumps, fusing back into the sky and turning into nothing.

"We all know. Dave, Lydia, me. We know she's living there."

"Well how could you not know? She's got the lights on at night and the stereo playing. Probably the whole damn town knows she's there."

"You can see the lights from your house?"

"No. But I can see them. I walk around. I figure other folks walk around, too."

"Have you seen anyone else walking around? I never see anybody walking around. Tourists, maybe. Everyone from Toclep is always driving. I don't think anyone's noticed. Besides, even if they were walking around, they wouldn't be walking beyond your fence. On your property."

"I guess it doesn't really matter if they do. Thought it did at first. But she's a citizen. She's got the right to move out of her house without telling anybody and go away. She's got the right to file for divorce, if she wants. Not that I think that's always the answer." He shrugged. "Sometimes people ought to try to work things out. Course, I reckon her situation doesn't really allow for reconciliation." He was tossing small stones over the edge of the cliff. He couldn't hear them hit; they simply disappeared into the sky below him.

"Sounds like things were pretty bad."

"Yeah. Well, I can't say I'd have expected much more from Rich Cafus. He's not a human being. He's a snake. He's a liar." Tom's mind made a quick detour to the past. It dipped in and out. He watched Rich's clumsy investigation methods at the cabin, looking like he was looking but not looking at all. Rich hadn't even bothered to page through the journals that Ezra kept. It was Ezra's habit after the war to write volumes of words in hopes of explaining what he thought life did to people and how people reacted to life without thinking. They were not the words of a crazed lunatic. Rather, they were the words of reason. It was Rich who came up with the word cult and it was Rich who had influenced the state police that it was a double suicide and that there was no reason for them to bother with it because he had it all under control. Rich was present at the autopsy. That had always bothered Tom. There was no reason for Cafus to be at the autopsy. He wasn't a forensics expert, but he was there. He made the statements to the press about Ezra and Patty and Kristie and Daisy and the rest of them like Ezra was Jim Jones and the whole lot of them were part of the family. As Tom could remember, the newspaper had stated that Ezra had tried to convince everyone else to kill themselves but had been unsuccessful because the others had been too drugged up to go through with it. It also stated that "this" substance and "that" drug had been seized from the premise, which seemed odd to Tom because he had never seen any of them using drugs. The story painted eerie pictures of Ezra as Charlie Manson and Mose as Tex Watson. Tom had burned the newspaper that day and had never purchased another. Rich had scared those people out of town and out of reach, scattering them like chaff in the wind while, at the same time, scaring the townspeople back behind their own doors.

"It doesn't sound like you're the only one who doesn't trust him."

"I just don't know what Brenda thinks she'll accomplish by waiting. I mean, I'm sure that Rich was pissed at first. I'm sure he's still quite angry because his big, fat, detective mind can't drum up any clues. Seems that Brenda's a little smarter than he gave her credit for. But that doesn't really matter. What I can't understand is why she just doesn't just confront him. Get a lawyer, walk into the sheriff's office, and have the lawyer present him with the divorce papers. That's all there is to it. I don't understand all this sneaking around."

"Like you said, he's a snake. She doesn't trust him."

"So, she'd have a lawyer right there. She could let the divorce papers eat him from the inside out. That's what they do, you know." He had been looking down into the lake but when he came to that he lifted his head. Roadside Girl saw he was talking into the sky. "All that wondering. Hell, what did I ever do? I didn't do anything. And then the papers and I still didn't do anything. I just sat wondering. The more I sat the more I wondered and the more I wondered the more I sat. And she was running around downstate forgetting all the good things we had in our life, forgetting the past like it was an embarrassment, forgetting everything—our life, the farming, the canning, the laughing, the horses. Hell, they were her horses. She wanted 'em, now I got 'em—red and gray daily reminders of my screwed up relationship. And what reminders did she take? Nothing. None of the photographs or books or . . . " he paused. "Yep, from the inside out." He sighed. "Like a big old tapeworm." He stopped talking. He sat there and she sat there, too. Quiet. They were both breathing through their mouths and their throats were dry.

"That was the past. That's over now."

"Some things are never really over. Besides, I don't want to forget my past. I think the past is as important as the future. You're the one who was saying that people rush too quickly into their lives. Well I'm saying they rush right out of the past forgetting what made them in the first place. I've had a good life. Had probably a little more tragedy than usual but all in all, a good life. That's what I told Sarah. Don't know why you would ever want to try to wash away your past. It's you. It's what makes you. Of course, there are things we don't want to remember. I s'pose that's exactly what Brenda wants to do. Wash it away. Make sure the stain is gone."

"That's right. She needs to get rid of it. She needs to shed the horror. But you, you're a different story. You don't honestly believe that it was your fault that Sarah divorced you? Maybe it didn't have anything to do with you. Maybe she just needed more space, more time."

"We all need more space. Whole god damn world needs more space. That's not what marriage is all about. And, she sure didn't get more space by running down state and marrying someone else. I'm the one who ended up with the more space."

"As far as you know she is as unhappy with him as she was with you." He didn't say anything. "I didn't mean that she was unhappy, Tom. I just meant . . . ."

"I know what you meant. This isn't about me anyway. I just can't figure out why Brenda doesn't march into his office and stab him with the divorce papers. It's a helluva a blade."

"Must be some reason."

"I guess. I didn't mean to make it sound like . . . well . . . you know, that Sarah is still ripping me up. Just saying that it did. That it was hard. It's hard soup to swallow. Hurts more than your throat. I just think the past is important that's all. That's all I'm saying." He looked out over the valley that cradled Moose Lake. "It's what I know about life through Sarah that makes me smile about things with you." He said to the valley. The words slipped out off his mouth and drifted to the dark waters below him.

Roadside Girl was looking at Tom. He hadn't moved, except for when he had pretended to be a bird. He had been perched on that rock with his knees pulled up in front of him. His dark hair, which had been frosted by time, hung onto the corduroy collar of his tan jacket. The jacket hid the shape of his body, but she was looking through the jacket and could see that his skin did not sag at his sides above his belt. She saw his long arms that were more bone than anything else and she imagined how his arms looked as he baled hay by himself. This year would be the last year for that. Next year she would help him and so would Dave and they would make short order of that work. She noticed how one shoulder looked a little higher than the other. He sat on that hard rock the same way he would, sometimes, smoke a cigarette—crouched like he was sitting in air, his elbows on his thighs, the cigarette slowly burning. He would sit that way long after the cigarette was gone and when he moved out of the position he creaked and lurched in deep knee-bend pain. He had a patience that was manifested in the little things he did—like the crouch, like the silent sitting, like his two-hour, front-porch coffee. He moved slowly, not because he couldn't move quickly but because he didn't have to.

"D'you know that one of your shoulders is higher than the other?"

"Yeah. I broke it. Maybe twice."

"Maybe, twice?" What does that mean?"

"Maybe. No point in going to a doctor for something she's going to throw in a sling and tell you not to use. I don't have time for that. I've got work to do."

"Like what, Mr. I-start-farming-at-ten-thirty. Start late and then quit when you feel like it." She was smirking and so was he, though she couldn't tell because he faced away from her.

"Well, like taking care of tomatoes. They need patience more than anything. Wouldn't want to rush them through their season. Lose half their flavor that way. Nope, you got to take your time with 'em. But when they're ready, they're ready and they need to be canned. Can't do that one-handed."

"Tomatoes, huh. That it?"

"Hey now. Watch it. I work, sometimes. Get the hay in, don't I? Anyhow, I only gotta do what I gotta do. No more, no less. Like I was saying, I fell skiing once, a few years back."

"I didn't know you skied."

"I don't. This was cross-country. I was zipping down the Lakeside Trail, you know halfway up Bayside Road." She nodded. "It was night and we were skinning through the birch trees and I lost Sarah. So I scooted back up the hill, not the big hill, that little dip of a thing after the first open area. She had fallen and the whiskey bottle she was carrying in her back pocket broke, so she was trying to get all the glass out of her ass and pocket. I turned around told her I'd see her out at the lake and BOOM. Same hill I had just gone down sent me wheeling through the air. I landed right on the tip of my shoulder like I wasn't smart enough to fall down. Damn thing's been crooked ever since. I'd liked to say that it was sloppy skiing, but the truth of the matter is I probably had one too many. Oops. I'm a statistic."

"Lydia came over and pulled the damn thing so hard, I thought she was pulling my other arm through my body. I wasn't s'posed to move it for a while but that's nearly impossible." He shrugged, "so it's crooked."

It seemed like he hadn't told a story in a thousand years. It seemed to him that he hadn't talked about himself in longer than that. Roadside Girl moved down next to him on the rock. She put her arm around him. They both felt good. In the crisp, dry October air, they felt like soft, balsam boughs.

"You know, Sarah made a big mistake."

"I know." He was going to say more but he didn't want to think about Sarah anymore. All he wanted to think about was Roadside Girl. Her hair hung off her face and down over her shoulders. He liked the fact that her eyes could never make up their mind what color they wanted to be. Today they were blue with the sky. Tomorrow they might be green or brown or copper.

"I like you Tom Gern. I don't want you to take that the wrong way."

"What way is that?"

"I don't know, just not the wrong way."

"Okay then, I'll take it the right way."

"That's like you, Tom." They sat enjoying the sound but not the feel of the wind. They watched the air and the trees and the cliffs and the water and the sky and they sat there in the simple sun and high clouds above Moose Lake listening to a few birds talking in the woods. Roadside Girl still had her arm around Tom, and they both had their hearts around each other. Their minds ran off to their own universes and own dramas that played through their own skies.

The drive to Marquette was one of watching trees. Tom and Marguerite and Matthew sat in the front seat of the paneled Country Squire. In the back, staring blindly out the windows, sat Ezra and his two newfound friends, Kristie and Daisy. There was an awkward, painful silence of dread and anti-climax in the car. Marguerite held Tom's arm all the way to Marquette and Matthew held the steering wheel and they both held on in white-knuckled fear, neither wanting to release their grip for fear that they might spin off into the universe. Ezra sat between Kristie and Daisy; he actually felt like saying something, anything to cut through the grim heaviness of the car. He looked into the rearview mirror but never made eye contact with his father, who was sadly hypnotized by the narrow pavement that divided the woods of the north. Kristie had her arm snaked through Ezra's. She would have held his hand but she didn't want him to feel her cold, sweaty anxiety. Sometimes, she would glance forward but only enough to catch Ezra's shape in her peripheral and then she'd turn back to the flashing parade of trees. Daisy had her arms crossed as if touching Ezra might give her the disease of war. As if it might give her the sickness that sent people away, never to return or worse than that, to return in body but not in soul, like Krebs had returned not being able to tell his mother that he loved her because he really felt nothing at all—not being able to pray and not being able to believe there was a God. That was what Daisy feared, even though she didn't believe in God. Daisy had her upper body turned away from him and leaned her head against the window, sending streaks of blue fog up the side of the glass, muddying the trees.

"You guys are acting like this is a funeral. It's not a funeral. I'm not looking forward to this either, but I'll be back and everything will be like it was before." The sad thing was that everything wouldn't be the same as it had been. He'd be back all right but there were things happening that he couldn't see, and those things would change his life.

* * *

Ezra had a waking dream, where he saw fire and inside he cried, "Fire! Fire!" The flames were small but in each second the wind licked them higher and higher into the air like an artist painting trees from the bottom up. Ezra ran around in circles screaming, "Fire! We gotta put out the fire!" But no one seemed to hear him. The people were wearing green, fireman uniforms that didn't seem to protect them at all from the flames or the heat and their fireman hats didn't have brims. There were people inside the fire and Ezra was yelling to the firemen that they had to get those people out. A baby. I hear a baby. We've got to get those people out. He was shaking his arms and stomping around the firemen. Then he noticed that none of the firemen had faces. Their uniforms had somehow absorbed their faces in camouflage. When he went to one of the firemen and grabbed his shoulders and shook him, his face came back like a reverse Etch-a-Sketch and Ezra saw that he wasn't a fireman at all. The fireman was a child whose eyes brimmed shock-white and bled tears. The kid/fireman acted confused and started to scream, but Ezra couldn't make out the words. He could only make out the rhythm and the terror, which was saying, "Let me go, let me go. God let me go." Then he noticed something really peculiar. The firemen's hoses weren't shooting water. They were shooting fire. He stopped shaking the kid and looked around to see that he, himself, was the only one with water, but it wasn't enough to put out the fire. It wasn't enough to do anything. He was carrying a wooden bucket full of water, then, suddenly, he couldn't move. He was frozen. Something knocked him to his knees and he died. Yet, he didn't die. He awoke in thick whiteness that wouldn't allow him to move. He could see out of the corner of his eye that there were many people waiting in the whiteness but he didn't know what they were waiting for. There were muffled sounds that gave the feeling of turning a record backwards on a turntable—backwards and backwards, slowly. Some shape to his right was darker than the other white images that mingled and melted together in one wall of light. Then there was black and the black was Rae Miller's Bar. He could hear the voices but couldn't see the faces. He could smell the floating flavor of hamburgers and french fries drifting hand-in-hand with cigarette smoke. He tasted the oiliness of the air that only moved with the passage of one person then another through the bar door. It was crowded and everyone, even he, was singing. He could feel hands on his back and in his hands. Then it was light again and he was standing in the empty nook of their property looking at the large piece of granite that towered above the grasses that would feed their cows, saying that it takes a glacier to move a mountain. He turned full around and watched the fence hug the land and felt the plank arms soothing him. He was home. He was alive.

* * *

Ezra knew that he would be home again. He couldn't explain why, but he knew he would be. What he didn't know was that everything wouldn't be the same. There would be winds of change that came, howling-wolf, out of the Crescents like they were the crags of the Carpathians. He didn't know that his father would have an uninvited dinner guest feasting at his table. He didn't see the commune of friends. Why would he? He would come back from the war and resume a country life, eating apples and chewing on long slices of yellow-green grass. He would build a little house in the back and help with the farm. He couldn't see that there would be interference. That there was something else he would have to do, just as he had to do this. He didn't see the past clearly enough to realize that it showed him his future. All he had to do was look backward and he would see forward. But how would he have known that? He was only a kid himself. He was no different than the shaken face that came out of nothingness in his dream. Yes, he would come back to Toclep. Why there, is hard to say, but he would come back. Unfortunately, his country-boy life would be left in a puddle of gasoline somewhere in the green forests of Vietnam with a bunch of other country-boy puddles, all splashing around forgetting about what they used to be. All splashing together as black, leather boots trod through them, mixing and mixing and forming one giant country-boy soul in the middle of the other side of the world.

"You know, this is kinda my last chance to talk with you guys for a while. I have a feeling that Ma Bell isn't going to be dropping off any apple pie to us over there and I kinda doubt that Mr. Lukis is going to be a daily occurrence, either." He was trying to keep it light. That would be best. Keep it light. Keep it superficial, if you can. Though, that was probably impossible.

"I remember when I had to get on the train to go to the Big One." Ezra's father seldom called it World War II; he always referred to it as the Big One, which had a way of desensitizing it somewhat, as if it hadn't been a war at all. "There must have been a thousand of us in Marquette. All standing in line wanting to get over there, wanting to rush right into the war and kick some Jerry butt. This is a little different though, isn't it?"

"It's all stupid. That war, this war." Daisy said to the window, stretching the blue mist higher, to the weather stripping.

"Well, we didn't think it was stupid. We didn't really know what it all meant, but we didn't think it was stupid. There were people dying over there. Not soldiers. People. People being killed. People who had had lives just like our own and had lost them and everything else."

"I know, we studied the war," she whispered so he couldn't hear.

"I'm sure you studied the war but it isn't like the books. The books weren't there. We were there and people were dying. People just like you and me or they had been like you and me before the war. Then the persecution, the long cattle excursions—it was like they were shipping meat to the factories in Chicago."

"Stop it, Matthew." Marguerite squeezed into Tom's arm.

"I'm not proud that I was there. I'm not stupid enough to believe the people I shot my M-1 at were any different than I was, but that's war. It's not right but that's the way it is. Some people, who would have died, didn't. And they didn't die because we, the big we, the

United States, stopped it. There was a monster in Europe but we stopped it."

"Yeah, well Nixon would have us believe that the same threat is upon us."

He looked at Marguerite and saw the sadness in her eyes. "This isn't the time or place for this discussion." He wasn't angry; he was just saying what he believed. "I'm not sure our President," he emphasized the word, "truly believes that this is anything like the Big One or that we should be there at all. I'd imagine it's a mighty worrisome chess game for him. The rest of them at the top, I don't know, but he inherited this."

"Well I know. A bunch of fat cats pushing the sons of America off to die." Daisy grew angry every time the word "war" surfaced its ugly, dragonhead. She hadn't even realized what she said and Marguerite moved uncomfortably in front of her. "It's not their blood." She was angry to be riding in the back seat of a station wagon taking another human being, her friend, off to get on an airplane to join the effort. It fact, she wasn't sure exactly why she was there except that she felt like she had to be.

"Please. Do we have to . . . ?" Marguerite's voice cracked.

Tom was sitting next to the door. Though he was looking out the window toward the passing trees that raced by in columned thousands, he didn't really see any of them. He knew they were there. They were always there and always would be there.

* * *

The trees turned into men and the men marched along this highway and every highway in America. The tree-men were urgently following some great, blind-faith cause into battle, but they were worried and confused because they couldn't see the cause. It raced in front of them somewhere, so they followed it, trying to catch up to it. Maybe, once they found it, they would decide it wasn't a good cause. They could choose then to join it or beat it up or turn-tail and run back to the quiet, timbered forests from which they came. In the trees, he saw Ezra. He kept seeing Ezra. All the man-trees were Ezra. They were running and stumbling over each other. They weren't anxious; they were out of control—panicked, destinationless, running. He could see fire ripping through the trees in a fulminated circle, from all sides. Tearing the bark from legs and arms and spitting molten chunks of earth through the masses, breaking them in two, separating head from trunk, crushing chests and limbs. He watched a million Ezra's get their heads torn off by Charon spears—movement ends, top falls off, body crumbles to the ground. He could see the slow transfer of forward motion to downward knee drops like the tree-men were genuflecting at the altar of their God. A God that would pound his iron-wrath fist directly down on them and they would shatter into tiny, hollow pieces of thin porcelain in the green, chess fields of life.

Tom saw it over and over again. He saw it in the clear, bright sky and in the red forests. It wasn't the trees he was seeing. It was the life, the life of his drafted brother, who collapsed like a card table. And maybe there was more to it than that. Maybe, it was everyone who was undertowed into the waxing tide. Maybe it was the whole country, the whole world about ready to explode and melt away like a ga-zillion atom bombs and hydrogen bombs lighting up . . . "the rockets red glare . . . " It was his brother, but it was more. It was the melting eyes, the disintegrating bodies—the skulls exploding like mushrooms hit by a golf club, and, worst of all, it was everybody gone—the earth coming back to life, all by itself. Sprouting trees and rivers cleaning themselves, cleansing the poisons from their blood and the animals gone with the people—pied-pipered off. It was the ringing silence of a million years. It was everything, gone. Everything, except him.

All the man-trees were his brother. All the tree-men were him.

* * *

They were coming into Negaunee. They would sweep through Marquette before the dip to the Sawyer Air Force Base. They would stop and have one last family supper—one last chance to say grace together and pass each other the salt and pepper. It wouldn't be one of Marguerite's home-cooked meals. It would be the potato blandness and over salty gravy, the pseudo-hominess of a restaurant trying to be something it is not. They didn't know now but they would know when they got there that it would be the skeleton Last Supper of every non-uniformed soldier headed off to war that day.

Kristie didn't seem to notice Negaunee. It was as if Negaunee wasn't there at all. But she did notice how the car had seemed to slow down. She hadn't looked over Matthew's shoulder, but she was positive that he had decreased speed. He was trying to prolong the silence that was trapped inside the car. She turned to look at Ezra's profile. He sensed her look and turned a smile in her direction. She tried to smile too, and did with her lips, but her eyes were holding the strong funeral grimaces of a Catholic procession line after the Rosary.

"I don't know about you," she whispered. She spoke softly so no one would hear her. Daisy had most of her body turned toward the window and Matthew and Marguerite's attention was focused on their bloodless knuckles that wanted nothing more than to turn the car around. She moved her head so her lips were touching his ear. Her soft, dry lips sent an unseen quiver through his nervous system. Her lips filled his veins with sand like his whole body was asleep. He was paralyzed. "I wish," she shifted her eyes around the car. "I wish we would have slept together." She quietly kissed his ear, which sent a coursing stream of electricity through his body.

"Me too," he breathed. His lips moved and she saw the words but not one sound issued from his lips. She squeezed his hand and far below the surface, under the sand he could feel the squeeze.

She looked at him, strong in the face, and he was looking forward into time, then she turned back toward the window. She remembered back to the northern-lighted sky after Chicago. They had stumbled through the dark trees, run into one another in the night, and tried to find pieces of wood without reaching their hands into the unseen ivy at their feet. He had taken her hand and they stopped.

* * *

"Look. Look through trees." He pointed with his words to the circular, faint blues and washed yellows and muted reds in the sky. The lights circled and seemed to come from all directions at once. "Not much as beautiful than that." They could both hear the night bugs and the attempted hush of their muffled swallows in the shining stars.

"Not much." He could see her face as she peered into the sky and he remembered the hollow, dented skin of her throat.

"Not much, but you." He didn't think about it. He simply bent forward and kissed that spot as softly as a violet petal. He couldn't see it with his eyes but he could with his mind. She let him kiss her neck, even though, she should have collapsed because inside of her all her bones had turned to quicksilver and were flowing toward her feet. She dropped the few sticks she had and pushed him against a tree and kissed him, eyes staring into black eyes.

Kisses had been it, though. When they were skinny dipping, all three of them had glazed their bodies off each other raising electrical urges. The skinny dip was supposed to be fun and not sensual but it had been both for all three. When they came out of the water, they warmed their naked bodies by the fire looking at each other. Each of them was cautious and they packed their excitement away in the catacombs of their minds. As they lay in the tent, each listened to the other breathe. They couldn't help it. Kristie had slipped her arm across Ezra's waist when she thought he was asleep. He was lying sideways and his eyes were open, but he didn't move. He pretended. When they woke in the morning, Ezra had his arm around Daisy and Kristie had her arm around both of them. They had slept cheerfully.

The weekend at the farm when they had received the D.O.D. blow and felt its aftershocks had turned them into sister and brother. The fact that they were never alone, always three, did not help. Daisy had been wearing her flaring war-anger yet at the same time wanted not to. On the second night in Toclep, the night after each had tossed and turned in conglomerate, erotic dreams of romance and world destruction, there was truth.

"I really like him." Kristie said to Daisy as they lied together in Uncle John's bed. "There's something I can't explain about him. It's not his looks. It's something inside, but it's different than anybody else I've ever met."

"I know. I can't explain it either. I want to wring his neck. I want to kiss his lips. I want to be angry with him. I want him to touch me. I want to touch him. But I can't. It's like he really does know something that the rest of us don't. And damn that bothers me."

"Then you're . . . you know, sexually attracted to him, too."

"That would be a yes. I know you are. And I almost, I never

thought about this before. I almost started something that night we were camping but . . . I wasn't sure. And hell I don't want any jealous feelings toward you or from you."

"I couldn't tell. You're so harsh to him."

"It's because I care what happens to him."

"You think we could share?"

"Maybe, early we could . . . but it doesn't matter, now. We've got to go back tomorrow and he's getting shipped off. It doesn't matter, now." They would come back to Toclep for another visit before the trip to Sawyer. However, that trip would be filled with awkward silences and misdirected conversations about nothing.

"Maybe." The last words had made them both cold and Kristie hugged Daisy and held her as they both ran could-have-been movies through their heads.

So there had been no sex. Only strong feelings of attraction and wanting like Whitman's pent-up aching rivers.

As they pulled into Marquette, Kristie was dreaming of the long kiss—the pulsing of bodies together in the cold, blue sparks of broken glass, shocked and startled and refreshed like a bath of menthol fingers. She saw herself quivering in skin that was too loose for her body as he brushed his feathered hands over her, brushing her lines and curves like soft, oil paint. She was over-excited. She wanted it to stop because she was in a car full of people. At the same time, she wanted it to last forever like she was in a bed with him. It was a dream. She felt a rippling, warm sensation in her breasts. No, they hadn't made love, not out there, but they had in Kristie's cloudy dream.

* * *

Dinner was a quiet, tongueless meal of food that under any other circumstance would have had flavor but today had none. There were twenty-six glassy, sad, fear-filled eyes swimming around the clinking and clanking of butter knives and forks against plate-stone. There was under-breath mumbling like everyone had halitosis and didn't want anyone else to know. There were looks from one table to the next that all said the same thing. There were kids who didn't know what they would see tomorrow and parents that hoped their kids would see tomorrow. Had there been an organ gently playing Amazing Grace, the whole thing would have been the melancholy pall of a casket. The only eyes with spirit were the eyes of the soon-to-be soldiers who knew the story of the little steam engine that could. They had to believe they were coming back. They had to. If not, they wouldn't come back at all or they'd come back in a black, zipper bag. As the cars left the restaurant they should have been equipped with miniature, magnetic flags with dark crosses on them. The stream of cars from this restaurant and that cafe seemed like a solid line heading toward the air force base. It was as if all cars headed in the same direction. Some cars skirted off into long, low motels that lined the road between hell and Sawyer—one more night together before the flight in the morning. Others drove right to the base, dropped off their son and tears like laundry and drove away with a pocketful of emptiness.

Matthew Gern knew better than to prolong the agony. He had seen it before. When he had shipped off to the Big One, he had watched Clyde Lampardson hold his mother like they were velcroed together. As if there would be a terrible ripping sound if someone had tried to separate them. They had hung and clung and she had cried and he had tried not to cry but couldn't help it because he was scared. Matthew had watched them. He had waited so he could board the train with someone he knew. So he could go off to war feeling like he had a friend in tow. His parents had hugged him in Toclep before he had gotten into the Lampardson truck. His good-byes were in the past. His tears were mixed with dirt in the driveway in front of a large, white house that belonged somewhere else. There seemed to him to be so much silence on the platform where hundreds of people were saying, so long—it's been good to know you. Then, they were all on the train and the whistle blew but nobody heard it and arms waved and it was still silent. The war ended and Matthew came home and Clyde Lampardson was the only person from Greenstone County to die in the war.

Matthew didn't need the long drawn-out silence of sitting around a motel room with his sunken-eyed wife and draft-shocked sons. And Marguerite didn't need to stare at her son all night, watching him go through every stage of his life: birth, baby, child, adolescent, teenager, teenager, teenager, teenager and have the record skip there for ten hours as she tried to muffle tears into her pillow. That wouldn't do and Matthew knew it. They had gotten Ezra a single at the Cozy Inn. He would spend his night alone. He might sleep that way. At least, that's what Matthew thought. Ezra would face the monster himself because that's the way it was going to be, anyway. Matthew would drive back through the dark trees with the road-hum lulling Marguerite and Tom into the crevices of their minds and they would face the ghosts in the morning. Marguerite wouldn't sleep, but at least she wouldn't sleep in her own bed.

There were tears and tight, bone-crushing hugs. The good-byes were said. Marguerite fought them.

"See ya," she kept saying. "You be careful."

Matthew knew that careful was the wrong idea. You be lucky, he thought. Then he took her hand, pulled her away, and said very quietly and calmly, "You need to say good-bye. It's okay." He hushed her with his soft voice. "It's okay. Doesn't mean anything but good-bye, but you need to say it." She was crying. She hugged him.

"I don't want to say it."

"I know you don't. But you've got to. You've got to say those words so you're not sorry that you didn't say them later. If you don't say them now, you may never get another chance. Now, tell your son good-bye."

She rocked Ezra like a baby and breathed, "good-bye," over and over in his ear.

Behind Marguerite the girls were talking to Matthew.

"We're gonna stay." Daisy whispered to him. "It's not an emotional thing. It's not sad. We're gonna stay an make sure... well, and make sure..."

Matthew didn't say anything at first then he asked, so softly that Daisy could barely hear him, "How will you get back, your car's in Toclep?"

"We'll hitch hike. It'll be okay. We've done it quite a lot. There's two of us." She ushered her finger back and forth between her and Kristie.

"I'd say no. You know, I'd say no normally though that wouldn't stop you." They both looked at him with yes in their eyes. "Don't know exactly what his mother will think of this but he's my son, too. I'd stay myself and talk to him about the whole thing but it would break Marguerite in two." He looked at his wife hugging her child then blankly said "You know how to reach us if you get into any trouble."

"There won't be any trouble, Mr. Gern. We just think that he might want the company. It won't be the silent company of the ride over. We're all kids." She couldn't believe that she phrased it that way but she had and it was true.

"Thanks." He reached into his pocket and pulled out a twenty-dollar bill. "Make sure he gets something to drink tonight, okay." It was a secret pact—a pact better off not known by Ezra's mother. Matthew Gern knew they were not kids. They were what the newspapers were calling the youth of America. They needed to take care of each other. They needed to stand together. They weren't going to let Ezra sit in the yellow quiet of a motel room on some lonely highway, waiting to face the Green Knight, himself. Matthew knew more about this night than any of them knew, and that's why the proposition was okay to him.

Everyone walked to the car. Matthew directed Tom to the back. Marguerite got in the front and closed the door. Matthew stopped on the other side of the car. "You be careful." They couldn't hear him in the car. "Write your mother. I know you'll be fine. I trust you." Then he did something Ezra had never seen him do before. He pointed to his eye and slipped behind the steering wheel. When the girl's closed the back door, Marguerite turned to Matthew. "It's okay," he said. "It's okay." Matthew put the car in reverse and Ezra waved, his left hand shielding the sun from his eyes, until the car was enveloped in light and disappeared into the horizon. Daisy and Kristie weren't waving. They let Ezra do that.

Ezra thought about his father putting his finger to his eye. The thought sailed with him across the universe and he saw it, everyday. He could see the lips of his Dad's eyes mouthing, "I love you." When he got back he would ask his father and Matthew would say, "I used to do that to your mother—a finger to the eye, then to the heart, then to her. I-Love-You. We finally just shorten the message to one finger to the eye. I hadn't used the signal in a long time. But, it was called for."

The car was gone. His parents saw the light of day disappear which was okay because they didn't have to face each other all the way home. There wasn't a word spoken. Ezra and Kristie and Daisy stood for a long time in the gravel of the Cozy Inn, looking out at the setting sun, which no one had noticed had been in the sky all day.

"Think we'll be able to buy anywhere, tonight?" Ezra asked.

"Think we'll be able to buy everywhere tonight. D'ya see that restaurant? Big old funeral. Yep, there'll be a party tonight unlike any Irish wake you've ever imagined." Daisy had a way of dolling out honesty like the government dolled out draft cards.

"Let's go to the room first." Kristie said.

"Yeah." Yeah was a butterfly that floated just over their heads.

It had rained in the night. Lydia walked around her house, which hunkered down for the winter, while Dave cut the grass, probably for the last time of the season. This morning she could see her breath, like coffee steam, drift out of the shade into the sunlight. Her flannel lined, Levi jacket covered her. Dave was in shirtsleeves and the bottoms of his jeans were soaked up to the knees.

"Might be a little wet for that," she yelled over the yard. Sam Adams turned his head but Dave didn't hear a word she said. She cupped her megaphone hands over her mouth and tried again. This time Dave heard. He reached up with his foot and pushed the piece of makeshift metal against the spark plug. "You think it's too wet to mow?" She yelled into the now quiet air, her voice banging around the yard between the trees.

"I don't. But you seem to." He bent down and lifted the front of the mower to see how much grass was stuck to the roof of the mower's mouth. When he lifted the wheels off the ground, the not-so-air-tight gas tank lid let gas seep out and puddle and gunk on the flaky paint of the mower. "Looks okay from here."

"Dave." She stopped because she got a strong whiff of grass. The cut-grass aroma was running around the house like children happy to have the snow gone and that smell took her thoughts away for a second to her childhood and left the word, Dave, drifting about the yard.

* * *

Her gray-haired mother, whose hair made her look like she was a hundred but whose skin and hands looked like those of a seventeen-year-old girl, was able to make smells like grass in her kitchen. Spring smells in the middle of winter that spoke, "Look outside; it's May." Lydia looked down at her own hands. How old was she now? That was such a hard question to answer. It depended on whose time scale she used. Her hands were replicas of her mother's hands—long, thin fingers with smooth, strong knuckles like old gears and soft, transparent nails. As a little girl, her hair stuck up in tufts around her head, not like other girls her age. She remembered the cabin in the Maine woods—out away from the townspeople, out in the old, crippled hickory trees where the townspeople said witches lived. She played by herself in those canopied woods. Trees often turned into giants and stumps into dwarfs and she always had someone with which to talk and play games within the trees. The trees never laughed or gawked or made fun of her. The trees never ogled in disbelief or moved off the dirt path away from her. The trees were friendly. They weren't like people. They were easy to live with.

She remembered farther back to rocky, open fields that rolled one onto the other. Immovable, giant stones stood sentinel over the far-reaching grasses, which faded into the sun and sank deep in the sea, like a rock thrown into a swamp. Her mother had been young then. Her black-red hair, long, with no signs of the gray winds of time and her hands, her hands had been exactly like Lydia's were now.

Lydia could remember no father. In that respect she was like Roadside Girl. Lydia and her mother had been pushed from that land by changing tides and pushed out of the next place by the same tide that continued to grow and intensify and strangle with strictness and adherence. She was used to that tide. It was the tide of the people. It was the tide of knowing just enough to know nothing at all. It was the tide of too much of one God, the tide of closing doors, the tide of throwing the past to the wind as if the wind could carry it away.

*** * * ***

Lydia was now looking at her hands. They were her mother's hands and her mother's mother's hands, hands that floated from time to eternity. The smell of the grass reminded Lydia of that and it made her sad.

"Yeah." Dave stood by the quiet, dead lawnmower. The lawnmower that was like a wood tick, sleeping for dormant years ready to catch the smell of passing blood, to be awakened with the urgent need to jump for its life and lock onto something with flavor, something with nourishment.

"Just about last night. You didn't have to worry about me. I would have been fine. But I'm glad you came up to the door. You pushed his fury away. I'm not sure if it was that he saw you as a witness or saw you as the child he wished he still was. Whatever it was quelled his anger. I just wanted to say thanks."

"He's afraid of me." Lydia stifled a laugh and Dave's face grabbed a little dust of disappointment from the sky and tightened. "He is. He's afraid of my eyes." She could see he was serious, so she tightened her face back into seriousness. She could remember how people had treated her as a child. She could remember knowing things that adults would never know or that they had known but they had forgotten as soon as they turned into adults.

"What do you mean, Dave?"

"I'm not sure if he knows it or not, but I'm afraid of his, too. Doesn't matter. His eyes were screaming bloody murder. Not when I was on the porch, but after that, when I was in the yard. It scared me, but it scared him, too."

Lydia closed her eyes and saw Rich's face in the dark living room. Her eyes had adjusted and she could see his wide pupils stretching and filling up the white gelatin of his eyes. They weren't focused on her. After Dave's interruption, Rich's eyes did little fox-focuses back to her every so often. Though for the bulk of the one-sided conversation, they were locked on something beyond the screen. Then, for a flash, she thought, they were locked on something beyond this world. "What?" She hadn't meant to say it aloud but she had.

"I think he's afraid of little kids."

"You're hardly a little kid, Dave."

"You know what I mean. I felt something really spooky last night when I was sitting in the truck. I thought, here's a house, dark as a coalmine, and there's a man sitting inside, by himself, waiting for something. I asked myself what he was waiting for and something said you." He pointed. "A wave of scared hit me and I jumped out of the truck and ran up to the door. And you know what, he was lurching at you like the wolfman."

"You're being a little over dramatic, aren't you?"

"No. That's what I saw when I got to the door. Him in forward motion, swelled up like a cat ready for a fight. Inside, I was yelling don't touch her. Don't you dare touch my . . . " The word spilled out like corn syrup, clear and slow with trapped bubbles of air, "mother. I don't know why I thought that, but I did." Lydia wanted to say something but Dave continued without so much as a breath. "I locked eyes with him then. I never took my eyes off him. Not for a second. It was like there was a coyote in the barnyard. Nope, I didn't move my eyes until you were in the truck. I don't think I even blinked. And I think that, even in the darkness, he could see that I hadn't blinked. He could see that I could see," then one slow word, "everything." Dave shuddered in the cool sunlight. "I saw something bad inside him. He knows I saw it and that scares him. It scares me, too."

"You don't have to be afraid of Rich Cafus, Dave. He won't bother you. He's like a fly."

"That's what scares me. He's like a maggot-laying fly." She wanted to walk over and put her arm around him and tell him everything would be okay but she wanted him to finish so his mind would be free of the incident. "I saw something last night, like you see somebody's gold tooth when they smile." Roadside Girl stepped out of the sauna and broke the conversation.

"Hey Dave, why don't you get up a little earlier tomorrow and get the chain saw running? Better yet, get up on my roof with a hammer and fix those shingles." She was standing on the shaded, wood step in her bare feet that had lost their summer toughness. She could feel the strings of wooden sinew under her feet. Her flannel pajamas didn't keep her warm in the morning air and she tightened her arms across her chest. It was obvious that she had just come from bed because her hair was melted to her head like she had just popped out of a toaster.

"Nice hair. Are you sure you don't need a hat?" He laughed. It broke his seriousness. "Maybe I will. It looks like some of those shingles could use fixin'." Then he turned back to Lydia and he spoke to her. Roadside Girl couldn't hear him. "I saw death last night, and he knows I saw it. That's why he was so scared." That was it. He turned back to the mower with the clayed gasoline on its body. He pull-started it back into its echoing life. Before Lydia turned away, she noticed that Dave had forgotten to say something and he called out through the wall of thunder, "you're welcome," then moved off with the echoing mower away from her.

"I'm glad you're up." Lydia called across the yard like she was on one boat and Roadside Girl was on another and they were passing each other on a river. "Why don't you throw some clothes on and take a walk with me."

* * *

As they approached the creek they could both see that Brenda was getting braver. She was now not only outside but also sitting in full view in the sun on the east side of the mountain out past the sweat lodge. She was sitting in an old, metal porch chair with a book in her lap, but she wasn't reading. She wasn't looking down; in fact, her face was turned up full volume to the morning sun that was peeking over the tops of the trees. When they got to her they could see by the wet grass that she had moved her chair two times to be in the sun. She had on big Sorrel boots and oversized blue jeans and Ezra's military jacket. She looked like she had lost something.

"New clothes?"

"Well a woman can't wear the same thing day in, day out. Can't alter the boots but a little needle and thread time on these pants and they'll be all mine." The sun was good for Brenda's face. Lydia didn't remember how beautiful she was and now in her new clothes, she looked more beautiful than ever. It was a somewhat homely beauty, but it radiated all the same. In fact, Brenda looked more like a girl playing dress up than a woman. The radiance around her made it hard to tell whether the sun was lighting her face or her face was lighting the sun.

"Whatcha reading?"

"I'm not. I'm holding. I thought that it would look a little better if someone wandered along. And look, somebody did, eh?" Brenda looked fresh. Clean. Happy. She didn't look like she was afraid. Roadside Girl had visited and Brenda had talked and talked. Nevertheless, Brenda hadn't looked like this before. If she had, it was on that day that she sat on the bottom of the ocean out under the hemlocks in the perfect isolation of nature.

"So what are ya doing?"

"I'm just sitting here. Sometimes, it's nice to just sit on a Saturday morning."

"It's not Saturday."

"Saturday, Wednesday. Not that it makes much difference what day it is. All kind of the same to me."

"Sunday."

"Yeah. It's nice to just sit and look at the grass and the sky and the fence." She said it as if she had lived in the cabin her whole life—as if she were an old farmwoman who might look out across the fields of Montana to her lodge pole fence in the distance—Little House on the Prairie. "And do nothing. Just sit."

"Brenda, I saw Rich yesterday," Lydia said.

Brenda looked up without fear at the mention of Rich. It made Roadside Girl wonder if Brenda had forgotten who Rich was.

"I went to the house. He's not looking all too stable. Sitting around in the dark, drinking beer."

"Well, I guess he hasn't changed too much, has he? Always was sitting around in the dark. You know, I don't hate Rich. I should. I should despise him. I should cry. Damn him, damn him to hell. But he's going there for what he did to me anyway. And for what he did to Ezra—for what he's done to this town."

"What d'ya say?"

"Nope. I don't hate him. I pity him. I pity him. What he's . . ."

"What'd you say about Ezra?" Lydia had stirred her own memories the day before and, now, here was the bowl of memories again. She could hear Dave running over sticks in the backyard through the trees and it made her think of ribs breaking.

"Well, I guess I have a lot to say today." There was an awkward calm about Brenda. It made Lydia feel uneasy and it made Roadside Girl unexplainably glad, confident in herself. "It's too cold to sit in the house but there are a couple of those folding chairs in the storage area under the stairs. Maybe we could have a little Pow Wow out here in the grass. Maybe Roadside Girl could make some more coffee." And, she thought, we could all sit in the warmth of each other as the sun dances its way into the yard.

They sat in a semi circle facing the sun. The speckled coffeepot was cooling in the damp grass that needed cutting. Roadside Girl had offered to go get decaf but Brenda had opted for full strength. The coffee smell swirled around in the blue, sun-lighted steam that looped its way into the sky.

"Rich has got some skeletons. He probably never thought

his bony, hidden friends would come back to hack him up like he was in a Sinbad movie. But they will. They will." She moved into a slow tale matter-of-factly. "I've been afraid of crows," she said. "I've been scared to death of crows for a long time. Not just any old highway-variety crow sittin' on some decaying, scaggy carrion. Nope, not those crows. But two crows in particular that are always sitting in the tree in our—no, his front yard. Sometimes they're perched on the garage or birdbath or between the house and the sauna. But no matter, they're always around. You go over to that house right now and those two crows, bigger than usual, are there. I never realized it before, but those crows are the same black birds I saw suspended upside-down in mid-air, twenty years ago, above the baseball diamond."

Roadside Girl looked confused because she didn't see the connection between the crows and what had happened to Ezra. There was no reason for her to make such a connection. "I saw them that morning. I'd been out with Katrina and when I was walking home I saw those birds in the distance." Lydia listened intently. "God, I felt cold that morning." Brenda said. "Anyway. The birds at the house, they're the same birds. Not the same kind of bird, mind you, but the same exact birds. They've been around that house ever since we moved there and before that they were at that place of Bole's we used to rent. I can't recall not seeing those birds after that morning.

"They used to come into my dreams, too. I thought they were coming to get me. I thought they were calling me out. Telling on me, 'she sneaks drinks during the day, Richie. She's been lying to you. She's sleeping with another man.' The more I thought about it the more I realized that the ugly birds had been around long before that. I didn't know that the crows weren't cawing for me." She laughed a little. It wasn't a distant, awkward laugh. It was a real, honest chuckle. "No one knows for whom the crow caws, it caws for thee," and she laughed again. "Saw that movie . . . with Gary Cooper, I guess . . . about a month ago. I didn't know it would make so much sense to me today.

"Anyhow, that's just it. The crows weren't there for me; they were there for Rich. Watching him. Spooking him. I've dreamed about the birds over and over and my guess is, so has Rich. I had a dream the other night. It's kind of hard to keep track of time these days. The crows came to me and scared me, at first. Then, I realized they only came to me to tell me that they weren't my birds. I've always hated those birds with their black beaks and black bodies bleeding together in one mass of shiny blue-black darkness. Their black, beady eyes separated, split on different sides of the beak, both looking at me from different angles. Hahhh." She shook. "And that cawing. That screeching, blood-curdling screaming like they were in pain. It would vibrate through my body and raise my hackles like I was a wild animal.

"The birds came to me in a dream, and I started writing. I started thinking about my past. I hadn't done that in a while because...well because, my past hasn't been too good, you know?" Roadside Girl had gotten a pretty clear picture of Brenda's married life and she nodded her head. Brenda pulled her coffee cup to her lips. The coffee was tepid, but she drank it anyway. "In the dream I saw the crows as clearly as I see you now. And I realized they weren't crows at all. They were Ezra and that girl, Patty. They had always been Ezra and Patty and that's why they had always watched the house. I was in my dream, too, but more important were the birds.

"I saw Rich in his brown, county uniform circa 1978, no 'stache. Others gathered and they were all laughing. I'm not sure who all of them were, but one of them was Seiler Stephenson. You remember old Seiler, don't you Lydia? Dumpy old Seiler, who never lost his baby fat or his baby brain. I know it was him in the dream cuz I've never known another man that big in my life." She patted Roadside Girl's hand. "They used to make fun of Seiler at school. They'd bray like a horse when he went by, *Sssssssseiler*. They'd do that and Seiler would pretend he hadn't heard and turn his face down as he walked on. Story goes that good old Seiler got caught, well, you know, doin' it with one of his daddy's horses. Rumors like that sail through high school hallways faster than water comes out of a faucet. Anyway, I know it was Seiler because I can still remember his stupid Hardy-harhar laugh. Broken. Laughing but not laughing like he was afraid to laugh or didn't know how to laugh or like it reminded him that everybody was always laughing at him.

"My guess, if I was gonna guess, would be that the other laughing boys were Wiles, John not Tim, and Eric McCrogey. In the dream, I watched them—three, maybe more, pounding Ezra with ax handles like they were laying track for the Trans-American railroad. Patty was trying to fight herself free but one of them cracked her on the head and she collapsed in the grass.

"Patty was from out of town. She didn't even hang out here. She just happened to be in Toclep on the wrong weekend. I remember seeing her parent's, dead and silent, wondering what the world was coming to. And two months later that news from Jonestown came. Poor people. They probably tied the whole thing to cult mentality just like Rich tried to do. I say tried, because his effort is foiled now. God, they were so sad looking when they packed their baby into the back of the mortuary van to transport her to Kalamazoo, a nation away.

"Yeah. Tragic." She paused then started again. "I know it sounds weird but I saw it. I saw it all like I was there. Because I was there, at least in my dream I was. There's more though. I watched them beat Ezra and I watched him die. But he wouldn't die. He turned into a fire and floated above their heads and they all stopped and they were all scared. And I guess the fire turned into those crows. Always those crows in the yard. Well, one of them came in the dream and spoke with a voice that I knew but I hadn't heard in a while. It was Ezra's voice and he said, 'everything will work out.' I believe him." She stopped. Lydia had seen like situations, which had ended with similar results, in her past. So many years ago she couldn't remember all the names.

Roadside Girl's intellect told her there must be more but oddly enough they all sat in silence. So she said, "I don't mean to sound disrespectful or like I don't believe you, I do." Roadside Girl began, "I believe you had this dream just the way you said you did. I also don't want to sound like I know anything about the psychoanalysis of dreams. But couldn't this all be scapegoating? I mean Rich hurt you. He hurt you a lot. You've been watching these crows and seeing them in your dreams. So, the two come together one night and unite in one prophetic dream that seems to nail Rich to the cross. It seems elementary to me. Like I said, I'm no Freud but it seems like you're subconsciously transferring your anger and hate to the most likely suspect. That, and you're lying around a deserted house that everybody's been calling haunted for years. I'm not sure all of this would fly in a court of law. Maybe, over in Newberry at the nuthouse, but . . . "

"It's a prison now." For the first time Brenda's voice sounded distant.

"What?"

"Newberry. It's a prison. They closed the mental institution." She wasn't angry or disappointed with Roadside Girl for her disbelief. The whole thing did sound like something with which Freud would have a field day, but she could see that in Lydia's eye there was something of relief. "There's more. Remember in '78 how everyone lit out of here like the town was on fire? Ezra's friends scattered to hell and high water. You even left." Brenda turned to face Lydia. "Those people were more scared for their lives than the rest of the town and they had every right to be. But it wasn't just them. In fact, as Rich started the investigation Wiles, Bower, McCrogey, and Stephensen all vacated. Vanished. Disappeared like they'd never been alive. My guess is that most of them have been working as carpenters and fix-it men, doing under-the-table work for money with no taxes and no social security. Or they're all in Canada. It wasn't so hard to get into Canada in '78, not like '70. Not like they would have to be in hiding. No one ever accused them of anything. They could all be living fine lives with wives and children and social security and all of that with big, fat, suicide crows flying around their dreams. Nope, nobody accused them of anything, nobody but me, right now. Anywho, I hadn't thought about it in a while. In fact, I never thought about until I was writing in my journal. It seemed so everyday, I was so used to it, I just didn't notice."

"What? What seemed so everyday?"

"Well around Christmas time, Rich got a phone call. I was upstairs."

"Last Christmas?" Lydia asked.

"No. Christmas '78. Remember that year, all that snow? Oh, I guess you don't; you were out east, weren't you?"

Lydia nodded. "We had the storm of the century that year there, too."

"Well like I said I was upstairs and the phone rang. Rich was talking and laughing. Just one of the guys, I figured. I came downstairs to iron, and I could hear the end of the conversation from the other room. Rich was talking and said, 'Nope. Nothing to worry about here. Yeah. I cleaned up the loose ends, the bulls stayed out of it. I took care of the autopsy.' I thought when he said that he was talking about the investigation. That he had gotten the autopsy done and everything was how he expected it would be."

"It still sounds that way to me." Roadside Girl's skepticism hung in her tone.

"Like I said, it did to me, too. That is until he said good-bye. Then he said, 'no one needs to know about all that shit.' He paused and lowered his voice and whispered, 'that son-of-a-bitch isn't gonna bother us, now. I fixed that for sure. Toclep'll be just another small town by summer. No need. Yeah, well it's damn good to hear your voice. Merry Christmas Croges, you madman.' It never even crossed my mind. I didn't even say anything because I thought that Croges, Eric McCrogey, still lived with his parents out on Harmen Road. But he didn't. I didn't think about it that day or any other day since. Not until the dream. Not until I was writing in my journal."

"It's hardly more than circumstantial. I didn't hear an admission yet."

Lydia chuckled a little at Roadside Girl. "You tell her, Perry Mason."

"There's one more thing that came up. You remember when that bald guy tried, God I don't know maybe he did, to take all those people off to meet the mother ship, or something like that? Heaven's Gate or the Starship Enterprise or something."

"We got you, what about it?"

"I was watching the coverage on CNN and Rich came in and looked at the set. He said, 'stupid leftover hippies. Bunch of lost, stupid people don't know their heads from a hole in the ground.' He turned around and walked out of the room.

"Well, that's something, Brenda. Let's go call a lawyer. Looks like you've got the case all tied up here." Lydia rolled her eyes at Roadside Girl.

"Then he said, clear as from you to me, 'gotta fix those problems 'fore they get started. Gotta fix them before they get out of hand. Just like I fixed Ezra.' He stopped abruptly. I think he thought I wasn't listening. He stopped dead and changed the subject. He walked out of the kitchen and into the garage. Just a little, what would you call it, Freudian slip and there it was lying on the table like a turkey dinner. I didn't say anything. I took that one "I" and slide it behind the stacks of fear and never bothered cleaning the shelves to get to it. In fact, I had forgotten Rich had even said it. But it came back to me recently."

She stopped. Lydia said very calmly and evenly, "I knew. I've known it for years." Roadside Girl looked at Lydia then at Brenda. She knew Brenda was not scapegoating. Brenda stood up and unzipped her jacket.

"Would you heat up the coffee?" Brenda handed the pot to Roadside Girl, who took the speckled can and walked across the path that led to the sweat lodge. She saw something that she had never seen before but it only registered in her subconscious. There were tiny blades of grass pushing through the hard-packed path that lead from the lodge to the fire pit. They wouldn't amount to much before winter, but they were there. Where they hadn't been before.

"You should watch how much coffee you drink. Caffeine and stress are hard on babies. God knows you have enough of the latter."

"There is no baby." Brenda's face looked like it had been drawn with a pencil that had never been lifted from the paper—just one continuous line. She wasn't distraught and she wasn't crying. She wasn't distant or happy or sad. "I lost the baby two nights ago."

Lydia couldn't say anything. She wanted to, but didn't know what to say. So she stood there. Her eyes were focused on Brenda's belly and she could see there wasn't a baby. "It's okay. I don't feel like the baby has died."

"That's denial, Brenda. You've got to let that go. It'll be all right. We'll get you through it. I'm sorry, I'm so sorry."

"No it's not like that. It's not that I think the baby's still inside me. It's just . . . well . . . I'm alive. The baby brought me to life. Maybe that's the only reason there was a baby, to bring me to life. But baby or no baby I'm alive. I'm free. I'm free of Rich. I'm free of cigarettes. I'm free of the crows, and I'm free of the baby now. That probably sounds bad, but it's true. I'm alive and I have a life that I can begin. It's been beginning since I came here, since I came to see you. I feel good enough about myself today to come out and sit in the sun. Not out in the woods but right here in the backyard. It's possible, not probable, but possible that someone could see me from the road, but I don't care. Because I'm alive. I'm part of the big, living human. I'm no longer a severed hand. And you know what? It's all that baby's doing. I would have loved that baby. After you told me to put my head to the window and I finally did it, I knew I needed that baby. I would've smothered it with molasses love every second of its waking days. But she's gone now. There isn't a thing I can do about it. Not a thing. She's gone and all she's left me with is my life. Isn't that beautiful? My baby gave me my life, not the other way around."

Lydia was astonished. She was shocked. Then, she was proud of Brenda in some sordid way. She could see the sunshine in Brenda's eyes and the sunshine was coming out of her not reflecting off of her. When Roadside Girl returned they all sat in the sun, which was faintly warm on this autumn morning and drank steaming cups of coffee. They wouldn't think about the consequences of the dream over the Freudian-words. They wouldn't think about the baby. They wouldn't dream into the future. They sat and talked about Toclep. What was happening today? They didn't talk about the cabin or the fires or how Mose Paxton had been one of the funniest men either had ever met. Brenda remembered that the few times that she had sat around that fire pit with Katrina and the rest of them. Times so long ago that they had nearly been edited out of the history books of her mind. Forgotten in rubble. But the rubble was being cleared and it would not break into the rest of conversation. There would be unseen passages through the woods, opening up all around her now. All she had to do was look around, they would be right in front of her.

It was still technically daytime; the sun was hidden beyond Captain's Peak and was arching its way into the water beyond the mountains. Massive shadows stretched across Gern property eating all the brightness and allowing the night cold, which had climbed into its den this morning, to creep back out of the ground. Tom sat quietly in the semi-darkness of the kitchen at the door that had stopped being a door when it sprouted legs, and became a table. He was looking at the dark cigarette burns that had changed the color and the character of the table but had never really burned into the surface or left the indentation of fire. He was eating leftover chili and thinking about how his father had always put too much pepper in his chili. It wasn't that it was so hot. It was that the flavor of pepper overshadowed and killed every other flavor, so the chili was tasteless red water with squishy, maroon beans. As a child he had let the beans float around his mouth, trying not to notice that their texture was like that of hard grubs he had seen in photos from *National Geographic*. He had always tried to swallow them without feeling them in his mouth. He never could do it. So, he would have to gulp them down or discretely get them into his napkin and then to Asha, who would softly pant unseen by Matthew or Marguerite. Asha always sat on the boy's side of the table knowing that table scraps would be coming from there.

Tom was frozen over his bowl when Lydia knocked on the door and entered with Roadside Girl behind her. Roadside Girl sat on the bench next to Tom. Her legs straddled the bench and her body faced him. Lydia, opposite them, began to tell Tom what Brenda had told them. Tom sat with his mouth agape and his head tilted like a dog. Every so often he would flare his upper lip but even that was a flare of confusion. He sat in disbelief for half an hour while Lydia talked. Without speaking a word, his squinted eyes and open mouth said, "I don't get it? You mean he killed Ezra?" His face looked like it didn't know who Ezra was or why she was telling him this story. Tom continued sitting that way for five minutes after Lydia had finished.

"I don't understand. What're ya telling me?"

"I guess I'm telling you what you've wanted to know for years. Now, you know. Now you know you were right. It wasn't simply suicide."

"Of course I was right. I know my brother didn't commit suicide. Jesus, are you telling me that Rich Cafus killed my brother? Is that what you're telling me?"

"That's what we're telling you. He and a few others who skinned out shortly after the incident because they were afraid they might say something they shouldn't or they thought Rich couldn't control it. He almost did, though."

"You're shittin' me, right? Rich Cafus did this?"

"You thought that, Tom."

"Not exactly. I thought he did a shitty job investigating. But this, Christ almighty." Tom looked over at Roadside Girl and she was nodding her head. She looked so serious that it made her look like someone else, entirely. It made her look twenty years older than she was. He had seen the serious face before and he was seeing it now for the first time, on her. "And Brenda told you all of this?"

"You know it's true. You've known it for twenty years. Maybe not that Rich had done it, but that it had been done. Certainly you don't need Brenda to see that?"

"No, I guess you're right. But I never really thought it was

Rich. Thought he might not be telling the whole truth but . . . right here, flopped on my dinner table, twenty years too late?"

"It's not too late, Tom. You know now."

"So?" He waited but no one said anything. He thought the question was pretty clear and that it didn't need much more elaboration, but neither of them answered. "So, what do I do now? Where do I go from here?"

"I guess Brenda's asking the same question. You need to call somebody. This needs to be taken care of."

"The police? Is that what you're telling me?" In his mind Tom heard a nearly comical telephone conversation. 'Hey, Tim this is Thomas Gern over here on 52. Your sister's been living out in my haunted house and she's had a dream that . . . ahhh . . . her husband, who beats her . . . yeah . . . yeah . . . you know . . . . well she's had a dream that Rich Cafus, her husband, killed my brother. Could you get me the sheriff on the line, deputy?'

Tom had stopped talking. He hadn't noticed but to Lydia and Roadside Girl the break caused mild anxiety.

Lydia broke the silence. "You need to call the FBI or somebody, a lawyer."

"I ought to go over there and string him up myself. String him up just like he strung up Ezrie and my life."

"That's a great idea. You just march right over there, tell him what you know and that you'd like to make a citizen's arrest. Then you can ask him if he'll kindly put the gun down. We don't need a relapse of the sickness from the seventies."

It had been so long that Tom's first strike instincts of revenge and pain had faded like old wallpaper. They were just images lingering around the back of his mind—little gray moths floating out of an old clothes closet. He was angry but at the same time he was relieved. His brother had been the scapegoat of bad luck in Toclep for years. Tom believed there had been people who suspected foul play, but they had hid their feelings as if their feelings were the sun playing hide-and-seek behind the Crescent Mountains. They could see the light, but it was so far away and they couldn't get to it from where they were, so they pretended that it wasn't there. Besides, if it had happened once, what would keep it from happening again? That's just how the people thought.

"I guess I don't know who I should call. I need to think about this."

"That's not a bad idea, Tom." Lydia stood up from the table; Roadside Girl was still sitting. "People ought to always think before they act. Not enough of them do, though."

"You want me to stay?"

Tom looked like he didn't understand the question. Then he said. "No. I think I need to sit alone for a while." Lydia was careful not to slam the door when she left. Tom sat dumbfounded in his kitchen, looking at the table.

He tried to clear his mind. He tried to see into the past. Unfortunately, he hadn't been there. Mose had said that Ezra had gone to get Patty at the bus station. The buses still stopped in Toclep then, down across the river in front of Will's. Her bus was due to come in at seven and when they didn't come back that evening, Mose figured they had gone to the lake. Ezra liked the lake, and where else would anybody go in Toclep? "Somewhere where you could see all the stars, man, right? Right. That's what I figured. Stars, man." Mose spoke in a yeah-man voice that was easy to hang onto in the north, where the intrusion of styles and language and slang were slow moving before the satellite dish and cable television invasion had made change electro-shock. "Didn't really think anything about it. Said he was picking her up, man. That's all there was to it."

That was what Tom had. Then there was the telephone call.

* * *

His mother didn't scream. She just stood there with the phone hanging like a right fielder's mitt in a game where everyone on the other team batted right-handed. She held the phone and

Tom heard the line go blank and the dial tone and then the beep, beep, beep of an empty line. It had been two months since Matthew had stopped breathing on a Tuesday morning and now there was the empty phone line calling another one in.

"Mom. What is it?" She just stood. It was the only thing she could do. He took the buzzing phone from her hand.

"It was Amanda Tiffelson. She said," Margurite stuttered. "She said she was sorry about Ezra. She said it's tragic to lose a son." Margurite began to shake. Then it happened—everything broke inside of her. When the police knocked on the door five minutes later, she was crying in a chair.

The universe became frantic movements of light in Tom's head. Light that asked questions of what and how then reflected off everything else and ricocheted around—going everywhere, going nowhere. Then there was movement in one direction then another and not knowing why he was moving or what he was doing or how he was going to get his mother, who someone had filled with a half ton of broken glass out of the chair in the kitchen.

She didn't say anything when Officer Lund told her that Ezra along with Patty Ballantyne had, presumably, committed drug-induced suicide by hanging themselves from the backstop of the baseball diamond. She didn't even hear him say that there appeared to be some bruises on them. She didn't hear him say that the investigation was already under way and that officer Cafus was in charge of the investigation and had been down there, meaning the school, all morning.

She hadn't said a thing since she had stood with the baseball-mitt phone in the yellow light of the kitchen. He had to go into Falls Creek to sign some papers because his mother couldn't seem to understand what was happening. Tom felt like he was moving a million miles an hour in a burning stream of energy through space and at the same time he felt like there had been a force that stopped all his movements and that he was pieces of a broken planet floating aimlessly without orbit in a vacuum. When he got back to the house, his mother dragged her feet across the kitchen floor and sat at the table. "I'm gonna have some coffee," she said. "Do you want some coffee?"

"I'll get it mom."

"You better let me do something, Tom. I have to do something." The phone rang. "Tom, take that phone off the hook. I don't want to talk to anybody. I don't want anybody to bring food over here. I can't take that again." He thought that it could be the police, that they might have found something. But it had been too quick, hadn't it. Nothing could be found that quickly. Besides, they could drive on over if they had something. Hopefully they would be able to get there before the news traveled by word of neighbors like Mrs. Tiffelson. He picked up the phone, heard a voice, and then, as he heard the little voice disappear, he hung up the phone and pulled the receiver off the stand.

"It'll buzz for a while," he said.

"It's gonna buzz forever."

He wanted to tell her that Ezra didn't commit suicide, but he wasn't sure she could hear him, so they just sat there in the kitchen. So much time just sitting in the kitchen. How many years of a person's life are spent just sitting in the kitchen? He wasn't sure how long they sat like that, but, finally, he decided he needed to go out to the nook and see what was happening with the others. Who was there, anyway? Daisy, Kristie, Mose, Phil. Jano had gone back downstate. Mose had been Ezra's closest friend since his return from Vietnam. There were some other people he didn't know. Probably the police had already been there, but he needed to go anyway to tell them they could stay as long as they wanted.

As he walked along the fence he could see the police car and as he got nearer to the house he could hear voices.

"So what d'ya all do? Get so high that you thought it'd be fun to kill someone? I don't think this is suicide like they're callin' it over in Falls Creek." He spoke loudly. "I think this is homicide. I think that some of you freaks, some of you leftovers, got a little too much LSD or PCP or PBB and ya got crazy, did some things that you shouldn't have done. Made a mess."

"Don't go pinnin' nothing on us, man. We didn't do anything. We were here last night. All of us."

"Sounds like a pretty airtight alibi, boy. Of course, all of you can vouch for each other, I'd expect no less."

Mose Paxton was no boy. He had lived through two bullet holes. He had dragged himself through fire swamps to serve his country. He had done his time in hell. "Don't have to talk down to me, officer. I know I'm black."

"Don't be getting uppity, boy. I think you all got something to worry about right now. Namely murder. I don't want anybody running out of here before I finish up this investigation." Though he said it, he hadn't meant it. That was exactly what he wanted. He wanted them all to run away, scared for their lives. "Those bodies were pretty bruised, and you can bet we'll get to the bottom of this."

"Are we under arrest, sir? Because if we aren't under arrest I don't think there's anything that says we gotta stay."

"You think you're pretty smart, eh? You just keep thinkin' that way. Maybe it will help you when you're serving time down in Jackson. Hear it's real nice down there." Their eyes flared wide in terror. Their mouths were open. They all looked like children.

"Go easy, Officer Cafus. These folks got nothing to do with what happened." Tom had come along the fence, listening to the conversation. In the eyes of everyone he was a kid—Ezra's kid brother.

"I'm not sure this is the best place for you right now, son."

"Don't son me, Rich. I'm no boy, either. You're not talking to my shell-shocked mother. I've just lost my father. Now I've lost my brother. And I'm telling you these folks had nothing to do with what happened over there at the school. My guess . . . ."

"This is an emotional time, Tom. I don't know that I'd be speculating right now." What Tom didn't realize was that Ezra had a sure-fire way to get Mose and the others packed and running. Running so fast that they wouldn't even turn their heads to see what they had left behind. And it worked. It wasn't instant. If they would have lit out of there on the first day, suicide would have turned to double murder and one of those folks from out of town would have sat in front of a local jury and been sent up the proverbial river. Rich was well aware of his strategy.

Tom tucked his mother into bed and sat brushing her hair with his hand. He tried to talk to her about how his father used to yell at him. "'Leave your poor mother alone, Tom.' You remember when Dad used to say that? And you'd say, 'yes, leave me alone. I don't have time to dance, Tom. I've got cookies in and a sauce to stir. You want it to burn to the pan?' Do you remember that, Mom?" Marguerite didn't respond. She stared nowhere. "'Always under you mother's feet, Tom. I swear you're gonna grow up to be an actor or a circus entertainer. That's what Dad would say.'" However, Tom didn't. He grew up and dropped out of college after his father died in order to take care of the farm.

He sat on the edge of his mother's bed and watched her tiny breaths rise and fall under the quilt she had made when Ezra was in Vietnam. He grew up to have his brother turn into a ghost of epic proportion. He grew up and realized that things fall apart that's what they're made to do—man made or God made, that's what they are made to do.

He awoke in the dusty light of early morning in the room that would someday be his room and looked at his mother, peacefully sleeping beneath the covers. He would leave her. He would let her sleep. He would walk over to the school. He would call the sheriff's office. He would look after the horses and cows. He would get life started again. He would walk out to the nook.

When he got back at noon his mother was still not out of bed. This was peculiar because his mother was always up at dawn. When he had left the house at seven-thirty he thought, good she's sleeping. He peeked around the corner to see her tucked nicely under the covers. That was about all he remembered. The next thing he knew an ambulance from Falls Creek was taking his mother out of the driveway with no urgency—no cloud of dust, no flashing lights. Stroke. However, Tom always knew that it hadn't been a stroke. Her brain hadn't stopped. It didn't matter what the doctors said or the autopsy showed. Her brain never stopped. Her heart did. It broke during a morning phone call and spilled out all day until there was nothing left. Nothing left but emptiness.

* * *

As Tom looked back on it, he saw how the well-oiled machine worked, smoothly, quickly, quietly. It was a conveniently ignored machine that, in fact, was never noticed. The respective migrations of Brian Wiles and John Bower, of Seiler Stephenson and, finally, Eric McGrogey were also never noticed. Why would they be? They were working age. There were no prospects in Toclep. They had nothing to do with Ezra Gern. So no notice was taken. He thought about his poor mother getting the news of her son's death over the phone from a Mrs. Tiffelson rather than from the police.

Tom was still sitting in the kitchen; his stained chili bowl dried in front of him. He was a farmer. That was all. He had bad luck in a string. He lost people like they had been marbles that had rolled under the piano and had fallen down the cold air vent in the living room. He needed to decide what to do, but he didn't have to decide right now. It had waited twenty years; it could probably wait more with the patience of time. He stepped out of the kitchen and onto the porch. The air was cold. He would need a jacket. He lit a cigarette and leaned against one of the support posts that held the roof. He could see a sliver of the moon through the trees in front of him.

"Hey." He hadn't seen Roadside Girl sitting in the darkness at the far end of the porch, her legs stretched out and her back leaning against the house. "Quiet, eh? No cars. Tourists gone."

She had been to the barn and had two horse blankets wrapped around her.

"Yeah. Quiet."

"Sorry I didn't take off. Thought you might want to talk. Or you might not want to talk, but you'd have someone to sit with either way."

"I don't have much to say."

"That's what I like about you, Thomas Gern. You don't have much to say. But when you do, you say it and then you're done with it." He was still standing at one end and she was sitting at the other. His cigarette lit his face as he took a deep drag and ignited the burning ash. He was already cold.

"You know I've never been very good about knowing what I want. Never really got things to work out like I thought they would in my childhood dreams. Never made it through college. Never had the successful marriage. Never had a family. I know you don't think that's very important. Maybe it is. Maybe it's not. The Gerns started this town. You know, this property and that property and those mountains were all Gern. Now there isn't a Gern left. I've got legacy up the wazoo, but nobody to give it to. These took my dad," he held up the cigarette. "Ezra took my mom, and Rich took my brother. Somehow it just doesn't seem fair. Somewhere, maybe, there's a God and he looked down on me and dealt my cards out of a Tarot deck by mistake and I got a full boat, death over the hanged man. And that God said to himself, 'that looks like a fair hand. Thomas Gern, he got himself a real fair hand.'" He dragged. The words stuck in his throat, captured by cigarette smoke. "I'm not sure if God thinks that my fair hand just came around because now I know what happened or not. But if he does, he's wrong." He stopped and looked out at the moon. She got up and went inside and came back with his ragged jean jacket. In the darkness she looked like an Indian from an old black and white photo, draped in blankets.

"Put this on. I don't think this has much to do with God, Tom. You know I don't believe in that stuff myself. I think it has to do with nature. People die. Your family died. Part of it was unnatural. Part of it was a lie. But the world is still ticking on. You don't have to stay here, but you do. Your idea of legacy is grand, but it's not your land. It never has been. And when the whole thing comes down, the land's going back to its real owner and so are you. You believe in that God stuff . . . ashes to ashes dust to dust . . . that's what God is. God sounds like time to me. Be that as it may, there's more than that. You know something now that maybe you always knew, something that you hid in the stacks of hay in the barn. You know something now that maybe a handful of people believed in '78. Now you've got to do something about it, but it won't be as easy. You and Brenda. It's your baby, so to speak. Your baby together. I don't know that you should rush right out like a headless chicken and stumble on this thing. I don't think you need to feel that you were dealt a shitty hand. If your God is dealing out hands, he probably only uses one deck of cards. That'd be my guess."

He grinned. "Who made you so smart?"

"I'd like to know that, myself. I'd thank 'em." She was serious.

The sky was clear and they could see each other's breath in the speckled, blue night. It was cold and it felt good and somewhere the curtain had come up to reveal a new day. Somewhere, the sun was shining on wet grass. But Thomas didn't need the sun to shine right now. The sky and the air would make things clear. He didn't know what he would do or when he would do what he would do. What he knew for now was that someone had put the balancing weight back in his soul. Someone had made things equal. Maybe that was his hand from God?

In 1882 sand and hemlock trees were the only things around the mouth of the Raspberry River. The area had been trapped and over trapped by the French and when the beaver disappeared, so did the French. The small sand beach hidden by large logs of driftwood could hardly be seen. Leaning white pines and red pines enveloped the river, which drifted slowly on the edge of the Crescent Mountains into Superior. The hills of the Crescent Range were old mountains. Some of the oldest rock in the world edged its small cliffs and river bottoms. Both were worn by erosion and time.

In the autumn of 1882, after three days of paddling, Lionel Gern turned his trapping canoe up the Raspberry to see if any beaver had returned to the area. None had. What he found, instead, were two jagged, green railroad ties that shot under his canoe and into the rock bank of the creek. At the bank of the creek was one small, fox-colored spot on the green that had been polished by moving sand. What he had found was not beaver; it was copper.

Lionel extracted about three hundred pounds of copper without too much effort. That spring he took his money and laid claim to one square of land, 640 acres. He was hoping to capitalize on a port city, at the mouth of the Raspberry. In the spring of 1883, the Ohio Copper Company purchased that same 640 acre square, from Lionel. They gave him a finder's fee and began mining about seven miles up the river just before Twin Falls. Lionel in turn took the money from his sale and his finder's fee and bought two more squares just west of his original purchase.

Unfortunately for the O.C.C., the area never made a profit in copper. There were a couple more finds but after eight hard years of linear mine shafts and virtually no metal, the O.C.C. called the operation a loss and scrapped all mining. In 1895 a small German company named Abendessen purchased the mineral rights and tried unsuccessfully for seven more heartbreaking years. Abendessen wasn't as lucky as O.C.C. and the venture left the entire company bankrupt. Even though Lionel had found the original copper and had noticed it angling into the rock, like copper does, he had forgotten. All the mining ventures had shafts that poked straight into the sides of the riverbank and the surrounding area. Though some copper was extracted, most of the time the blasting and digging shot through the narrow capillaries of copper into rock that yielded no more metal than it did bananas because the vein was angling over the miners' heads or under their feet instead of running in a straight line in front of their faces.

In the early 1900's, when copper mining had been perfected somewhat, The Johansen Company of Calumet hit a large vein about nine miles from Lionel's original discovery on the Raspberry. Crescent City formed around the mine. The mine dumped its tailings into the Abundance River and scraped the inside of the earth bloody. Now, the mine was the major unemployer of the area. It had been dying a slow death, and people had been leaving in continual streams as the corporation tried to prolong the death by solution mining. Of course, copper has lost its value and its usefulness and the continuation of operations was simply the company trying to hold onto a past that no longer existed. This was unlike the past of Thomas Gern, which seemingly was holding onto him.

The copper upon which Lionel Gern had paddled still angles under the riverbeds and into the mountainside that is now the property of the state.

About the time Abendessen pulled out of the area the Linman Company of Chicago, a major logging operation, pulled in. They had to purchase land at the mouth of the Raspberry from Lionel Gern who had bought the 640 acre square back from the bankrupt Abendessen Company in order to set up the transport mechanisms for wood and the living quarters for some two hundred lumbermen, forty-seven women, and seven bars. That was the beginning of Toclep, which took its name from the metal projected footwear the loggers wore on their boots to scale the giant, northern trees. Lionel took his money from one sale and purchased one more square of the Crescent Mountains that land locked much of the internal area, which was now the park. When he purchased the land he got the mineral rights, thus keeping Linman from hacking down every giant hemlock, every towering sugar maple, every healthy oak, every white pine, red pine, and red cedar they could get their greedy loggers gloves on. Within fifteen years most of the area had been cleared and what was left was a sprouting land of white-tailed deer and paper birch, popple, and ash with the scatterings of newly planted jack pines peeking up between stumped forest turned prairie. When the trees were gone most of the city dried up like an August stream but a few people stayed and the city shrunk, fell apart, and was rebuilt. By 1925 the town was less than half the size it had been in 1910. People who stayed went to work in Crescent City or managed to milk a meager existence from the others who stayed in the town. Lionel Gern had enough money and plenty of land. He tried unsuccessfully to be a farmer. He had preserved some of the land and some of the trees. He had saved the mountains, forgot about the copper, and had had four children. Some of those children died early deaths and two bought more land and one had children that lived. Sometimes procreation was biblical in proportion for the Gerns, it was not.

One year earlier, Ezra had been throwing stones from the sweeping sandstone of Sunset Rock. He had watched the stones break through the calm and flutter into the clear darkness. The water accepted the sand-colored stone and wore it like engraved crystal wears its pattern, knowing that the patterns and the glass are one and the same. Sometimes, he would set pieces of dry wood afloat and watch them disappear into the freshwater sea. He would watch them for an hour or longer, until the waters that were ever flowing pulled them out of sight. The surfaced submarines of wood seldom, if ever, washed ashore. They were grabbed and escorted until they lost buoyancy, bobbed off-balance, and sank into the cold depths somewhere out past the horizon. He used to dream about being the dried, barkless, white, sticks that were so light with air. The sticks were like whipped chocolate. There was nothing to them but air and weightlessness.

Sometimes he watched rocks slowly guided by underwater gravity flutter out of sight; he could imagine his eyes bulging in the increasingly cold water. Five feet, ten feet, twenty feet down and the pressure trying to suck him into himself and pull his eyes out of his skull. He could feel the pain like being swatted with a two-by-four in the back of his head as the pressure and cold worked together to pull him down. Drown bodies in Superior often never surface. It's not because fish eat them. It's because the water is so cold that decay doesn't occur and, therefore, nothing produces the oxygen that makes bodies float. The weight of a body is dragged to the bottom the same as a rock released from your hand, fluttering like a butterfly out of sight into a cold, dark, watery grave—crushed with vacuum-like pressure beneath thousands of pounds of pressure per square inch.

Ezra would watch the rock dive for the bottom wondering, sometimes, if there was a bottom. He could feel the cold and, then, the cold would disappear with the pain of some mighty water god trying to press his ears together at his nose and squeeze his head until his eyes popped out as if they were the throats of some exotic South American frog. He'd forget there was a world above water and all the oxygen would be wrung out of his lungs. His speed would increase as he went farther into the pressure, deeper into the darkness. He'd dive like a summer swallow. Dive-bombing, kamikaze to a bottom that he would never feel when he reached it because there was no bottom. There was nothing to stop him.

Now he tossed pebbles into green water and they disappeared the second they hit the surface. The pressure would be different here—the color, the depth, the cold. It would all be different here. He half expected the stones to rise back out of the water and float on the warm, slow-moving river surface. He wouldn't sink like a steel battleship here. He would bob at the surface and the fish would pick him apart slowly at first and, then, as more realized he wasn't escaping to the bottom, he would be torn apart as if he was saturated bread thrown to seagulls. He threw another rock. How fast could he be to the bottom here? The rock disappeared the moment it hit the surface and Ezra knew that was how long it took to get to the bottom. It was not like the torpedo in the clear water that took the color of anything until it simply became darkness. It was not that water. It was the green, clay water that looked more like cream soup than a river. It had viscosity that would clog his eyes with green-darkness. He wouldn't see anything. It would be like the swirling brown-reds of having his eyes closed tightly in mid-day for half a second. Then it would be instant green darkness. There would be no pressure, no cold, no air-sucked lungs. It would be like sinking in oil, like the LaBrea Tar pits opening their mouths and swallowing in slow, mucky warmth. It would not be the cool, clean death of Superior. It would not be the forever-preservation, the floating, sunken eternity of clear water. It wouldn't be refreshing and that's what he had always dreamed that sinking like his sandstone rocks would be, like wintergreen.

There were no dry, beaver-barkless branches to set afloat in the green tar. He took live, white wood and hacked clean, narrow ships with his K-bar then tossed them into the quiet current of the river off the side of the Swift. He was not quite sure if he was still on the Mekong or if he was on another river. It sure seemed too narrow to be the Mekong to him. He did know he was always going the wrong direction. He'd put his tiny boats, reaching over the side, onto the water. The sticks floated like they sat above it and not in it, and they would run off, always in the opposite direction, away from him. He could see them drift out of sight. He trusted the wood. The wood had always known where to go. From Sunset Rock, it would paddle itself into the open water and open sky and open universe. It would join the big water in search of itself. It would, eventually, turn into a rock from the weight of the water that it took on and plunge itself down to the other sticks that searched the depths. It would sink into a new universe, a universe of the past and the present and the future, which swirled in great, looping circles on top of themselves. He knew the universe could be seen. Most people didn't know there was anything to look for or would search in vain—linear lines forward, linear lines backward. They would not see the millions of billions of universes that surrounded and stacked on top of each other like interlocking magician's rings. That didn't really matter to him, now. Time could stand still and other peoples' losses were inconsequential. What mattered was that the rocks disappeared. That the ships of K-barred wood drifted in the right direction and the PCF Swift drifted in the wrong direction was what mattered.

He had told Sergeant Billings that they were moving in the

wrong direction. He had watched the water get smaller around him, the edges forcing their way to the boat, which was an odd whaling ship of unroped harpoons and barbless spear guns. He wasn't quite sure how far in they were going but the sticks told him that they were moving in the wrong direction. There was no universe up river. The universe was down river. That's why the water flowed that way. It knew where the universe was. It knew where it was supposed to go. The sticks knew that and they followed the water to eternal life. It wasn't just him or his whaling ship, either. It was all of them. All the dark images that had no distinct shape or nationality were moving in the wrong direction.

"Billings, sir," he said though he hardly recognized his voice or the use of sir. Both were instinctual sounds that he was sure he had uttered with his first breath, which he was sure all of his kind had muttered for generations with their first breaths. He was quite sure that when he had first said, "Mama" that he had actually said, "Mama, sir." He could remember being asked questions in biology class and responding in a clear, loud voice, "Sir, no sir. The cerebellum does not control respiration and circulation, sir. That is the medulla oblongata, sir." And so when he spoke, the natural sound of "sir" was fixed with verbal speech like an "ah" or an "um." No one noticed the word that was part of every sentence. It was as if the Standard American English sentence had three parts, subject plus predicate plus sir equaled proper grammatical structure. It was an unnoticeable mid-tone buzz that was adrift in all the air around him that he never noticed until there was no sound at all and then he noticed with shocking ferocity. "Sergeant, sir. I believe we are moving in the wrong direction, sir." Ezra had been saying it for days. No one was quite sure how many days, seeing the boat had seemed to have a special providence to simply circle in time.

"Don't call me sir, Gern. I'm not a sir. You want me to get shot or something? If you want to call out sir you talk to that Navy officer back there."

"Oxford." The Sarge called backwards on the Swift boat without turning his head. His words, caught in the air, hung until the back of the boat caught up with them. "Oxford."

"Yea, Sarge."

"Oxford." The Lance Corporal, whose hair had grown out since Ezra had first been assigned to the unit, had the distinct look of a young professor. If he had only been wearing a light brown, corduroy blazer with a blue, button-down collar, his horned-rimmed glasses would have projected Ph.D. like loudspeakers at a Pulitzer Prize ceremony. Oxford was twenty. He was a college dropout who had lost his freedom to lack of funding and one semester of work in Edwards County, Illinois. "Oxford. Take Gern to the back of the boat before he drives me crazy and send Burton up here with his M60." He looked down at the peelings of bark that were edging the large, green, metal wall. "Goddamn soldier ought to be peeling potatoes somewhere in a C.A.P., not playing Rat Patrol on a Navy Swift."

"Yes, Sarge. His watch was just about over anyway."

"This isn't a factory, Oxford. There aren't any shifts here except the shift of death and he's manning that pretty damn well. Needs to get his head out of his ass."

Oxford and Ezra walked through the cabin to the back of the boat. The Sergeant could hear them talking because the boat was trolling slowly up the river, but he couldn't decipher what they were saying.

Ezra wasn't shell-shocked. He wasn't afraid of dying nor was he afraid of firing his gun, though there was some sort of revulsion within him when he tore the trees to pieces with the scattered metal that burned out of his recoiling M16. The bullets tore through trees and made them fold over like they were bowing to him as if he were king of the world. The trees always reminded him of Mrs. Jaslo's discussion of MacBeth's prophecy. The trees would come alive. The trees would attack.

The trees were alive but they weren't alive with the sound of music. Sometimes, they would spit fire from tiny, black eyes that were everywhere. Behind trees, between trees, below trees, above trees, Maggie's underwear was in every tree. They would spit fire that became the blinking eyes of demons and he would fire into the trees knowing that the way to kill demons was not with a gun, but he did it anyway. He would chop the trees with lead axes that were too numerous to count. All he would hear was the hell fire of his gun until someone behind him would scream that it was over. Ezra would continue to fire, hacking away at trees, clearing land, stopping the trees from their attack that was inevitable because it had been prophesized.

The day before, after being attacked by the trees, he had dug some of the mashed bullets out of the interior sides of the boat. He didn't know much about the tiny missiles that had become splattered and chewed pieces of lead gum in the boat walls. But sometimes he wondered whether they were AK47 or M16. He wondered what the difference would have been. He wondered if his rocket axes ever made it past the trees and into the chest of another human like himself. A human from some small town in Vietnam that had a name in three parts like the rivers did. Toh Cle Po. Or if the bullets only tore through God which wouldn't be that bad, because God could replenish himself, because God could make rivers and trees and people and life and Ezra couldn't, nor could his enemy. All he could do was tear trees into splinters and turn men into dissolving effervescence. "Diffusion is the solution to confusion," he said to himself. He wondered if there was an enemy beyond the self. He wondered why he had this enemy. He wondered why he had become a lumberjack of green, river trees and yellow-white eyes of fire. He wondered if there was a God or a Devil, if there was good or evil or if all of it had been made up by insane generals to scare the child-hearted and reinforce the terror of an open, night closet. The whole world was an open, night closet. The whole world ended beyond the banks of the river, in the darkness of the trees, in the darkness that had always been there and always would be there no matter how many trees he chopped down with his M16. The trees hadn't caused the darkness. He guessed that the generals had.

"We're going the wrong direction," he said to Oxford.

"How can you know? How can you know which is the right and which is the wrong direction? They're all the same. All the directions are one. They all lead to the same place."

"No they don't. Water is the spirit road of man. Water leads to true spirit. Watch." He took a piece of slippery, white wood that had been stripped of its skin out of his pocket and threw it in the river. "See. The wood runs with the water. What'd I tell you? Yet, we run against it."

"What'd you tell, what? All I see is a stick floating with the current."

"Yeah, but the stick is running in the other direction. It's running in the right direction. The current of man is running in the wrong direction. We can stop that if we believe. We can stop it. If you don't believe what you see, believe what you feel. Can't you feel it? Can't you?"

He looked at Ezra closely. Oxford's eyes were shiny hematites that peered over his thin nose from behind the glasses that were not army issue. "We're moving. The boat's moving, Ezra. River's got current."

"I know the boat's moving. I'm not stupid nor am I insane. That's not what I'm talking about. Were you ever in a fight when you were a kid?"

"Yeah."

"You ever in a fight when you were a kid when someone said, all right meet me after school at the bike rack?"

"No. I mean . . . I usually backed out of those kind of fights."

"Why?"

"Well, because I had time to think about 'em I guess. I mean...there was no real anger left after school."

"You ever met the VC?"

"No."

"How do you know you hate 'em then?" He asked curtly.

"They're our enemy. I kill them or they kill me. Easy as that."
"You believe in God?"
"Yeah."
"You believe in the God in the bible?"
"Yeah."
"Love your enemies, do good to those who hate you, bless those who curse you, pray for those who mistreat you. That bible?" There was a sharp break then a terse addition. "We're going in the wrong direction I tell you. Do unto others. Would you want someone boating up the Bonpas River blasting a cannon through the trees and out onto the wheat fields?"
"No. How do you know what rivers run through Edwards County?"
"How can I not know?" He paused. "You wouldn't. So why is it okay for you to do the same thing here?"
"You didn't answer my question."
"You didn't answer mine."
"Okay. So, it's not right. However, Sergeant Billings might disagree with you."
"That's because he doesn't see. He's a lifer." Ezra threw a stick into the water then whispered to Oxford, "I don't think any of the lifers believe in God. Any God."
"You're driving him crazy with this right and wrong direction shit." They were standing on the back of the boat watching the slow wake creep behind them. It would have been better to travel at night but there was no way to navigate the river. They would have run aground in the thinning, twists and bends of the river that closed in on them more and more as they moved upstream. "He doesn't trust you."
"I don't trust him."
"Quite frankly, neither do I. But, we're in NVA area. Hell, the Sergeant doesn't even know where the NVA are and he doesn't know where we're going anymore, been so much movement. But he's the only one ever been in combat before."
"This isn't World War Two."

"You ever been in combat?"

"All of life is combat. We don't need to know anything about combat. All we need to know is that we're going in the wrong direction. We are being lead in the wrong direction."

"And all you can say is we're going in the wrong direction which scares him and me and everybody else. I don't want to die, Ezra. I gotta lot of things to do, yet. I know we're going in the wrong fucking direction. Hell there's only one right direction and that's back to the world. But I can't have you pulling a Flanagon on me. Freakin' out. Disappearing out there like you were Houdini or something."

"I'm not freakin' out. It's just that everything's flowing in the other direction. Everything. We keep going this way and we're gonna die. It ain't gonna be my fault or your fault, but it's not gonna matter much who's fault it is because we're all gonna be dead."

"Jesus, Ezra. What are you, the little steamboat that couldn't? We've made runs like this before. It's not impossible."

"We knew where our troops were before. We knew there were troops. It's not a case of possible or impossible. It's a matter of right and wrong. And right now we're heading in the wrong direction. Flanagon's better off than we are. At least he knows where he is."

"No he doesn't. He's lost. He went in and never came out. He's dead."

"Woods never killed anyone. Darkness is what kills." He was saying it but he didn't believe it. Back in the world, when he lived in Toclep when his world wasn't the world of MacBeth trees but was the world of the trees that never killed anyone—he would have believed it. But now, the trees killed. He had watched them kill. They had tried to kill him. Not everyday but enough to know that these trees had changed. They were not the trees of his childhood—the weak dying trees he and Tom had kicked over. These were the trees of Tom's nasty dream ride.

"Nope the woods haven't. But Flanagon and the woods aren't

the only two out there. If the Charlie didn't get him, the way he thrashes around, he probably got ate by a snake or went dinky do. Either way, he's dead as a doornail by now."

"Ok. So he's dead. We're heading into hell. What's worse?"

"Death is worse, Ezra. There's still a chance we can get out of hell."

"You're wrong. There's never a chance to get out of hell. There will be no harrowing." Ezra thought Oxford should be lecturing about dead Russian writers. Death could not be worse than hell. Maybe it could be worse than this place, but this place wasn't hell. It just looked like it.

He knew they were going in the wrong direction. He knew that by going in the wrong direction they were inviting death to come and play with them in the woods and that death knew these woods and all woods better than they did. Death had always known the woods because death had known the darkness between the trees and the darkness between the trees was evil. "We're going in. But we need to follow the wood. We need to get out." He threw another strip of white into the green oil of the river and watched it float out of sight. It was flowing out, on the shallow green water, past the trees that had become his enemy, past the warmth that would allow him to become the food of fish, past the green into the blue that was universe upon universe. It would flow forever into the sky of the sea until it was soaked into those infinite universes, until it became a part of that infinity and part of the whole. The sticks were all running in the right direction and he knew it. They all knew it. They just hadn't looked around to see. No, they weren't going in the right direction. There was only one right direction and it was out. It was in the tiny, white boats that were making a path toward the sea like migrating salmon.

They both sat on the back of the boat and watched the green water like it was a sunset disappearing into the horizon. The river snaked and disappeared behind corners long before it went out of sight. A curve and gone, another curve another sunset. They must have watched twenty sunsets disappear behind the boat into the green sky of unfamiliar trees—trees with no name. A place that never existed to them before and would be lost in fragmented memory for the rest of their lives.

"If we didn't keep chopping it down with the cannons it'd be beautiful." Oxford said to the quiet wake.

"It's still beautiful," Ezra said. "It's scary, too."

"Yeah." His voice sounded like he smoked but he didn't. "I never knew there was a scared like this. When Flanagon left I pissed my pants. I heard someone screaming and calling out for him in the trees and I pissed my pants. I wanted everyone to shut up. I wanted everyone to let him go. I didn't want the attention attracted to us. You want to know why? Not cuz I was scared for him. No siree. I was scared for me. I can't have you freak out on me, Ezra." He stopped as he counted in his head. "Only the Sarge, I don't always agree with his judgment. I never have liked sergeants. They're all off their rocker. But I just don't need you to drift away with your sticks." He didn't notice that he was hanging onto one of the drying, naked pieces. "You, Me, Charles, 'Bama, Wholesale, and the NFG."

"What's that new guys name?"

"Olshelfski or Oldschedski, something like that."

"NFG."

"Right, NFG. At least until he kills something. Anyways it's just us and them. As soon as they Navy boys drop us off." He lifted his forehead to the trees. "I'm pretty sure there's more 'n six of them. We've already lost half of us. I don't wanna pee my pants again. I don't wanna be here, anymore 'n you do. I don't wanna die. Shit man, I'm only twenty years old. I should be a junior this year, a junior, not a fucking Lance Corporal. It's like being in some comedy about war, except it's not funny. Every time someone gets shot you jump in rank. And every time that happens I say, I don't wanna be a fucking sergeant. I don't want to lead this shit. I'm pretty sure the Sarge is on the up and up. He's got more kills than you and me." He paused. "I don't wanna be a sergeant. I don't wanna die."

"You're not gonna die, Oxford. Leastwise not here."
"You guaranteeing that?"
"Ever heard of Mt. Vernon Outland Airport?"
"Yeah."
"I give you my word as a gentleman."
"I'll take that word." Oxford wanted the handshake. He wanted the deal complete, so he stuck his hand into Ezra's side. Ezra shook it.

He wished he could guarantee them all. He wished that he had a gentlemen's agreement with God. But there was no such handshake. All he had was the darkness that surrounded the boat in mid-day, a blackness enshrouded in the tarpaulin underbrush of nameless trees, a darkness that scared him. He had that darkness, but he also had one fleck of a dream he had nearly forgotten. He had seen Oxford in his dress uniform getting off a bus at some unremarkable American airport that looked like every other unremarkable airport he had ever seen. He remembered it clearly because behind Oxford painted on the cinder block building were the words, Mt. Vernon Outland Airport.

Ezra wondered again about being a rock in this river, sinking to the bottom. Would he plunge through the green skin then bob near the surface bathed in warmth and not be able to sink? If so, he would force himself to sink by blowing all the air out of his lungs but would the water tighten around him, would it let him sink? He'd have to force himself to dip below the surface, eyes open, but he wouldn't be able to see anything in the green oil. He, finally, would sink but not know how far because he wouldn't be able to see anything. He would touch bottom, something that he never imagined doing in the endless waters of Superior. It wouldn't be very far below the surface. He'd be able to tell that because the water would still be warm and there would be no pressure. No pressure at all. He'd turn his head upward and not be able to see into infinity. He wouldn't see darkness or light. He would see nothing at all because that's all there was to see. If he were a rock, he would sink into the muck that held the earth together and suffocate below its warm suction. That wasn't the rock he wanted to be. He wanted to breathe the clear, colorless water of Superior. He wanted to be in those universes and jump from one to another. But it didn't seem possible to him now. The only thing that seemed possible was to float in the wrong direction because everything was moving that way.

The weather had changed. The bright, cold sun would allow work to be done in shirtsleeves but wouldn't allow standing around to be done that way. The grass had already changed to the dry browns and now the trees were following. Pigment was running from the leaves like watercolors in the rain. Things weren't fading. They were exploding. Fire had taken the trees and would have them for a couple of weeks before they burned out into winter death. That is, all but the oaks that would strain to hold their leaves forever. And they, too, would if the soft, spring leaves didn't push their grandfathers to the ground.

Tom was unable to concentrate. Twenty years, he thought. I don't know why this is coming up now. Twenty years it's slept. Twenty years and the dreams had come and gone like seasons. Twenty years and his anger had softened into talking to the cabin that sat quietly in a nook at the corner of Gern property. Now, spastic dreams of red swarmed through daylight thought, playing a child's game of Bloody Murder. He hadn't been bothered by it for years except when he had been in places where the townspeople were gathered. Then, he would stab tiny insinuating comments into the sky for them to try to ignore. He didn't even take himself to those occasions very often. He kept to himself and people forgot that they really did like Thomas Gern, that Thomas Gern had only become a loner out of necessity. He could feel himself growing back into the town. He would have to. He had to fix something that had been broken for so long that nobody even recognized that it was broken.

"Damn it." He said. He put his book down. How many times could he read the same lines and not understand what they said? How much time would he have to waste trying to understand Carver's paragraph about the affairs of husbands and wives, which he didn't need to read anyway because he already understood the dynamics of marriage all too well: the poignant loneliness so acute that it made you notice flaws in the glass of windows.

He hadn't been to talk to Brenda since he had gotten the story from Lydia. Was it accurate? A narrator twice removed isn't always that reliable, but for some reason he trusted this one. He had half a mind to forget the whole thing, to let it die, to let it blow in the wind and sand, again. Unfortunately, he had to talk to Brenda. He didn't want to. He had to.

* * *

The good thing about jean jackets is that if you don't outgrow them they can last forever. This one had. Tom tried to remember how long he had had the jacket but he couldn't put a stamp of purchase on it. He thought that the jacket might be as old as he was—maybe older. It may have come down, an heirloom, from his great grandfather. That's how jean jackets were. He patted his pocket then searched the kitchen with his eyes, looking at the cover of his book, which had a man with a hard hat, smoking a cigarette. Then he looked at the table that used to be a door and the stained, cracking linoleum, the drying dishes that were never put away. He walked to the refrigerator, opened it, and peered into the light. No cigarettes in there, he thought. He always checked the 'fridge when he had lost something. He would sometimes find a book or a wallet or a half-eaten sandwich that he thought he had left on the table.

"Brenda. I've got to go talk to her." He slapped his head and forgot that he was looking for his cigarettes. He grabbed a paper sack and walked around the kitchen tossing in items that he had purchased just for her and items that were simply lying around the house that could be eaten: jars of tomatoes, one of three unsliced loaves of bread, strawberry jam, jerky. He went to the 'fridge again and pulled venison from the freezer, eggs, mustard, candles. "Candles?" He said as he stared at the box of dinner candles that shared a shelf with cheese and butter and condiments that he never used. He picked up the mayonnaise. "April, huh. Well, at least it's not two years old." He set it on the counter. He closed the 'fridge then opened it again. "Cheese." He grabbed it and threw it into the bag. Then he grabbed the special treats. Nutty-Bars—eight, individually-wrapped containers of two in a yellow box for only a dollar nineteen. Popcorn. He didn't like popcorn but figured popcorn was easy. Pretzels. No fat and never go stale. He turned to go out the door again. He saw his cigarettes but it didn't register that he had been looking for them. "There's plenty I'm forgetting," he said as he stepped onto the porch.

* * *

The sky had changed colors. It had moved from that late summer white-blue to the high cloud pall of autumn. The sun was completely white and the temperature actually changed when he stepped into the sun from the porch. It wasn't like the Michigan summer when you might try to hide from the heat in the shade of a tree and find that the shade and the unshade were the same hot. When he stepped onto the ground he felt the hardness of change under his feet. He looked behind the house to the patches of flame that blazed out of the hemlocks that would never change, that would always be green, that were perpetual life. He walked across the field and looked at the bowing and brown sheaves of corn. They had stopped competing for sunlight with the sunflowers that were still holding their heads high to the sky, towering far above the corn, casting shadows onto the whispering, paper-dry sheaves that spoke in the gentle winds. The hay was cropped short and looked like the stubble of a young army recruit. The cows looked like they were pasted onto the fence that was glued onto the sky that was painted onto a canvas in fading hues. He shifted the bag from one arm to the other, wondering about the eggs.

Brenda heard his footsteps on the wooden porch and could feel the vibrations run up the stairs to the loft where she was cleaning when he arrived. He could see clearly through the windows that were letting light fill the cabin, heating and drying and giving comfort to the entire space that lately had stopped its complaining about lack of use. Everything likes to be useful. The faucets no longer screamed from dryness nor did the floorboards moan from lack of sun. The house had life.

"Bren? Brenda?" Tom peeked his head through the door.

"Up here." Her voice sounded like spring. She was holding the bed spread over one arm and was pulling the sheets off the bed. "Laundry day."

"God. I didn't even think about that. How've you been doing laundry?"

"Like they used to in the old days." Her face glowed and he noticed that she was more attractive then he remembered her ever being.

Of course, some people grew into beauty. It wasn't something that everyone had in youth. Some have it and lose it. Some don't have it and gain it. Some never lose it. Some never have it. There were really not many that never had it, only those who didn't look for it. Tom drifted back to the long-gone Rae Miller conversation.

"Wash tub." She finished.

"Sorry. I didn't mean to make you Laura Ingels."

"I like it. I really do. It makes me more conscious about my clothes, or should I say Ezra's clothes? And about everything, really. It's good work. Whatcha got there?"

"Oh, food." He had forgotten that he held the bag and so

stared at it momentarily as if he was holding a baby skunk. "I've been kind of lost lately. Forgot I bought all this stuff." He set the bag on the wall between the living room and the kitchen.

"I guess Lydia told you what I told her, eh?"

"Yeah." A silence held in the air like a violin note. It was surrounded by quiet and seemed to be alone in the universe, separated from time and space—vacant but dissident. Brenda came down the stairs holding the materials that enveloped her at night. The stairs did not squeak and her feet did not click on the wood. It was almost as if she floated from the loft to the floor next to Tom.

"I wanna hang this comforter outside. Come with? We'll talk."

Again he said, "Yeah." And he stepped in behind her as she carried the comforter outside to a line a Tom had never seen before. He noticed the line was not in the open but was directly behind the house so as if the wind was blowing the clothes would be hitting the house.

"Hope you don't mind. I needed to be able to dry my clothes."

"I guess we need to do more than talk. We need to act. Time's come to take care of things that you came here to take care of, which I didn't think had anything to do with me. But in actuality, have quite a lot to do with me. S'pose we're into something together that isn't connected. Or is connected. I don't know."

"You know what to do?"

"I've known what to do just about every moment of my life. I know to plant the hay and to bring the hay in. I know to feed the cows and bring the cows in. I know to fix the fence when the fence needs fixing. I know to can when the vegetables need canning. But I don't know how to fix time when time's been stolen. I don't know how to replace esteem like it was a tractor tire. I don't know a thing about the law of man but I know a little about the law of God. The law of God says thou shalt not kill. The law of God say does unto others. The law of God doesn't say thou shalt not ra . . . " He didn't want to say the word. He slid by it like it didn't exist. It was closer than the murder. It was sharper. It was worse. "But God must have been sleeping on that one. There's been some infractions and those infractions need to be absolved. I'm not sure how to go about all of that. Not from here, anyway."

"I'd like to stay right here and forget about the whole thing. Forget not forgive. I'm on my way to forgetting. Doing my laundry, for me with my hands, helps me do that. Walking in those trees helps me do that. Having slow, simple time of no distraction or all distraction helps me do that. Forgetting is sometimes hard to do, but I'm trying. Forgiving is another story. Some things are unforgivable. Even if I was God, I wouldn't be able to forgive him. I guess Rich is lucky that I'm not God."

"I got a lot of God to throw around for a guy who isn't religious. When was the last time you stepped into a church?" He didn't wait for a response. "Only to deliver vegetables to St. John's. I'm saying, all of it amounts to a hill of beans. We need to end the facade. We've suffered—you, me, my mom, my brother, Patty, and the rest of those folks who lit out of here on a rail because they were scared and now I know why. The laws haven't changed. I'm not some naive kid who just took over his father's farm and his mother's canning and his brother's . . . I guess I never took over anything for my brother. Nobody did. Huh?" It wasn't as much of a question as it was a consideration. He looked like an animal that was incapable of cognition. "You've been beat up and . . . ." Again he stopped like it was impossible to form the word on his lips. He saw for a moment the most heinous crime he could imagine and Brenda was the survivor of that crime. Brenda now had to carry the sin of her oppressor with her for the rest of her life. Sure she'd like to forget it, he thought, but she'd never be able to forget it all. There would always be a piece of it floating around her soul. "And that's all new. It's domestic though. It's your word against his. But so is the other. Lydia said FBI but I don't see how the FBI is going to run in here and find twenty-year-old evidence that disappeared because Rich destroyed it."

"So. Maybe the answer isn't in the law. Maybe, it's in us."

Tom was going to ask what she meant, but he didn't. He

stood with the question dripping from his eyes and carved across his face and stuck like saliva on his lips. He looked around the yard and noticed the long grass surrounding the house. "I should mow this grass," he said rather absently. He looked at the house that had its eyes open to the world. He looked at the clothesline that said, "yes there's life here." He looked at Brenda. Her hair hung just below her shoulders and in the windless brisk air she looked like a teenager. He waited.

"You know, I saw your brother that morning. Strung out like a black scarecrow stretching his arms to fly but not being able to move. Suspended in time, suspended in air, suspended in death. The papers never said anything about him having his arms outstretched. But they were. They were outstretched and motionless. How's a person do that to themselves? I've seen your brother plenty of times since then. His face glints from the black sheen of a crow that watches Rich everyday. If your brother wanted revenge, he would have gotten it already. I don't think he wants revenge." Tom looked at her like she was loony. He thought that the response was Ezraesque vision talk with no logic or string of reality.

"Sounds kind of flaky, Brenda."

"Let it sound anyway it wants to sound. It is what it is. I think your bother wants truth. Your problem and my problem are only connected because your murderer is my rapist." She didn't flinch when she said it. She was detached and matter-of-fact. "The person who stole Ezra's life also stole my life. Maybe that's the way it had to be. Don't ask me why, but that's what we have in common." Her voice changed a bit. "Apart from growing up together and sitting next to each other for two years." Then it changed again. "I've been sweating. In my house, which was never really mine; in my sleep, which he robbed too; in my thoughts, which were his thoughts; in everything I've done for years—I have feared him. Now it's time for him to fear me. I'd sure like him to sweat a little."

He wasn't quite sure what that would do. He wasn't sure what she meant. He thought it sounded like revenge. He didn't know who to contact. He didn't know what the law could do after twenty years. He was pretty sure there wasn't a speck of evidence except the word of a distraught wife against her husband who had been sheriff in Greenstone County for years. Brenda had been there almost a month. The nights were cold. Soon she would have to have a fire. The cabin with its cracks and holes would be drafty, winter living. He didn't really know how comfortable it would be. Ezra had never spent the winter there. He had died before the first winter after the cabin's completion. He had died.

"You know people have crazy lives." He said in a low, scratchy voice that changed into a monotonic lecturer's voice. "Most people see tragedy. It's all around them. Some get to experience it one way, while others another. It's not all Richard Cory tragedy or Romeo and Juliet tragedy. Most people, they experience what those around them would call non-dramatic tragedy. But you know, it's all the same. One kid, like Dave, his mother leaves him and then his father, who can't see any other way, kills himself with a copper-mine cough. Another kid, like Roadside Girl, loses her mother to an unknown sickness, never knowing her mother or, even, who her father is. You get beat up, trapped, forced. I loose my father to cigarettes, my brother to the devil, and my mother to my brother. Lydia, she's always lived alone. Never had anyone else to share her life with. Always lost everything—not here but other places. Rae Miller's alone. She lost her husband and then lost her lover who she had never made love with. People lose others all the time to different things at different times. People fall apart just like things fall apart and there's nothing we can do about it. Nothing. It's all tragedy. It's all life. I would guess that there isn't life without tragedy. There's only life without realization. There are those who pop out of the big tragedy, they're the ones who realize and move on. Then there are those who don't. Those are the ones who walk around and mumble to themselves cursing this God or that or mankind or life or death or the dead or the living. Doesn't really matter what they curse as long as there's something to curse. Those are the people who have let the tragedy eat 'em. And that's too bad. But there is no life without tragedy."

"What about Rich?"

"Rich's tragedy is the worst kind of all. It's knowing that you have caused misery in those around you." He looked at Brenda. "Even those you love." He thought about how he loved Sarah and how she had left him. He remembered that young love of the early days and projected that love onto Rich and Brenda as if they were he and Sarah. "It's that and the can't-get-the-blood-off-my-hands tragedy that'll haunt him, forever."

"But Rich has never . . . "

"You don't think that Rich has seen the crows that you say you've seen? If they are real crows, the kind that come to you in the night, and they watch and caw in horrible gazing black eyes, like you say, he's seen 'em. If you think they haunt your nights and you've got nothing to haunt except, excuse me, the sin of passivity." It was the wrong thing to say and he knew it, but he couldn't see it any other way. "Then think about how they must haunt his nights in terrifying screeches. He's carrion in his dreams except, unlike carrion, he's alive. He's torn to pieces by his past. His crows are more than two. They are as endless as his sin. We should feel pity for Rich. Even though he's a son-of-a-bitch, we should feel pity for him because he's like Prometheus; he's tied to a rock and those birds are tearing out more than his liver."

She tightened her eyebrows in a grotesque squint that said I'm not sure I understand. "Pro-what-a-ma?" She shook her head as to say it didn't matter. "You really think he's seen the crows?"

"Maybe not the same crows you've seen but some crows, yes. Another shape, another color but just as scary and always there. He's not different than you or me. He's not a twisted, crazy, freak of nature. He's only a man. And men have fears. Just like you and me. We're not unique. We all live with tragedy. That's why every time you read a book or see a movie about the person that seems to have everything going wrong in their life, you say I know that story. I've lived that story. You look around at other people and you think you . . . you probably don't get it because you haven't lived it. But I get it. I've been there. And when you say that the person standing across from you shakes his head, inside. No, he says, *you* don't get it. I've really lived that. I've really been there. And you both walk away like the other one doesn't know anything about tragedy. But that's not true. It's not true at all."

She stared at him. This was Thomas Gern talking, she wondered, quiet stay-behind-the fence Gern. Maybe he was right. Maybe all of life was tragedy and the differences in people came through those who suffered because of it and those who lived because of it. She didn't think about it but she moved from the yard back into the cabin where the bag of food was balancing on the half wall, sighing "put me away, there's frozen meat in here." The sun was still filling the room. He followed her because he didn't really know what else to do. They had to decide how to handle this situation. Maybe she should just file for divorce and live in the cabin and forget all the rest. But that probably wouldn't do. It probably wouldn't work for her with Rich in town or for Tom with the ghost of high sin wearing a badge for the people. No, he was quite sure that wouldn't do. The price for his sin was surely higher than that.

The situation was ironic. The situation called for a sever-the-head-and-the-body-will-die philosophy. The question was where was the head and what was the best way to sever it? It was the story of Sir Gawain except the Green Knight wore an elected badge and a brown uniform and there was no green sash. Tom had never liked Rich but he had always trusted the law. He saw that too in his story of tragedy, the law didn't have faults. People had faults. It just happened that this person worked for the law that worked for the people.

"So what should we do?" Now the question came from her.

"I think you and I and somebody with a clear head like Lydia should make some phone calls and then take a ride into

Marquette or somewhere if we need to and hear what some fancy-schmancy lawyer has to say about this—all of this. I think before we go in there you should write down everything you told Lydia."

"Already have."

"I don't think we should necessarily confirm our stories. I don't know that there are any stories except the truth and your truth and my truth and Rich's truth are all going to be a little slanted."

"You think a lawyer will know what to do?"

"He'll know better'n you or me. At least he'll know the law. I was angry at first. I wanted to rush over there and shoot the bastard. Sit in the bushes with my shotgun and BOOM. Cut him right in half. No more Rich. But Lydia's right about that. Can't be taking the law into my own hands, vigilante man. Nope, I'd guess that someone who knows the books will know what's best."

"So that's it?"

He shrugged his shoulders for a response. "You need to get a fire going in here. Take the bite off."

"I'm confident but not that confident. Not until we have some answers."

"Gonna be too cold to wait for answers."

"It was pretty cold all summer," she said. "Shivered down to my bones all summer long over there on Pine Street. Think I can make it a few more days."

"Gonna be longer'n that."

"Ya never know." She said.

"I'm gonna wander over to Lydia's. She's probably not home but I may as well check. She knows more about this sort of thing than I do. I only know farming. You wanna walk with me?"

"Got groceries to put away. Stop by when you come back. I like company these days." He turned to leave. "Tom? Thanks." She sounded like she was finished he waved a silent okay. "Hey." He stopped. "I'm not sure Lydia told you, I . . . ." She didn't feel bad about it, and she didn't want him to feel bad about it either but it was weird news not to cause that skin-crawly feeling. "I lost the baby." His mouth dropped. "It's all right. I never wanted the baby. It's okay. I just wanted you to know." She had the look of confidence on her face. It was not the look of a woman who has just lost a baby. And he saw that.

"Then, I'm not sorry," he said, and he wasn't.

Oxford stood with his horn-rimmed glasses and his college haircut stuffed into his metal helmet and, instead of books, he held an M79 by the strap. The village had beaten mud paths like sidewalks between three bamboo shacks. Trees grew among the hootches and the compacted mud seemed to sneak into the forest and disappear.

"Don't burn it yet. Not finished looking around here."

"Search and destroy. Search and destroy. Let's just burn the mother and get out of here." Wholesale wasn't listening to the Sergeant. He was screaming at Oxford.

There were four dark-haired bodies—barefoot and in ragged farmer's clothing that had been threadbare before it had been ripped apart by the rapid fire of .223 rounds. They were trophied on the ground like in old photos of big game hunters.

"Aw fuck! Gern get over here."

"What is it Sarge?" The sergeant was standing by a well in front of the middle hootch. He had surveyed the bushes and trees, and now held his .45 Colt out toward Ezra. "I don't want that."

"You're going down Gern."

"The hell I am. Send the NFG. He's smaller than I am."

"Take the Colt. You're going down. You've done it before."

"Give the experience to someone else."

"Take the Colt; you're going down."

"I haven't seen you clean that pistol. When was last time you cleaned it? I haven't seen you clean it."

"The Colt's clean. I cleaned her this morning." He fired three or four shots from the colt. No one was counting.

"Jesus Christ. I went down last time. Send the NFG. He's small."

"I'm not sending some green grunt into a tunnel. The kid doesn't have a confirmed kill. Now take the Colt. That's an order." Ezra grabbed the gun and pulled the flashlight off his belt. He saluted the Sergeant.

"God damn it Gern. You know better than that."

"I sure do, Sarge. Where the hell's the entry?"

The sergeant was staring at a bush on the other side of a garden of unidentifiable vegetables. He pointed. "Oxford. Search the hootches. There's probably an entry in one of 'em. When you find it, you stay there. Wholesale. Start looking under the bushes out there." The Sergeant was pointing into the black trees. "There's a reason why no one's here. Watch for booby traps and everybody on rock 'n roll." Unconsciously, everyone thumbed his fire-selector to the rear. "Bama. You take the NFG and patrol the perimeter. There's no one around and that makes me nervous as hell. I do not want an unexpected firefight." Ezra was hunched at the entry to the tunnel. "Gern you go down there and take a look around. Take no prisoners."

When Ezra disappeared everyone above ground thanked God they didn't have to go down. The Sergeant knew better than to send the NFG. The kid was from New Jersey. The only time he had even seen a gun was in basic. Always send the hunters, he thought. Wholesale was cocky but on more than two occasions his M16 had jammed because he hadn't cleaned it properly. It was the kind of mistake which got soldiers killed. It was the kind of mistake that deer hunters didn't make and the Sergeant knew that. Two dark eyes at another entry of the tunnel underneath some ferns watched Ezra go down. The teenage girl rocked baby with her hand gently over its mouth. She cocked a .38 revolver and waited to die like her family had just died.

The tunnel was tight; Ezra hardly needed the ladder because

there was no place for him to move. It was like he was trying to squeeze down a laundry chute. At the first elbow he cranked his body around so that he was moving headfirst. The flashlight dimly illuminated the packed dirt walls. Ezra crouched looked at his compass and drew blueprints in his mind. He breathed through his mouth so as not to make any sound. He wasn't quite sure if his light could be seen on the other side of the twists and curves that cut his ability to see. Three yards after the elbow where he turned around there was a tunnel to the right and a tunnel to the left. "You fuckers." He tapped the flashlight against his right thigh, "Righty tighty," and turned right. A short tunnel. A few boxes of US Army rations were stacked at the end. Just refuge that had fallen off a boat or slipped off an APC, he figured. He turned and went to the other off chute. Short tunnel, went nowhere. Ezra continued his descent. He came to a "Y" and knew that there was no way he could know if there were any NVA in the tunnel. He went left and crept slowly clockwise through the system. He passed a large room with six weaved sleeping mats and two Soviet rifles, then came to a small food store and was stopped dead by the shaft of the well. He turned around. No sign of Charlie. Ezra squeezed down two other dead-end off chutes. When he rounded another corner his flashlight shined on two brown eyes. The girl had stuffed the revolver in the waist of her pants in order to hide her child beneath an empty basket. Ezra judged her to be fifteen.

Above ground Oxford stood over the main, interior entrance nervously tapping his foot. He pointed his M79 into the mouth of the cave. Wholesale had not found another entry and the Sergeant knew damn well that there was another entry.

Ezra was pushing the girl in front off him through the other entry. He turned his flashlight off and called, "Coming up. Coming up. Prisoner first."

* * *

"A thousand fucking tunnels down there but nothing else. Just a hideout to get away from people like us."

"Hideaway my ass. The gook had a gun didn't she? I say waste her before anything bad happens." Wholesale pointed the girl's revolver at her head. The girl was talking but her frantic Vietnamese words sounded like screams of intonated cee achs.

"I told you not to take prisoners. What the hell are we supposed to do with her?"

"Put the gun down, Wholesale. For Christ sake you already killed the kid's family. Don't you think you've done enough damage for one day?"

"Them or us Gern."

"Them or us? What were they gonna do? Knock you down with their bamboo rakes?"

"You were there when Mayers was telling about his buddy," Wholesale yelled. Got torn to pieces by a bomb that some Charlie bitch had in her basket. Carryin' it just like a fuckin' baby and BOOM his arms and legs were swimming in the sky. Not for me, man. They all need to die. Kill the gook and let's torch this dump."

"Aw shut up—the both of you. Bama get on and radio it in. And all of ya put your fucking helmets on."

"Stop your fucking screaming, gook." Wholesale hit her with the butt of the revolver. Her lip split open and she crumbled to the ground. He was bending to do it again when Ezra stopped him.

"Knock that shit off."

"Prick 25 ain't reaching anything, Sarge."

"Just pineapple the damn thing."

"Close it off?" They were all pointing to the tunnel. The Vietnamese girl saw them pointing. She watched as Oxford pulled the M26 grenade off hit belt. She made a futile run for the tunnel screaming. Though Ezra didn't speak Vietnamese, he thought it sounded like baby.

Oxford rolled an M26 down one corridor and Wholesale did the same at the other end. The Sergeant pulled the pin on another, held it for a two count, then dropped it down the well. During the commotion the young girl ran into the trees—her angry black eyes searching for safety.

"Where's the girl?" The Sarge yelled. "Jesus Christ Bama, what the hell were you doing?"

"I was watching you smoke it. I didn't think she'd run off."

"Wouldn't you?"

"I knew we should have killed that bitch." Wholesale added. "I say we burn this place." Wholesale didn't wait for an order. He pulled a small can of lighter fluid from his pocket, squirted it on one of the shacks and lit it up with his Zippo. He acted like he was lighting autumn leaves that he had raked into curbed streets. Wholesale didn't seem to notice that the leaves were houses. He didn't remember that he, too, had come from a dry, wooden house that would spring into unstoppable fire if someone set it ablaze. Ezra shook his head as the house jumped into flames. He was surprised at how quickly the bamboo took to fire.

He thought about the old, bamboo fishing poles with their red and white bobbers that hung on the wall of a barn a million miles away. He liked fishing. He liked sitting with his father in the small rowboat on the calm, clear water holding onto the long stick of bamboo. That bamboo had come from somewhere. He knew, now, from where. He couldn't imagine throwing the poles into a fire. They were too perfect. Long and slim. Flexible and unbreakable. If they were people they would be the kind of people that everybody liked, the kind of people everybody wanted to be around. In fact, when he had gotten his Zebco casting rod, he learned that he didn't like fishing that way. It wasn't like it had been before. The silent sitting, suspended twenty or thirty feet above giant rocks by a thin epidermis called water. He remembered sitting and not talking to his father for two or three hours, looking at the water, hoping to catch something, but not really caring whether he did or not. He looked back at the burning shack and left his father in the blue water of another world. It was as if the bamboo and the fire were old lovers who hadn't seen each other in years, and they raced into each other's arms and embraced each other in uncontrollable passion.

Wholesale moved his hand slowly with calm gestures, flicking the hot flint wheel of his dirty Zippo that no longer had the wink of polished metal. After each light he clicked it closed and the tight-fitting sound of the metal flicking shut could be heard through the fire, which was now not only eating the bamboo but was also sucking all of the moisture out of the air around them. The fire began to overpower the normally deafening chirps and caws of the forest.

"I don't know why you're doing this."

"What's done is done." Oxford said. "These folks are dead." He jerked his head toward the bodies. "Nobody gonna live in these hootches, now."

"Jesus Oxford, you're as bad as Wholesale. These folks were just farmers. Just like my parents and your parents. They weren't our enemies. They weren't NVA. They were simply farmers."

"And now they're nothing." Wholesale said.

"Oh that's great. Why don't we leave the hootches? These people didn't do anything wrong."

"What? Didn't do anything wrong, what do you mean? The fucking trees spit metal at us all the time. Where do you think those bullets come from? You think the trees are pissed at us?"

"Well if they aren't, they should be. Shit, you don't know if it's VC or Semper Fi shooting at you half the time. Can't ever see anything. You don't know the enemy from someone who'd serve you a chicken dinner. Fucking supreme command in Washington that's our enemy. Not a bunch of poor old dirt farmers like these."

"That anti-war ideology is great when you're in fucking San Francisco or Chicago, and you can carry a sign around and whine and cry about the government who paves your roads and collects your garbage and delivers your mail and builds your sewage systems so you don't have to root around in your own shit like you were a pig. But quite frankly, it's destroy or be destroyed. It's a basic natural instinct that Darwin, you've heard of him haven't you, calls survival of the fittest. I don't wanna die. And if I have to kill a few gooks who don't deserve to die in order to stay alive and I get to torch their fucking houses as a payback, I don't have a problem with that. You sleep with you're fucking eyes open. Take care of what looks like your enemy and maybe you'll be able to close them and dream." Wholesale moved on to the next house. "You know that it would be untrue, if I were to say to you ... " He flicked the wheel of the Zippo in front of Ezra's face and continued yelling in lounge singer style, "girl you couldn't get much higher, come on baby, light my fire."

They didn't even notice they were yelling to each other but it was a necessity. The sound of the fire was eating all the space that usually surrounded their words. Oxford's yell sounded mundane, like mowing people down and burning their houses was something that he did on dates back in high school. Wholesale flicked his Zippo open like he was Captain Kirk ready to be beamed back to the Enterprise. "God damn. Campfire in Cambodia."

"Were not in Cambodia."

"Yeah, Smart guy. You know where we are?" He didn't give Ezra enough time to answer. "I didn't think so."

"Best defense is a good offense," Bama said.

"The saying is the best offense is a good defense."

"Hey Gern. Stop standing around with your thumb up your ass courtin' your girlfriends and get to work." The sergeant made it sound like they were laying brick at a construction site, like the green metal helmets were the new and improved OSHA standards. "Let's burn this shit and get out of here. Before that gook bitch gets back with some of her neighbors."

They had their backs to the pair of brown eyes. The hootches were burning and they stood there and watched them like they were sitting around a campfire. She was fixated on the grave of her daughter, listening to the funeral march of the fire. Then she was gone. The eyes disappeared.

"Let's get the fuck out of here before the party comes back."

"Let's hump."

* * *

A young girl silently serpentined between trees, following the seven Marines. She moved when they moved. When they stopped she stopped. When nightfall came Billings ordered the NFG first watch. Unfortunately for all of them, he had his neck slit by a teenage girl when he accidentally drifted off to sleep. He bled peacefully in the night.

The girl tossed both of the NFG's grenades, one directly after the other. The first killed the Sergeant in the middle of a dream about his eight-year-old boy. The boy was swinging a baseball bat when the explosion shattered the Sarge's helmet.

Wholesale thought he heard something before he died, the same grenade that had torn the Sergeant to pieces sent one fragment of metal under Wholesales left arm. His flak jacket had not helped him.

"Everybody hit it!" Ezra yelled.

"Charlie and Bama had been alive before she let loose with the NFG's M16. Now pieces of their flesh were scattered all over the place. Soft spongy gray matter would feed birds and insects in the morning.

"Ezra?"

"Oxford that you?"

"You okay?"

He had been okay. Then Ezra's spinal cord answered the question as it shut down all circuitry in his body. He turned into jelly and slopped to the ground face first. Ezra was hit.

"Ezra!" He watched Ezra fall to the ground in the broken strobe light of M16 fire. Oxford waited for a sound and there was none.

* * *

At daybreak Oxford was humping deeper into the forest. Lost. Even if he could have picked up the pieces of all the marines he couldn't see any way he could have gotten them out. Ezra had promised him that he would live. And by leaving the others, Oxford had made that prophecy come true.

The girl looked down at Ezra, the only one of six marines still breathing. She sat patiently and sharpened a stick of bamboo. As she did, she watched her life and her mother's life and her father's life disappear in a vision of black smoke. She envisioned the tunnel as it caved in on her daughter and touched the bamboo to Ezra's stomach. His body jerked as she leaned against the bamboo in one downward motion. The weight of her body jammed the bamboo through his mid-section. The stick glided through his skin like it was butter and Ezra let out a horrible scream that woke him for one moment as she anchored him to the ground. Though he had passed out, his body jerked in spastic, electrical shocks.

The girl walked back to the smoldering houses. She sat down on the packed dirt and began digging. Two days ago she had been the daughter of a farmer. She had not been their enemy. However, she was now.

Thomas stood in the darkness of his old bedroom. It was late, somewhere past midnight and before dawn, when everyone slept in deep eye-shaking dreams. No cars moved. Toclep was like other small, northern towns. When the tourists were in town, cars sometimes sputtered down the roads at two a.m., but once the season was over the town returned to the struggling-to-get-by winter that began in late August and lasted until early July. People tucked themselves in early and got up early.

When the days changed, the people changed. Most never noticed the change. In the summer they would yawn, "that fresh air sure makes ya tired, eh?" However, it wasn't that summer air was any fresher than winter air; it was that summer days began with a sunrise at five o'clock and stretched out on the horizon staying light until eleven. Winter days, on the other hand, didn't light until seven-thirty and they burned out before people even got home from work. Though most people didn't even realize it, they were far more tired in winter. No, it wasn't the fresh air or the lack of fresh air; it was the light and the lack thereof, which influenced the body and changed people without them even noticing.

Tom looked across highway 52 to the sleeping town of Toclep, which was bathed in the purple and yellow hues of street lights that were far enough apart to allow for large swoops of darkness to fall between them. The middles of the small blocks were dark, the houses were dark, the yards were dark. The sky was clear.

He had watched the big dipper move across the sky, watching it slowly turn upside down and drift over his house and out of sight like a flock of birds. The sliced moon rose late and was now far beyond his house, behind Captain's Peak, running after a sun that it would never catch. Though there were streetlights, they hung like drooped autumn sunflowers with their heads down and there weren't enough of them to blaze into the sky and block the strength of millions and billions of light years.

There were three bedrooms upstairs. The one he slept in faced west and north across the field toward the mountains. In his mind it was still his parent's room. It allowed him to watch his hay grow and his garden bloom and his five cows chew. The other two bedrooms sat down the hall that split left around the old banister, which was missing one rung. Matthew had sawed Tom's head free from the grips of the cherry railing and had never replaced the rung. The room to the right was Uncle John's; no one had slept there for years. It was an uncomfortable room with a dresser that still called to Tom, "Look over here." The one to the left was his and Ezra's old room. That's where he stood now.

He had taken the news from Lydia as if it were the score of a game of which he already knew the outcome. There had been no storm and though there might be one in the future, there was now utter calm. The bunk beds that had once been in this room were gone now. And like Uncle John's room, no one had slept here in years, either. Thomas Gern was not a moper. He was not a whiner. But tonight, as he looked out the window, he realized that he had let life slip through his fingers like sand. It had raced through his digits and out into the air where it swirled with the wind and disappeared. So much time gone, he thought. So much time alone. Now he was middle-aged though Rae might call him a pup. He had lost his youth when his father raced out of his life in less then two seasons. He had dropped out of Northern to come back to a farm and a mother that Ezra should have been able to take care of without Tom, but couldn't. Tom had always thought that Ezra was smarter than he was. He had always thought that Ezra had something special—that Ezra was stronger. He had always wanted to be Ezra, because Ezra was like a light. Tom had been wrong, though. Ezra hadn't been the strength. If Ezra had been the strength he'd be here now, but he wasn't. Tom had been the strength. He had held life together by himself. It wasn't his fault that he couldn't keep everything together. There were other factors. If Ezra could have been there for him and his mother, for the farm, for himself, the paper clips of life would have turned into epoxy and their lives would have had adhesion. Unfortunately, Ezra had been in another world and that world came to a screeching halt in the late seventies. It was the destruction of Tom's world.

He looked down 52, away from town. A dark figure moved along the road. At first, he thought it was a bear and he squinted behind his glasses to try to bring the shadow into focus. But the figure was standing erect and bears only stood that way to see better or smell higher. This figure was walking not, sniffing or looking. Besides, bears had bad eyes and would stick to their nostrils' trail at night: head down, body following. The image brought a memory of Tom's grandfather who had told him about Waynaboozhoo, the spirit man of the Ojibway.

"Waynaboozhoo awoke on one of his many journeys in the giant trees to see Bugwayjinini. The trees were hemlocks like those that scooped up the Crescent Mountains. And their canopy was so high that a maple tree could fit underneath them. Bugwayjinini was tall and stood like a man." Tom remembered his grandfather's high nasal tone.

Tom pictured the slumped, stupid looking creature as his mind replayed the one film reel he had ever seen of Big Foot—the dark figure with long arms running away from the camera. He wasn't sure whether he believed in Big Foot or not but as a child he had believed the story his grandfather told him. It was a story that his grandfather told him to pass the family heritage on to the next generation. The story had come from Lionel Gern's wife's father, Nibi Ozid. Nibi Ozid had not been a medawin or a chief; he had been an ordinary Ojibway as Tom was an ordinary farmer. But these trees and these shadows were the right trees and the right shadows for such a story.

"Most people never see the beast sent by Gitchie Manito. Bugwayjinini appears to those in need of help—those who're lost. Most never know him because he is sent only to the Indian, like me, Tom. Bugwayjinini is the oldest brother, the protector, the helper sent by the creator to help Waynaboozhoo, to help those who searched for truth in mountains and forests. He who treats nature with respect, like a brother, has nothing to fear, for Bugwayjinini will help guide the lost."

Tom knew the legend and that the legend applied to the Ojibway, but his Ojibway was a long road backwards. Bugwayjinini would help guide his brothers but not those who were not his brothers; they would never see Bugwayjinini. "But we are all brothers," Tom had told his grandfather. And his grandfather had been lost for words because he knew it was true.

Tom remembered another image. The picture of the Boggy Creek Monster pounding on his doors and windows, shaking Tom's world as he knew it, scaring the hell out of him. Was that the Bugwayjinini that would come to help him? Or was that another story, altogether. It was the story of the Bogeyman—not one of nature but one of the devil. Bears, wolves, mountain lions, they did not attack people's houses and Bugwayjinini was not animal, he was spirit. No, animals did not attack people unless they could not tell the difference between people and danger or people and food. They did not bang on windows or doors; they were part of nature. Bugwayjinini might be walking up this road. God knows Tom could have used him.

Tom looked out the window again and searched the highway for the lone figure but it was gone. Then he saw it again as it disappeared into the yellow light of Church Street. He wondered where the hell it was coming from and where it was going this time of night. For all Tom knew, it might have been the Boggy

Creek Monster heading into town to pound on the windows and doors of Rich's world.

He left the room and returned with his cigarettes. He opened the window then remembered that he had already attached the storm windows. He sat on the dresser and looked around the room. The reflection of the red stump of ash glared off the window like the taillight of a car. Every drag was like stepping on the brakes. He looked at the double bed and saw the bunks of old and he remembered.

* * *

"Ezrie? Ezrie?" He whispered above him.
"Yeah, what?"
"Just checkin' if you're awake. Are you awake?"
"Are you stupid? What do you want?"
"Nothing. Just checkin', that's all."
"Tom?"
"Yeah?"
"Shut-up and go to sleep."

It was a conversation that had happened over and over and over again in his youth. He'd hang his head down over Ezra until Ezra got so annoyed that he would grab Tom by the hair and yank him out of the bunk, and Tom would land with a crash on the floor.

"Are you two out of bed?" Matthew's voice came up the stairs. Tom had imagined him standing at the bottom with one hand on the railing and the other on his hip. "Don't make me come up there."

"Isn't me Dad." Ezra yelled. "Tom's out of bed." Tom would try to scramble back into the bunk but Ezra would keep knocking him down.

"You're gonna get it, Ezra. One of these days you're gonna get it."

He would stretch his legs up to the underside of Ezra's bunk, when Ezra had the top, and push up and down by extending his legs until his knees were locked, bouncing Ezra up and down. Ezra would hang his head over the edge, looking at him.

"Stop staring at me."

"I'll stare at you if I want. Stare, stare, stare, I'm staring at you." Tom tried to reach up and grab Ezra's hair to pull him off the top bunk. But Ezra would grab his arm and swing him out to the middle of the floor where Tom would land with a large, hollow thump. They'd hear movement downstairs.

"What the hell's going on up there? I'm coming up if I hear one more noise." There would be no more noise. Tom would sneak into his bed. Matthew Gern seldom acted on a threat, but Ezra and Tom feared he would. They feared his look in times of anger or disappointment. They weren't afraid of the belt. They were afraid of his voice that deepened and creaked like the floor. It slowed and sunk and hurt them because something they had done had hurt him or Marguerite. They were afraid of the infinite silence, the hundred-year dinners where no one spoke except the forks and the plates and everyone would try not to have them chatting, either. Matthew wasn't much of a talker to begin with, but when he tightened the clamp of silence, comfort levels felt like barometric pressure falling off the scale.

* * *

Like most people in Toclep, Tom was not a late night person. But tonight he didn't feel like sleeping. Lydia had helped. Phone calls had been made. Questions had been asked and answered. Appointments had been scheduled. The lawyers had told her that the FBI would have to have more information to have anything to do with the case because it wasn't really a matter that crossed state lines. It would be something for the state police. Wheels were in motion.

He looked out the window again. He and Ezra had been like brothers everywhere in the world. They were the sons of a son of a farmer. They grew up, went to school, came home, and worked. They were like other people in Toclep, simple without anything too exciting ever happening in their lives. Then the war had come and taken Ezra away like World War II had taken his father. But when the war sent him back, Ezra had changed. Though Ezra had been a little different than the others in Toclep, though he had idealistic visions of peace on earth, goodwill toward man, so did a million other kids in America. That was not unique in those times. No matter, he returned and he wasn't the same brother who had pulled Tom out of bed or the same brother that stared across the fence at Rae Miller as she read her daily mail or the same brother who pulled weeds out of the garden. His obsession with peace, with tranquility, with right and wrong, had devoured the old Ezra. His search for heaven or nirvana or samsara and karma, or whatever, had taken him away from the real truth. The real truth that there were people right here and now that needed each other, that relied on each other for life and death, that survived on the smile and the tear, the handshake and the hug. That truth wasn't mystical or hard to acquire. It was everything and everyday, and it was how those days added up and fell apart. The truth was in the trees and mountains and rivers and lakes. The truth was in mother and father and brother and friend and lover and child. The truth was in work and play. It was in actions and thoughts. It was bigger than words. It was bigger than hiding from reality, and at the same time, it was small enough to fit into every house in Toclep. Exciting things didn't happen in Toclep any more than they happened in Sidnaw, Champion, or Eagle River but exciting things really don't happen to most people. They only happened to people on movie screens, but those people aren't people at all. They're shadows of people—stretched and distorted.

 For twenty years you've been the ghost of Ezra, he thought. You don't even have enough balls to face your own townspeople. For twenty years you've hidden behind this plank fence and tried to make your own truth as if the real truth was not good enough for you. For twenty years you've tried to kill yourself with loneliness, burying yourself in work and crucifying yourself with martyrdom like there was nothing else but burying yourself in work. Maybe it's Ezra's fault that he's dead. Rich helped him into physical death sooner, but that year, 1978, was my poison apple, not the fruit of truth or the fruit of knowledge but the fruit of Snow White—the fruit of death. Now, it's time to wake up. It's time to look around. It's time to stop crying over what my father would've called spilt milk.

Tom cleared the blurriness from his eyes and saw the dark figure again. Who the hell is that, he wondered? Where'd he come from, where's he going and what's hell is he doing this late at night? Again he watched the figure in the dark starlight of the open road. The person was visible but not distinguishable. He walked slowly. There was no lightness to the figure, only tight darkness. The figure absorbed all the light from the stars. Maybe it is Bugwayjinini, Tom thought. Maybe Dave or maybe my great-grandmother sent him here to help me, to help us. The figure merged with the darkness as the road closed and was caved by trees. I like a night walk, too, he thought. Then he thought about the feeling he got when he encountered a black bear at night. Even though a bear probably wouldn't bother him, he'd feel scared all the same. A bear doesn't know that I'm not part of his nature, he thought. As far as they can tell, I'm no different than a deer or a fisher. I just smell different, that's all. I smell dangerous.

Tomorrow would struggle to be a clear day. The sun would try to push, but cold would not be shoved into the corners of the woods, under rocks, into streams, or behind shadows. The trees would burn their yellow-reds and scarlet-orange fires, but the sky would be cold. The wind would carry what was left of the land's heat out into the lake where the waves of Superior would gulp it away and replace it with the winter cold that was buried in her depths. Tomorrow the town would wake up like yesterday and put coffee on and scrape sleep out of the corners of its eyes and move into the autumn day, the day that cried to everyone in the same whisper. "You're getting older. Look at you. You are the trees, you are the browned grass, you are the faded sky. You're getting older every second, so it's important that you live your life. You haven't forgotten how to live your life, have you? I fear that you'll wake up some time, like Thomas Gern did last night, and see that you've let the warm knife of life slide through buttertime and sever you from your past and your future, both of which are the same thing: your life." And though not many would hear it; that's what the day would whisper. That's what days always whispered.

Rich had not been sleeping well. When Tim asked him why he looked so dragged out he replied that he had the flu, which was not odd for this time of year. Many of the school kids were out with the flu. Unfortunately, it had not been the flu that was stuck in Rich's craw. It had been the crows. The crows were increasing in intensity. They were no longer like jays or the robins. They hung on indefinitely. He had seen them off and on and then off again over the years but he had not to let them bother him. Now the crows were coming every night, every nap as if Brenda, in leaving, had sent them to him. Now they were larger. They were more prominent.

His dream, which had come to him in different forms over the years and had just about faded out of existence, was back in dreary, full-spectrum color. It had mutated into a phantasmagoric abomination that was grinding his bones. The character, with which he spoke in many dreams, had rotted and turned green-black. There was now a putrid, yellow pus coming from the man's mouth and coming from the hole under the man's ribs. Rich and the man no longer spoke in matter-of-fact, business-like tones as if carrying on affairs of numbers. Their conversation was frantic and urgent. It was impatient and worried. It was cluttered and anxious. He no longer strode easily to the figure and walked quietly in conversation. Rich stumbled away now. The dream was full of running—all the time running away from the blackened body. Rich had even stopped in his dream and waited for the man, who still seemed calm, to catch up with him because it was inevitable that he would. But that had done no good. When the man caught up to Rich, which he always did, Rich was forced to run again. So, Rich just kept running in his dreams. He would run until he was out of room, as if the space of his mind was finite like the space of his head.

The dreams always ended in the attic or on the roof of some building where Rich tried to climb higher, tried to escape. They ended with nowhere to run, no way to escape, no speed to free himself.

He had stopped in his dream and when the man approached, he saw neither the man from the dentist office picture book nor the shirtless, young soldier. He looked straight into the figure's eyes and he saw himself—a decaying, black corpse that looked both mummified and moist with swamp rot. The himself he saw was chasing him and being chased at the same time. Rich saw that he was the pursued and the pursuer.

Lately, he had to sit up in bed and hope that the images would go away. He would get out of bed during the night and dry himself off then walk around the room shivering as the air wicked away the rest of the moisture. Then he would fall back into his damp sheets afraid to close his eyes. He would stare at the gin bottle, which had become his teddy bear. However, his eyes would close for him, because he was tired. Once, he had noticed that the rotting Rich that chased him was being chased by the man from the blue book and the soldier, who walked effortlessly, without concern with a girl who had swollen, busted, cheek bones, and Brenda. He was sure it was Brenda. Behind her were others, but he couldn't recognize them. As they came for him, Rich stared in disbelief. He'd run but it felt like he had been strapped with bungee cords and when he turned around they'd still be there. They were all calmly walking, and he had put no ground between himself and them. No matter how fast he ran, the space between them only changed in its diminishing.

"What do you want?" Rich called to the rotted man.

"You."

"It's not right. It's not right. I used to come for you. We used to talk but you were different. You weren't me. You were him." Rich didn't point but both knew which him they discussed.

"Yeah, but something's gone wrong. There's somehow a new variable." The crows floated softly above their heads. They weren't menacing in the least. They floated like beautiful, blue seagulls that were lighted from the inside.

"I know the new variable. It's her." Again there was no need for him to point because they weren't really speaking to each other. They never opened their mouths. They only opened their minds and all the words from all the minds flowed in a tidal wave of great clarity and confusion, of screams and hushes.

"Maybe it's her? Maybe it's them?" The eyes of the man, which appeared to look inward for thousands of miles, responded.

Rich no longer cared whether the man would try to get out of it. Now, it was more important for him to escape, for him to get away. Although, every time he tried, it had ended the same way. Impossible. He could remember conversations with the other dream man and how the dream man had told him the law was bigger than he was. He never believed it. Now he did believe. He believed there was nothing he could do but wait. Multitudes of dreams like that had washed his shores since Brenda had left and had increased intensity since his meeting with Lydia. He could hardly close his eyes without seeing these images.

Then there had been last night's dream. The dream of being watched. The dream that opened a deep, sewn scar. The dream that had forgotten to retreat all the way into his soul and had accidentally dropped a white envelope onto the floor into reality at the base of the stairs.

He had been on the run. When the rotting man finally made it to his door, Rich ran up the stairs, locking the door to the bedroom. When he pushed open the door, there was the line of people standing and waiting behind him on the stairs, so Rich fled to the attic. As Rich knew he would, the rotting man came into the attic. Rich scurried on all fours like a squirrel onto the roof, but the rotted man already stood there. He was behind him and in front of him. He knew every move before Rich could make it.

"There's no place to go," he said to Rich. "I hate to say the word, but it's hopeless."

"No it's not." Rich's voice whined like he was a pleading, junior high kid. He squatted and jumped from the roof.

"Look you're not the first person this has happened to. I'm just trying to save you the effort."

"No!"

"Down is where you're headed anyway. I don't know why you always run up, up, up, when you gotta go down? You've been told that, right? He told you that, didn't he? He must've because he can't lie; it's beyond his capabilities. He was supposed to tell you that."

When Rich was on the ground he was no longer in his back yard. He was behind Will's. The rotted man stared down at him from the roof and now two of the others were in front of him. The girl with broken cheekbones who was no longer bruised and the young soldier, fully-clothed in a green army jacket and blue jeans. The girl had red-brown hair with distinct highlights that blended into the rest of her dark hair. The man was Ezra. The two were surrounded by Rich and four other blackened bodies, whose voices he recognized like his own fingers. Rich was in the dream, yet watching the dream. Rich was the main character, the writer, the narrator, and reader all at the same time. He was the critic and the criticized. He was the assailant and the victim.

"Bringing more of your freaks into town, eh? Don't you think we have enough of your Hara Krishnas leeching onto our town? Huh? You may be a Gern and we can all accept that, can't we boys?" They shook their heads in zombie slowness. "But the rest of these folks Ezra, I just don't know. Got yourself a spook and a wetback over there. Got yourself a couple of whores from God knows where, sucked in some of the folks 'round here, too. Includin' my cousin Katrina who seems to be sleeping with your wetback buddy. My Uncle Steve, he's not too hip on this whole thing. Can't say that I am either. Nope, I don't like that. Don't like that at all. You got 'em all believing that you're God or something. Got 'em selling their things and suckin' your dick, I s'pose. Is that what's goin' on, honey? Got you all out there suckin' his dick?" The darkmen were sharks moving in circles around Ezra and Patty.

In his dream there was no time between words and actions. They were pouring in, mixing together. He wasn't sure if he had really said these words or other words. He wasn't sure if he was saying them in the dream or watching himself say them in the dream. It was a blender of scenes.

"Fuck you rednecks." He saw the spit, a patient spider moving across a circle before it spread out on his face. Now, he remembered. Patty's words pushed Eric McGrogey. He hit her so hard that she crumpled—motionless, like heavy, wet clothes into Seiler Stephenson's arms. Seiler laughed his broken, unsure laugh. Ezra was a young man in the dream. He no longer assumed the shape of the man from the dentist office book. He moved with slow ticking motion like single frames of a film flashing on a large, white screen and clocked McGrogey on the side of the neck with his forearm. McGrogey dropped immediately to his knees and the film was now running faster than time. Eric would have gotten up. He wanted to, but his spine kept telling his legs, to stay down. His dizzy eyes watched as John Bower hit Ezra. The spikes had been removed from his ten. Ezra collapsed. The dark bodies moved and closed around Ezra, around the girl. Rich was with them.

As he stood outside of his dream and watched the five men grow and swallow Ezra, he became Ezra and he was pounding on himself. Then he was standing on the roof of Will's, watching them pull the bodies and the bodies were he and he pulled them and he watched himself pull himself.

He awoke in a flash of white light to his dark room and sat breathing with emphysema. He watched the room to make sure that no one was coming in through the window or the stairway door. Before he was shocked into his erect position, before the dream lightening flashed out of view, he had heard something. What he heard had saved him from the rest of the dream. What he heard probably saved him from a night aneurysm or a heart attack. Now, there was just darkness and open-eyed silence. He was wet again. When he finally realized no one was going to chase him into his attic, he got out of bed and dried off. He walked down the stairs. That was when he saw that the dream had not retreated entirely to its night roost. At the bottom of the stairs on the Berber carpet was a white rectangle that screamed in the silent darkness. Rich stooped at the landing. He had the envelope. It was real. He could feel it in his hands. He walked into the kitchen and turned on the overhead light. If he could have seen outside, he would have seen the two crows under the small willow tree, whose eyes had just popped open.

The kitchen had the tinny, echoing emptiness of an empty beer can being set on a counter. The floor was dirty from spilled beer and tipped Ramon noodles. The wastebasket was full to the point that the compacting boot would no longer push the garbage together. He opened the refrigerator and the light spilled out into the other light. There was nothing in the 'fridge but beer and condiments. If he wouldn't have had his mind somewhere else, he might have asked why there were so many condiments. When did they use all of them? He stared into the refrigerator with one hand on the open door and the other holding the white envelope. Then, without thinking he walked away. He wasn't sure if he had closed the door or not. He just turned away and looked into the glossy darkness beyond the kitchen window. The light from the kitchen spilled out onto the grass, but Rich couldn't really tell that.

He opened the envelope that had not been sealed and pulled out the single piece of unlined paper. It made the sound of a crushed, brittle maple leaf as he unfolded it to the blue ink. He read to himself:

Rich—we've been watching you. We know what you've done. In the distant past, in the near past, in the now past, we've watched you. There's death in the air you breathe. We've watched you for years. Since that night, September 1978. You remember us, don't you? And then beating your wife, forcing her down, how could you? Things are going to come down pretty fast now, Rich, because we've had enough of watching you.

With no respect whatsoever,
The Crows.

He read it only once. The letter and his arm dropped with the dead weight of gravity and he released the paper from his hand. It sat open to the world on his kitchen table. He knew the handwriting, well. It was Brenda's. Brenda had come into the sleeping house and stood at the bottom of the stairs. She had placed the ghost-like letter on the floor and looked up the corridor to a shivering and frantic, dream chase. She was here. She was in town. She was no longer afraid of him. She was after him. She had been inside his dream. She had seen the crows. She was cheating. He didn't say anything. He didn't mumble to himself. He slumped out of the kitchen. He had no energy to be angry. It had been scared out of him in tiny drops of cold sweat that had been absorbed by his sheets. The light of the kitchen went off. Rich sat on the couch in the living room in the darkness between midnight and daylight trying to remember where he had put his pistol.

The crows closed their eyes when the light of the kitchen disappeared. There was a dark figure walking slowly down the quiet of highway 52. Stepping softly in the star shine as a cigarette eye glowed from the upstairs window of the white house behind the plank fence. When morning came, Rich was still sitting on his sofa. Eyes open. Looking nowhere.

Ezra had been at school but now he was home with a five-day trade of books and papers for broadaxes and mallets. There were a couple of inches of snow on the ground. If looked at from a distance the snow seemed to cover everything, up close it weaved its way into the stiff, tall grasses like dandruff. The ground was hard. It had become part of the rock that reached from beneath the shoreline into the cold water of Superior. The sun, long gone over the mountains, was no longer visible from Sunset Rock as it sank below the horizon, which it would do within the hour. Birds no longer sang. They clattered and seemed to bite at each other when they spoke in their short, cold breaths. It was hat and glove weather and Ezra, Tom, and Matthew were wearing long johns and thick, brown jackets in the fading light of old-fashioned construction.

Even after Ezra had been home a while and his wounds hid beneath his scar and clothes, he would sometimes jerk with spasms of sharp pain. Whether it was real pain or memories of real pain was hard to tell from the outside. However, from within, Ezra would feel like a wild dog was tearing the raw, red meat off a steak bone.

The gnashing teeth of pain bit Ezra. His body jumped. Ezra dropped the end of the heavy piece of hemlock he had hoisted above his head, stretching his body out, lifting the framework to the skeleton of the cabin, leaving his side open for an attack of angry dogs. That's what had happened in the last hour before sundown.

His father couldn't help his reaction. The log swung up and nearly pinched his gloved hand between two, wooden battering rams. It just missed Tom, who was carving plug-nails out of maple, as it crashed to the floor. Tom escaped with a shocked breath that steamed out of his blue stocking cap. When he got to the floor, Matthew pulled off the thin, worn, leather glove, which had been cut cleanly. He had a nasty blood blister that was swelling and spreading like an oil slick on the fleshy web between his thumb and forefinger. The next time he swung his hammer, pain would jolt through his arm the same as hitting a baseball with a cracked bat. "God damn it, Ezrie." The log had bounced off the bottom of his ladder and Matthew had had to jump from where he stood five or six feet above ground. He held his hand and was writhing in pain, tightening his face like he had a lemon in his mouth. He was trying to push the pain down inside as he bit his tongue to hold back the tears that were in a wild dash for his eyes. "You gotta warn me when you're gonna do that. I could lose my hand. Or worse than that, my other son." He looked over to see if Tom was okay. Ezra was holding his side and was bent over on the ladder, swallowing in gulpy, loud swallows. The log was now on the ground and not moving. Matthew was still holding his hand. "Sorry, son. I didn't mean . . . it wasn't your fault. But someone could really get hurt. You okay?" He was still gripping his hand as he walked over to Ezra who was hunched on his ladder. "You want to call it quits for the day? It's gettin' dark. We can hoist this up there tomorrow."

Matthew didn't make decisions for Ezra. He knew that his son should probably take it easy but he also knew that work was good for him. It took his mind off the place that it often trailed back to when it was quiet—that unknown, dark, forest with swelling pain in a little clearing and an M16 striking, striking, striking. Then, darkness and small, jerky breaths waiting to die, not knowing what happened, not remembering the past but for the burning mouth of hell. Matthew wondered if Ezra was busy enough in school to keep from drifting back there or if, when he studied at night, he would turn the page of a book and see himself stapled with bamboo to the forest floor.

"I'll be okay. I just need a little breather." He looked down, "Sorry Tom. You okay?" Tom nodded his head and looked at his father whose eyes were shiny with pain. Ezra straightened his body and tipped his head back as he took an eyes-closed breath of air through his nose. "Mose is supposed to be coming up tomorrow or the next day. It'll be a lot easier to get these supports up when he gets here."

"Ya know," Tom said, "I could help with those, too. It's not like Ezrie's any stronger than I am."

"I know you could, Tom." His father knew that actually Tom wasn't as strong as Ezra.

"Yeah, but why bother when Mose can throw the damn logs on his shoulder and lift 'em by himself. And crack a joke while he's doing it."

"He's right about that, Tom. Mose is about two of you and three Tim Conways rolled into one. Feel sorry for him though, every time that poor kid comes into town the place swells up like a child with the mumps. It's as if they'd never seen a man walk on two legs before. Poor Mose has to put up with a town full of ornery folk who think cuz he's black that he's, he's ... hell I don't know what they think, 'cept whatever it is, it's not very nice. All those church-going folk. It doesn't make any sense to me."

"Me neither. Not like we're gallivantin' all around town either. Don't go much farther than Rae's, to tell the truth."

"What else is there in this town?" Tom commented.

"Got a point there."

"Worst part of it is that our bar full of drunks got nothing better to do than moan about their lives. A bunch of people who ought to be proud to have a couple of Purple Heart veterans in their presence, but instead only have a bunch of under-their-breath comments and snickers. Ta hell with them Ezrie, that's what I say. Ta hell with them."

Ezra imagined a live heart, something like the chicken-heart, ten feet tall, sitting at the bar—purple as violets, pumping. He remembered meeting Mose at the infirmary and Mose telling the story of dragging himself through the dark swamps because he was more afraid of the NVA than he was of snakes. If he stuck to the swamps, he had told Ezra, he'd probably stay clear of the VC. At least, that was what he had thought before he ran into three different congregations of Charlie, as Mose called them. "Ta hell with them," Ezra mumbled, unconsciously repeating his father. "All that to get back to this." His words were lost in the universe, floating through infinity.

"Mose keeps his cool. He doesn't seem to mind." His father said.

"Guess not. He likes coming up here. Says he'd like to stay. When I talked to him on the phone yesterday, he said that it was, what did he say . . . something, man, really something. Mose doesn't have a lot of skills. Went to a bad school and didn't like it."

"Who didn't go to a bad school?" Tom interjected.

"True. Mose said he liked being here, learning how to build houses the old way. Said you're the first father he's ever known that treated him like a father ought to treat a son."

"That's a mighty nice thing for him to say. He's a good kid. I mean man. You tell him if he wants to stay, there's room. If he doesn't have a job down there we got a cabin to build up here. Doesn't pay much, though."

Ezra was learning on the job. His father had spent all his free time helping Ezra learn how to hew and shape logs. He would come home after work and walk through the kitchen with a quick peck on Marguerite's cheek and be in his overalls and walking out the door before she had even turned around. Matthew liked this work. They had skipped Deer Season this year. None of the three seemed to mind because the construction had been time spent together and work they enjoyed. Matthew hadn't used the skills since he was a boy, when his father and he had built a small hunting cabin out near Forgotten Lake, which now belonged to the park. He had to search lost corners of his mind for how to form the notches and fit the logs and shape the plug-nails. He had to remember which logs were best for which part of the house. Ezra's cabin was no little, square, hunting lodge either. It would have a loft and electricity and plumbing, all of which made the construction more difficult. Matthew wanted to do it right and Ezra wanted to do it the way it had always been done in the past, the way the barn had been built. In order to do it right, Ezra had to become a patient spectator, watching his father with the broadax. Matthew's consistent and effortless swings chipped perfect Lincoln Log grooves that fit together like folded hands. He would hold Ezra's arm as he swung the broadax, showing him how to move his elbow and wrist to keep his bites into the wood even. Ezra would look at the logs and select one for a support log. He and Tom would bring it over to his father and Matthew'd say, "Not that one, Ezrie. That son of a pup ain't big enough. Ya need yerself a big one." He'd put his hands in front of him, holding an invisible medicine ball. "That one you got there is a side log. Throw it on the side log pile." And Ezra started forming a pile for side logs with the mistakes he brought his father.

"Okay, let's get this log up there," Ezra said. "I'm okay." This time Tom supported the log in the middle as Ezra and his father tried to maneuver it into drop position, so it would fit into the hewed lock grooves at the end and not be off-kilter or unbalanced. They didn't want to have to rock it into position. Once a log dropped into the grooves it didn't want to be rocked. Matthew had hewed the grooves so that they were tight, so when a log was in position, it was in position and it wouldn't need any shims to even it out. They didn't all work that way, but he wanted them to and many did. That's why the house took so long to build. It was a house and tight fits.

"Fits snug as a bug. Just need to pound 'er in a little. Snug it down good and tight." The log had been about sixteen feet long and if it hadn't have dried for a year they would never have gotten it above their heads. "Gonna take more than a tornado to knock this house down. Long after Toclep is gone, this house will still be standing. It'll look around this clearing and say, I'm here to stay—be just like that rock over there."

"What's next, or should we pack it in?" Ezra was standing on top of the log now, pounding it down with a six-foot log that still had branch nubs to hold onto. Matthew was standing on the ground watching Ezra use the primitive ramrod. He stood in sawdust from handsaws and graying wood chips from hewing and he lit a cigarette. Matthew was a big man. Even from where Ezra sat above his head he looked large. He had silver-gray hair that had been dark in his youth but now shined with a tint of yellow: smoker's shine. It wasn't as stained from the nicotine as other people's Ezra had seen, but it was noticeable. Matthew had worked most of his life as a farmer and a builder and finally took the job with the state for security, for the benefits and the retirement he would never get a chance to use. Had he known that he was going to die early and his wife would follow, he probably would have never taken the state job. But he was of the generation that had seen the economy bloom and wither. He was of the nest-egg generation. There would be a rainy day and he would be sure to have money for it. Unfortunately, his rainy day came and his money went in almost a straight line to Tom's pocket. But he didn't know that was going to happen, so he took the job as a forest inspector and regulator. He was large and overweight and his skin was darker than his sons' skin. He was almost a caricature of himself. Sometimes, when he went swimming he would look comically gigantic, his large stomach hanging over his swimming suit and his skinny, chicken legs trying to support the upper body weight of Jack's giant. Neither of the boys was as tall as Matthew.

"Hard to say. I guess now that we have that support in we can work on rafters, but that can wait 'til the light of tomorrow.

Building log-rafters is a dog." He said and sighed. "That one there'll give us something to stand on." He was motioning to the one they had just dropped into place. Ezra finished pounding in the support and came down to stand next to Matthew and Tom who were looking through the frame to the pile of logs. "We've got to get some large logs for those rafters. My grandfather always said, when it comes to top logs, the larger the better. I'm gonna have to trust the man."

"Yeah," looking out at the pile Tom realized that the logs were stacked like firewood.

"Right you are boy. Looking out at that pile, I'd say you boys got some restackin' ta do. Looks to me like all the big logs are on the bottom. Well, now ya know, don't ya."

"Learn something new everyday, damn it."

"Let's just take a few minutes to survey what we've got before we rush out of here." They examined the frame and the pile of logs and the work yet to do. "This isn't gonna get finished before summer's over. More work here than building a regular stick construction."

It had taken them most of the summer to hand shovel the crawl space and secure the footings. They stood within the bare minimum of a skeletal frame. No one had hurried to finish the job. There had been hay and corn this year, gardening and horses and cows which all had taken summer's time. Ezra tried to work on his own but his father would show up shaking his head with his hand on his chin. Ezra would scurry around with "whats" and "what's wrongs?" coming out of his mouth and Matthew would tell him that if he wanted it done right he should hew grooves like this or double stack logs for strength or use a different size log for that. The list was infinite. Ezra was the apprentice. His father, though his expertise came from forty years earlier, was the Merlin.

"Yeah, we're lucky we can even work this late in the season. Not gonna get too much done in four days, but I'm glad I came home last night, anyway."

"Geez, I almost forget you were even gone. I've been gone so much myself. They're getting ready to log between Falls Creek and Houghton again. Mighty shame. Those trees are just starting to look good."

"I've seen some decent sized hemlocks up that way."

"There are now, Tom. In five years won't be anything but birch saplings and jack pine. There's a helluva a lot of bear in that area, too. I wonder where they're all gonna go?"

Tom smiled. "Somewhere close I'd bet."

"Any wagers on the Toclep area? Give Les Smalley a whole new group of bear to eat out of his dumpster." Matthew was reaching for where his wallet usually was.

"Finger-lickin' Smalley'll have all the tourists over there watchin' his stinking garbage get devoured by bear and then one of those stupid tourists will get out and try to get a picture of his son feeding marshmallows to a bear like it was a horse and somebody'll get mauled. Then we'll all have to strap on our rifles and go on a no-holds-barred, wild bear hunt and kill every bear within three counties."

"Ezrie, you're gonna call him finger-lickin' sometime and he's gonna clean your finger-lickin'clock."

"That's all he does, isn't it? Get himself one of his own greasy burgers, like he was the Big Boy himself or something, and drive around in his truck dripping grease and goo, lickin' his fingers as his hands slip around the sloppy steerin' wheel."

"Speakin' of burgers, we ought to get this mess cleaned up before our supper gets cold."

Tom asked, "we having some of Les' finger-lickin' burgers?" They all laughed.

There were days when it seemed like they didn't get any work done at all and days that seemed like they would be able to finish the whole house in a week which, of course, was impossible. Mose would be in tomorrow or the next day, and they would get in two or three days of solid back breaking work. They would get some rafters up, maybe. They would look at the logs that were left and see if they needed to select and fall any more trees for next year's work. There was snow that covered the hard ground now. They had ground it into their work area under their boots and compressed it into dirt. They picked up the tools and stored them under visquain in the skeleton of the house.

"We'll have to get up early and get a good amount of work done tomorrow, before your mother fills us with turkey and stuffing and gravy and everything else that brings on a good nap." The three men walked out of the nook along the fence line looking at the hard ground that stretched across the field and made them shiver like it was a frozen lake. The pasture approached the fence that planked the foot of the mountain. "Ezrie, what do you think you're gonna do up here after you graduate?"

"Not really sure. I might be able to find something, though. I know there's not much that isn't tightening down."

"Like that everywhere. Just want you to remember, you don't have to live up here. It's not like you have to take care of your mother or me."

"Hadn't ever considered it. It's just that it's my town. I live here. This is where I want to live. I've been away and I can't say I really liked being away." Then his voice dropped in tone and pulled away like a shooting star jumping to the speed of light and he was a hundred, million light years away. "I'll come back here and try to put me back together again, try to figure out who I am and why I am and what went wrong and how to fix it." He was serious, and the comment was what worried Matthew Gern about his eldest son—the son who had gone away a teenager, to a war he had been against, and came back a silent man, with violent memories and a hole that went all the way through his body and into his soul. Matthew worried about all the king's horses and all the king's men not being able to put Ezra back together again. The house, construction, school, they all had occupied Ezra, but what would happen when all that was done? What would happen when there was only time and memories and Ezra and space? Matthew wanted his son close. He never wanted him to disappear into the woods, off the path, on the other side of the fence again. However, he knew that a man with time on his hands only goes to one place, the place behind his eyelids—the place of dark, gray considerations where reality mixes with dreams and dreams with nightmares and when it is all stirred together it is hard to tell which is which. When Ezra wasn't working on the house, he would become a Greek statue at the fence in pensive silence, staring out into nothing and seeing everything. Matthew had watched him turn into rock and then become invisible as he stood at the fence.

"Not me," Tom jerked Matthew back into the now.

"Yeah, Tom's gonna be an actor. Gonna go out to Ho-Lee-Wooood and win himself an Oscar Meyer wiener." Ezra laughed and pushed Tom's left shoulder.

"What's your degree going to qualify you to do, anyway? Communications? What's that? I can't say I know of anyone with a Communications degree," Matthew said.

"What you mean to say is you don't know anyone with a degree. I know it's Toclep. I'll be the first."

"Smart alecks always get their ass kicked, Ezrie. Remember that."

"I do. Believe me, I do. I'm not really sure what it will qualify me to do. Talk, I guess."

"You don't need a degree to do that, Ezra." Tom laughed and turned around in front of Ezra. "You've never had trouble talkin'. Only trouble you've ever had is sayin' the right thing at the right time."

"Yeah. I'll say the right thing to you, ya punk." He put Tom in a headlock and they struggled along the fence in jest.

"All right you two. Knock of the shenanigans. Let's get this wagon train moving a little faster toward the dinner table." They cornered the fence and started to walk into the cold wind that blew off Superior. Matthew thought that there would be plenty of time to worry about the future, tomorrow or the next day or when the future came.

As Matthew, Ezra, and Tom neared the house, the lake spit cold, damp air which it would continue to spit well into January before it froze far enough out for someone to think the whole thing was frozen and for the wind to become dry, cold, brittle. It was rare when the entire lake froze. That was the kind of winter that froze the marrow inside of bone. That was the cold wind that Matthew feared had blown into his son and would rear its ugly head every time Ezra stretched his arms above his head.

"You know I never read the *Tao Ching* before I went to Vietnam. Of, course, I never read anything else, either. I should have, though. I should have known something. But I didn't know anything. Just some simple philosophy. I guess that's what philosophy is, isn't it? Simplistic knowledge that we should all have in the first place." Ezra was sitting with his back to the cabin. His sweat lodge, freshly completed, domed to his right. The sun was down and the night air was cold and free of bugs.

"What do you mean simplistic knowledge?" Daisy asked. "If philosophy were so simple everybody'd be able to grasp it. The whole world would be able to grasp it. There wouldn't be any need for wars or weapons or any of that jazz."

"I'm just saying, a little knowledge of a few simple words, a little belief of a few simple words would have saved me a lot of trouble. The *Tao Ching* says, know when to stop. That's what it says, all right. Know when to stop. Now, if we'd just pay attention to that . . . everything would be all right. Know when to stop. And you'll meet no danger." Ezra pointed his finger across the young fire. "Then . . . you can endure."

"How can we know when to stop? Sounds like religious hubbub. What you are saying is simple, I'll agree with that. But determining when to stop? That's a bit of a problem, isn't it? I mean if you would've known when to stop you wouldn't have been laid out flat and pinned to the mud of Vietnam like a bug for observation. Because you wouldn't have gone to Vietnam in the first place."

"She's got a point there, Ezra." Mose's voice crackled with the fire. "I mean the way you've told that story about motoring upstream and driving those people batty with the whole stick thing. Seems to me . . . Well it seems to me that you would've stayed in college to avoid . . . ."

"Seems to me, too." Daisy added. "Whole lot of babbling."

"She's got you. I mean...you would never have been on that boat . . . . You would never have gone into that tunnel. You'd never have burned that village. And you'd never have been gunned down."

"And that's just it, isn't it? If I had stopped pushing then, I would not have been poked to the ground. I wouldn't have climbed out of there. And I probably wouldn't be here right now. I wouldn't have met Mose."

"Not true." Daisy said. "You had already predicted that you would be back here. Remember that day in the rain when you brought Kristie and I out here to show us this place? You had already seen this."

"That's right," Kristie added. She was sitting away from the fire, picking slow notes to the stars on her guitar.

"True, but I didn't know the circumstances."

"Well shit, Ezra, if that's how your logic works. Hell, I can manipulate some philosophy be it eastern or western to fit every scenario of my life. I'm not arguing with you there."

"Yes you are."

"Shut up and listen to me. I agree. If we all knew when to stop, things would be better for all of us. It just sounds like you're grabbing snippets of information and fitting them to snippets of your life. Everything is out of context."

"Everything is always out of context."

"Oh God, Ezra, don't start that. Take your own advice and stop." Mose laughed.

"You're so serious." Daisy shook her head at Ezra. Her copper hair was tied in one thick braid and laid on her back. The young, yellow flames of the fire shaded her light freckles and splashed her eyes with brightness.

"Point well taken, Ezra. According to everything you've just said, you knew when to stop and didn't so you got stapled to the ground. But who knows if you would have your circumstances might have been completely different and we all might not be sitting her right now. You may never have met Mose. Quite frankly, you might be dead. But you're not." Kristie said. "I don't think knowing when to stop would have helped you that time."

"God, loosen up you two. You guys drip with seriousness. It's a campfire. Can we just look into the flames and enjoy the heat and each other?"

"It's possible." Ezra said. He looked in-between the flames into the darkness of the fire. He spun in vertigo to the burned out hootches in a place of memories that was halfway around the world. He jerked in one not-very-fluid motion and everyone around the fire turned to look at him.

"What was that?" Daisy asked.

"A memory. Just a memory, that's all."

"Isn't just a memory makes you jump like that. What was it?" Mose looked at Daisy. He knew the kind of memory that would make someone want to jump out of his skin. He shook his head at her, but she didn't notice.

"I felt my insides. I felt my insides move up and down."

"What? Right now? You okay?"

"No."

"What's up? What do you want us to do?"

"No. Not right now. I'm okay." Ezra seemed to be talking to the inside of his eyeballs. "I tried to stand up. But . . . but I couldn't, you know. I couldn't stand. I was stapled into that mud. I couldn't even realize at first why I couldn't move. I searched around with my scrambling eyes, looking for something. Something I would recognize. But there wasn't . . . wasn't anything. Nothing. Then I saw the Sarge. I lurched forward toward him.

And I mean lurched. Because I didn't know at first . . . I didn't know that I had been stuck, ya know? Kept trying to move and every time I tried . . . ." Ezra tightened up his face. "It hurt. It really hurt." He swallowed hard. "I couldn't move laterally. I could only move up and down. And when I did, I could feel my insides. I could feel my belly on the outside and the inside. I could feel it slipping. When I finally pulled myself off there were ants and leeches eating away at the hole. And you know what? I . . . I couldn't feel 'em." He whispered. "They were eating me and I couldn't even feel them. I found out there were maggots all around the other hole, the one in my back. Never felt them, either. Well not then. Few days later . . . when everything started itching, I could feel them, I guess. But I didn't know what they were. I have no idea how long I was stuck on the ground or how long the bugs ate me. Absolutely no idea." Everybody was staring at him. Kristie had stopped playing and had turned around. Mose was thinking, don't tell this story. Don't go back there. Don't take me back there. Please, Ezrie don't take me back there. However, Mose had made his wish too late.

"I guess the bugs eat at all of us."

"Anybody ever ask you specifically what happened?"

"Huh? No. I don't think anybody really wants to know. I think that old saying . . . there are some things better off left unsaid came from a grunt."

"Everybody's always talking about the war in generalities. Nobody ever wants us to know how awful it is."

"I don't want to know how awful it is," Daisy said.

"It's not that. I mean . . . have you ever talked about it?"

Mose thought about himself. No he had never talked about it. Not to the doctors. Not to the people in the infirmary. Not to his preacher. Not to his mother. Not to anybody. No one had ever asked him to be specific. No one had ever really wanted to know. "People don't really want to know the truth. It's better if they don't." He said.

"Why is it better?"

Then Ezra interrupted. "I was laying there. Taking deep breaths. I couldn't remember how I got in such a position. All I remember was that girl. The girl . . . I imagine her running into the woods." He stopped. The fire cracked like breaking sticks. "Bang, bang." He shouted. "Bang, bang." Then, only the sounds of the fire popped. "That's what I remember. I don't even know how we came to be where we were. Wholesale . . . that's all I remember. All I remember is I pulled up to my knees and tore a bunch of dried blood loose from my body. It took me a long time to figure out how to get from a kneeling position to a standing position. I tried to pull the stick out of the ground . . . so I could stand up straight. But I wasn't strong enough. I was like a tree planted by streams of water. I had to get off my knees. One, two, three and I jerked. One, two, three and I jerked again. It was like I was working the fence line. Except every time I pulled, electricity shot through me. I don't remember how long it took. But I do remember waking up bent-over. Standing but bent . . . and I looked down to see the bamboo was still secured through me and into the ground."

"Ezra?" Mose groaned.

"The next time I woke up. I was sitting on my ass with a fence post running through me. I was sweating like crazy. It was hotter than hell. And I was confused because I didn't know what to do with the piece of wood that was . . . sticking out of my body. Hey, I said. Hey, I don't know what to do? But there wasn't anybody listening. Only Sarge and Wholesale and . . . and I picked up the Sarge's helmet. I . . . I don't know why. Then I thought about the inevitable. Life, death. I couldn't make it if I tried to maneuver through the forest with the bamboo sticking out of me but if I pulled it out I was worried that all my guts might slide out of me and pool at my feet. So I left it in." They all sat silently for a moment. The sky had grown dark. Only the light of the fire broke the darkness.

"I went to a tree and I . . . I positioned my back so the bamboo was sticking out, touching the tree. Then with everything I had and as quickly as I could, I fell back against the tree. One jolt of lightening shot through me. But it worked. When I woke up it was dark, and I was on my back next to a tree with most of the bamboo sticking out of my stomach. I took my K-bar and slowly sawed. I sawed and I sawed and I sawed over my belly. I barely could grip my knife. I think I sawed my way into eternity. I was sweating. I cried. When the bamboo gave, I had a clear hole in my stomach and I kept putting the K-bar in the tube. I couldn't believe it. I just sat there and looked at the tubular hole."

"That's enough." Mose said. "That's enough, Ezra."

"I don't know what happened after that." Ezra droned. "I walked until I came to a river. I remember thinking... I remember thinking I should have buried the Sarge and Wholesale and the rest of 'em. I stood and watched the water. I watched sticks float by and I knew. Then... then there were two flat bottom boats by the river—both were riddled by bullets. Women were decomposing by the boats. But I couldn't think about them because I was decomposing, too. I took the clothes off the women. I remember doing that. Their bodies were stiff like popsicle sticks. I stuffed cloth into holes. And I got scared. I got scared and I pushed one of the boats out into the river and then fell into it. I almost missed. Almost fell into the river. But I didn't. Nope, I didn't. I followed the current and kept thinking about the sticks leading me out. I kept saying that the sticks would get me home. They wouldn't let me die. And I knew I'd be okay. I'm not sure how long I floated. I do remember sitting in the tiny boat in water halfway up my ass and water only two inches below the edge of the boat. But that's about all I remember."

"I think that's more than enough." Mose said. "In fact, it's far more than enough. I gotta...I gotta go...." Mose stood up.

"Hey where you going?" Kristie asked.

"I just gotta go, that's all." And he walked toward the cabin. Ezra was still staring into the fire. He didn't even move his head when Mose walked away. He, in fact, didn't even hear Mose. He just looked into the spaces between flames and he saw himself. Kristie stood confused looking in Mose's direction and Daisy joined Ezra somewhere in the fire. It was the only time anyone had ever asked him what really happened, and it was the only time he had ever talked about it.

"I was thinking back in time last night," Tom said. Roadside Girl sat across the table from him and coffee steam was twisting above her cup. "I was thinking about how I've let my life slip by me like a passing car on the highway. I was thinking about when you and me replaced those fence posts over there in the corner. I was thinking about what you said about people being spiritless and that term came to my mind." He chuckled. "Rocket eyes. People lost with glossy, photograph eyes sitting behind the steering wheels of their lives without a clue as to which direction they're going or why they're even going. I think I told you that everybody wasn't like that. Well, last night I was looking out into the sky and I realized that maybe everyone is like that. Even the ones who say they're not, like me. They are. They're just so rocket-eyed they can't even see themselves." He was standing looking down at her from the other side of the table. He picked up his coffee cup and walked to the door grabbing the jean jacket on his way out to the porch. It wasn't as if he was in mid-sentence, not even as if he was in mid-thought, but it seemed to her that he was.

"You've got a pile of history that just flopped out of nowhere onto your plate. I don't think you're like those people I was talking about." She followed him out to the porch and they both sat with their coffee, hanging their legs over the edge like it was a dock jutting out into water.

"Yeah. I am. I've been watching myself die since my father

crossed over that summer. I just never realized it. I never went back to college. I simply sat down with a big plate of sorrow and feel-sorry-for-myself and watched, staring into the distance as if a grass fire was burning everything around me, and I never did a thing to stop it. I wasn't rushing into the fire like you said; nope I was doing the opposite, which resulted in the same thing."

"Come on Tom. What were you going to do, turn into a cure for cancer? You still don't know what happened the night Ezra was murdered. How were you going to stop that? It may have been a matter of circumstance, for all you know. And your mother... well, how would you have known? She still had you, but somehow that wasn't enough. What could you do with all those variables?" She was sitting right next to him. Their knees fused together to make one leg.

"I don't know. All I know is I'm dying or I've died already. Every move I made in last twenty years...." She rolled her eyes in disbelief. "Last night I saw something. I saw that if I didn't want my life to swim by me so that when I looked back from my deathbed it looked like one ugly day. If I didn't want that to happen, I had better start living like things matter."

"You do live like things matter. You were happy when you were married. You can't say you weren't. You were living life then. You like living here—your farm, your freedom. And what about now?"

"That's what I'm talking about. I'm not talking about retiring to the grave. I'm talking about living my life. Starting today and living my life."

He looked into her eyes. They had made up their mind to be green today. They reached out and hugged the dull sky and reflected back in granite. Her hair hung in her face and he pushed it back behind her ear. He noticed the look on her face. It was one he had seen a hundred times but he didn't know where. However, he did know that he loved her.

"I've got some business to finish up for Ezra. When that's over, I'm going to try to remember who I was or who I've become or anything about me that I can. This summer has brought it on. You've brought it on." She smiled. "I've never thought. I just went through the motions. I was alive. I just didn't do anything with my life. I wasted it. I don't know what the answer is. But I'm by myself. I don't have any money. But I do have five cows, thanks to you." She felt a rod of gold bloom in her chest. It was that precious liquid she would always have swelling in her heart to remind her that she had done something for him. "I can do anything I want. I guess I always could. I just never realized it until last night. I wonder how all this would have played out if I hadn't come home from college, if I would have stayed there and finished my studies, but I didn't. I came back and stayed back, by myself."

She was looking down at her leather boots that were tied like blocks around her ankles. The wool socks climbed out of the leather and gripped the thick white tights that were under her green, flowered dress. "You're not really by yourself." She whispered into the corduroy collar of the Carhartt that covered the dress. No one would ever know whether it was a dress or a skirt.

"What d'you say?"

"I said," she raised her voice. "You're not really by yourself."

He looked at her for what seemed to him like one one-thousandth of a second and what seemed to her like fifteen minutes of speechless silence. He smiled, not with his lips but with his upper cheekbones. She bent forward and kissed him on the forehead as if she were his mother. They looked at each other as if neither one of them could figure out what had just happened.

"I'll help you live, Tom."

He didn't look at her. He sat back down where their legs joined into one and his head faced 52, which was blocked by the plank fence. He appeared to be looking at something but actually he wasn't looking outward at all. He was looking inward. Roadside Girl sat in the same fashion, gently bouncing her thigh, which was his thigh, peering nowhere. They sat like that until the warmth went out of their bodies and the cold of the sky seeped in, and they got up and went inside.

She was beautiful. Tom was quite sure that he had never seen anyone as beautiful as she was. It seemed funny to him that he hadn't really recognized it before summer. It had sprung on him like a bobcat. If she walked down Clarion or any other main street in America, no one would have seen her like he saw her now. No one would have stopped and jerked his head around saying, "that's the most beautiful person I've ever seen." But now in the light of his kitchen, all he could see was her beauty. He couldn't even see the room because of her brightness.

"When Ezra returned from Vietnam he had changed. He was distant. He was even what you might call scary. But I still liked him. I'm not sure he had all his marbles left after everything he saw, but that's hardly justification for death.

"Why do you think they killed him?"

"I don't know. Coincidence? Maybe he ended up at the wrong place at the wrong time and he probably said the wrong thing. He had the habit of saying things without thinking. He didn't really care how the other guy saw things. Always thought he was right." He was playing with a heavy, pottery ashtray. It was glazed green and black on the inside and fringed in red on the outside. It had been his father's ashtray. It usually sat at the end of the table where the table tucked into the cupboards and there was a small nook filled with old yellow cookbooks. "And you know, most of the time he was. Right that is."

"Is there more than what Brenda told us?"

"I'm not sure. I mean . . . I remember that Mose had said Ezra had gone in to get Patty. She was a friend of his from Kalamazoo. So Ezra and Patty were alone. I know one night somebody lit some small fires in a semi-circle around the cabin. That was after everybody had been out there for a couple of months. Mose said he and Ezra raced out and were pelted with rocks and sticks from the woods. They managed to put the fires out though. Some folks didn't like them hanging out back there because no one knew what they were doing, which was nothing. Folks in small towns don't like not knowing what everybody's doing. You know that. Toclep wasn't too happy about it; they thought Ezra was Charlie Manson. They were disappointed that my father had let it go on so long but he was sick and died and that left Toclep no one else to blame. One night Daisy, Kristie, and Katrina went into Rae's and got assaulted or something like that. I guess that was the second time something like that had happened. By the time Rae got out there everybody was gone. Rae had left Barb, Barb Nieson, she's dead now, to watch the bar and had driven the three girls back. I'm not sure why that wasn't reported, but I have a pretty good idea now." There was a pause.

"That's all you know?"

"I wasn't here. I only happened to be home from Northern that weekend. I know what Brenda said. I remember the quick investigation. I know now but didn't know then that Wiles, Bower, McGrogey, and Stephenson left town like jackrabbits. I know that Rich has always avoided eye contact with me."

"Pretty circumstantial."

"I guess." He lit a cigarette and watched the smoke drift off the end into the cone-shaped light that floated above the center of the table. "You know when I was thinking about my life last night. I thought about the fact that Ezra was partly responsible for his own demise. I mean, if he wouldn't have been trying to create Utopia in the nook, none of this would have happened."

"Jesus, Tom. That's oversimplification. Ezra wasn't doing anything wrong."

"But what he was doing upset people. I'm not trying to justify what Rich did."

"I don't think I'm hearing you. Are you saying because he was trying to live in . . . ." She was looking for words and found them though they sounded a bit contrived for the situation. "In unobstructed harmony with his friends that he is at fault for what happened? I'm sorry Tom, that's the dumbest thing I've ever heard."

"Maybe. I'll agree that I don't see everything as clearly as I should, but . . . ."

"Don't even say it. I don't believe that he's at all responsible and neither do you. Neither do you, deep down."

He didn't say anything. He thought that she could see more clearly than he could. She was removed. She wasn't caught up trying to decipher events that happened twenty years ago.

"I saw something funny last night." He changed the subject. "I was standing upstairs in my old bedroom, the one above the living room. I was looking out the window and thinking about all this and I saw someone walk up the street. It was odd because they came up 52 like they had walked from Ironcloud, quite a walk. The other thing was that it must have been two-thirty, three o'clock. I saw the person turn into town and walk up Church Street. I guess that isn't so crazy. But then about twenty minutes or a half-hour later, I saw the person again. Walk out of the city lights and up 52." He paused like he was finished and she took a breath like she was going to say something and then he continued. "Then about two minutes later I saw another figure come from nowhere, least it seemed that way because I was looking out that way, away from town." He motioned with his head toward Ironcloud. "Must have come from Clarion, but where the two were going. . . ." he put his hands in the air. "You got me. Nothing out there 'sides Lydia's. All park and white tail 'til you get to Terry Sikes', park and black bear from there to Spider Creek. Hell that's twenty miles or more of nothing."

Roadside Girl had a smirk on her face. "I was the second person. I wondered myself who'd be out walking at that time of night until the person turned down the two-track to Ezra's. Then I knew it was Brenda. Should have been able to tell it was her just from the way she was walking."

"Brenda? What the hell was she doing in town?"

"Good question. I was just wondering why she was up. I'd been down at Sunset Rock. Went out there to watch the moon rise and think." There was a space like she wanted him to ask her what she was thinking about. "Fell asleep on the rocks and woke up in shivers. Cold running straight from the rock through my bones."

"It kind of scares me that she was in town. I thought she didn't want to take any chances. That's a hell of a chance."

"Yeah, I guess it is. I didn't know she was coming from town last night. But just being out is kind of chancy."

Thomas stood up. "I'd like to know what the hell she was doing in town. It doesn't make any sense that she would sneak in there in the middle of the night."

"Well then, let's take a little walk." They were both standing; the light over the table was mingling with the faint light that was coming in the windows. They walked out the door and he looked at the fence. She took his hand as they walked out behind the house. "You know what I was thinking about last night?" Her voice skipped in the slippery grass like a young child. "You." Then she amended the word. "Us. I was thinking about us."

He squeezed her hand. He hadn't held anyone's hand in quite some time. Her hand felt good in his rough fingers.

He didn't want to leave the field. He wanted to stay right there and swing her around like they were in some epic movie and the kinescope was circling around them taking in all the angles of their happiness. He was lucky to have her around right now. His life was being shaped and he could tell that it was she that was shaping it. He didn't want to see Brenda. Unfortunately, he had to.

When they got to Ezra's, Brenda was pouring steaming hot water into a galvanized tub that smelled like vinegar. "Thought I'd do the windows I could reach." The sun was fighting with the clouds and was, at present, losing the battle. Steam rushed into the air from the tub and quickly disappeared. It was still very early in the day. "What's up?" She was smiling. She looked like she had lived here all her life. Oddly, she had spring in her voice.

Roadside Girl spoke first. "We were just wondering why you

went into town last night. Thought it odd that we'd been rather careful and now . . . well now, you weren't being careful."

"It was safe. I didn't go in there until the bars were closed. Besides, we've talked to people." She didn't look at them. "I just went and dropped a little note off to . . . to Rich."

"What!" It wasn't a yell or a scream, it was only a rather loud exclamation that resounded off the trees and hushed the birds, momentarily.

She smiled. "Yeah." Her eyes had a twisted look then came back to normal. "I just dropped off a note. And you know, I don't think he's sleeping very well. I could hear him thrashing around in his bed."

"You were in the house?" It didn't matter who said it; they were both thinking it.

"Just for a second. Only long enough to leave the note on the floor."

"What? Are you insane?" Tom said as he hit his hand against his head.

"Just wanted to give him something to think about."

"Like what?" Tom asked. Roadside Girl was standing beside him with the same stupefied look he had.

"I wrote that I was watching him. That I knew what he did. And I signed," she laughed like it was a joke. "I signed it the crows."

"I'm not so sure that was using you head, Brenda."

"I think it's over. I called the state police about ten minutes ago from Lydia's. I told them what I knew. I told them everything. About Ezra and Patty. I told them about the phone call—his comment. I told them everything Katrina told me. I told them he had been beating me. I told them he had raped me. I told them that Joe Willerstein, attorney at law, said they were who should be contacted. Yeah, they've got to come from Ironcloud. That will take them a while. But a Captain Preston Struggis told me that they would be over this morning. He asked me if I was somewhere safe and I told him I was as safe as can be." She was smiling. It was the peace, the calm of someone who had finally made the decision to kill herself. "And I am."

"My God." There was a frightening gap. "You've been to his house. He knows you're in town, and you've called the police?"

"And told them everything," she added smugly. She bent back to the steaming water that was easing its combustion with the cool air. Then she looked up again. "I left two notes last night. I forgot. Not sure he'll get the second; I put that one in the mail slot. It just said, murder 1978 and I've called the state police."

Tom was frantic. He was worried. He was bouncing off walls. He was running small circles as fast as he could. He was envisioning all the possible outcomes. He was seeing a desperate man with a sheriff's badge and a couple of guns and two crinkled notes. He dropped his head and tried to look calm. He could not. "Jesus Christ. And you're calm. You need help. Let's go." He took Roadside Girl's hand and jerked her behind him. They stopped. He held his finger up like he was trying to make a point. "I don't know if you think you are indestructible all of the sudden, but you're not. Get into some warm clothes right now, and go out and sit on that hillside where you can see the cabin but can't be seen from the cabin." He let go of Roadside Girl's hand and stepped forward. "What are you waiting for? Go now." All of a sudden Brenda's composure broke. She looked worried. Panicked. "Go! I'll send Dave out to sit with you. You watch for him." Tom turned toward Lydia's. "She needs her fuckin' head examined. She's made a mistake. But it's made. I'm gonna call Lydia. You find Dave and get Lydia's twenty-gauge and load it. Don't bother wasting any time telling Dave what's happened. Just tell him to go find Brenda on the hillside. Tell him simply to shoot at anybody that isn't Lydia or you. Anybody. He doesn't have to hit anything, just tell him to fire in the general direction. Nobody, not even Rich, will head across a field if slugs are whizzing by him. Then you and me are going to town. Lydia will see much clearer than I do, just like you see clearer."

Her face had gone pasty. When she swallowed he could hear it. "You think it's that serious?"

"Well, it's serious enough to kill two people and try to hide it for twenty years. I guess I'd call that serious." He was frowning. The morning had twisted through some rather murky area and both of them were foggy from lack of sleep and distant from lack of judgment. Minutes before he had been thinking about Roadside Girl's beauty. Now he was thinking about death.

The morning, which was wet with time, had been one flowing movement that had stopped abruptly at the front door of the story and a half Pine Street house. By the time Tom and Roadside Girl got to the house, Lydia was already there. Her truck was parked in the front on the curbless grass. Mr. Berge was standing behind his window wondering why Lydia was standing on the front stoop of the house next door.

Tom and Roadside Girl had cut through the back of the sleeping churchyard and the childless elementary school which was usually filled with running, knee-scraped kids and the screaming chains of synchronized swings. They had cut the corners and the yards and were now coming around the back of Rich's house. It seemed to rotate and swing them around to the open eyes of the front windows where Lydia stood looking.

Roadside Girl looked up and was shocked as she reluctantly noticed the two black birds sitting heavily with slouched shoulders on the fake dormer above Lydia's head. They were so black they didn't look real. They looked like animated and slick—formless like oil. They hung their heads down over the drip-edge, as if they were trying to see the upside-down world that Lydia was viewing. Roadside Girl and Tom did not come straight at the door. Lydia's strict posture was a flashing, yellow, warning sign that blinked, "do not enter." Lydia had her hand on the door but had not opened it. She gave the impression of being suspended magically in the air.

As Tom and Roadside Girl came down the narrow sidewalk that cut in front of the kitchen window to the front steps that were hardly a porch, they moved in lost time. Tom turned his head to see an incredible, blue-white flash that came from the clutter on the table of the empty kitchen. He shook his head once and the light was nothing more than a small piece of unlined paper. He couldn't see the writing but the note signed by the crows was on the kitchen table. Roadside Girl had turned away before the letter could grab her attention and was looking at the willow, which wept in the center of the yard. When they came behind Lydia, she turned.

"He's not doing anything." She whispered. "Not yet. He hasn't seen me because he hasn't looked up, but he knows I'm here. He knows we're all here."

"What's he doing?" Tom's was trying to find the ground between a foggy whisper and a soft speaking voice. His voice was to rough and low to find the middle tone.

"He's sitting. He's talking to himself. He's shaking his head that way and this way like he's having and argument with himself."

"Why don't we go . . . ?" Lydia didn't wait for Roadside Girl to finish.

"He's got a piece of paper in his hand." Tom and Roadside Girl looked at each other and shook their heads knowing it was Brenda's note.

"Number two." Tom said. "That's the note telling him that she's called the state police. Telling him that an investigation has been opened. Telling him that he really does have something to worry about."

"Yeah." She stopped and swallowed. "Well that piece of paper is lining his fingers that are gripped around the handle of his pistol. The gun is hanging like a dead cat between his legs and his other hand is trying to push his forehead back to his ears."

"Is he . . . ?"

"Gonna shoot himself. I'd guess that's his plan. Quick and

easy, no investigation," Lydia finished Roadside Girl's question. "Or shoot whoever comes through that door."

"What?"

Lydia interrupted. "I don't know. I sure as hell don't want to get my head blown off trying to stop him." Tom thought about his legacy: a flopping, headless fish out of water.

"It's pretty obvious that he's not very stable. He's got problems and needs help." Lydia knew that the help would have to come from her. It was the kind of help she had always given in towns like this. It was the kind of help that had usually brought trouble and change.

"Yeah," Tom added, "I thought the same thing about Brenda this morning."

They could've stood there all day talking about the apparent problems of Rich Cafus. However, the odds were that they didn't have all day. Rich had gotten the first note in the darkness of morning. He had gotten the second when he had glanced at the mail basket that was behind the shiny, brass, mail slot beside the door. It had been sitting there in the basket all alone. He looked at it for a long time as the sky grew into lightness—one envelope with no writing. No stamp. It leaned against the wire basket in perfect loneliness. It was the same loneliness he felt as he pulled it out and realized it was the same kind of envelope that had fallen out of his dream onto the landing of the stairs. After he read it, he went up stairs and found his holster where he had left it the night before, draped from a hook on the back of the closet door, but his side arm was not in its sheath. He had looked around the room and remembered that he had been hiding the gun in his t-shirt drawer because it had been yelling at him. Telling him what to do because it wouldn't shut up. He walked spiritlessly down the stairs. His body had so much weight that each step, not just the third one from the top, creaked as his foot touched it. He was angry. He was angry at her. He was angry at his life. He was angry at Eric McGrogey for hitting that girl. He was angry at himself for letting it go so long. He was sorry. Sorry for the whole thing—for everything. And most of all he was hopeless. There wasn't a speck of light that came to him to say, "You've got a chance." Not one speck.

Now he sat trying to make himself do something that he really didn't want to do but thought he had to do. Head bowed, he sat shaking his affirmatives and negatives to the voices that were arguing minor points of life and death in his head. Lydia knew the police would soon be there and that would make things worse—more desperate. Even though Rich never imagined there could be a more desperate.

Lydia had a flash of standing over Rich—dead. She knew she wasn't going to get shot. She made up her mind without telling the others that she was going to do something. Something would be better than nothing, she thought. She knew it would have to be her. She was the only one who could do anything safely, in this situation. A bright, red light was saying, "danger" in her mind and it had little pictures of Tom and Roadside Girl all over it.

"Well," Lydia turned so quickly that there wasn't an instant for them to react before she opened the door and stepped into the house. Her move had been just like the morning, a series of actions that had all become one, fluid motion. The crows on the dormer startled and flew into the willow where they could look through the front door. Tom's futile and broken Lydia went unheard before the black-tubed spring of the storm door pulled the aluminum closed behind her.

"Stay back, Lydia." His movements weren't frenzied. They were nearly methodical. His wrist clicked like machinery as the barrel lifted from the floor and pointed in Lydia's direction. "I don't want to shoot you, but it doesn't really matter to me if I do, because I'm not gonna be around to have to deal with it." His words ticked like his movements—slow drips of emotion showed in his strained face, his face that was as full of confusion as it was with rabid wildness.

"You don't want to shoot me. I haven't done anything." She

spoke in soft, calm flute-like tones. Her words had the feeling of elevator music as if she knew that he wouldn't shoot her. "Shooting me or shooting you, that's not gonna do anything for you, Rich. If you kill me, then you have to kill you, which you want to do anyway. That's not really what I mean though. If you kill yourself you won't be getting away from any of this. None of it, Rich. You'll be getting away from jail but jail isn't what's haunting you."

"What do you know? You don't have any idea about what's haunting me. Do you know what they do to police officers in prison? Do you?"

Her tranquility was frightening. It scared Tom and Roadside Girl and it scared the hell out of Rich. "I know that prison isn't Disneyland. But it's life. Death is a flash of nothing, Rich. A flash that lasts a million years and you'll be in the flash. And heaven or hell—if you believe in either, won't matter, because once you're within that darkness you will suffer mercilessly at the hands of your own soul."

"There's no heaven for me."

"You're right, Rich. There's no heaven for you. No heaven right now, that is. But how do you know there's a heaven anyway?"

"This isn't about heaven or hell. It's about me. It's about life and death and my future in prison. There's nothing beyond right now."

"Isn't there? Why do you think you're going to prison, Rich?"

For a moment, just a flicker it sounded like he might cry. Then it was gone and his voice strained, "Cuz I've done something wrong." His face looked like he wasn't sure if what he had done was so wrong.

"See Rich. You've admitted it. Now you just have to be sorry. That's all. You just have to regret it."

"Just have to be sorry, that's all what?" He was pouting. He didn't know that he was but Lydia saw his bottom lip shake and could see his chin pulling down the sides of his mouth.

"That's all. That's how you get out of darkness."

"But this isn't about darkness." He stuttered like he didn't know what it was about. He shook his head just slightly and added in a furrow-eyed voice.

"Isn't it, Rich? Everything is about darkness and lightness. It's what our days are built on. It's what our world revolves around."

"Not this."

"Is that why you've got a gun in your hand, because you're afraid of prison? Not because you've done something wrong and now you see what you've done? Not because you're worried about eternity, but because of prison?" She waved her hand at him like she was dismissing him. "Well you sound like a kid, Rich. I thought there was more to it than that. I thought there was more to you than that. Prison, eh? That's what you're worried about? Prison's only years, Rich. You've already spent years in your own prison—what's a few more? Eternity, that's forever. That's what you should be worried about." He saw Tom and Roadside Girl's shadow move into the upper panel in the storm door.

"Punishment. It's all punishment."

"Is that why you think we're here, to punish you? We're not here to punish you, Rich. We're here to save you—to save you from yourself. To save you from eternity."

He tightened the grip on pistol. "You don't have that power."

"No, we don't. You do. Only you."

"No I don't. They told me. He told me. I don't."

"Who told you?"

"He did, the man from the dream. Ezra or whoever." Outside, two pale silhouettes framed Lydia's body. He thought that they were the silhouettes of Tom and Roadside Girl, but they were the silhouettes of the crows that had adjusted themselves to the meeting of lightness and darkness in the doorway. Rich looked at Lydia and saw three heads. He had seen her for years. He spent time, not necessarily as friends but as acquaintances with her since . . . well he was not sure since when. He knew that she didn't believe in God. Yet, here she was trying to sort out heaven and hell for him. There she was talking about eternity. He knew she didn't like him and never really had, but here she was trying to save him. "Why are you here? Why are you trying to talk me out of this? What's it matter to you?"

"All life matters to me, Rich. It always has. It matters to all of us—me, you, Roadside Girl, Tom, everybody in Toclep, everybody in the world. It's all we have when we're here. Then we're gone and there's, there's . . . ."

"Heaven or hell? You don't even believe in that."

"Eternity, Rich. That's what's left."

"You're trying to fool me. Well I'm not stupid, Lydia. This isn't a movie. It's not gonna end pretty. Because it's real, it's life." He was shaking the gun at her. "And BOOM! It's death."

"I'm not trying to fool you. You're right, I don't believe in heaven and hell. But it's all darkness, Rich. When you leave here there is no light. It is all darkness. And that darkness lasts longer for some than for others. That's why we act the way we do. And you're right, it's life but as soon as you make it death, you have no idea what it is. Just that it's darkness and that darkness might last forever. And that's a long time."

"You don't think I'll do it. You think I'm chicken."

"Now you're talking like a kid again. Listen to yourself, threatening me with your suicide. You're right. You're right I think you're a chicken. I won't lie to you. It won't matter much once you've pulled the trigger. I think you're chicken and that's why I'm here. That's why we're all here, because a chicken would pull that trigger, Rich. No doubt in my mind."

Roadside Girl didn't say anything but she wondered if provoking him was the right thing to do. She was watching Rich's reflection in the fireplace glass.

"I'm not a chicken. I just don't want to go to prison."

"You don't want to go to prison, but you want to die? That's interesting, Rich. It would probably make a good psychological study for some graduate student somewhere."

"They can perform that study on a dead man." He made one

swift movement with his arm. The barrel of the gun went from Lydia to his head. As soon as she saw the movement she screamed his name and dove at him. It was not a Superman-type drive; rather it was as if she was trying to tackle him. The hammer clicked and the cylinder moved and the gun went off. Rich crumpled with Lydia lying across him. There was a splatter of red on the arm of the couch and against the wall in the distance. Tom and Roadside Girl were inside. They pulled Lydia off the body. All the movements were movements that they would never remember making.

Roadside Girl looked at the wall and saw a bullet hole clear and precise that went into it and feathered out on the other side through the refrigerator. The clean whole seemed odd to her, but she didn't really know why. She looked down at Rich, who lay crumbled on the couch, bleeding from the top of his head, which he still had. She looked confused. For some reason that she would never be able to explain, she reached out and touched the top of his head. It was solid.

"He missed." They were quiet words that the other two heard but didn't understand. She repeated them three times in cold, straight syllables, which they could almost see come out of her mouth. She kicked the gun. "He missed." She yelled.

There was a wound that cut into his skull but had not cut through it. Like other people in the face of shooting themselves, Rich had frantically and nervously tried to get the gun to his head, pull the trigger, and not be obstructed. He had failed. He had passed out from the shock of the bullet and his expectations. He was alive and the gun was against the far wall.

All movements were liquid lightening.

"Good grief," Lydia said. "Get a towel. We need to get him to Falls Creek. ASAP. Let's go, let's go, let's go, let's go. Get a couple blankets, too."

Mr. Berge was now in his yard. His body looked thinner than it looked through the glass. He had heard the gun shot. He had to put his shoes on and find his jacket but now he was standing there with wonder eyes.

"Your truck's got a topper doesn't it, Harold?" He nodded his head. "Good, back it over here by the door. We've got to get him to the hospital." He stood there like he didn't understand her words. "Now." She yelled. He moved, unconsciously, with the command.

Lydia and Tom rode in the back of the small pick-up with Rich, his arms tied to his sides, and his ankles tied together, covered in blankets as Mr. Berge raced toward Fall's Creek. Roadside Girl sat on the front steps. She wasn't quite sure what she should do. She called Tim at the sheriff's office. She called the state police though they were already on their way. She called the hospital. She told Mrs. Berge what happened and told her not to go into the house. She got in the truck and drove down Ezra's two-track and walked behind the cabin. She didn't bother telling Brenda what had happened. There would be time for that. When the police arrived on Pine Street that morning, Roadside Girl sat on the front porch where she had stood earlier this morning, staring at Dave. She looked around the yard as the police arrived. It was going to be a long day. The police went into the house, and she held Dave's hand as she searched the willow tree and the dormer, then the yard for the crows that were no longer there. She didn't notice it was a cool morning until one of the officers offered her his coat, because she was shivering. She took the jacket and slipped it over her Carhartt. She shivered anyway. It wasn't the cold of climate that had her shaking. It was the cold of life.

Roadside Girl wiped the condensation from the window inside the sauna shack. Large, shapeless flakes danced their ballet to the ground outside her window. Halloween was gone and with it, the ghosts. This was the second snow and already the large flakes were gathering together and covering the grass. The geese had been right. Autumn had stayed nice, slowly waltzing from warm to cold, blue sky to faded jeans, leaf detaching rain to quiet snow, which would now take all the sounds from the woods and muffle them. Autumn had moved like a weasel for all of them, especially Rich. It had been a seizure of crack-the-whip, which had thrown them askew from their previous tracks of life, at least inside. Now a man who had been sheriff was being held for psychological observation. There was a permanent indentation that cut across his head where no hair would ever grow again. He rocked nervously. He no longer sauntered calmly like Wyatt Earp. State police officers asked questions and searched for people and hovered in Toclep, bending and picking up twenty-year-old pieces of a jigsaw.

Autumn had been a whirlwind for them but, for itself, it had been no different than it had been last year or the year before that or the years before that when Lionel Gern had not cared about the snow growing at his feet because it made logging his land easier. Autumn had not changed, had not burned itself out like a falling star that shoots once across the sky. It had not jumped its track. Autumn had moved in its five-thousand-mile-an-hour orbit around the sun, tipping its hat to the south, bowing out of summer in slow color to the burnt browns that were being insulated from the harsh cold by the snow. It had been like that last year and it would be like that next year. Autumn had not rushed itself out of season. The people had rushed through autumn but autumn had been in no irregular hurry to pass its baton to winter.

Dave wasn't awake yet. When he got up he'd be yelling in kid-joy, running and dressing at the same time to rush into the wet, soft flakes that kids love immensely more than adults did. He would never again be asked to hold a gun in defense of someone. He would never again sit crouched in the woods with a gun for anything more than a whitetail or a grouse. He held gold in his heart from summer: a gift from a cow. He held insight—knowledge from eye-to-eye contact with Rich, knowledge no one else ever would. He forgot that he had ever had any other mom than Lydia and though he hadn't grown in inches that fall, he had in knowledge and silence grown into adulthood, which he dipped into like cold water then retreated.

Roadside Girl watched the flakes fall and cover the arms of the balsam and hemlock—weighing them with heavy sweaters. The grass peeked through the cloud of coverage on the ground but would soon disappear if the snow kept falling and sun kept hiding. The ground wasn't frozen and wouldn't hold the solid water for long, but today it would stay. Today there would be paths of green through clouds of snow from where the body of an early snowman, who would stand—though shrinking from the sun—for most of winter. Roadside Girl got out of bed and stocked the fire that was but ashes. She stuffed the mouth of the small Franklin until it was full. It would catch by itself. A little fire went a long way in the small rooms of the sauna shack. She stepped out onto the small wooden porch in her flannel pajamas and leather Minnetonkas that were shiny smooth on the bottom. Her arms squeezed across her chest trying to hold warmth in vain. She heard the sound of geese that were getting a late start for the south. Of course, they knew when to go and when to stay. Now it was time to go. She looked out at Sam Adams. He seemed indifferent about the snow as it touched his coat and disappeared like candles being snuffed. She imagined that she could hear it sizzle off his back. It had snowed before but today was the first day of winter in the north. According to the calendar it was November, but it was the birth of the new season and the death of the old, which would be born again and again in the years ahead. She dressed slowly, pulling on wool socks and tights that would hide under her long skirt. Lydia's truck was still in the driveway, completely surrounded by an endless mote of unbroken snow. There was a light on in the kitchen.

Lydia was drinking coffee. She poured a cup for Roadside Girl and they sat at the oak table looking out the kitchen window at the falling sky. They were glad to have each other. Some people yearned for somebody like Roadside Girl and Lydia and the quiet moments they had with each other. Not simply content, but truly happy.

"It's none of my business, you know." Lydia started with a preface that said it was her business. "I'm just curious about Tom. About what's going on."

"I don't know." There was no hesitation. "I think I love him. And from there, I just don't know. I'm going to let my feelings play out. Maybe I'll get hurt and maybe I'll get hugged but either way I'll get what I want, life."

"People are talking, you know? They always do in small towns. Rae Miller can attest to that."

"They can talk all they want. I'll be happy and so will Tom and they, they will wish that their relationships bloomed like ours." They both sipped their coffee and Lydia agreed with a nod because she knew Roadside Girl. The kitchen smelled like bacon. There was a cast iron skillet on the stove full of bacon grease that Lydia would save just as her mother had saved it. There were dried and drying plants hanging like butcher-shop chickens in all the windows and from the drying hooks in the ceiling.

Antique pestles of marble and rock sat in small bowls scattered across the counter, lined with different colored powders.

"And how does Tom . . . does he feel the same?" Lydia didn't need to hear the answer. She already knew it. She just wanted to hear Roadside Girl say it with confidence.

"I guess he does." She saw that look in Roadside Girl's eyes. That look Lydia had watched grow from the child to the woman she was now. It wasn't Daisy's look; it was another. They had time for only one cup of coffee before Lydia left for work. However, in one cup of semi-silent coffee, they assured each other that everything was all right—that neither had been scratched by the falling leaves. Roadside Girl watched Lydia leave. There was a large rectangle of brown-green in front of the house. Before she turned away she noticed that it was as if Lydia had left no tracks in the snow. Lydia would mend the broken worlds of Toclep. It would take time, but she would do it and she would stay there until the glaciers came again because there wouldn't be any tides to wash her away this time.

When Roadside Girl passed Ezra's, a truck sat sleeping in the falling snow. The chimney of the house had a trail of gray-blue smoke drifting out between the trees into the darkness of the winter woods, weaving blue threads up and out of the mountains. The curtains were open and she could see Brenda standing at the sink. She had her head down diligently working. Her face was strong. Not like the Brenda she remembered from that summer night at Rae Miller's. She had lost that summer sickness. But it would be back. Brenda would feel it again. It would sweep in and out like waves to remind her of a weakness she let control her, to remind her not to close her eyes or run deep to the closets inside her for safety. The sickness would stay with her like herpes but it wouldn't flare into fire. It would just settle in the background, a reminder that she would need to shine outward. Brenda didn't looked up and Roadside Girl went and knocked lightly on the window. Brenda didn't startle; she smiled and waved an invitation with a soapy hand.

"Hey." Roadside Girl peeked through the back door. Next to the door there was a calendar, it no longer read, September '78. In small, green letters under snow-covered prairies of Yellowstone it read, November '98. Brenda had decided, with the offer from Tom, that she would stay at Ezra's until she felt like she wanted to go somewhere else. There was nothing to pay but the taxes. It had been that way for Tom and now it would be that way for Brenda. Tom would figure out how pay the utilities. There were some boxes she had brought from the other house, but most of the other life she had left where it was. She brought her sewing machine and she was slowly altering what was left of Ezra's clothes to fit her. She would plant a garden in the spring, and though she wouldn't notice, Tom would notice that the path from the sweat lodge would have a thin carpet of bright green in late May. By July no one would ever know that grass hadn't grown on that path for twenty years.

In front of the Pine Street house there was no "For Sale" sign. The house stared vacantly, and even Mr. Berge didn't bother to look across his driveway into the dark, reflective eyes of the house. The crows were gone. They might have been sitting on the ledge of the psych-lockdown or they might have dissolved back into the sky from where they had come or they might have flown down the road to another man or woman who needed to be watched. Wherever they were, Brenda had not seen them.

She had gone into the house only once to look at what she wanted and what she never wanted to see again. There was brown, dried blood still splattered on the wall and when she opened the refrigerator, it looked like someone had taken a cannon to it. The house would sit alone and quiet for a long time. When the "For Sale" sign finally did go up, it would sit with lack of interest for another three years. That was how houses that weren't on Superior sold in Toclep, bloodstain or not.

Ted Russell had been down the two-track a couple of times, and Brenda had sat politely mewing over books with him. She never told him about her pregnancy and had pushed her crutch-like sexual reliance on him to platonic. Ted didn't seem to mind. Though sometimes, his urges did. He wasn't hurt that she wanted space, didn't everybody? He was younger than she was and he could wait. There was nothing else in Toclep to do but wait. He would chew thoughts in his mind repeating, this too will pass. He was glad that she still wanted to see him, and he hoped that she would want more than conversations, that she would want to know love like it was supposed to be.

There were divorce papers flying like ducks, somewhere, and a court case lingering in the future dependent upon Rich's overall stability and whether the police would be able to round up the scattered grains of McGrogey, Wiles, and Bower. The Montana police had already picked up Seiler Stephenson with a worried and anxiety-ridden statement that admitted he had only been there. The rest was in the future somewhere. Floating like the snow. Roadside Girl didn't stay. She just stuck her head in because that's what neighbors are supposed to do, check on each other.

"On your way to Tom's?"

Thomas Gern was leaning against the fence. He had one boot up on the first rung. She could see him as she rounded into the clearing. He was looking out at the town, leaning against the one thing that had never let him down, the one thing that had always been there. He didn't move his leg from the time she saw him in the distance until the she stood in much the same manner with her leg on the fence, looking out at Toclep. The snow was melting on his shoulders and covering his hat.

"What're you looking at?"

"Everything, I guess. Toclep's a good town. I locked myself out of it, but it's a good town with good folks."

"Yep." They were both looking out at the town and the road as if they were talking to someone on the other side. "That's why I've always said I want to stay here. It's beautiful. The town and everything else—the trees, the hills, the quiet, the water, the sky. The everything."

"The town. The town and the people, they're good, too. I just forgot there was anybody but me alive." He turned toward her and smiled. "But there are other people and those people live just like you and me. Those people wake up and see their lives, too. We were talking about people rushing through life. We all do it too much and we don't even realize. Then one morning, bang, it hits you. Some people like me are lucky. Their bang comes before they're too old to hear it. Others aren't so lucky and they can only talk about the could-have-beens when they hear their bang. Thanks to you I'm awake. I'm alive."

"Yeah. Well I got a bang this morning when I rounded those trees." She jerked her head to indicate which trees. "And I saw you standing out here in the cold, white sky like you were waiting for me. You don't have to tell me you were. I'll just let my mind tell me."

He didn't tell her. He turned and looked into the sky. "It's winter now," he said. "I saw the geese heading toward their barn." He started to head toward the house.

"Where ya goin'?"

"It's coffee time, don't ya know." When they got inside he had to remove his glasses and clean the moisture from the lenses. "You know that whole thing with Rich is rather sad. I feel sorry for the guy." She didn't say anything because she could tell that Tom actually had sorrow in his voice. "He woke one morning and his wife was gone. Then he banged around wondering where she was, got a note from her, tried to put a bullet in his head, has two murder charges hanging over him like vultures.... He woke up one morning and everything he thought he had was gone."

"But...."

"I know what you're gonna say. I know. He brought it on himself, but that doesn't make it any easier to take. I know it's silly and I know I'm biased about it but he and Brenda agreed on something. I know she didn't get a picnic out of it. And I don't know what to think about that but...." He paused and looked into the living room and kept talking. "But if your husband was in a tragic accident and paralyzed from the neck down, would you leave him? I guess that's kind of how I see this. But that's not right, is it? Nope. Even if Rich does come out of this thing with some shine of sanity, what's left for him? Nothing. He would have been better off not missing. Not because he will have to go to jail. He fully deserves that, but because he has nothing, absolutely nothing to show for his forty-some-odd-years on this planet. He's got a bushel basket full to the handles of nothing."

"He reaped what he sowed, Tom. He was a bad man. He deserves to go to jail because he killed two people. He deserves to be left for dead by his wife because he beat her and . . . " She didn't want to say it, so she didn't. "Maybe it's hard for you to see because you're not a woman. But it's his boat."

"I don't think it has to do with being a man or a woman. I think it has to do with doing what you say you're going to do."

"Well, there you are. He never kept his end of the bargain. Never. And for that he gets a king-sized helping of nothing. He's a son of a bitch. He's lucky to get that."

"You're right. And you know you are, but I can't help feeling sorry for the guy. Even with all the bad he's done and all the pain he's caused."

"And that's why I love you, Tom."

She took both his hands in hers and held them tightly. They both felt the temperature rise, surround them, move through their bodies, and radiate like the morning sun. She had felt this way standing in the growing warmth of Sunset Rock. It was the heat of nature. The life that others rushed through or left behind in excited anticipation of something greater and grander than what really is, was theirs. They had found it in each other because they needed the same things. She was strong. He had seen more than she had. They were the knives and forks of liveliness. She was looking into his face with eyes that reflected the brown table. Her eyes shined and said I-know-something-you-don't-know and Thomas saw the eyes and recognized them clearly. He knew he had seen them before. He had watched them all summer. They had fallen in love with him and he had fallen in love with her and there wasn't a thing either one of them could do about it.

Printed in the United States
3813